THE SOCIETY FOR

SOULLESS GIRLS

THE SOCIETY FOR

SOULLESS GIRLS

LAURA STEVEN

DELACORTE PRESS

Text copyright © 2023 by Laura Steven
Jacket art figure copyright © 2023 by Robin Macmillan/Trevillion Images; moth copyright © 2023 Wirestock/iStock/GettyImages Plus; gold leaf texture copyright © 2023 by Katsumi Murouchi/GettyImages; blood splatter copyright © 2023 by Jose A. Bernat Bacete/GettyImages; other images used under license from Shutterstock.com
All rights reserved. Published in the United States by Delacorte Press, an imprint of Random House Children's Books, a division of Penguin Random House LLC, New York.

Delacorte Press is a registered trademark and the colophon is a trademark of Penguin Random House LLC.

Visit us on the Web! GetUnderlined.com

Educators and librarians, for a variety of teaching tools, visit us at RHTeachersLibrarians.com

Library of Congress Cataloging-in-Publication Data is available upon request.
ISBN 978-0-593-70391-5 (paperback) — ISBN 978-0-593-70393-9 (ebook)

The text of this book is set in 11.3-point Sabon LT Pro.
Interior design by Megan Shortt

Printed in the United States of America
1st Printing
First Edition

FOR THE GIRLS WHO WERE BORN ANGRY

BUT IT IS THE SAME WITH MAN AS WITH THE TREE. THE MORE HE SEEKS TO RISE INTO THE HEIGHT AND LIGHT, THE MORE VIGOROUSLY DO HIS ROOTS STRUGGLE EARTHWARD, DOWNWARD, INTO THE DARK, THE DEEP—INTO EVIL.

—Friedrich Nietzsche

PART I

Roots

CHAPTER 1

Lottie

Every kid has a moment in their childhood when they realize just how terrifying the world can be. A moment when they realize there are far scarier things out there than bigfoot and bogeymen and monsters hiding under beds. For my grandparents' generation, it was pretty much the entirety of World War II. For my parents, it was the Cold War. For my friend Shannon, it was the unconscionable existence of the Teletubbies.

For me, it was when a girl from my hometown died in the North Tower murders at Carvell Academy of the Arts.

Nineteen-year-old Janie Kirsopp was a quietly intelligent violinist in her first year at Carvell. Her parents had driven her the hundreds of miles from Sevenoaks, our small town just south of London, to rural Northumberland, said tearful goodbyes to their shy, uncertain daughter, and promised they'd have the best Christmas ever to make up for their time apart. Janie had begged them to take her home, said she'd made a mistake and that she didn't want to be so far away from them, that she'd request a transfer to one of the elite music programs in London instead. They had kissed her on the forehead and told her to stick it out for a couple of months and see how she felt then.

But in a couple of months, Janie was dead.

I was only nine when it happened, but I remember how her pretty, hooknosed face had dominated newsstands across Sevenoaks. Photos of Janie on holiday in Spain as a child, of her toothless first school picture, of her performing at the Royal Albert Hall with the National Youth Orchestra. Splashy headlines about hot new leads in the case, about prime suspects and grisly forensic evidence.

The notion of murder was completely abstract to me until I saw my own parents crying at her funeral. They knew the Kirsopps from church and had attended Janie's christening when she was a baby. They could still remember her white tulle dress, her ivory sandals the size of seashells, her shining, cherubic eyes as she was baptized. And now her body had been shattered at the bottom of a cold stone tower hundreds of miles away.

That was my before and after. I was just a child, yet my understanding of reality shifted on its axis.

Janie's death was the second in a string of four unsolved murders that ultimately led to Carvell's closure. So my parents understandably had reservations when I announced, less than a decade later, that the soon-to-be-reopened arts academy would be my first choice of university.

Well, "reservations" is putting it mildly. My mother threatened to saw my legs off if I so much as mentioned it again.

At first they thought I was messing with them, playing the kind of cruel joke only teenagers have the genuine apathy to execute. Then, when I was invited to interview at the academy, they flatly refused to drive me up. I'd always been stubborn, so I caught three different trains until I was within throwing distance of the campus, then got a taxi to take me the rest of the way.

A shiver had run down my spine as Carvell Academy came into view at the end of the sweeping driveway, the spires and crenelations of the North Tower silhouetted against a gray autumn sky. There was something so alive about the old convent, something that swooped and pulsed like a murmuration of starlings. I'd always romanticized the university, despite its history; it brought to mind old parchment and knee-deep piles of crunchy red leaves, cellos and dark windowpanes and snow.

The thing that made me fall truly in love with the campus, swiftly and irrevocably, was the cat. There were rumors that Salem, a sleek black Bombay known to have wandered around the campus before the school's closure, was actually immortal; her soul was said to be the same as it was hundreds of years ago, back when the convent was still operating. The tour guide told us that Salem stalked the same route around the priory every day, visited the same glade every afternoon to bathe on the trees' sun-dappled branches and curled up in front of the log fire every evening after a little nip of brandy and milk. When I saw her slinking along a window ledge of the chapel on my campus tour, I felt as though I was witnessing something ancient and sacred, something tapped into a supernatural pulse. I wanted to be part of that more than anything.

Be careful what you wish for, as my beloved Goosebumps books used to say.

Now I could practically feel Dad's apprehension as we pulled up that same sweeping driveway on my first day as a Carvell student. He gripped the stitched-leather steering wheel so tightly that his knuckles turned white. I knew he was thinking of Janie—tulle dress, tiny sandals, cherubic face, dead body. I knew he was thinking of how he would never survive if that was me. I knew he was wondering if it was too late to fetch my mum's hacksaw.

After I was offered a place, my parents eventually came around to the idea of me attending Carvell. They weren't happy about it, exactly, but they didn't expressly forbid it. Despite its ten-year closure, Carvell still offered one of the most prestigious and competitive English literature programs in the country, with published authors and internationally acclaimed academics among the glittering new faculty. Before the closure, there was one eccentric lecturer—Professor Sanderson—who taught a gothic literature seminar that was rumored to send students mad. I didn't tell Mum and Dad about that one. Especially since most of the original professors were set to return this fall.

Plus, the nightlife was practically nonexistent—there was just one student union and a couple of old-fashioned parlors on the campus—so the chances of me choking on my own vomit or drowning in a river after a night of partying were slim. The field hockey scholarship sealed the deal. I was the star midfielder throughout high school, and my love of sports was secondary only to my love of books—Carvell offered me both.

Still, now that we were actually here, traipsing around Willowood Hall in search of my room, I could tell Dad was having second, third and ninth thoughts.

"Are you sure about this, kiddo?" he asked, lugging a box of books.

He looked up at the North Tower, squinting against the late-summer sun, teeth working at the corner of his mouth like they always did when he was nervous. He'd worked in construction for decades, so he was no stranger to physical risk, but it was different when it came to me. He couldn't even stomach watching me play field hockey. So leaving me at the site of Janie's death on the day of my nineteenth birthday—the same age she was when she died—was a little too much for him to handle.

I grinned, hoisting my field hockey bag farther up my shoulder. "Of course I'm sure, you goof."

In truth I was nervous too, but I didn't want to show it.

The apprehension wasn't just about the school's bloody

past, or what would happen if old demons came back to haunt it. I was also afraid that I would fail under the lofty academic pressure. Because the reality was that I'd lived in the same small house in the same small town all my life.

What if I didn't rise to whatever challenges were in store for me at Carvell? What if I was only a great field hockey player—and a great writer—in the small world of Sevenoaks? I was about to find out.

Fixing a confident expression on my face, I gave my dad a final reassuring beam and took a step in what I hoped was the direction of my dorm.

CHAPTER 2

Alice

Within fifteen minutes of arriving at Carvell, I already wanted to slit someone's throat.

The tweed-clad woman in front of me glared at her clipboard as though it had personally wronged her. "Name?"

I shifted on the heels of my Doc Martens. They squeaked conspicuously on the checkerboard floor of the cavernous entrance hall. "Alice Wolfe. Philosophy."

Judging by the woman's disdainful expression, I got the feeling she'd been roped into these tedious welcome greetings in the absence of any student volunteers. Which made sense, because I was one of the first students to walk through the doors in nearly ten years.

Her watery blue eyes scanned a list. "You're not on here. Did you submit your enrollment paperwork before the deadline?"

Through gritted teeth, I replied, "Yes."

She gave a terse schoolmarm tut, pushing her half-moon glasses farther up the bridge of her nose. "You mustn't have, because you're not on here."

Anger snapped across my chest like an elastic band, a hot, familiar sting. I couldn't keep it from my voice. "Well, I definitely did. So it must be a cock-up on your end."

At this the women inhaled sharply, as though the unsavory word had caused her physical pain. Eyelids fluttering with distaste, she replied quietly, "There's simply no need to be so rude. I *assure* you this is no fault of our administrative staff. I'm afraid you'll have to resubmit your paperwork."

I'd spent hours on that godforsaken paperwork the first time.

Breathe. Just breathe.

I lowered my voice and said, "I've already done the paperwork. Please, would you check again?"

She issued a tight grimace. "I'm going to have to ask you to step aside and complete another set of forms. There are a lot more students I have to see."

She looked down her nose at me, smug with self-importance, and the dam holding back my anger crumbled.

"For fuck's sake!" I snapped. "Would it kill you to check one more time?"

She blinked sharply, as though a loud bang had gone off. Then, lips curling, she disappeared into a small office behind her welcome desk.

As usual, there was a soft ebb of pleasure as I let the anger out, followed by the cold tide of guilt and self-loathing, a deep undertow of shame.

Then came the acute sensation of being watched.

Following a tug of paranoia, my gaze landed on a tall, bespectacled man in a walnut-colored corduroy suit who was staring at me with an impenetrable expression. I recognized him as Professor Dacre, head of the philosophy program; his headshot had been in the brochure. And he'd just witnessed my outburst.

Hands folded over his sloping stomach, he gave me a chastising head shake, like a disappointed grandfather.

"Such wrath isn't very becoming of a young woman, you know," he said in a crisp academic tone. He adjusted his mustard-yellow tie.

I glared at him, momentarily speechless.

Did he *actually* just play the "unbecoming of a young woman" card?

Before I could sling a low and dirty retort in his direction, the woman reappeared from the office, cowed. Without meeting my eyes, she said, "We found your paperwork. Accommodation office is in the Jerningham building. Inauguration speech is at four p.m. in the chapel. Attendance is mandatory."

The victory felt hollow. She handed me a dark-green lanyard that cheerfully proclaimed *I'm a new student!* and I scurried out of the entrance hall, head down to avoid the cold glares of the other students.

The campus was built in concentric semicircles around the grounds of a former convent, a proud stone building of stained-glass windows and ribbed vaults, flying buttresses and pointed arches, spires and towers and intricate tracery. The cobbled walkways were lined with black Victorian streetlamps and gnarled trees with branches like crooked bones.

Outside the entrance hall was a statue of Sister Maria, one of the last nuns to live in the convent before it was converted into an academic institution. Her stone hands were clasped in prayer as she stood vigil. The folds of her habit draped down to her ankles in rough-hewn ripples, and her chiseled face bowed in a way that made her eyes sink into shadows. The beads of the rosaries snaking around her wrists were fat, glimmering rubies, surrounded by shallow scratches where many a desperate thief had taken a chisel to the precious jewels. The attempts were fruitless; they may have been worth a fortune, but the rubies were embedded in the stone as though by some greater force.

Sister Maria had been the original North Tower victim, falling to her death a little over a hundred years ago. Whether she jumped or was pushed, nobody knew.

Laying down my monogrammed leather satchel on the cobbled courtyard, I stood against the statue for a few minutes, taking in great gulps of the late-September air and trying to gather my emotions.

Northumberland had always been home for me, and yet being here already felt all wrong.

I'd applied to the elite philosophy program as soon as Carvell reopened—if I was going to practice law one day and be a judge, if I was going to play god in the fates of murderers and victims alike, where better to cut my teeth than a place so famously steeped in death?

Plus, it was less than twenty miles from the town where I grew up and where my parents and brothers still lived. My mum had suffered from lupus since I was twelve, and it was getting worse every year. Even the prestigious universities in Edinburgh and Durham felt too far away. What if she took a turn for the worse and it took me hours to get home? What if . . . ?

I tried not to think like that.

After composing myself by Sister Maria's statue, I headed back to the car park and yanked my suitcase out of my beat-up Ford. I frowned down at the campus map. Willowood Hall, where I'd be living for the next year, was adjacent to the central priory. Right opposite the North Tower, with its turrets and crenelations and dark, dark past.

Nerves writhed in the pit of my stomach like vipers, but not because of the proximity to the site of the murders. I'd been on edge about my new roommate all summer—about what it would be like to share a bedroom with another person after eighteen years of my own space. Another person who could well be the devil, or worse, a snorer.

Friendship, for me, was a long game. Something that could not be rushed or fast-tracked. My affections were not the quick flint of a forest fire, but rather grew like ivy; a slow creep over many years, difficult to destroy with a barbed comment or a careless joke.

Ever since my best friend, Noémie, moved away, the thought of getting to know new people felt overwhelming. Noémie and I had known each other since primary school, and become properly close in sixth form. But having been born in Canada, she'd just moved back to Toronto to study, and I was already daunted by the crater she'd left behind. There had been an almost romantic layer to our relationship, limbs tangled as we slept, though we never kissed. Love-yous exchanged with a kind of fake casualness. I'd never entirely unpacked what I felt for Noémie, and I was a little afraid to.

Anyway, now it was too late. She was gone, and we didn't talk anymore, so what was the point of it all?

Back in high school, I never felt like I belonged. It was cool to look like you didn't try, like you'd just tossed on whatever novelty tee and dirty Converse you had lying around. I was scorned for trying too hard, for being too serious, for thinking too highly of myself. So I hoped my new roommate would be like me. I wanted someone I could discuss Sartre and Foucault and Nietzsche with while drinking red wine and whiskey. To speculate about the afterlife and the occult, and exchange beloved books and films. Someone who would make Northumberland feel so much larger than it was. Because if I couldn't go and study at Edinburgh or Harvard or Cambridge, Carvell had to be the next best thing.

When I found the room, it was still empty; no sign of my roommate yet. There were two single cabin beds bracketing a central arched window, each with a little rolltop desk tucked beneath the bunk. The carpet was a dark-green tartan and the walls were high and white. The window was open a sliver, and the smell of moss and rosemary and wild garlic drifted in on the breeze. It was at once achingly familiar and achingly sad. A connection to the Alice who used to make dens in the woods with her brothers, Aidan and Max, before Mum was diagnosed, before Max left for London.

It smelled of home, and yet I was not home. Not anymore.

CHAPTER 3

Alice

Just as I hoisted my suitcase onto the bare, rust-springed mattress, there was a pop of laughter from the corridor as someone fumbled with a key. The door lurched open, and behind it stood my new roommate and a man I assumed was her father.

She was tall and tanned, with long blond hair in french plaits. Fine-freckled and makeup-free, with a neat ski-slope nose and wide-set blue eyes. Denim shorts, despite the chilly Northumbrian breeze, and a tight black tank top. Slung over her shoulder was a Grays field hockey bag. All in all, she looked like a *Sports Illustrated* cover, and made me feel instantly dumpy and odd.

"Hi!" Her voice was light and mellifluous. Around her grinning mouth was something that looked a lot like sugar.

"I'm Charlotte, but everyone calls me Lottie. This is my dad, Dominic."

Dominic stepped forward eagerly, extending a broad hand. He was shorter than Lottie by an inch and wore a faded rugby shirt over pale-blue dad jeans, with the pink-cheeked look of the shamelessly outdoorsy.

"Hi! Dom! Great to meet you!"

Everything inside me groaned.

My new roommate was *cheerful*. From a *family* of cheerfuls.

"This is so cute," Lottie chirped, taking in the room with wide, wondrous eyes. "Oh my god, just adorable. I'm in love." Then, jabbing her thumb behind her, "Is that your car parked outside?"

Tucking a lock of hair behind my ear, I turned away. "Yeah. But I'm not going to Ikea with you."

I didn't know where the needless snark came from. I think she reminded me too much of the perky, popular girls who had spread vicious rumors about me in school.

She blinked in surprise. "Oh. I didn't—"

"No, I know," I interjected. "But it seems like that's the kind of thing you'd want me to do, so I just wanted to manage your expectations. The only Swedish things I care about are meatballs and Greta Garbo."

Stop being such a pretentious dick, I screamed internally, but it was no good. I was in full defense mode, performing myself so fiercely that she couldn't make me feel small for it.

"They have meatballs at Ikea," Dominic pointed out. He slung an expensive-looking weekend bag onto the empty bed, then tucked his hands into his jean pockets. "Though I have no idea who Greta Garbo is."

Lottie, who looked embarrassed by his admission, changed the subject. "I'm just *so* excited to be here. It's surreal. I can't wait for field hockey practice to start. And oh my god, the Refectory! Have you ever seen a cooler student union?" She laid her field hockey bag down on the desk with a clatter of wood. When I didn't reply to her almost offensive enthusiasm, she forced my hand with another question. "So where are you from?"

"Here," I answered, arranging a stack of books on my own little desk. "Northumberland."

Say something else, I urged myself, frustration ebbing like a current. *Stop being a joyless twat.*

"Nice!" Lottie smiled. "It's such an amazing part of the world." She paused, waiting for me to reciprocate the question. When I didn't, she glanced uncertainly at Dominic.

"We're from Kent," he said, still grinning that golden retriever grin, but there was a pointedness to his tone. "Maybe you can show Lottie around?" He tossed an arm over her shoulders, a bearlike act of reassurance that made me want to cry.

I did that. I made him feel like he needed to reassure her.

With a hot flash of shame, I suddenly couldn't bear to

be there a second longer, so I excused myself to go to the library.

"But we don't even have any classes yet . . . ," Lottie whispered, when she thought I was out of earshot.

"Don't worry, kiddo," Dominic replied. "You'll win her over. You always do."

Disappointment weighed heavy on me as I left the building. Lottie was nothing like Noémie. Noémie was deep-brown skin and cashmere sweaters, serious conversations and foreign films, the wistful smell of blue ink and old books, laughter as soft and smooth as butter. She was so much like me that it often felt like talking to myself. There was a unique kind of comfort in that.

And yet there was something eminently human about Lottie, an easy zeal I sorely lacked. Winding through the cobbled streets to the main convent, I continued the conversation with her in my head, imagining how a confrontation might play out. I always did this, always argued fiercely with people in my mind, mentally sparring with words like a boxer might practice punching.

The Sisters of Mercy Library was housed in the original convent, climbing in split levels up all three stories of the building. The upper floors were wraparound mezzanines, so from the center of the ground floor you could see all the way to the proud domed ceiling. There were wrought iron spiral staircases connecting different levels, and a hodgepodge of reading nooks with wingback armchairs and moth-eaten velvet footstools. Along one wall was a row of antique writing desks with little green bankers' lamps; beyond them, through arched windows, were acres and acres of gorse-pocked crags beneath a faded gray sky.

It was beautiful, but I could barely enjoy it. My jaw was tensed, my temples pulsed, every muscle and sinew taut and ready for a fight that wasn't coming. The exhausting anger is what pushed Noémie away in the end.

I should have known it would follow me here.

CHAPTER 4

My new roommate did nothing to alleviate the fear that I wasn't good enough to be at Carvell.

When I first met Alice Wolfe, she was stacking leather-bound editions of Sartre and Foucault and Nietzsche on her vintage bedside table, wine-red hair flipped over her face in a defiant wave. She wore a silver septum piercing and an unreasonable quantity of winged eyeliner. She was almost insultingly beautiful, albeit in a satanic sort of way.

Shortly after our scratchy first exchange, Alice left to go to the library, despite the fact that classes hadn't even started yet. I fought back tears; I was already so out of my depth.

As I hugged my dad goodbye, I felt an overwhelming tug toward home, an inexplicable franticness. I didn't want to be left here. I was suddenly very, very afraid, although I couldn't say of what, exactly. Something about the place felt innately hostile. The air was too cold and dry in my lungs, and that supernatural pulse was suddenly more unsettling than intriguing, a shadowy presence in the middle distance that vanished whenever I tried to look at it head-on.

It seemed completely impossible that just this morning, I was sitting having a birthday breakfast in my favorite Sevenoaks greasy spoon before Mum had to go to work. She'd been to the little jewelry shop on the high street and bought me a new charm for my bracelet: a little silver bumblebee. That's what they'd always called me. Their little bumblebee.

Now it dangled against my wrist, warm to the touch.

It had always been the three of us, and things would never be like that again. Sure, they'd always be my parents, and Sevenoaks would always be there for me to return to. But I had loved my friends, my school, walking my old dog, having breakfast with my mum and dad every morning. It had all been so easy, so safe, and now it was gone. The thought was so profoundly sad that it knocked the breath out of me.

"Dad," I mumbled into his broad chest. He smelled of home, and of our gray-bearded Labrador. "I . . ."

He gripped my shoulders and pushed me up off his chest, a certain ferocity in his gaze. "Just say the words, Lottie. Just say the words and we'll go home."

From the look on his face, I could tell he was thinking of Janie, of how she'd pleaded with her parents to come home, and how they forced her to stay. He wouldn't let history repeat in the same way.

I was tempted. God, I was tempted. But Carvell is what I'd been building to every moment of the last few years, ever since they'd announced their plan to reopen the school. Every grueling field hockey practice, every hour of mind-numbing exam revision. Every tear-filled fight with my parents about this decision.

Swallowing every irrational fear lodged in the back of my throat, I convinced myself that I was just being childish. There was no such thing as a supernatural pulse, and a place couldn't be innately hostile. My university experience would be what I made of it. All I had to do was approach my time here with the same passion and positivity I did everything else. My mum had taught me that raw enthusiasm can make up for almost any other deficit.

"Dad, it's okay." I smiled. "I promise."

Watching my dad as he shifted his weight from one foot to the other, I could tell he wanted to say something but didn't know how. I busied myself lifting books out of the box and onto the little writing desk. They suddenly seemed horribly juvenile compared to Alice's neat leather-bound stack.

"Kiddo, I . . . I found your scrapbook," he said, trying and failing to sound casual. My stomach tilted to one side. "The one with all of Janie's newspaper clippings. Is that why you're really here?"

Stacking my Raymond Carver paperback collection

beside a deep groove in the wood, I decided on a half-truth. "Kind of. I mean, I heard about Carvell because of her. But it's not *why* I'm here. It's an amazing school. One of the best—"

"—in the world for literature. I know." My dad sighed. "Please, just . . . I know you, Lottie. You're braver than I'll ever be. But don't go looking for trouble, okay? Don't go digging around in old mysteries. Keep your head down, focus on your work. Try to forget about Janie."

From the pain on his face, I knew he was thinking about her. I think he always was, in a way. And now it was all too easy to imagine me meeting the same fate.

But that was *why* I wanted answers. To give him and my mum—and Janie's family—the peace they'd been robbed of for so long. I was doing it for them. For Dad. To take some of that pain away. And call it hero complex, call it main character syndrome, call it whatever, but I genuinely believed I could do it.

"I'll be safe," I said, but I knew he wouldn't believe me in the slightest.

The tears didn't come in full force until he left, and I was alone in the bedroom I'd be sharing with a girl who had loathed me on sight. I hated to admit it, especially when I'd stubbornly told my dad I was absolutely fine, but this all felt wrong—not because of the historic murders or my capricious roommate or the strange, too-dry air, but because of me. I wasn't cellos and dark windowpanes, I wasn't leather-bound Sartre and wine-red hair, I wasn't Carvell. Everyone was going to sneer at me like Alice had.

Just as I was about to call my dad, to tell him to come back, come back, I've changed my mind, I noticed the view from our dorm room window for the first time.

My breath hitched in my chest.

We were directly opposite the North Tower.

CHAPTER 5

Alice

Dean Mordue stood in a tailored blue dress behind a polished walnut lectern. She was shorter and thinner than I expected her to be, but her shoulders were squared proudly, her chin tilted to the vaulted ceiling of the old chapel. Behind her was a vast rose window, glazed with cherry-red and forest-green stained glass, the whole thing divided into floral segments by intricate stone mullions. A black cat sat on the window ledge, peering in with vague interest.

Hands clasped tightly around the sides of the lectern, Mordue addressed the several hundred students packed into the pews.

"Many of you know of my own rich history with this school." Her accent was crisp and neutral, but there was a subtle Scottish rumble to it if you listened closely. "It was my very first faculty job, in its very first year of opening, which must be an inconceivably long time ago to your young minds. I had just received my doctorate in English literature from the University of Oxford, having been taught at undergraduate level by none other than J. R. R. Tolkien."

There was an audible gasp. I looked around at my peers, at the two stunned strangers flanking me in the pews, amazed they didn't know this already. It was almost as though they hadn't spent the whole summer researching Carvell and its faculty in immense detail. Weird.

The dean smiled warmly. "I arrived at Carvell bright-eyed and stuffed with wonder, ready to impart everything I'd learned. Shaping young minds was nothing short of magical to me. I still feel that way today, even after a long decade away from the place that has always felt like my home—both academically and spiritually. But, as they say, absence makes the heart grow fonder, and it is with immense gratitude that I welcome you all here today."

At the mention of the school's closure, the cold air was pulled taut.

A few pews over, I saw Lottie sit up straighter. By the looks of things, she'd already made friends with a couple of other girls. They were wedged tightly together in the pews, as though close physical proximity would cement their relationship faster. Something bitter curled in my stomach. People like Lottie would always make friends easily. It was my own fault I wasn't one of them.

I turned my attention back to Dean Mordue, who had let a misty silence settle around the chapel.

"The North Tower victims are with us today," she said firmly, but with a kind of defiant tenderness. "They will always be with us. Sam Bowey, Janie Kirsopp, Fiona Taylor, Dawn Middlemiss. I think of them every day. I pray for their families every night." She lifted a hand to the dainty cross necklace hanging at her throat. "They came—sorry." She took a quiet moment to compose herself, as though her emotions threatened to spill over. "They came to this university to give themselves better lives, and instead they lost them. This tragedy should never be shied away from, never be swept under the rug. May they never be forgotten."

She shifted on the stage, and it creaked beneath her pointed ankle boots. An old brown radiator sighed nearby. "That said, tragedy tourism will never be welcome on this campus. There will be no press interviews. There will be no photographs sold to the media. There will be no rumormongering, no childish speculation, no dishonoring the victims in either life or death. No putting their families through even more pain than they've already suffered. And finally, the North Tower is permanently out-of-bounds. Any student found breaching this rule will be expelled on the spot."

A murmur spread through the students like wind through rushes, but Mordue simply talked over it.

"First and foremost, we are here to *learn*. To grow. To think." She spread her arms wide. "We must never lose our thirst for knowledge, for understanding, for wisdom. So too must we strive for kindness, for sincerity, for collective purpose. And we must always look inward. We must study ourselves with rigor, and interrogate our flaws. We must become *better,* in all the ways it is possible to be so. We must not leave this school the same people we were upon arrival."

I shivered underneath my black wool turtleneck. A bat's gossamer wings fluttered in the rafters. As I peered upward, my gaze snagged on someone else's. The professor who'd witnessed my outburst this morning was watching me carefully. When I caught him staring, he didn't even have the good grace to look embarrassed. He simply smiled mildly and turned away.

Although the undertow of shame had mostly subsided, it rippled at the split-second interaction. A brilliant academic I had so badly wanted to impress already thought me awful. And who could blame him? My sharp edges were already snagging on the world around me.

Mordue clasped her hands together with an air of finality. "As I stand here, I am exceedingly hopeful and optimistic about the future of this school. How can I not be optimistic when I see the future in front of me? You are the future; the future is yours. Now go and claim it."

It was a rousing sentiment, one that brought to mind gusty autumn winds and choral music and black graduation caps tossed in the air.

And yet within weeks, that very future I was supposed to claim would be all but burned to ash.

CHAPTER 6

Lottie

Of all the hundreds of new students packed into the chapel for Dean Mordue's inauguration speech, I was the only one taking notes—and feeling extremely self-conscious as I did so. In my flared jeans, retro Adidas sweater and red beanie, I looked like an off-duty children's TV presenter. There was an honest-to-god packet of candy in my back pocket.

It wasn't cool to make an effort in Sevenoaks, but Carvell made me hate feeling so underdressed. I vowed to go clothes shopping with the student loan that had just landed in my bank account. I didn't own a single item of black clothing, which suddenly seemed like a grievous oversight.

Dean Mordue was finally talking about the North Tower murders, after twenty minutes of pretentious preamble in which she flexed her academic credentials with a shamelessness that seemed too much even for Carvell. My pulse quickened when she said Janie's name, and I started to bullet point the names of the other victims in my notebook—even though I'd studied the case for so long I knew them by heart.

"And finally, the North Tower is permanently out-of-bounds. Any student found breaching this rule will be expelled on the spot."

As Dean Mordue left the dais, disappointment crested in my chest. I'm not sure what exactly I had been expecting—for the dean to let slip a clue that would allow me to solve Janie's murder where the police had failed?—but her speech gave absolutely nothing away.

All I knew was that the chances of me staying away from the North Tower were slim to none. The tower was the reason I was here.

My phone vibrated in my pocket, and I pulled it out to see a text from Dad.

> Just getting a coffee at the service station. If you need me to turn around, speak now or forever hold your peace. (Kidding. I'll be there with a cup of tea whenever you need me.)

My nerves having settled somewhat since earlier, I popped a sour cherry candy in my mouth and forced myself to type out a chirpy response.

"Hey, what are you writing?" asked the girl next to me, gesturing to my notebook. She wore big tortoiseshell glasses and had long black hair and more piercings than I'd ever seen on a single human. Floral tattoos crept along the ridges of her shoulders and wound up her neck like wisteria. She wasn't gloomy like Alice, though. Her beaming smile and lilting Mancunian accent were incongruously sunny.

"Oh, erm, nothing," I said, tucking the notebook into my backpack and adjusting my beanie. "I'm Lottie, by the way."

Another wide smile. "I'm Nat, and this is my roommate, Sara." The girl next to her with tight ginger curls and a cream cable-knit cardigan waved theatrically. "We're already obsessed with each other."

Something childish in me glowered with jealousy. Why couldn't I have a roommate who described herself as "already obsessed" with me? Why had I been stuck with a literal porcupine?

Come on, Lottie, I told myself. *You had about fifteen thousand friends in school. Making new ones shouldn't be so hard.*

"What are you guys doing after this?" I asked, forcing my usual pep back into my voice as we stood and began shuffling down the pew. Carvell would be what I made it, and if I didn't find a lifelong friend in my roommate, I

could easily find more elsewhere. Friends were like Poké-
mon, right? I could just keep collecting them until one was
a shiny Charizard.

"We're going to get seriously pissed tonight at the
Refectory," Sara said, smearing garish red lipstick across
her mouth and pouting into a gemstone-studded pocket
mirror covered in smudges. "You should come!"

I grinned at her, this little flame-haired Charmander
with big potential. "I'm in. You can help me round out my
birthday in style, yeah?"

"It's your *birthday*?" shrieked Sara, as though I had
just announced my intentions to climb Kilimanjaro in the
nude. "Bitch, why didn't you say?"

This confused me, on account of the fact I had quite
literally just said it, but I laughed anyway.

"Right," said Nat, following me up the aisle toward the
exit. "Let's meet at seven to get you unbelievably fucked up."

Their friendliness settled the nerves in my belly to a
mere flicker. It was going to be fine. I didn't need my roommate to love me, as long as other people did.

(This was a complete lie. I'd always wanted to be loved
by everyone.)

As I left the chapel, I found myself wondering why I
hadn't told Nat and Sara what I was really writing in my
notebook. Perhaps it was Dean Mordue's cautionary words
about tragedy tourism and needless speculation, and it was
prudent to keep my cards close to my chest. Perhaps I realized how insanely narcissistic it was to think I could solve a

series of complex murders when professional investigators couldn't.

And yet I kept thinking about an idea from *In Cold Blood*, one of my favorite books. The fact that imagination was so powerful that it could open any door—and let terror walk right in.

The North Tower murders had gripped the nation. They were on the cover of every newspaper, at the start of every news segment. People discussed theories over hushed pints in bustling pubs, speculated over who had done it and why, or even suggested it was the work of a suicide cult. But when several years passed and the deaths remained unsolved, Carvell slipped out of the cultural zeitgeist the same way the Zodiac Killer did stateside. People just . . . moved on. But I never did.

What if it was *my* imagination that could open this long-sealed door?

What if the fact that Janie's death was so important to me was the key?

And if that key let the terror walk right into my own life, so be it.

CHAPTER 7

Alice

When I got back to my room Lottie was already there. She was tangled in a blue floral duvet cover she was trying to put on the bed. Although she didn't see me come in, thanks to the linen ski mask she'd inadvertently fashioned for herself, she must have heard my footsteps.

"Changing bedsheets is impossible, right?" she grunted. "Like, it's literally not a possible thing to do?"

She emerged from the sheets with a flustered harrumph, blond flyaways haloing her face. She glanced over at my still-unmade bed; I'd spent the whole afternoon meandering around the library instead of unpacking. "I think you're onto something. Just like, shunning bedsheets altogether. Jail cell chic."

I smiled tightly, hating that it was tight, hating that I

could feel my skin puckering around my lip scar, hating that there was nothing I could do about it.

"Yeah," I said, laying down my stack of library books on the heavily scratched desk. "I'd offer you a hand, but I'm rubbish at that stuff."

"What, like, laundry? Or being a good person?" Lottie grinned, then saw my expression. "I'm kidding! Oh my god, I'm kidding. I'm sure you're all sunshine and roses deep down."

I rolled my eyes, and muttered, "At least I keep my sharp edges on the surface, where people can see them. Unlike the girls in my high school, who . . ." I trailed off, realizing I didn't particularly want to share the worst moments of my teenage years with this near stranger.

"Ohhh, I get it," Lottie said slowly, with a triumphant grin. "*That's* why you don't like me." She stuffed a pillow into its creased case. "I remind you of the girls who were mean to you?"

"Don't psychoanalyze me," I practically spat, regretting it the second I did.

That's when Lottie's perky patience seemed to run out, and I didn't blame her. I knew I was making things difficult. Self-loathing beat in my skull like a pulse.

We continued unpacking for a few long, stony minutes. Watching her out of the corner of my eye, I saw a dazzling array of extracurricular paraphernalia: cross-country medals and grade eight piano certificates; a tennis racket and a trombone; a program from an amateur production of *The Rocky Horror Picture Show* that she'd starred in. I felt immediately and completely inferior. That was the kernel of truth at the center of my anger toward Lottie: I was jealous of girls like her. Girls who moved through the world with joy and ease.

I checked my phone and found a text from my dad. As it always did, my stomach flipped over. Texts from my dad usually meant something had happened with Mum; she was in hospital with kidney failure, or she'd had another seizure, or her vision had taken a nosedive. But today he was just telling me that I'd forgotten Alf, my childhood teddy I slept with every night, and did I want to come home this weekend to get him? He'd make my favorite roast beef, and I could tell them all about my first week. My heart twinged. I didn't know how to tell him that the decision to leave Alf behind was intentional. I fired off a quick message saying I'd think about it.

Noémie still hadn't replied to my text from earlier that morning. True, it was still early in Canada, but she was an early riser, waking at dawn for a long, slow jog every morning. And so for her not to reply to my text meant she really did hate me. A fist of grief opened in my chest, but I clamped it shut as quickly as I could.

Thankfully Lottie was far less stubborn than either me or Noémie, and she broke the silence first.

"Come on," she said, with that carefree grin. "I don't want it to be like this. I'm meeting some other girls at the student union in twenty minutes." She gave a little butt wiggle to indicate dancing. She really was exceptionally tall—at least six foot. Her whole body was long and muscular in a way that made my throat dry up. "You should come."

I knew I should say yes, just in the name of making things less awkward, but the thought of all those sweaty bodies made the belt around my chest tighten.

"Nah, I'm fine here." I gestured to the stack of library books on my desk. "I want to get ahead on the course reading."

Lottie laughed. "You're unbelievable. One drink! You can come for one drink."

"I do like to drink." I chewed my lip, thinking longingly of the softly lit reading nooks in the library. I could head there just before sunset, let the dusky lavender light drape over me through the arched windows. "But I really . . ."

Lottie folded her tanned arms. "Alice, come on. I'm not going to beg you. But I am going to guilt-trip you. It's my birthday." I looked at her in surprise, but she held up a palm as if to tell me not to bother addressing it further. "And I just left home, and I'm emotional, and I'm terrified that I made a big mistake coming here. So please. One drink."

The ease with which she shared all of these emotions momentarily stunned me. It felt like looking at a bright lamp head-on. It wasn't how we did things in our family. We skirted around the truth of our feelings, communicated through subtext and passive aggression, never apologized after an argument—just waited for the anger to naturally subside. It was a Northumberland thing.

Despite my involuntary eye roll, I caved under Lottie's emotional blackmail. "Fine. One drink."

CHAPTER 8

Lottie

The Refectory was a monstrous, magnificent place.

Not many student unions were housed in cathedral-style halls, with high, vaulted ceilings and arching stained-glass windows. It was dark outside, but the old Victorian streetlamps refracted broken light through the stained glass, casting strange kaleidoscopic shapes across the polished parquet dance floor.

It made my drinking spots back home look positively primitive. Flaky memorial park bench, this was not.

By the time I arrived with Alice, the holy space was already thronged with tipsy freshers, and I was desperate for a drink to round off the hard edges of the day. I felt emotionally wrung out from saying goodbye to my family, and from fretting over the fact that Alice thought I was tragic, and from finally standing in the shadow of the tower I'd thought about almost every day since I was nine years old.

"Bar?" I asked Alice, who was dressed more like an Ivy League professor than a cheap student.

"Bar," she confirmed.

From the grimace-set of her jaw, I guessed she felt as out of place as I did. Which was bonkers, because in her tawny tweed blazer, polished brogues and cigarette trousers, she looked like she had been born in a place like this.

I spotted Nat and Sara by the bar, white strobe lighting illuminating the orange frizz of Sara's curls. The four of us got a booth near the stage, and chatted about where we came from and what we were studying. Nat and Sara were both in the theatrical arts program and acted accordingly, all big hand gestures and performative laughter and Shakespeare quotes that didn't seem to make sense in the context.

At first I didn't find them that annoying—they were easy to talk to, at least, especially once I'd sank three drinks—but as I watched Alice visibly growing irritated, I began to see them through her eyes. They were try-hards, desperate to make a good impression, forcing friendships on the very first day rather than letting them grow organically.

Probably exactly how she saw me, too.

"So what made you choose theatrical arts?" asked Alice, with a curious twitch of her dark-red lips. Her

Cupid's bow was so pronounced that I found my eyes drawn to her slightly mocking half smile. She had that kind of cruel magnetism to her.

Then, when Nat announced proudly that "all the world's a stage," Alice mouthed along with her, as though she'd known all along what her answer would be. She caught my eye as she did so, and I had to bite down on my lower lip to keep from laughing. Even though I knew she was being cruel, it was briefly intoxicating to have a private joke with her.

It wasn't meant to last, though, because Alice's self-professed sharp edges were indiscriminate, and my turn to be on the receiving end rolled around faster than you could say *porcupine*. I'd been chatting about my field hockey scholarship, about how I very nearly missed out due to a knee injury, when she cut me off.

"I've never understood why Carvell offered sports scholarships," she said, as though innocently musing aloud. She rolled the ice cubes around in her tumbler. "It's an arts academy. Why does it matter how well people can hit a ball with a wooden stick?"

I was at least half a foot taller than her, but in that moment I'd never felt so small.

The trend of feeling like a philistine compared to Alice continued for the next few hours. I ordered vodka cranberry; she ordered whiskey on the rocks. I passed around a packet of Skittles, she looked at me as though I'd assassinated her mother. I leaped up to dance when a

Kanye song came on; she cast a disparaging look in the DJ's direction.

After an hour of loose-limbed dancing, Nat yelled, "I'm going to the bathroom!"

"Me too!" Sara screamed back, her eyes glassy. She was drunker than I realized, hanging on to Nat for support.

"I'll go get us some water!" I shouted, making a gesture toward the bar. It really was extremely hot; the hairs at the nape of my neck were sodden. Sweat pooled at the base of my spine and soaked through the waistband of my jeans.

As I stood at the crowded bar waiting to be served, I found myself tentatively imagining a future at Carvell with Nat and Sara as my friends. We'd hang out on the grassy lawns in front of the old convent, studying and laughing and sipping from little cans of pear cider. I'd go to watch them in their plays, or help them run lines in the dressing room, while they'd cheer for me at my field hockey matches. I allowed myself a private smile.

But the moment of internal peace did not last.

Nat and Sara came back from the bathroom different people from the ones I'd just been dancing with. They were high on something, erratic and jittery, with an owl-eyed intensity I didn't trust. As they took their places beside me, fingers rapping frantically on the polished oak like concert pianists, I tried to tell myself it was no big deal, but deep down my heart sank.

Then, over the sound of the thudding bass, I heard a nearby commotion.

"Oh my god!" Nat shrieked. She was staring somewhere over my left shoulder. "Oh my god oh my god oh
my god!" Her voice was a cocaine-addled air-raid siren.

"What? What happened?" I winced as she grabbed me
too hard by the back of the arm.

"Your roommate just punched someone."

CHAPTER 9

Alice

Music pulsed through the Refectory like a living thing. My brain beat against my temple to the rhythm of it; sweat trickled down the ridged white bones of my spine.

The Refectory had an ominous kind of sentience, breathing and shifting unnaturally. As the night wore on, the ceiling seemed to grow farther and farther away, and the walls grew nearer. It was as though a great hand had grabbed the roof like a fistful of clay and begun to stretch it upward. One of the stained-glass windows appeared to flicker and change, too. In the time it took me to blink, the Virgin Mary would go from the picture of innocence to a snarling serpent and then back again. Every so often, my vision would flash ruby red in a way that had nothing to do with the strobe lighting.

Panic started to climb in my chest, claustrophobia pressing in on me from all angles.

I had to get out of there.

I'd fulfilled my promise to Lottie of staying for one drink. In fact, I think I'd had four. Four cheap whiskeys scorching my gullet like paint stripper. The drunkenness didn't feel as good as it did when I was curled up in an armchair, reading Bertrand Russell and sipping Lagavulin. In that safe, quiet environment, the alcohol loosened my mind enough to let the ideas flow, to give my thoughts room to breathe and expand, but I still felt safe and contained.

This night was different. There was a wildness to it I didn't like, a rabid unpredictability.

Blazer slung over my forearm, I was pushing my way through beer-sloppy dancers to the exit when a heavy hand closed hard around my wrist.

For a blazing millisecond, I was back in my ex-boyfriend Chris's starkly lit living room, back in that awful moment, and my free hand went protectively to my lips, but I was yanked back to the Refectory with a painful twist of my arm.

A floppy-haired, slack-faced student in a white slogan tee was on the other end of the grip. His drunk eyes roamed over me, and he smiled lazily, and pulled me closer and yelled into my ear, "You're not going anywhere, gorgeous. You're staying here with me."

And then he leaned in to kiss me.

Repulsion roiling in my gut along with the cheap whiskey, I tried to twist my wrist free of his grasp, but even in his intoxicated state, he was still too strong, and I *hated* him for that, for this easy way he could control me no matter how drunk he was, and that hatred sharpened into a violent shard, and some animalistic fear took over everything.

The starburst of pain in my hand when it made contact with his cheekbone felt like power.

Then the circle of friends he'd been dancing with closed around us like vultures, and I realized just how outnumbered I was.

But they were *laughing* at him. They didn't believe I could seriously hurt him. And so even though I could tell I'd hurt him, he was forced to laugh it off too. After all, he'd been hit by a *girl*. It would be inconceivably embarrassing to admit I'd caused him any pain.

Their laughter was flint to a flame.

I wanted them to *fear* me.

Without any forethought or conscious intention, my hand reached out and grabbed an empty beer bottle. Gripping the neck with my palm, I brought the bottom of the bottle down on the side of a table with a satisfying shatter, so all that was left in my hand were jagged glass teeth.

Stepping toward the guy I'd just punched, I pressed the broken end into his stomach, just hard enough for him to feel the spikes as they were about to pierce his skin.

His eyes widened, and something monstrous inside me writhed with pleasure.

"Don't you *ever* fucking touch me again," I hissed.

The soft ebb of pleasure grew into a roaring warm internal gush.

I leaned forward, and the shards pierced his skin. He gave a yelp of pain, then quickly disguised it with a more masculine grunt as I stepped back and dropped the bottle to the ground.

"Harris, what the hell, bro?" yelled one of his equally intoxicated friends.

"Fucking psycho!" he snorted, shaking his head in disbelief. Then he turned to his group. "Did you see that? What a fucking *psycho*!"

I turned on my heel and walked away, relief and something headier coursing through me. I was pretty sure he wouldn't take it any further—to security, or to the dean—because that would be too humiliating for his fragile ego. I pushed through the gaggles of dancing bodies and left the Refectory, stumbling into the blurry night beyond.

Once the adrenaline had worn off, I was filled with shame.

Shame over what I'd done, but worse, because it had felt so *good*.

That split second of raising my fist, of cocking my arm, of throwing all my weight behind it, of making sweet, crisp impact . . . there was no denying how richly satisfying it had been. Every muscle in my body felt alert and was tingling with energy. Every overthinking synapse in my brain ceased firing for a moment, and there was only the raw physicality of the act.

And then, his fearful expression when I had pressed the glass into his stomach. I had stolen the power from him. I had righted a wrong. He had made me feel small and vulnerable, and I had turned it around with a dramatic swing of the pendulum.

Until that night, I had never hit another person before. Growing up, my brothers Max and Aidan had always grappled, always play-fought and wrestled with gleeful shrieks and grunts. Afterward they'd be so mellow, so happy, as though some primal desire had been released. They'd shovel dinner into their faces with a wolflike hunger before falling asleep the second their heads hit the pillow.

It was different for me, as the only daughter. If I ever tried to join in, Mum or Dad would pull me away, tell me girls didn't fight. It was just boys being boys. Boys were stronger than girls, and they didn't want me to get hurt. I was encouraged to sit quietly in a corner, painting pretty pictures, reading books about unicorns, watching my brothers tussle with a secret, shameful envy, a feeling of that same primal desire left buried.

So was it any wonder that by the time I was in Chris's starkly lit living room, or the dark, pulsing Refectory, I didn't know how to wrest my own wrist free? I didn't have the strength or the experience from years of harmless adolescent practice. I didn't have the muscle memory to fight back.

That night in the Refectory felt like a rusty pressure valve finally loosening, and I was afraid of what that meant.

CHAPTER 10

Lottie

I followed Alice out of the Refectory, and despite the tears stinging my eyes—this had been the worst birthday of my life, and I missed home so much already—I offered to walk back to the dorm with her.

"I'm fine," she snapped, in a particularly porcupiney manner. "Go and hang out with your new *friends*." Her tone made the very concept of friendship seem absurd and unreasonable.

"No, Alice," I said faux sternly, folding my arms against the chill of the night. "I want to make sure you're safe."

"How very noble of you," she seethed, her body writhing with a strange tension.

"Look, what's your problem?" I asked, raising my voice against the ringing in my ears. "I've been nothing but nice to you since we got here."

Alice shook her head, as though I could never understand her. Then she shot me a vicious look and swiveled on her heel, leaving me standing on the mist-slicked cobbles alone.

As I watched her walk away, a stubborn upward tilt to her pixie chin, I found myself not wanting to go back inside to find Nat and Sara. They had actively made the situation with Alice worse, Sara shrieking hysterically and Nat rolling up her sweater sleeves like she wanted a piece of the action herself. It wasn't just that they were high, I realized. It was that they were drama leeches. They loved the fact that my roommate hit someone on my birthday. I got the sense that they'd tell the story to their fellow thespians first thing in the morning, embellishing and exaggerating for greater effect.

Nor did I want to go back to the dorm, on account of my possibly encountering Alice summoning Satan for a cup of tea and a catch-up. If I was honest with myself, she utterly terrified me. Not in a *you look like you want to murder me but you're probably fine* way, but in a *you look like you want to murder me and you probably will* way. I decided I would sneak in when she was asleep—assuming she was the kind of demon who required rest in the first place.

Despite the cold, I decided to go for a walk around the old convent building and see the statue of Sister Maria, which was supposed to be insanely creepy. I wouldn't normally walk alone at night, but there were so many people milling around campus that it somehow felt safe.

As I gathered my bearings and started to walk, a silvery fog drifted around the tree-lined walkways in eerie whorls that licked at the feet of the convent. With the hypnotic plainsong of my footsteps on cobbles, I slipped into some kind of exhausted trance, my mind pleasantly scrubbed free of thought or precognition.

A few images broke through the haze: a cigarette butt smoldering warm orange at the base of a twisted hazel tree; a howler's moon hanging low and bright in the sky; Salem stalking up a drainpipe and through an open window on the third floor. When the black cat looked back over her shoulder before disappearing into the room, her eyes flashed a brief ruby red. I looked around for the source—a reflection of something?—but found none.

Before I knew it, I was standing not at the statue of Sister Maria, but at the foot of the North Tower.

I felt the sudden, stomach-yanking sensation of missing a step.

Why had I gravitated toward the North Tower with no conscious desire to do so? Was the pull of it so magnetic?

I felt insane just thinking it. Yet looking up at the tower from the wonky cobbles below, its proportions seemed all wrong. It stuck up too high above the rest of the convent and leaned slightly toward the north. There were no windows apart from the arched orifices in the observatory at the very top, where there had once been telescopes (the nuns got really into astronomy in the late 1800s).

It was from those open maws that the victims had fallen to their deaths.

At first, there was nothing in the incidents to point to murder. Sam Bowey died first. He was Janie's new boyfriend—a similarly quiet musician from County Durham—and he fell from the tower just weeks after they got together. Janie testified that she had broken up with him just hours before his death, and so, coupled with reports that he was failing his classes, the police believed it was suicide. Case closed.

Until Janie died too, less than a week later.

Her death was different, because her body showed signs of a struggle. She had finger-shaped bruises on her upper arms, scratches on her face and chest, and significant bruising around her neck. It was rumored that she had been hoisted over the windowsill by her throat.

At that point there were still no real leads, no genuine suspects. Nobody had seen anything suspicious; even the students in the dorms adjacent to the North Tower hadn't seen anyone coming or going.

The police followed all kinds of lines of inquiry to find a motive. It seemed a huge coincidence that two new lovers could be killed within six days of each other by a total stranger, so they started looking at other students who knew them both. Maybe someone in love with one or both of them who had acted from jealousy. That avenue was mostly fruitless—any evidence the police uncovered was flimsy and circumstantial at best. It was an investigation built on gossip and hearsay.

Finally, two weeks after Janie's death, Fiona Taylor and Dawn Middlemiss died on the same night. They fell within minutes of each other, their shattered bodies stacked on top of each other like a dreadful cairn at the foot of the North Tower. Their bodies had been ravaged by awful, almost subhuman claw marks. The police suspected there was a serial killer at large, and Carvell was closed with immediate effect.

Despite years of inquiries and investigations, the murders were never solved. The killer was never caught.

But now, standing mere yards from where those broken bodies had been found, an utterly ridiculous and yet frankly terrifying prospect came to me: What if the tower itself was the murderer?

It had overridden my conscious thoughts to draw me here. Was it haunted? Possessed? Or was I simply too intoxicated?

An owl hooted nearby, snapping me out of my reverie. Before I turned to head back to the dorm, another strange impulse overcame me, and I felt my body moving about five seconds ahead of my brain.

I closed the distance between the tall, arched doorway at the foot of the North Tower and grabbed the wrought iron handle. It was icy to the touch. When I tried to turn it, a rusting mechanism jarred.

Locked.

The brief spell broke. I let go.

Relief washed over me like a fine, cool mist.

I hadn't wanted to do that. I hadn't *not* wanted to, either, but it was still unsettling. A vague, pervasive sense of dread that I couldn't quite name.

Giving my head a good shake, I turned on my heel and walked straight into Dean Mordue.

Dean Mordue, who had said not eight hours earlier that any student caught sniffing around the North Tower would be expelled on the spot.

"Dean Mordue, I—"

"It's locked," she said in a clipped voice, holding up an ancient-looking brass key and wiggling it with an air of irritation. "Why are you here?"

I racked my brain for an innocent explanation, but nothing came. "I don't know. I was just drawn to it, I guess."

There was an agonizing split second in which I had no idea how she was going to react. She looked simultaneously on the verge of detonation and tears.

Mercifully, the latter prevailed.

Her shoulders sank as she sighed heavily, pinching the bridge of her nose with her free hand.

"I was so afraid of this." Her voice was quiet and watery, worlds away from the clarion pitch of her inauguration speech.

"Afraid of what?" I asked, practically a whisper.

My imagination galloped ahead of me.

Was she about to admit the tower was haunted? Or were the aforementioned vodka cranberries addling my judgment? Until this point in my life, I'd associated a belief in "hauntings" with general psychological instability.

Mordue tucked the key into the pocket of her peacoat and stared up at the North Tower like it was a lifelong nemesis. "That students would be fixated on what happened here. That Carvell would always be about the murders, not the learning. That . . . that the wound would be prodded so much it would never heal. God, sorry." Her hand went to her cross necklace. "I shouldn't be off-loading this on you." I could practically hear her tell herself to toughen up. "If I see you here again, you're gone. Okay?"

"Okay." I nodded. "Thank you, miss." Adding "miss" onto the end seemed an incredibly childish thing to do, but I had no idea how to address authority figures in this strange new world.

Scurrying in the direction of my dorm, I looked down at the baby pink wristwatch I'd worn since I was twelve.

Five minutes after midnight.

Something in my brain snagged on this, but it wasn't until I got back to Willowood that I realized why.

All of the North Tower murders had happened within five minutes of midnight.

CHAPTER 11

Alice

Lying in bed the next morning, I was acutely aware of Lottie's breathing. The room smelled of stale vodka and furred breath, and of the empty sweet wrappers all over her desk. I longed to crack the window, to let in that gentle, nourishing scent of rosemary, moss and wild garlic, but I was afraid of disturbing Lottie. Of inviting a conversation I wasn't ready to have.

In any case, assaulting a guy on her birthday was probably the final nail in the my-roommate-hates-me coffin. All right, so she'd tried to follow me out, offered to walk me home, but by then all I wanted was to be alone, not reminded of how awful I was by my too-nice, too-perfect roommate. So I pushed her away with a final verbal shove, and it seemed to have done the job.

If she was going to hate me, I wanted it to be on my terms.

As quietly as I could, I slipped on the same black turtleneck and beige cigarette trousers I'd worn yesterday, put the day's textbooks into my satchel, and headed out to my first seminar.

Introduction to Philosophical Theology, like all lectures and seminars, was held in the old convent building. Room 26B was a high-ceilinged, tall-windowed space with old-fashioned school desks arranged in neat rows. The slatted wooden floorboards creaked moodily under the weight of thirty students piling in.

Professor Anton Le Conte stood at the front of the classroom, studying the blank blackboard intently. He held a piece of brand-new white chalk between his thumb and forefinger like a pen, as though contemplating the first mark to make with it—like that first mark was symbolic somehow. I supposed it was. This was a blackboard left blank for ten years. It seemed to matter how that hiatus was broken.

I took a seat in the front row, wincing as I unfurled my fist from around the handle of my satchel. Punching people *hurt*. It was a strangely pleasant ache, though, like tired legs after a long walk.

Dressed in a sharply cut waistcoat and perfectly pressed slacks, Le Conte was a lean, spritely man with pale olive skin and flecks of silvery gray in his black hair. I knew he'd spent the last few years editing the *European Journal of Natural Theology* before being lured back to the place where he first established his name in the philosophical theology sphere. A paper he published during his tenure here, on the impact of modern philosophy on hermeneutics, was widely hailed. He put Carvell's floundering philosophy program on the map, and merely being in the same room as him carried an almost electric charge.

As he finally turned to address the room, a hush fell over the giggling back row. His gaze was intense, his movements careful and quiet. Authority emanated from him in waves.

"Why are you here?" he asked, not with the insistent boom of a classics professor but with the soft restraint of a man who knew his own power.

The question was met with silence; even the creaking radiators were afraid to breach the taut quiet.

"I know why *I'm* here," he said, gesturing around. "We natural theologians provide arguments for the existence of God based on reason and rationality. Where better to do so than a former convent?" He smiled out the high window at the woods and the crags beyond. "The place is steeped in all the inspiration I'll ever need. But why are *you* here?"

He looked around, taking in each of us individually, weighing us against some invisible measure. Then he asked again, "Why philosophy?"

Forcing any tentativeness out of the action, I raised my hand. He nodded for me to speak. "I want to be a judge."

His eyes bore into mine, dark and hawklike. "So why not a law degree?"

I met his intensity, leaned into the earnest core of myself, and hoped to hell he would approve of it. Because if I couldn't be myself *here,* where would I ever belong?

"Before I learn what to think," I say, voice low and clear, "I want to learn *how* to think."

It was the kind of statement that would have earned sniggers and eye rolls in high school, would've had me labeled pompous and pretentious, but Professor Le Conte gave a small, satisfied nod. The other students didn't look at me with ridicule; in fact they seemed begrudgingly impressed.

This is the feeling, I thought. *This is the feeling I would have all the time as a judge. Like people care about what I have to say.*

The rest of the class, though, left me a little deflated. I quickly realized I was already way ahead in terms of background reading. All Le Conte did was draw the lines between civil, natural and mythical philosophy for those who'd never heard of any of them. Concepts I'd been exploring since I was fifteen were presented as brand-new information. Still, part of me enjoyed the feeling of superiority it gave me. I'd always placed so much importance on my intellect, and having it affirmed gave me a much-needed bolster.

Five minutes before the end of the seminar, there was a lazy knock on the door. It croaked open before Le Conte could even address it.

In the doorway stood Professor Dacre, in his brown corduroy suit, mustard-yellow tie and off-white shirt.

The head of the program, who'd seen me verbally abuse a member of staff not twenty-four hours earlier.

For a fleeting moment, my stomach sank. Was he here to kick me out? Had he heard what I'd done to Harris? Coupled with the way I'd spoken to the woman in the entrance hall, I wouldn't blame them for expelling me from the program.

Yet he didn't even look in my direction. He smiled broadly around the room, exposing coffee-stained teeth, then nodded at Le Conte as he crossed to the front of the classroom holding a single sheet of white printer paper. They exchanged a few hushed words before Dacre crossed back to the door and left, leaving the sheet of paper in Le Conte's wiry hand.

Le Conte held it up and raised one eyebrow in a perfectly groomed arch. "Private tutor assignments." He laid the paper down on his squat walnut desk. "Come and find your name at the end of the session."

There was a faint flutter of excitement just below my ribs. Who would be my private tutor? Students worked closely with their tutors throughout their entire time at Carvell—it was really more of a three-year mentorship. I'd have been happy with Le Conte, but my top choice was Professor Lucille Arundel, who was doing groundbreaking work in the field of applied aesthetics. Before the university closure she was known for floating around campus in Grecian gowns, and had many thousands of pounds' worth of nineteenth-century art hanging in her office. After hearing that she'd be returning to teach when the university reopened, I'd mentioned her specifically in my personal statement.

As soon as the bell rang, I shoved shamelessly past my ambling peers and reached the list first, hoping beyond all reason that it would be Lucille's name next to mine.

But it wasn't.

It was Dacre's.

CHAPTER 12

Lottie

The morning after the North Tower drew me to its door, I had field hockey tryouts.

By the time I woke up around half past nine, Alice was already gone, and I was relieved. I couldn't face her after what she'd done in the Refectory—and the vitriol she'd spat my way as we stood outside. No doubt she'd be pricklier than ever today, doubling down on her actions instead of admitting fault. I didn't know her well yet, but that seemed like the kind of approach she'd take.

How was I ever going to be able to relax around her? She was gloomy and unpredictable, a melancholy violin strung so tightly she was always a split second from snapping.

Then there was what had happened last night, the invisible lasso of the North Tower. It was one thing telling my dad I'd be safe, that I'd do my best to avoid anyone who seemed a bit murdery, but what if that killer was a sentient tower whose will could not be overridden?

For now, though, my focus had to be making the field hockey team and fulfilling the scholarship requirements. I'd figure out Alice and the North Tower later.

As I traipsed down to the field, munching on a handful of Haribo Starmix, I found myself feeling jittery. Intellectually I had no reason to be nervous. I'd represented my county several times during sixth form, in field hockey, tennis and cross-country. The surgery I'd had on my knee last spring had gone well, and it was pretty much fully rehabbed. Plus there was the fact that competition wouldn't be as stiff as it would be at other universities, because there were no second, third or fourth years to compete with. And yet none of that eased the cramping in my stomach as the pitch came into view. There were already dozens of girls warming up.

The field hockey pitch was my domain. It was where I felt most confident and most powerful. I just had to lean into that. I hoisted my stick bag higher up on my shoulder and picked up the pace, hearing my dad's North London accent in my head.

You're nervous because you care. That's a good thing, kiddo.

But from the moment I started sidestepping in the warm-up, everything felt wrong. I realized I wasn't just nauseous from nerves—I was also nauseous from five double vodka cranberries and a terrible night's sleep. My feet kept tripping over themselves, and the turf blurred as I grew ever more light-headed. I made bad impact with the ball on my first few strikes, and the stinging reverberations up my arms made it hard not to yelp. The heat of the two coaches' stares bore into me, and when I glimpsed over, they were talking behind their hands. Probably saying, "What the shitting hell, we gave this bitch a full-ride scholarship and now she's playing like a concussed slug?"

There was also a strange tugging sensation just above my belly button, and my gaze kept flitting up to the shadowy outline of the North Tower. It felt as though something sentient had sunk its claws into me, and it didn't like that my attention was elsewhere.

I remembered the flash of Salem's ruby-red gaze with a shudder.

Supernatural pulse, indeed.

The tryouts never really improved, and while I ended up making the squad, it was as a reserve. Mortified and humbled, I tried to grab my stick bag as fast as I could and leave the pitch without having to show my reddened cheeks to anyone, but someone appeared by my shoulder.

"Chin up, chuck," said a low, broad Yorkshire voice. "Just a bad day. We've all had 'em, when you feel like you can't do anything right."

I looked up to see a short, curvy Asian girl in a dark-red top that said SPRINGDALE HIGH. She'd played sweeper on the opposite side to me during trials.

I smiled brightly, even though I felt anything but. "Yeah. Just a shame that day had to be today."

She snorted as she wiggled out her gum guard and snapped it into its plastic box. "I played so badly at county tryouts last year that I chipped my own tooth. With my own stick. That shouldn't be physically possible." She opened the silicone cap of her water bottle and took a big gulp, then wiped her mouth on the back of her forearm. "I'm Jen, by the way."

"Lottie. Lottie Fitzwilliam."

"I baptize you Fitzy." She made an invisible cross on her chest as though deep in prayer. "A load of us are going to the Grandstand after we're showered. You fancy it?"

"What's the Grandstand?"

Jen grinned. "The Refectory's demure grandfather."

"Demure grandfather" turned out to be an apt description of the Grandstand Parlor. If it was possible for a bar to wear velvet slippers and smoke a pipe, this place would do it.

Situated in a far-flung corner of the old convent, it was an oak-paneled, green-carpeted room solely for the use of Carvell athletes. There were faded pool tables with brass pendant lamps, antique dartboards with gold numbers missing, marble chessboards and intricately carved backgammon sets, and a roaring fireplace that made me want to curl up and take a catnap. The walls were adorned with old team photos from decades gone by, and a row of glass-front cabinets were full to bursting with trophies. The whole space smelled of woodsmoke and spiced cigars.

When I walked in, Jen and some of the other players from tryouts were dominating the chesterfield sofas by the fire, and Jen immediately called out, "Fitzy! Over here!"

I grinned from ear to ear. Maybe these were my people. My shiny Charizards.

The next thing I knew, I was at the bottom of the North Tower again.

Midnight darkness had descended on campus. I was on my hands and knees on the rain-slicked cobbles, clawing at the unrelenting stone with my bare hands.

Pain rocketed up my fingers and wrists like bolts of electricity. I let out an involuntary groan as I snatched them from the curved wall.

The last thing I remembered was leaving the Grandstand in high spirits after an afternoon of hilarity and banter. Jen had convinced me to go for a dance at the Refectory before we retired for the evening. We'd been sampling Lindisfarne Mead in the bar, pretending to be medieval monks—Jen's impression had me in stitches—and it had a profound effect on my intoxication levels. Once we got to the Refectory, there was just a confusing montage of red light, stained glass, pounding bass, sweaty skin, close bodies, and then . . .

Footsteps approached.

I didn't have time to process the confusion or fear; I just had to get out of the way before someone found me here again.

I crawled along the ground to the foot of the nearest tree and folded myself into its shadows. The dew on the grass was cold and wet as it seeped through my jeans, and I heard a snail crunch beneath my knee. My heart galloped in my chest; my pulse a high, thin staccato in my temples.

What the fuck is happening to me?

The sound of a key in a lock. Resting my palm on a misshapen gnarl, I risked a glance around the knotted trunk.

Mordue. She obviously performed a search of the tower every night at midnight.

She was the dean of the university. Didn't she have better things to do? Didn't she trust a security guard?

Then I remembered the aching sadness in her voice as she reprimanded me last night. This was personal to her. I made a mental note to check whether she had a connection to any of the original victims. Someone she'd mentored, perhaps?

She slipped inside and pulled the door closed behind her, locking it from the inside.

I waited for her silhouette to appear in one of the open

windows of the observatory, but the pain in my hands overtook me before that could happen. I looked down to survey the damage.

Even in the near darkness, the blood running down my fingers was unmistakable.

CHAPTER 13

Alice

Dacre would be my mentor.

The shame of my first day at Carvell came flooding back. It had started with cursing at the welcome-desk woman and ended in a free-flying fist—and a shattered bottle pressed into a guy's stomach. That ugly wrath had been Dacre's very first impression of me. Would he ever take me seriously as an academic? Would I spend the next few months or years clawing back the respect I'd lost? Or was I forever tarnished?

How thoroughly unreasonable for my actions to have consequences.

And yet as much as I was ashamed of what I'd done, the shame was still undercut with that terrifying sense of satisfaction, of rightness, of ancient scales rebalanced. I was afraid to look at that feeling any more closely.

After Le Conte's seminar, I went to the dining hall for a late breakfast. The room was much like the others in the Jerningham building, with high white walls and tall Gothic windows and scuffed wooden floors, only about ten times the size. It rang with the sound of clinking teaspoons and hungover laughter, and smelled of burnt sausages and ketchup and bad filter coffee. The scent made my stomach roil and clench, but I knew I'd feel better with some food inside me. I realized too late that I hadn't had dinner last night, which is probably why the four whiskeys had left me feeling so jaded. A headache had already begun to pound at my temples.

I grabbed some boiled eggs, a few slices of buttered toast and a black coffee the size of my head, then slid onto one of the long benches that filled the dining hall. Looking around nervously, I scanned the room for the guy I'd assaulted in the Refectory, but I couldn't see him anywhere.

I hope he choked on his own vomit.

The thought arrived in my head fully formed, yet I found that I truly meant it in the very depths of my chest. In that split second of vindictive malice, I genuinely wanted him to be dead.

Shrugging the feeling off like a coat, I forced a spoonful of yolk into my mouth, tried not to gag, and pulled out my phone. Still nothing from Noémie. I started typing a text to my older brother, Max, who was a third year studying fashion at Central Saint Martins.

But I didn't know how to finish the message. How could I possibly articulate the things I was feeling? He always told me I was a "sulky mare" (his words), but if he knew I'd almost stabbed someone . . . there was just no way he'd relate. Max had always been the life and soul of the party, the raucous karaoke and feather boas, the snazzy cocktails with tiny pink umbrellas. I was the one who felt like an alien half the time.

The idea of going back to the dorm after breakfast filled me with dread, but as it turned out, I was destined to run into Lottie that morning regardless.

When I entered the Sisters of Mercy Library, I saw her sitting in one of the green velvet chairs by the theology section, reading a massive purple book. Her hair was pulled up in a messy blond ponytail, and she wore a frankly horrifying fleece with a green-and-purple zigzag pattern.

As I walked past her to the spiral staircase, she glanced up at me, offered a tight smile, then looked pointedly back down at her book. For a moment I considered apologizing, but her stiff body language told me it would be wasted breath. I gripped the handle of my satchel even tighter, the ache in my hand still fresh and deep, and kept walking.

I headed up to the philosophy section, to check out one of the only books on Le Conte's list that I hadn't already read, only to find myself so utterly sapped of energy that I slumped down into the nearest armchair instead.

It was there, from that velvety perch, that I spotted the book that would change everything.

Bound in a woven emerald-green hardcover, the volume had an embossed gold title on its spine: *Soul-Purification Rituals in 19th-Century Convents* by T. A. Renner.

Something about the words *soul purification* gave me that academic flutter I'd spent the last few years of my life pursuing. Mysticism was very much in my research interests, and this sounded right up my alley. Plus, we were *in* a former convent that had been operational in the nineteenth century.

A quick scan of the introductory chapters outlined a purification ritual devised by a wrathful Sister Lois in the mid-1800s to rid herself of violent thoughts and impulses. It soon became popular in nunneries across northern England and the Scottish Borders, but fell out of favor for unknown reasons around the turn of the century.

At first, I found it strange that the book was shelved in the philosophy section. Surely it was more at home in theology? Or perhaps history? But then again, the very notion of having a soul was fundamentally a philosophical one.

The next chapter, "How the Ritual Was Performed," was any aspiring occultist's dream come true. It was essentially a how-to guide complete with diagrams, equipment lists and detailed instructions.

For the most part, it was pretty standard fare. Grinding wild ingredients like pimpernel and heather and rosemary with a pestle and mortar. Pulverizing a recently abandoned moth chrysalis, and then gently murdering a living moth in order to extract hemolymph from its arthropod. So far, so creepy.

And then it devolved into blood magic.

The final part of the ritual required the blood of a person they had wronged. This blood would be mixed with the pulped ingredients and then stirred into fresh elderflower cordial. One of these tinctures per moon cycle was said to eradicate wrath from the soul.

My heart beat a little faster.

I was no stranger to rituals. First there was my religion-questioning phase when I was twelve, during which I performed a series of elaborate chants intended to summon the Holy Spirit. Then there was my witchcraft phase, when I got heavily into moon manifestation rituals. I'd cleanse my space with sage smudge sticks, cleanse my body with a lavender salt bath, light candles and incense and pray to the moon herself.

In short, I'd always believed there was something more to the universe, something more than what we could see and hear and taste. There were mysterious energies and forces at play, invisible currents and complex webs, strings of light and dark that only a select few knew how to pluck and weave and snap. Maybe that's why I didn't immediately dismiss the moth blood tincture as irrational folklore.

Maybe that's why it lurked in the back of my mind for weeks before I finally acted on it.

CHAPTER 14

Lottie

Years of field hockey injuries meant I always had a well-stocked first-aid kit, so the first thing I did when I got back to the dorm after my harrowing midnight sojourn was clean and bandage my bleeding hands. Alice stirred a few times while I was opening sachets of antibacterial wipes, but she didn't wake up. I didn't know whether I was glad or not—she terrified me, but I would've appreciated some help.

And yet how would I have explained this to her? It probably didn't matter. She was a goth. They probably got off on this stuff.

My trembling hands were in bad shape. The nails were sanded down to stumps, and the soft skin on my fingertips had been ravaged into bloody frays. Bile rose in my gullet as I thought about how hard and how long I must have been clawing at the stone to do this much damage.

I had to stop drinking so much. Not only had a perilous hangover cost me a starting place on the field hockey squad, but those loose nights kept ending in the same place. A place that could see me dead if it got the better of me.

And who drinks *mead,* for god's sake?

Banishing the mental image of my parents weeping at my funeral, I swallowed a couple of painkillers and forced myself to get some sleep.

The next day I didn't have anything on my timetable until the English lit welcome session at three p.m., so I got up early—wincing as my bandaged fingertips brushed the duvet—and headed to the dining hall for a hearty breakfast. As I was pulling on a hoodie, Alice noticed my hands, but she didn't bother asking what had happened. It was a small thing, but it made me incredibly sad. If this had happened back in Sevenoaks, I would have had multiple relatives and about fifteen pals cooing over me by now.

With a sudden pang, I realized how much I missed my friends back home and made a mental note to call my best friend, Frankie, later. She was studying maths at Bristol and had probably shagged a quarter of the men and half the women on campus already. I longed to hear her tales of hedonism and debauchery almost as much as I longed to talk to someone I could be totally myself around.

Miraculously, Jen and two of the other field hockey girls—Alex and Mei—were already in the dining hall. They didn't look even remotely jaded; they could obviously handle their mead. I grabbed an extra-large, extra-sugary coffee and a sausage sandwich and slid onto the bench beside Jen with a grimace. "Okay, first of all, what the fuck?" Jen asked, staring at my bandages. "Second of all, what in the name of god? Third of all—"

"Yeah, I get the picture." I laughed, taking an enormous mouthful of my ketchupy sandwich. "Honestly, I was kind of hoping you could tell me. I had too much mead. Everything after the Grandstand is a blur." My insides squirmed at the half-truth.

"I was in the bathroom with you at maybe . . . half eleven? Quarter to midnight?" Mei offered, sipping from a steaming cup of herbal tea. "There were two other girls from the drama program snorting coke, and they kept trying to talk to you, but honestly, you were kind of blacked out at that point. Then this weird expression came over your face. Like you were doing an impression of someone else, I don't know. Your features just kind of changed. I went to dry my hands, and when I turned back to the sink you were gone."

My appetite rapidly diminished as she spoke, and by the time she stopped, I'd laid down my sandwich half-eaten. The way Mei described my face changing sounded like far too many horror movies about possession.

I had to get to the bottom of this. I was only a few days into my time at Carvell and already deeply afraid.

"Got to go," I muttered, abandoning my food and coffee while they were still warm.

The Sisters of Mercy Library felt like Alice, somehow. It was cold and achingly beautiful: tall mahogany bookshelves and green velvet chairs, antique writing desks by grand arched windows, the scent of leather-bound books and old parchment. There was some slow, moody orchestral music playing somewhere in the rafters—then again, that could've been my imagination.

I spent two hours browsing various sections in search of books that might (a) give me some ideas on how to start investigating ten-year-old murder cases and (b) help me understand what was happening to me vis-à-vis possible hauntings. For the former I picked up my favorite true crime classics—Truman Capote and Norman Mailer and Hunter S. Thompson—to remind myself of where the greats started their investigations. My heart gave a little flutter as I picked them off the shelf.

The latter was a less orderly research process, with many false starts and dead ends, but I eventually stumbled upon a book called *The Devil and the Divine: True Accounts of Possession and Exorcism in Religious Orders* by W. F. Burgh. I settled into one of the green velvet armchairs—muscles aching from yesterday's ill-fated tryouts—and read the first chapter.

It told of a demon-possessed Parisian prioress, Jeanne des Anges, and how she was exorcised in the church of Loudun. Nobles and priests gathered to watch the exorcist accuse the devil Balam of possessing Jeanne, to which Balam supposedly responded, "It is true, I am responsible for all the evil things that you are complaining about," and caused Jeanne to "contort her body grotesquely, horrifying the onlookers." Burgh's contextual sections explained that in the 1600s, exorcisms were both a public spectacle and a lucrative source of revenue, with "spiritual tourists" traveling hundreds of miles in the hopes of catching a glimpse of the casting out of a demon.

Jeanne's story went on to inspire many writers—exclusively male writers, I noted, including Burgh himself—to adapt it for mass entertainment. Alexandre Dumas wrote a four-act play titled *Urbain Grandier and the Devils of Loudon,* and Aldous Huxley published a book in the fifties called *The Devils of Loudun.* There had also since been a Broadway play, an opera, and a gratuitous X-rated Ken Russell movie from the seventies.

So many men profiting from the pain and fear of these women. It made my stomach curdle like off milk.

I laid the book down on the arm of the chair and tried to tamp down my rising dread.

Demonic possession. Was that what was happening to me at the hands of the tower? It seemed an almighty leap, but I was stalking the grounds of a potentially haunted convent and investigating its bloody past. It made sense that if possessions actually happened, I'd be a prime candidate.

I had just picked up the book again to read another chapter when none other than Alice came into the library. I caught a glimpse of claret hair from the corner of my eye, and my initial thought was, *God, it's really annoying how beautiful she is*—then I felt the stomach-dropping sensation I'd already come to associate with her. What was she going to do or say next that would make me feel two inches tall? Or was she going to apologize, to say something nice, to give me another flicker of satisfaction like the one I'd experienced when she let me in on a brief private joke? In fairness to her, she'd gauged Nat and Sara's nonsense from the outset.

After scanning in, she approached the place where I sat, eyes fixed on the spiral staircase just behind me. Nerves beat in my belly like moth wings, and I forced a stiff smile.

She slowed her steps, flicked her gaze in my direction and opened her mouth just a sliver as though about to say something . . . and then kept on walking.

I sighed inwardly, packing up my bag to leave. Demonic possession was nowhere near as stressful as my roommate.

CHAPTER 15

Lottie

Over the next few days, Alice barely said a word to me. She seemed to spend most of her time in the library. I saw her there a couple of times, hunched over a writing desk and scrawling essays in black fountain ink, but if she saw me wave, she didn't acknowledge it.

I found her so disquieting to be around that I barely spent any time in the dorm, and I knew it had to change. I was exhausted from being constantly on edge in the one place I should be able to relax, and I found falling asleep at night almost impossible. The one upside of this was that because I was awake when midnight rolled around, I didn't find myself unconsciously clawing at the foot of the North Tower. There was just a twinge of latent temptation, a subtle tug somewhere deep in my rib cage toward the building, but nothing I couldn't easily override.

Still, field hockey practice was like wading through black treacle because of the lack of sleep, and I knew something had to give. After my last lecture on Friday afternoon, I headed to the Grandstand, parked up in a comfy armchair with a half of shandy and called my best friend, Frankie.

"Charlaaay!" she exclaimed with a deep, throaty cackle.

She was the only one I allowed to call me Charlie. She liked it because "*Charlie and Frankie* sounds like a sitcom in which two kooky lesbians have sex and do crimes."

"Hey." I laughed, her familiar voice washing over me like sunshine. "How are you?"

"I'm good, my friend, I'm good!" There was a lot of shuffling and background noise. "Getting ready to head out for my, like, ninth night of clubbing in a row."

"Do you have five minutes to talk?" I asked, suddenly uncertain. I didn't want to intrude on her fun new life.

She made a little *pfft* noise. "Don't be a silly bitch. Of course I do! You're my home slice. My numero uno. My ride or die." I heard a door slam shut and the background noise abruptly stopped. "I'm in my room now. What the jolly heck is occurring? Just as, like, an FYI, I have already consumed half a bottle of Tesco's cheapest vodka. So keep it simple. I have murdered a significant quantity of brain cells in the last week."

"So you're loving Bristol, then?"

"Dude, *yes*. It's mega." I heard the flick of a cigarette

lighter and a sharp inhale. "When are you coming to visit? Where even is Northumberland anyway?"

"Really far from Bristol." I laughed.

"So get on a train. You're not a Victorian pauper."

"Well spotted," I conceded.

"So what's up?" She sucked on her cigarette as though the elixir of life was hidden at the bottom.

I groaned deeply, then took a sip of my shandy. "My roommate already hates me."

"Understandable. You're hotter than like, eighty-five percent of the population."

I quirked an eyebrow even though she couldn't see me. "Only eighty-five?"

"Fine, eighty-seven."

"Very generous. But yeah, we got off on the wrong foot. I think she just immediately thought I was some idiot with a field hockey stick—"

"Accurate."

"—and made up her mind to hate me from there. Also I think she was, like, bullied by popular kids in school or something. And she thinks because I'm in the eighty-seventh percentile of hotness and also play sports that . . . I'm going to be the same."

"Okay," Frankie said levelly. "And do you like her?"

It was a complicated question. Obviously the answer was no, because Alice was an incredibly intimidating and unpleasant presence, but I couldn't deny being intrigued by her. She reminded me of the woods: vast and beautiful and dark, but overgrown with defense mechanisms: thistles and hogweed, poisonous mushrooms and gnarled roots. Talking to her was like grabbing a fistful of nettles.

"I don't think I do," I admitted. "She punched a guy in the face on my birthday."

"In fairness, that makes her sound awesome."

"Well, yeah, but what if she punches me?"

Frankie snorted. "Then you'll punch her right back. You've never backed away from a fight."

"No, but I've also never actively pursued a fight." I nodded hello to Mei, who'd just walked in with a tall, black-haired guy in a rugby shirt. "Love thy neighbor, or whatever. Kindness is always my first instinct."

"Exactly. Just go be you, Charles. You'll win her over in the end."

When I got back to the dorm, Alice was cross-legged on her bed, a red highlighter poised in her hand as she read a textbook. I'd never seen a red highlighter before, and could only assume she imported them directly from Dante's fifth circle of Hell.

"Hey," I said breathlessly, before I could talk myself out of it. She pressed her forefinger to the page to mark her place and looked up with a distant expression. "I just wanted to say I'm sorry we got off on the wrong foot."

She frowned, peering at me as though I was faintly stupid. "But you don't have anything to apologize for."

"Okay, well, I'm saying it anyway." I smiled. "Even if you don't think we can be friends, I'd at least like us to be amicable. I mean . . . surely you don't want things to be this fraught?"

She gave the slightest sigh-nod of acknowledgment.

"And I warn you," I added, "I am one persistent son of a bitch. I will continue to be nice to you against your will until you like me."

After considering this for a moment—a moment in which I wondered how she could possibly object to this benign sentiment—she nodded once more and went back to her book.

It wasn't an apology, but it was a start.

Later that night, we were both in bed by ten. Rain was pattering on the window like a thousand tapping fingertips. I was reading the demonic possession book I'd checked out of the library, while Alice was lying flat on her back in her full-length red plaid pajamas, staring at the ceiling.

"Do you ever get . . . impulses?" she asked mistily. "Like . . . violent impulses?"

I laid my book down uncertainly. This conversational path was particularly unnerving. I suspected Alice knew that and got a kick out of making me uncomfortable. Was she calling my bluff on being nice to her no matter what? Pushing the boundaries of my kindness?

"Sure," I replied cautiously. "Like when you're standing

in a high-up place and your imp says, 'But what if you jumped?'"

She turned her head to face me, and the dim lamplight cast half her pixieish face in shadow. The elfin upsweep of her brow line was particularly striking tonight. She genuinely looked like a cartoon villain at times. "I mean, that's a strange thing to say when we're mere yards away from a place where four people fell to their deaths."

I flushed pink. I guess it was.

"Also . . . your *imp*?" she asked, the slightest frown tugging at her forehead.

I rolled onto my side to face her, propping my head up on my elbow. The pulse beating in my temple echoed in my palm. "Yeah, the Imp of the Perverse. Like in the Edgar Allan Poe story?"

Her expression remained blank.

"Basically, everyone has an imp in their mind that urges them to do the worst possible thing in any given situation," I explained. "Like a mother standing at the top of the stairs holding her baby, and she suddenly thinks, 'You could just throw him down.' It doesn't mean she hates her baby, or that she'd ever actually act on it. It's just the imp, right? Baudelaire explores it too, in 'Le Mauvais Vitrier': '*C'est une espèce d'énergie qui jaillit de l'ennui et de la rêverie.*' 'It's a kind of energy that springs from both boredom and fantasy.'"

"So we all have an imp?" Alice asked, as though the notion filled her with immense existential relief.

I nodded. "Mine's called Steve."

A sudden burst of laughter from deep in her chest made me jump. She looked just as surprised as I did, as though she'd forgotten what the sensation felt like.

"Steve?" she said incredulously, with something like genuine glee on her face. "Why *Steve*?"

"Just a particularly impish name, isn't it?"

She shook her head, but she was smiling. It changed her entire face, crinkling her usually cold eyes and scrunching her nose up in a way that could, at an absolute stretch, be described as cute.

"Night, Lottie," she chuckled, turning over to face the wall.

For a few moments, I felt a warm glow of triumph. I'd appeased the cartoon villain, if only for a moment. And I'd proven that I wasn't just some idiot who'd waltzed in on a sport scholarship.

But the satisfaction didn't last, because as soon as I flipped off my own lamp and tried to fall asleep, Alice's original question worked its way back into the forefront of my mind.

Do you ever get violent impulses?

Her imp was different from mine and most people's.

It was different because she listened to it.

She indulged her vicious streak without hesitation.

She punched people in the face. She hurled cruel comments for no reason. Falling asleep just a few feet from her suddenly seemed an incredibly vulnerable thing to do.

Still, after the previous night's mead bender and the subsequent jaunt to the North Tower, exhaustion tugged at my eyelids, and before long I succumbed to sleep.

I awoke once again at the foot of the North Tower, with the knowledge that something was seriously wrong.

It was well after midnight. Dawn lilac crept up from the horizon. Birds chirped somewhere overhead. I glanced around fearfully for Mordue, but she was nowhere to be seen.

I was lying flat on my back in the shadow of the gnarled tree, damp grass soaking me to the skin through my white pajama top. Cold had burrowed all the way into my bones until they were stiff and aching.

There was a searing pain at the top of my clavicles; the feeling of a hot knife carving into me.

Dread pooling in my gut like an oil slick, I slowly raised an icy hand to the spot that hurt.

Right at the bottom of my throat was something hard *protruding* from my skin.

Panic lurched in my chest. What *was* that?

But I didn't have time to examine the fear in any more detail. Mordue could appear at any moment. I had to move.

My limbs were numb and uncooperative as I dragged myself back to Willowood, blocks of ice lodged in my lungs.

The door to the dorm was still open a sliver. At the sudden warmth inside the building, pins and needles prickled up my arms and legs. With a sick sensation in the pit of my belly, I crossed to my writing desk and grabbed the small magnifying mirror I used to apply makeup. I held it up to the agonizing spot between my clavicles, took a deep, painful breath and looked at the damage.

At first, my eyes couldn't make sense of it. But there was no mistaking what it was.

A ruby rosary bead.

CHAPTER 16

Alice

The morning after Lottie and I chatted about her imp, everything felt brighter for the briefest of moments. Some of the omnipresent tension in my shoulders eased just a fraction, and I was grateful to her for being the one to make amends—even though it was almost entirely my fault there was friction to begin with. The last week had rattled me, my violent outbursts blazing without warning, and I didn't want to let any more animosity stoke the fire.

I wanted to believe I could do it. That I could overcome the anger and make a friend. I just had to put myself out there. Because as much as I liked to pretend otherwise, I needed companionship. I needed company, and comfort, and affection. And I wasn't living under my parents' roof anymore. Affection was no longer a guaranteed daily occurrence. I had to fill that void somehow.

"Morning," I said to Lottie, if not cheerily then at least civilly. I tugged a tailored tweed waistcoat over a crisp white shirt with an oversized collar.

But Lottie, who was lying flat on her back, staring at the ceiling above her bunk, said nothing. She was inexplicably wearing the hideous green-and-purple zigzag fleece in bed. For a split second I wondered if she was breathing, but when I saw her chest rise and fall, I knew she wasn't dead. She was just ignoring me.

The familiar stone of resentment dropped into my stomach. Lottie was probably having regrets. Regrets about apologizing, about engaging me in conversation, about living with me at all. *Why* did I start that conversation about violent impulses? I'd been an idiot to think someone like her could be friends with someone as spiky as me.

"Fine," I muttered, disguising the sting from my voice as best I could. I grabbed my satchel and a little trilby that matched my waistcoat and left the dorm before I could do or say anything I might regret. Still, I couldn't resist a whispered "fuck you" as the door closed behind me.

I'd always had a short fuse, and I'd always had violent flashes whenever I felt wronged. When Emily Marshall snickered at me in the school hallway, I'd dream about slamming her head into the lockers, imagine how satisfying that metallic thud would be as it reverberated up my arm. When my boss at my first retail job screamed at me in front of customers, I'd fantasize about stabbing him in the face with the end of a broken coat hanger. (My violent revenge fantasizes were usually face-based.)

Now, after being shunned by Lottie, the violent urges waxed and waned all day. When the giggling cheerleader-type cut in front of me in the breakfast line, looking me up and down as though I were a piece of shit she'd trodden through. When Professor Latheron ignored my raised hand for a whole seminar, instead favoring the boys in the class. When a girl in my political philosophy workshop gave me a scathing look when forced to partner with me on a pre-sentation. I wanted to *hurt* them. I wanted them to pay for making me feel small.

Anger was a constant current. It felt fundamental to me as a person, a force of nature I couldn't live without, like gravity.

After classes were over, I went to the library to work on an anti-realism assignment. It wasn't due for another month—I was shocked at how long we had to write essays compared to sixth form—but I was itching to sink my teeth into something intellectually starchy. Maybe that would distract me from the gnawing chagrin.

Entering the library, I nodded hello to Kate Feathering, the omnipresent librarian with sleek dyed white-silver hair and black lipstick. She was in her midthirties, and wore clichéd librarian outfits with a quirky twist of personality: soft, oversized tunics paired with jeweled skull brooches and knee-high platform boots. I often thought I'd like to be her friend, but she gave off intensely cool yet emotionally distant aunt vibes that even I found intimidating.

I found a writing desk in front of one of the grand arched windows. It was a cold spot, but the view of the dramatic crags and sprawling woodland brought a kind of familiar peace. No matter how churned up with rage I felt, the Northumbrian landscape always made my troubles seem insignificant. I imagined it was like looking at Earth from outer space, the sheer scale of it a dizzying display of perspective and irrelevance.

As soon as I pulled out my favorite pen and started writing a plan for the essay, I fell into an easy rhythm, and for the first time in days, my heart rate slowed, becoming less erratic and more like the steady beat of a metronome. I always felt best when it was just me and my thoughts and an empty page.

After a few minutes, or maybe hours, a hand tapped me by the shoulder, jolting me out of my sanguine state. I flinched, and the shock of it made me bite down so hard on my tongue that I tasted blood, hot and slick and tangy.

I swung around viciously, the shock replaced by that seething fury, to see a dark-haired guy staring at me in confusion. With his brown eyes and light stubble, he looked *exactly* like Chris, right down to the preppy polo shirt. My heart pounded fearfully.

"I, uh, sorry, I just, I wondered if I could borrow an ink cartridge?" He held up his fountain pen.

It was such an innocuous request, and it should've

placated me instantly. There was no threat; I could stand down from flight-or-flight mode. And yet I didn't. The adrenaline scorched through me like acid, and it was all I could do not to jam the nib of my pen into the side of his neck. I stood from my chair, gripping the pen in my hand.

"*No*," I seethed, my voice low and almost serpentine.

He took a confused step back. "Ohhhkay. Forget it."

My pulse thundered in my temples. His face melted from his own to Chris's to the guy in the Refectory on the first night, and I thought of hunters and of prey, eagles and mice, and which one I'd rather be, and before I was even aware of what I was doing, I was shoving his chest with the heels of my hands.

He staggered back, stunned. "What the . . . ?"

Stop stop stop stop, urged a distant voice deep in the back of my mind. *He's not Chris.*

I shoved him again, harder, but he was ready this time and planted his feet more firmly so that the impact juddered up my arms. His face still wore a mask of surprise, not rage, but I felt like a dog backed into a corner by some invisible danger nobody but me could perceive.

Then someone else touched my arm, and I spun to face its owner.

Kate Feathering, the librarian.

Her expression was impenetrable. There was steel in her eyes, but instead of a tongue-lashing, all she gave me was a terse shake of the head and a look that told me to walk it off.

I stuffed my belongings into my satchel. The guy I'd shoved walked back to his desk, still shaking his head in disbelief.

I took the long way back to Willowood, feeling like I was wrapped in barbed wire.

When I got back to the dorm, Lottie was out at field hockey practice, her stick bag gone from the window alcove.

Splayed on her unmade bed was the chunky purple volume she'd been reading when I first saw her in the library nestled in that green velvet chair. Dumping my satchel on my desk, I crossed to her bunk and read the gold-lettered spine: *The Devil and the Divine: True Accounts of Possession and Exorcism in Religious Orders*. Frowning, I wondered how this could possibly be on her reading list. Historical context for a piece of literature she was studying, perhaps?

Whatever its purpose, it reminded me of my own peculiar library discovery: T. A. Renner's depiction of the moth purification ritual. Devised to rid desperate nuns of violent thoughts and impulses.

Searching my memory archives, I couldn't remember reading about whether the ritual had actually *worked*.

CHAPTER 17

Lottie

The North Tower was the killer. I was sure of it.

The sleepwalking and the unconscious lure could have been explained away, could have been rationalized with science and psychology, but this? A ruby in my throat? There was no other explanation; that supernatural pulse had dug in its claws.

After I saw the ruby in the dim light of the dorm, it took a while for the fear to really build. At first there was a sense of disbelief, of there's-no-way-this-is-actually-happening, the kind of existential denial you'd feel while watching a loved one die in a horrible accident. My brain shut down to protect itself. Instead of worrying about what the ruby meant, I changed into a fresh pair of pajamas, shoved the filthy, sodden pair into my laundry hamper, splashed some warm, soapy water over my face, and climbed back into bed as if nothing especially untoward had happened.

It was only then, lying in the silence with my pulse beating raggedly in my temples, my heart fluttering fiercely, that the pain and fear really sank in. The ruby felt like it burrowed deep, too deep, as though it had roots wrapped around my windpipe. My lungs tightened and my breath came in shallow rasps, tears tingling at my ears as denial slowly lowered its veil.

Stifling a sob, I tossed the duvet off me, tugged on my dad's old fleece, stuffed my feet into grubby old trainers, and slipped out of the dorm. The hallways were deserted as I made my way to the communal bathrooms, squinting against the harsh glare of the fluorescent strip lighting.

When I got to the bathroom—too warm and overly damp but empty—I unzipped my fleece and had to stifle a gasp. The area around the ruby was pink and angry, flecked with little specks of dried blood. As I swallowed, the ruby rose and fell around the lump of emotion in my throat. The room fuzzed around me as my vision blurred, and I had to grip the sides of the sink to steady myself. Years of field hockey meant blood didn't scare me, but there was something so perverse, so *wrong* about the way the ruby looked and felt. As I thought as much, its roots gripped around my windpipe ever tighter, and it was all I could do not to cry out.

The pain was worse when I looked at the ruby head-on. There was stinging around the wound and a kind of bone-deep ache; a panic-inducing sensation of being impaled on something sharp and metallic.

Gripping one hand even tighter around the lip of the sink, I got as close to the mirror as I could. Then, with my free hand, I pinched the gem between my thumb and forefinger—and pulled.

It was only the slightest tug, a tentative attempt at extraction, but the shrieking pain bent me at the waist.

The agony was visceral, and almost . . . *sentient*. Like the ruby was hurting too, and sharing its pain with me.

Whimpering like a wounded animal, I clapped a hand over my mouth and ran back to the dorm.

Now the panic was real. It had climbed inside me, pulled on my skin like a jacket.

What did this mean? Would I be the North Tower's next victim?

None of the original victims were reported as having rubies lodged in their throats. None of the autopsies could've missed such a thing.

Unless the police were keeping it from the public— the kind of detail that would sort the liars and attention-seekers from the genuine leads.

By the time I finally managed to drift off, pink dawn light glowed behind the curtains.

As I slept, I dreamed things that felt less like dreams and more like memories. They were just fleeting glimpses, mostly: aging, sun-spotted hands illuminating a manuscript with a tiny paintbrush; those same hands digging a hole in a wooded glade; a faceless body falling from a great height, the black folds of their habit flung skyward like a cape.

I woke the next morning having slept in jagged fits and starts, the ruby in my throat burning red hot.

Dimly aware of Alice saying something and then leaving, I stared at the ceiling in an exhausted trance, palm resting on the ruby as it rose and fell with my breath. I was afraid. Deathly afraid.

After lying there for what could have been one hour or seven, I turned on my side and reached over my bunk for the magnifying mirror, hoping beyond all rationality that the ruby might have disappeared. Maybe I'd hallucinated the whole thing, like the weird dreams I'd had, and that the thing I felt through the skin of my palm was just a regular pimple.

Of course, nothing had changed. The area around it was a little less pink, but it was still firmly rooted just above my clavicles, glimmering a vicious red in the grayish daylight.

There was something about the size, shape and bloodred hue of the ruby that looked familiar, and with a sickening lurch, I realized where I'd seen it before.

I was still wearing my fleece from the trip to the bathroom, so I tugged on my flared jeans and some trainers and headed out. The sun was high in the sky and the air was enjoying a final late-September burst of warmth, but I still felt cold to my core. On the cobbled walkway I passed Jen and Mei from the field hockey team. They smiled hello, but

I could barely bring myself to lift a hand in a half-hearted wave.

As I rounded the corner to the statue of Sister Maria, my worst suspicions were confirmed.

One of her rosary beads was missing. The one right at the center of her throat.

These were rosary beads that many a desperate thief had tried to extract over the centuries; the rosary beads that were said to be held there by some greater force.

And somehow, by that same greater force, one was now embedded in my neck.

CHAPTER 18

Alice

October came in a ferocious gust of orange and red. Long gone were the oilseed rape fields rising and falling over the countryside like sunny yellow parasols; now the plowed fields were dark and brown, the sprawling woods aflame like a brilliant phoenix. Trucks of maple firewood arrived on campus, and the evenings hung with the scent of blackberry crumble and log fires.

Lottie and I hadn't spoken since our conversation about mind imps. While the initial smart of her rejection the next morning had worn off a little, I still couldn't bring myself to say hello again, to ask about her day, to offer anything that might be rejected or scorned. We moved through dorm life as though the other didn't exist.

Unlike when I usually cut people out, however, it made me feel a little sad. I had genuinely enjoyed talking to her about my violent impulses. She'd offered a perspective that was so fresh and nuanced it had cast my innermost demons in a slightly less monstrous light. She'd intrigued me. She'd made me *laugh,* something only Max and Noémie were usually able to do. To have that brief promise of friendship so swiftly snatched away felt a little like loss. That brief promise of affection, of companionship . . . I could barely admit to myself how lonely I was. How my skin almost hungered for the comfort of human contact.

Then I started to notice that Lottie was behaving a little strangely. Over the next week, a couple of times I woke up around midnight to find her missing from her bed, even though we'd both gone to sleep around eleven. Was she just going to the bathroom? Or was she sneaking out? If it was the latter, I had no idea why she felt the need to. I was just some stranger she shared a room with, not her mother. She could come and go as she pleased.

One thing that did irritate me was that she left the door open on her way out. The first couple of times I got out of bed and pushed it shut, in case she was just at the bathroom without her key, but by the third I was so annoyed—and a little unsettled—that I locked it too. If she was sneaking out, she should be taking her key. She should be showing me the barest trace of respect by at least attempting to keep me safe.

I was woken around three in the morning by a frantic knocking at the door. A flare of anger opening in my chest like a rose, I gritted my teeth, slid out of bed, and padded over to the door, preparing to snark at Lottie for leaving it open in the first place, let alone forgetting her key.

The words died in my mouth when I saw the state she was in.

Her pale-gray pajama shorts were damp and dirty, as though she'd been lying on wet grass, and her knees were grazed and pink with fleshy blood. Clumps of mud and twigs in her blond hair framed her face, and her eyes were blood-shot and swollen from tears. She had her arms wrapped around her waist and was shivering uncontrollably.

"Sleepwalking," she muttered flatly, not meeting my eyes as she pushed past me into the room.

"Shit, are you okay? Your knees look—"

"I'm fine," she snapped. "I just need to get my . . ."

Flicking on her bedside lamp, she knelt down on the floor, which must've stung her knees badly, and pulled a first-aid kit out from under her desk. Sitting back on her butt, she got to work cleaning the wounds with antibacterial wipes, as though this sort of thing happened every day.

"Is there anything I can do?" I asked, on the verge of going over to help her, before swerving toward my bunk instead. I perched on the lip of it, legs swung over the side. "With the sleepwalking I mean. I could lock up at night and hide your key so you can't get out."

Lottie finally looked up at me, her gaze milky and blurred, and choked out, "Yeah. Yeah, that would help. Thanks."

For the most slender of moments, I wanted to go to her,

to hug her, to tuck her hair out of her face so she could see what she was doing. To comfort her. To feel another person's skin on mine.

But I couldn't. She hated me just because of who I was. And honestly, who could blame her?

In the dim lamplight, I could just make out something nestled in the hollow of her throat, just above her clavicles. A necklace pendant? But there was no chain. A cut or bruise? Narrowing my eyes and leaning a little closer, I realized it was the deep-red hue of a ruby. It glittered as the pool of light caught it from different angles.

"What's that on your throat?" I asked, feeling a little uneasy for no discernible reason.

Her hand flew to the place where it sat, a look of fleeting terror on her face. She recovered quickly and said, "Oh. Dermal piercing. Field hockey girls talked me into it." She smiled weakly and got back to sticking plasters over her knees, angling her body away so her back was to me and I couldn't see what she was doing.

Messaged received, said a snarling voice in the back of my mind, but I wasn't so sure. There was something odd about the whole thing, but I couldn't put my finger on what.

The next morning I decided to extend an olive branch. It was around eight-thirty, and she was sitting cross-legged on her bed, braiding her hair with a tiny compact mirror balanced on her grazed knee. She wore a giant faded T-shirt that must have belonged to her dad, that inexplicable fleece, and a fresh set of frayed cotton pajama shorts. There were shadowy bags under her eyes.

Fastening the gold buckle on my belt, I picked up her library copy of *In Cold Blood*. She was using a postcard as a bookmark and was about halfway through.

"I loved this book," I said, and she froze at the sound of my voice. "Although did you hear that the lead investigator has since claimed that many of the scenes were totally fabricated by Capote?"

Lottie shrugged, a hair grip balanced between her lips. "I still think it's a masterpiece." There was a defensiveness to her tone I didn't quite understand.

"Oh yeah, of course," I replied hurriedly. "The landscape of creative nonfiction wouldn't be what it is without him. What did you think of . . ."

I trailed off when I saw what was lying folded on top of *Fear and Loathing in Las Vegas*.

A dorm transfer request form.

"Oh," I said flatly, placing *In Cold Blood* back on top of the request form and turning to my bunk to hide the scarlet sting of humiliation on my cheeks.

Lottie sighed, snapping the compact mirror shut. "I mean, you can't have thought this was going well."

"Guess not." Hot tears prickled behind my eyes, and I blinked them fiercely away. What happened to *I am one persistent son of a bitch. I will continue to be nice to you against your will until you like me*?

"Alice, come on," she said darkly. "You don't exactly

seem like you want to be living with me either. I could tell from the second I walked in here that I wasn't what you wanted in a roommate."

I met her bullishness with my own. "The feeling seemed entirely mutual."

"That's not fair. I tried to make an effort. I invited you out for my birthday drinks. And then you ruined the whole night, and you still haven't apologized."

Sliding moonstone rings onto my fingers, I frowned. "Why would I apologize? I didn't punch *you*."

Lottie swung her legs off the bed, wincing slightly. "Forget it. I just think it's best if we live with people who we have more in common with." Her phone started ringing, and she glanced at the name on the screen. "My dad's calling. Would you mind giving us some privacy?"

"Fine," I snapped, grabbing my black plaid scarf. "Go and cry to your dad."

The soft ebb of pleasure. The sharp stab of shame.

But instead of looking wounded at my cruel jab, Lottie *laughed*.

"Oh, fuck off, Alice," she said cheerfully, before stabbing the green call button. "Hey, Dad!"

Pride smarting, a flash of white anger burst through my skull. I wanted to smash something, wanted to throw her stack of books through the window, wanted her to yelp in shock as the splinters of glass rained down around us. The intensity of the urge stole the breath from my lungs.

I hope her dad dies.

The thought shot through my head before I could discern where it came from. I was deeply, deeply afraid of that snarling voice. I was deeply afraid of myself.

Before I could say or do or *think* anything else I might regret, I grabbed my satchel and left for my first seminar an hour early. The hazy rain soaked me in an instant, beads clinging to my eyelashes and the blunt ends of my hair, but I didn't care enough to open an umbrella.

Self-loathing followed me out of the building like a shadow. I was doing to Lottie what I'd done to Noémie. I was like this with my family, too, sharp and scratchy and mean. Perhaps I was spikiest to the people I was closest to because I was trying to find the limits of their love— pushing and pushing to see how much the boundary would give.

It made me glad that Lottie and I weren't close. I'd only end up hurting her too.

Campus was quiet as I walked to the dining hall in search of coffee. Black poplar trees lined the walkway on both sides, and from one particularly gnarled branch a row of moth cocoons dangled like sleeping bats.

The sight awoke a dormant thought in the back of my mind: the purification ritual.

Perhaps the nineteenth-century nuns were onto something. Perhaps their creepy moth blood tincture could round off the edges of my sharded anger, could shrink my violent impulses down into something I could control. Most likely this was absurd wishful thinking, but the part of me that had always been drawn to the arcane loved the romance of the idea.

And what did I have to lose? If it didn't work, all I'd be left with would be a dead moth and a vague sense of silliness for believing in it to begin with.

To kill some time before class, I decided to go to the library and read more about it. When I arrived at the philosophy section, though, the book was not where I expected it to be. Instead of being neatly lined up on the bottom shelf, it was lying facedown and open on the floor, spine bent awkwardly back on itself. Frowning, I propped my satchel on an armchair and bent down to pick the book up.

It was open on the very last page I'd looked at: "How the Ritual Was Performed."

I wondered which of my fellow philosophy students had stumbled upon it. And why did they leave in such a hurry that they left the volume lying around like a piece of old junk?

The page was exactly as I last saw it, with one tiny, significant exception: the droplet of blood in the bottom right corner. A small smudge, as though someone had pricked their finger on a spindle and then tried to turn the page.

The sight made me smile. Someone had tried to perform the ritual. I knew it in my bones. There was someone at this school as intrigued by the occult as I was. For some reason, this knowledge bolstered me.

In a moment, the decision was made. I was going to attempt the ritual too.

CHAPTER 19

Lottie

I felt bad about the dorm transfer request, especially because Alice seemed to think it was all because of her. It partly was—our conversation about violent impulses lingered in the dark recesses of my mind, peeking its head out from the shadows whenever I tried to fall asleep—but mostly it was because I needed to get away from the North Tower. I thought that if I could maybe transfer to Nettlebank or Rosemary Green, one of the halls farthest from the main campus, then maybe the tower's grip on me would loosen.

After I got off the phone with my dad—I hadn't let him know anything was wrong, because he'd only worry—I hid the ruby in my throat with a pashmina.

That morning I had my first session of the infamous elective in gothic literature—the one notorious for sending students mad. Both Dawn Middlemiss and Fiona Taylor had taken it before their untimely deaths. Professor Sanderson's seminar was hallowed ground, and it felt important for me to tread it carefully. Just flipping through the list of lectures in the course outline made me shiver: "The Castle of Otranto, Birthplace of Nightmares" and "Edgar Allan Poe's Terror of the Soul" were later in the semester. I could hardly wait.

The classroom was filled with hideous miscellany: sheep skulls and Baphomet figurines, rusty pentacles and a plague doctor mask, coffin-shaped mirrors and curious insects suspended in amber. Sanderson was also a collector of morbid ephemera: death notices and obituaries; long, sad sonnets and torn-up wedding photos; sepia-stained letters to orphanages begging them to take in a possessed child. These terrible collages hung in black frames on the stark white wall, any references to literature circled in blue fountain ink.

Our first seminar was on *The Strange Case of Dr. Jekyll and Mr. Hyde,* a novella I knew almost by heart.

"Evil," said Professor Sanderson, spreading his arms wide at the front of the classroom. Tall, pale and raven-haired, he was informally dressed in black jeans and a T-shirt, with studded black leather cuffs around his wrists that looked like miniature dog collars.

"What does the word mean to you? And how far would you go to eradicate it if you found it within yourself?" A curious lip curl. "Or would you simply . . . submit?"

The classroom was packed with curious students

watching Sanderson hungrily as he spoke, as though he was a cult leader we were only too happy to follow into the dark.

As Sanderson gave an overview of the text, I noticed his voice had a peculiar rhythm to it, an unnatural cadence, pauses and inflections in subtly awkward places. It was as though he spoke with an unpredictability designed to keep you from falling asleep.

"How*ever*." He sucked his bottom lip between his teeth, narrowing his eyes and nodding to himself. "However, we will not *sim*ply be analyzing pretty sentences and prodding at wishy-washy themes. I couldn't care less about the duality of man. A flat, *life*less concept. Likewise, Stevenson's writing style is of little interest to me. What I *am* interested in is the impact of the gothic on the world around it. The power it had to corrupt."

The air in the classroom was pulled taut as a corset.

"In August 1888, a stage adaptation of *Jekyll and Hyde* opened at the Lyceum Theatre in London. An actor called Richard Mansfield played both roles. His performance was said to be so utterly horrifying that audiences left the theater in absolute distress."

Picking up a piece of chalk, Sanderson wrote *J&H play* on the left side of the blackboard, then drew a circle around it.

"The murder of Martha Tabram—a crime believed to be the first committed by Jack the Ripper—took place just two days later." He wrote *murder of MT* on the right-hand side and circled that in white too.

He turned back to us and shrugged. "Of course, to the modern mind, these two events seem entirely independent of one another. But at the time, the public drew connections between Stevenson's story and the medical manner in which the Ripper removed organs. One paper reported that after watching Mansfield's performance, a well-dressed young man threw himself from a bus that was traveling at speed, convinced that the repulsive-looking man he found himself sitting next to was either Dr. Hyde or the Whitechapel Murderer. Another gentleman wrote to the *Telegraph* suggesting that 'the perpetrator is a being whose diseased brain has been inflamed by witnessing the performance of the drama of Dr. Jekyll and Mr. Hyde.'"

Sanderson turned back to the board and drew a stark white line between the two circles.

"It would be easy to dismiss all of this as a simple matter of Victorian hysteria. Perhaps it was. Or perhaps the Whitechapel Murderer really *was* inspired by *Jekyll and Hyde*." His black stare was hard and bright. "Personally? I believe that the gothic has an almost supernatural power to corrupt. To unravel, to violate, to deprave.

"To my mind, a story is not a story until it is shared. There is an esoteric current that flows between author and reader, an arcane golden thread whose nature we cannot truly grasp." He gestured to the line on the board, stabbing at it with his piece of chalk. "*That* is what we'll be studying in this class."

A final, vampiric smile. "Try not to go insane."

CHAPTER 20

Alice

Gathering most of the ritual ingredients was simple enough.

On a weekend visit home, I slipped the marble pestle and mortar from the kitchen into my overnight bag and pilfered some of my dad's gardening shears. I made fresh cordial with my mum, using lemon, honey, sugar and pretty elderflower heads. We drank most of it that afternoon; I stoppered four vials' worth from the dregs in the pan.

There were pimpernels, heather and rosemary scattered throughout Carvell's wooded grounds, so it was a simple case of snipping samples and collecting them in small glass vials I found at a local hardware shop. I returned to the gnarled black poplar tree and plucked one of the moth chrysalises from its perch, grinding it into a fine powder while Lottie was at a hockey match.

The book also called for sage, fern and philodendron

leaves, which were slightly harder to find, but I eventually found a sun-dappled glade in the woods where all three seemed to have been planted a long time ago.

I enjoyed this period of foraging immensely. I felt connected to something ancient and spiritual, something much larger than myself, walking the same paths as the nuns before me. Maybe, I thought, that was the real power of a ritual: the intangible connections it forged between souls. It was at once grounding and liberating.

Killing the live moth was the least pleasant part of the experience. I had to do it in a way that would keep the arthropod intact in order to be able to extract the hemolymph, which meant I couldn't just swipe at it with a rolled-up newspaper as my dad did at home. I settled on capturing a beautiful turquoise and red-spotted *Zygaena* I found fluttering in the glade, sealing it inside an old jam jar and waiting for it to asphyxiate. I stuffed the jar in the back of my wardrobe, beside my tarot decks and healing crystals.

The guilt I felt in the time it took for the moth to die reassured me that I was not, in fact, a psychopath. I felt no pleasure or satisfaction in murdering an innocent being.

Finally, all that was left to collect was the blood of a person who I had wronged. For days I carried an engine oil dipstick around in my pocket, waiting for an opportune moment. Accident-prone Lottie was sure to cut herself shaving, or come back to the dorm with another field hockey injury—a bloody nose or a broken tooth perhaps.

But the right opportunity never arose, and I soon realized that if I was to progress with the ritual before my new roommate arrived, I'd have to take matters into my own hands.

I really didn't want to hurt Lottie any more than I already had, so I instead settled on Harris—the boy I'd almost stabbed in the Refectory that first night.

After another visit to Youngman's, the now-familiar hardware store, I created an innovative contraption using two silver rings and a drawing pin. I stacked the two rings on my middle finger, then slid the flat part of the pin between the two so the sharp point was pointing outward, into my palm.

Finding out which dorm Harris lived in didn't take very long. I followed him as he left his Victorian literature seminar and tailed him back to Hume, a few rows back from Willowood. I considered trying to slip past the keypad entry system behind his group of friends, but it would've required me to get too close, to lose the element of surprise. Besides, I wanted to get Harris alone. This next part would not benefit from an audience.

The old Victorian streetlamps gave the poplar-lined walkway an orphic glow, illuminating the drifting haze of mist that hung low beneath the branches. There were few people around: a group of giggling girls staggering in the direction of the Refectory, and a couple of guys snogging beneath a tree. I was sure I saw Professor Dacre and Professor Le Conte walking together, heads just a few inches apart, but they disappeared from view before I could ascertain whether their rendezvous was also a romantic one.

Wrapping my coat tighter around myself, I sat on a memorial bench opposite the entrance to Hume and waited for Harris to resurface. I knew it could be a while, so I'd brought along the book from the library. For some reason—inexplicable foresight or pure gut instinct—I hadn't checked it out of the system officially. I didn't want anyone to know I'd been reading about the ritual.

Still, I wanted to read more about why the tincture fell out of favor in the late 1800s—whether there were any mysterious dangers I could be letting myself in for. The section on the first purification ritual ended abruptly, however, making way for a much longer section on ill-advised chastity rituals that ended up poisoning an entire convent in Cumbria.

Baffled, I carefully flipped through the pages again, until I noticed that there was a narrow gap between the how-to for the tincture and the chastity section, as though pages were missing. A closer look showed a few frayed edges of paper still tangled in the stitched binding.

Someone had ripped out a section. Why? What did the missing pages say? Did they explain what the ritual actually did? Outline the side effects?

An icy frost crept up my spine. Who would tear pages from the book like this?

I racked my brain, trying to remember whether the

book had been intact when I first stumbled upon it. Had the pages been torn out by the person who'd left it face-down on the ground and smudged with their blood? Was that why they'd been in such a hurry?

This discovery didn't put me off performing the ritual, even though in hindsight it certainly should have. It only made me more intrigued than ever.

I was so absorbed in the book's mystery that I almost didn't see Harris leaving the Hume building. He wasn't alone, but there was only one other guy with him. They both had dark-green kit bags hoisted over their shoulders, and Harris's friend carried a dirt-caked rugby ball, which he twirled around in his palm as they walked.

It would have to do. It might be weeks before I could get Harris alone. It was now or never.

CHAPTER 21

Lottie

Trying desperately to get back onto an even keel after the ruby incident, I threw myself into field hockey as best I could.

The first thing I noticed was that the lassoed-stomach sensation, the one that tugged me toward the tower while I was down on the field, had grown more intense since the ruby had appeared in my throat. It had spread to my head, too, a flurry of unwanted thoughts like *I need to get back to the tower* whirring through my mind like a blizzard in summer.

Despite these unsettling developments, I started to perform a little better in practice. Nowhere near my old Kent County levels, but a definitive improvement on the lurching nausea and clumsy strikes of tryouts. Several of my teammates noticed the ruby in my throat, but I parroted the same story about a dermal piercing—only this time, my goth roommate had talked me into it. There was a chance I could get caught in the lie, but the odds of Alice ever talking to my field hockey friends seemed incredibly slim. She was far too spooky for sports, and seemed to disapprove of them as a concept.

The first home match came and went, and while I was only subbed in for the last five minutes, it was so delightfully normal to be out there running around in the rain and dirt, not thinking about anything but the game. I felt like myself again, if only until the final whistle blew.

Still, the reason I was here at Carvell sat heavy on my chest. I had to do Janie justice. I'd been distracted by my own pain and fear, my convictions that the tower was somehow to blame, but I knew it sounded absurd to the outside ear. I had to find some kind of proof. I felt the need to solve the murders more urgently than ever; a visceral tug from my ribs to my sternum.

One brisk blue afternoon, I headed to the campus bus stop. There was a newspaper archive in the nearest town dating all the way back to the early 1900s, which meant all the local coverage of the North Tower murders was also held there. I'd already read every single thing on the internet about the murders, so I wanted to trawl through old articles looking for any peculiar references—to possession, to the tower, to the supernatural pulse, to dark forces. Had any of the witnesses or faculty members been concerned that there was something larger at play? Had any of them dared vocalize those concerns? Maybe the dusty old archives would throw up something the internet had missed.

Riding on the bus away from Carvell, I couldn't focus on the beauty of the rolling landscapes because the lasso around my stomach tightened with every passing mile. Nausea roiling, my breathing grew shallower and shallower, as though my body was protesting being this far from the North Tower. As we approached the outskirts of town, it became so bad that my vision danced and blackened, and I had to grip the seat in front of me to keep from passing out.

Then, with a sudden internal snap, everything stopped. My vision washed back with a wave of blue sky, and the nausea cleared immediately. It was as though the invisible lasso had been stretched as far as it could go, and I'd passed some kind of threshold where it could no longer keep a hold on me.

After that, everything felt a little brighter, my thoughts a little clearer. I hadn't realized how much of a shadow the North Tower had cast over me until I was out from under it. It brought me immense relief; it *was* possible to get out from under it. If this all got too much, I could just leave. Ruby or not, the supernatural pulse hadn't dragged me under just yet.

But I didn't *want* to leave. Not yet. Not without justice for Janie and her family. For reasons I couldn't quite articulate, being on the campus, burying my own roots there . . . it only solidified my resolve. An insistent, bone-deep desire.

The local newspaper archive was a small, musty building attached to a redbrick parish church. The sandy-haired, middle-aged man working behind the front desk looked appalled that someone had dared to enter his lair. Judging by the dog-eared stack of historical novels beside the computer and the ring-marked coffee mug that said GRUMPY OLD MEN'S CLUB, he was not used to being disturbed.

Nonetheless, he led me begrudgingly to the back room and left me alone in the dank, windowless room filled with shelves upon shelves of file boxes and clippings. It smelled of old paper, sawdust and something oddly sour.

Everything was labeled diligently and chronologically, so it didn't take long to find what I was looking for. I grabbed four file boxes from the years of the murders and took a seat.

Reading the first few pieces about Sam Bowey filled me with a sense of vicarious dread. There was a brief but generic statement from Mordue about the tragic suicide of a promising young student; she had no idea what was still to come. The first piece itself was a small column on page four. Carvell hadn't yet secured its place in the region's dark history.

Then, Janie. This was front-page material: the death

of two young lovers within a week of each other. And this time, the body showed signs of struggle.

As the weeks drew on and two more students fell, the case dominated the papers. Page after page of information, including a timeline of events—of which I took a photo with my phone—and sympathetically written profiles of all the victims. There were also details of a memorial service at St. Mark's, which I realized was the church next door to the archive.

I read an entire year's worth of coverage, but there was nothing in the papers that I didn't already know about the killings, and nothing that could possibly be considered a reference to the paranormal. And I was an English student; I was used to reading into things.

The one useful piece of information I did glean, however, was the name of the local reporter who had covered the story: Peter Frame. I jotted his name down in my notebook and headed out.

I stopped by the front desk again on my way out, and the crotchety man actually sighed at me as I said, "Excuse me?" in my peppiest voice.

"Yes?" The word was clipped with irritation.

"Does Peter Frame still work for the paper?"

"No, he moved to the *Gazette* last year." He peered impatiently at me over wire-framed glasses.

I had what I needed.

On my way back to the bus stop, I stopped by a small

newsagent's and found a copy of the *Northumberland Gazette*. Peter Frame was listed as crime editor, with a phone number, email address and postal address. As well as a giant stash of pick-'n'-mix, I bought a copy of the newspaper and tucked it in my backpack.

Even if the archives didn't have any answers, Peter Frame might.

CHAPTER 22

Alice

Swallowing the breath that hitched in my throat, I approached Harris and his friend quickly before they could storm away, the drawing pin warm against my palm.

"Harris!" I called, voice low and clear in the misty dusk.

His jaw clenched when he saw me, but he obviously didn't want to lose face in front of another guy, so he just said, "What do you want?"

"To apologize for the way I acted at the Refectory that night." I arrived in front of him with a forced smile. There were only the faintest tinges of yellow bruise remaining around his left eye socket. "I'm sorry. I'd had a bad night."

His hand went to his stomach defensively. "Whatever," he muttered, glancing at his friend, who I could tell was trying not to laugh.

"No, really." I spoke quietly, trying to prevent a cluster of passersby from overhearing. I knew an audience would rile him up, and truth be told, I was a little worried that he'd try to hit me back. "It was wrong of me. I should have just rejected you politely." God, even when I was trying to be sickly sweet, I was still kind of a bitch. I pressed on. "I know I hurt you when—"

"You didn't hurt me, you stupid bitch," Harris practically spat. The muscles along his shoulders rose and tensed, like a dog getting its hackles up. Salem stalked past us, giving the situation a disdainful glare before rounding the corner with an emphatic swish of her tail.

"Okay," I replied, trying to meet vitriol with calm, even though it went against every instinct I had. "Well, I embarrassed you, then. And I'm sorry."

This time he actually did spit. A fat glob of saliva landed just to the right of my Doc Martens.

"Fuck off," Harris snarled.

"Dude . . . ," muttered his friend.

"What? She's fucking *pathetic*."

The violent urges rose to the surface again; the need to lash out, to hit, to hurt, to give my pulsing anger an outlet. I forced myself to take a deep breath and focus. There was more at stake here.

Harris started to walk away, by which point his friend was gaping at me. I didn't recognize him from the Refectory that night, so there's every chance he was confused by the level of tension in the conversation.

"Okay. I will fuck off." Heart pounding in my rib cage, I extended my hand with the spiked ring contraption, hoping he'd take it. "But first . . . truce? I promise I'll never come within ten feet of you again."

The next few seconds sprawled into eternity. Lip curled in disgust, Harris looked down at my hand—the way my fingers were cupped disguised the drawing pin nestled between the rings—and back up at me, hatred plain on his face.

Then he rolled his eyes, as if he couldn't care less about me either way.

"Fine." He reached out and took my hand with more force than was necessary, and I leaned into the extra force to make sure I hit my mark. The pin pierced the pad of his palm, and he yanked his hand back in shock. "What the *fuck*!"

Feigning confusion, I looked down at the drawing pin. Nothing. Not a drop of blood.

I tried to match his own surprise. "I'm sorry! It must have been the engraving on my ring or some—"

Shoving chest-first into me in a way that brought bile to my throat, he hissed in my ear, "Stay the fuck away from me, psycho." His body was hot and big against mine, his breath sour with old coffee as I pressed back against the rough wall.

This time, I didn't bother trying to tamp down the violent urges coursing through my body. I leaned into them with full force as I lifted my hand and slapped him clean across the cheek.

This time, the drawing pin drew a hot, red stripe of blood.

This time, at the stunned hatred in his eyes, I really was afraid for my life.

His arm swung out, hand curled in a claw like he was reaching for my throat. I ducked under it and ran faster than I'd ever run before, nearly tripping over Salem as I rounded the corner.

Voices shouted after me, and there was the clomp of trainers on cobbles, the tenor of male shouts. My satchel smacked against my thigh as I sprinted for a dense snarl of poplar trees, then wove through them to the convent entrance, heart leaping in my chest. My footsteps were too loud and quick on the checkerboard floor of the entrance hall, echoing through the cavernous space.

I chanced a quick glance back. They didn't seem to be following me, but that didn't mean Harris would just leave it be. He seemed the type to hold a grudge.

My pulse pounded a painful tattoo as I finally came to a stop, gasping for breath as I crouched in a stone alcove that obscured me from view. There was a reason I did not participate in sports. My lungs burned, my throat constricted, and I felt for one brief moment like I might be dying. How did Lottie do this every day? Of her own volition? Then again, I suspected she was quite into pain, judging by the piercing in her throat.

Once I had finally caught my breath, I looked down at the drawing pin in my hand.

There was a dark smear of blood on the thin, gold tip; not much, but enough.

Smiling to myself, I pulled a glass vial out of my pocket and slipped the pin into it with a satisfying clink.

Now I had everything I needed for the ritual.

In a few hours' time, I could be a whole different person.

CHAPTER 23

Lottie

Peter Frame agreed to meet me in town after he finished work. I found him hunched over a table in a little tearoom, tucked on the ground floor of the dark stone town hall that loomed over the high street. Frame was jowly and gray, with heavy eyelids and pouch-like bags under dark-brown eyes. He wore a plain white shirt, unbuttoned at the collar and in desperate need of an iron, and a black trilby with a few locks of stringy hair hanging loose beneath it. As I got closer, my nostrils winced at the scent of unwashed grease.

Still, the bloke was doing me a favor, so after ordering a coffee, I fixed my trademark sunshiny grin on my face and offered my hand cheerfully. It felt much easier to slip into my old persona without the North Tower looming over me.

"Mr. Frame! Lottie. Thank you so much for agreeing to meet with me."

Instead of taking my hand, he gestured to the wobbly school-style chair opposite him and said nothing. On the table there was already a plate covered with scone crumbs and empty packets of butter, and a teapot with spidery cracks all the way up its belly.

"I just wanted to have a chat with you about the North Tower murders," I said, rearranging the pashmina around my neck as I took a seat. The back of my neck was sweaty from the walk, but I didn't want to expose the ruby to any curious questions lest he immediately dismiss me as one of those Youths with Piercings He Did Not Understand.

"Aye, fine," he said with utter disinterest.

I swallowed hard. I'd prepared a list of questions about his interviewees, and whether there was anything they'd told him off the record, but now that I was here it didn't seem like the right approach. It had been so long ago, and he likely didn't remember precise details.

Instead, I opted for a single broad stroke. "What do you think happened?"

Frame reached for a small bowl of sugar lumps and popped a crumbling brown cube straight into his mouth.

"Aye, well, all crimes against females are sexually motivated, aren't they?" he replied, crunching the sugar cube like a horse. When I frowned involuntarily, he sighed, and said, "It's basic Freud."

I couldn't have disagreed more, but again, I needed to keep him on track. "Right. Of course." Holding back an eye roll required so much effort that I had a small but not insignificant aneurysm.

He gave a flat smile. "So, I think one of the professors was grooming them, maybe assaulting them, and when they'd threaten to go to the police, he'd kill them." He nodded to himself. "It's basic Freud, isn't it? Absolutely basic."

I had to wonder what Freud he'd been reading, because it certainly wasn't Sigmund.

"Did you tell the police your theory at the time?" I asked.

"Aye, they said they'd look into it. But they couldn't find evidence to back it up."

"Was there a particular professor who came to mind?"

Frame shrugged. "I've always found males who teach art to be a bit . . . not right. Not right at all."

I pressed my tongue to the roof of my mouth, careful not to let slip any clapbacks that would stop him talking— although I was beginning to suspect he had nothing valuable to offer anyway. "Maybe. But not all the victims were girls. You think that happened to Sam Bowey too?"

"Now, Sam . . . I reckon that was his bird, Janie. She wasn't right either. Mental, like. He tried to have her committed within a week of meeting her."

This was a piece of information that hadn't been printed anywhere—not even in the national coverage.

Every hair on my body stood to attention. I lowered my voice. "Really? I hadn't heard that."

"Her parents wanted it kept out of the press. I said we should print it anyway, but my editor was afraid of a lawsuit." A low *pfft* as he reached for another sugar cube. "Sheer cowardice, in my view. The public had a right to know she was crazy."

My teeth gritted at the ugly word. "I suppose they didn't want it to turn into trial by media. If it had gone to court, it would've colored a jury against her before any evidence was shared."

The Contempt of Court Act had been passed to prevent this very thing: the media unfairly prejudicing active court proceedings. It would've been on the mind of Frame's editor.

Purple blotches appeared on the journalist's sagging cheeks. "It would've colored them against her with good reason. Sam Bowey is dead because of her."

"Maybe," I replied, fighting hard to keep my cool. "Maybe not. But the last thing Sam Bowey's family would have wanted is for the case to be found in contempt and thrown out."

Frame sneered at me. "And I suppose you know that from your decades of journalistic experience, do you?"

"No," I replied indignantly. "I know that from doing my research."

"Research, eh?" He gave me a patronizing look as he

leaned forward. "Why didn't I think of that? Why didn't I, in my years of reporting on this case, think to do some research?" White spittle foamed at the corners of his mouth, and something like hatred burned in his eyes.

I got up and left before my coffee even arrived.

CHAPTER 24

Alice

The library would be the best place to perform the ritual, I decided, in part because I didn't want to risk Lottie walking in on me midflow, and also because it just *felt* right, with its arched windows and distant orchestra. It was a much more spiritual place than a dorm room filled with field hockey sticks and half-empty bottles of lukewarm wine.

I was a firm believer that it mattered where these things took place. A big part of the moon manifestation rituals I used to do was the cleansing of the space with salt and herbs, sage and smudge sticks. During my "do I even believe in God?" phase, there was a decent chance I was never able to summon the Holy Spirit because I was hiding in a bathroom with my older brother, Max, pounding down the door. The unrelenting soundtrack of "I need to take a shit!" was perhaps not conducive to a sacred religious experience.

When I returned to the main building just after eleven, the air inside the quiet convent was cold and still. The central corridor—with its scuffed parquet floor and faded green runner carpet—was lined with busts of famous alumni who stared at me as I passed. My fingertips grazed the crypt-cold wall, its texture rough against my skin. I thought of the stone wall at the end of Chris's street, where I used to perch as I waited for him to come and meet me. At the memory of him, my stomach churned with unspent anger.

There were only a few students in the library, hunched over rolltop writing desks lit with little green bankers' lamps, textbooks and flasks of hot drinks scattered on neighboring tables. I recognized one girl, Amanda, from my philosophy course, poring over Nietzsche and looking thoroughly miserable. In a quiet corner near the fine arts section, Hafsah al-Hadi from my ethics seminar was in a huddled conversation with a pretty ginger-haired girl, who was clutching her notebook like a weapon.

Other than that, the library was almost wholly deserted; most students were probably dancing in the Refectory at this hour. I climbed the spiral staircase to the second floor, where the philosophy section was housed.

Taking a seat in one of the velvet armchairs, I unclasped my satchel and retrieved the tincture. Notched into the elastic pen slots were three other vials of simple cordial, hemolymph and ground florals, but I hadn't retrieved any-where near enough blood to make another full dose of the tincture. It might not even be necessary; perhaps one dose would be enough to round off all my sharp edges.

Still, I had several reservations. I had swilled the tip of the drawing pin in the elderflower cordial until the lemon stripped the blood from the metal, but it was a tiny amount, not even enough to color the liquid pink. I was sure I'd prepared the tincture correctly, but would there be enough of Harris's blood for it to work? I was also unsure whether the elderflower cordial would be made in the same way it was in the 1800s. Would the sugar have a diminish-ing effect? Did it used to be served sharp and tangy? And the quantities had been so vague in terms of the florals and herbs. A pinch of this, several heads of that. As a majorly type A person, I liked to know I'd done things properly, by the book. But in this case, the book was old and vague and missing several pages.

There was only one way to find out.

Before I drank, I took a few moments to center myself. I always did this before a ritual; meditated for as long as it took to clear my head, then visualized what I wanted to happen with as much clarity and specificity as possible.

I imagined a calm, logical mind, free from flintlike anger, free from violent twitches and desires; a mind I could devote to thinking and learning without fear of what it might tell me to do next. A mind fit to be a judge someday.

I imagined joyful relationships without the fraught

tension, without constantly pushing the other person away with my impulsive barbs. I imagined the freedom to love softly.

Unstoppering the vial, I lifted it to my lips and drank in one deep gulp.

For a moment, nothing happened. There was just a sweet, floral aftertaste with the slightest metallic burn. The gentle turn of pages somewhere nearby. A cleared throat. A vague sense of foolishness.

Then, with a sudden roar of internal thunder, I convulsed with pain.

Searing-hot pain that began in the depths of my chest and spread outward, as though every muscle in my body was being shredded by a fork of lightning. I bent over at the waist, trying not to scream at the racking pangs, the grinding in the bones, the deadly nausea. An absolute horror of the spirit.

Time slid, losing form. As the world narrowed and deepened, the violent urges dancing at the back of my mind came to the forefront, larger and larger until they obscured everything, until there was nothing but the color of blood, the urge to hurt, to kill, to exact revenge. To level the whole world.

And then a gaping maw of darkness opened and swallowed me whole.

CHAPTER 25

Lottie

After my meeting with Peter Frame, I caught the bus back to Carvell. I climbed onto the faded single-decker Arriva to find Salem perched on the frontmost seat, peering out the window at a nearby pub garden as though she was above it all. I tried to sit next to her, this supposedly immortal being, but she hissed when I got within three feet of the empty seat. Wary of angering a supernatural beast, I tucked myself away into the back row instead.

As we approached the university, the tower's shadow fell over me once again. There was the tightness in my lungs, the lasso around my stomach, a sense of impending doom that lessened and lessened the closer we got to the school. As though something deep inside me was relieved to be going home.

The idea made me shiver. I knew something was horribly,

horribly wrong. I knew I was not wholly myself anymore. I knew the ruby in my throat was doing something inherently terrifying to me. And yet I couldn't quite admit just how afraid I was, because I had to stay. For Janie.

Once we were back at Carvell—I could've sworn Salem nodded at the driver as she disembarked—I went to the Grandstand and sat in the corner farthest from the roaring fire. I ordered a Fentimans ginger beer, then allowed myself to briefly unravel the pashmina, fanning my face with my notebook in a desperate attempt to cool down. The ruby was bothering me a lot; a deep, bright scratch whenever I swallowed.

Tuning out the drunken rumble of the men's rugby team, I filled three pages of my notebook with every detail from the meeting. Most importantly, the revelation about Sam Bowey trying to have Janie Kirsopp committed.

That pearl of information filled me with unease. Had she been suffering from the same disquieting experiences as me? Had she been sleepwalking? Had she been washed through by a sense of impending doom and found herself unable to cope? Had she opened up to Sam about her fears of possession, and he'd thought her undeniably insane?

I wished I'd kept Frame calm long enough to ask more questions. To be detained under the Mental Health Act you had to pose a serious and imminent risk to yourself or others. How had Sam gone about it? Had he told a school counselor? Social services? The police? No, I thought—the police couldn't have known, otherwise they never would've believed his death was a suicide. Perhaps the revelation had come later, once Janie herself died.

I still couldn't quite figure out how this nugget of knowledge fit into the wider case. After all, Fiona and Dawn had died after Janie, so she couldn't have been the serial killer. There was nothing to suggest they were even known to Janie. And besides, Frame didn't seem like an especially reliable source. Had he exaggerated the extent of Sam's concern for Janie? Maybe Sam had only chatted informally to a counselor, and Frame had blown it out of proportion to make it seem like a bigger journalistic scoop than it was. That could be another reason his editor had refused to print it.

And yet . . . it felt substantial, somehow. It reaffirmed my ideas about the tower's sentience, about the luring, maddening effect it could have on people. There was a weight to the revelation that both unsettled and comforted me; I was not alone.

Then again, it could just be confirmation bias. I had found something that fit my existing theory and shoe-horned it in to fit. That felt easier to believe, somehow.

Because if Janie really had gone through the same thing as me . . . what was to stop me meeting a similar end?

I sat there in the Grandstand for hours, working through all of these ideas and developments on paper. My hand cramped, and I had to replace my ink cartridge twice, and by the time I'd run out of mental steam I had filled half the notebook. Bleary-eyed but clear of mind, I looked up at the grandfather clock by the fireplace and realized with a start that it was nearly four in the morning. I was the only patron left in the parlor, which didn't close until the last person had finished their drink. The young ginger barman stood polishing glasses with a dishrag, looking thoroughly pissed off.

As I got up to leave, I nodded my head in apology before I realized that I was not the only person still drinking.

Professor Sanderson, from my gothic literature seminar, sat by the dying fire, staring grimly into its embers. The orange light danced in his onyx eyes as he sipped at something amber-colored in a crystal tumbler, a single cube of ice clinking against its rim.

Strange, I thought. The Grandstand was supposed to be for athletes only.

The first thing I noticed when I stepped outside was that it was not as quiet as it should've been at that hour. I couldn't quite make out individual noises, but there were shouts and cries in the middle distance.

When I rounded the corner to Willowood, I saw the source of the commotion, and a trapdoor opened in my stomach.

Three police vans were parked around the base of the North Tower, blue and red lights flashing against the sinister old stones. There was already yellow and black tape forming a perimeter around the trees, and several clusters of people—some crying students, some police—surrounded the scene. Dean Mordue was wrapped in her black peacoat, trying in vain to convince the onlookers to disperse.

I didn't have to ask what had happened. I knew deep in my gut.

Somebody else had died.

PART II

Branches

CHAPTER 26

Alice

I woke up in my own bed in the small hours of the morning with no recollection of how I got there.

My head pounded with a constant hammering behind my eyes, at once dull and sharp, like a fishhook through my skull. Every part of me ached. I sat up gingerly and pressed my fingertips into my pounding temples, then ran a palm over my aching ribs.

That's when I realized how bad things were.

My white shirt was covered in dark-crimson blood; a great circle started at the collar and arced down to my naval, as though I'd vomited terrible scarlet. I touched my face gingerly; it too was crusted in blood.

Lottie, to my surprise, was awake and pulling on a gray Sevenoaks class hoodie. In the dim light of the moon outside our window, she hadn't noticed me stir.

"What's going on?" I groaned. A glance at my wrist-watch told me it was a little after four.

She turned to look at me. All the color drained from her face at the sight of the blood, something like understanding settling over her features. I'll never forget the hoarseness of her voice as she said:

"They just found a body at the bottom of the North Tower."

The world froze on its axis.

I was covered in still-wet blood, with no memory of what had happened between the library at midnight and the dorm room at four a.m.

Heart palpitating painfully in my chest, I asked, "What time did I come back?" God, I was thirsty. My voice rasped and rattled in my throat.

Lottie stared at me. I couldn't read her expression: fear or excitement or crow-like curiosity.

"I don't know," she said slowly. "You don't remember?"

"I had one too many whiskeys at the Refectory." The lie slipped out of its own accord. I had no idea how many knots it would later tie me in. "I fell and hit my face on the way home." I gestured to the mess of my shirt. "Nosebleed."

"Who were you at the Rectory with?" Her tone had taken on a careful quality. I thought of her stack of true crime books. Did she think she had woken up in one?

When had she woken up, anyway? How had she heard about the body so quickly? Had I missed something?

Or had she been sleepwalking again? The thought brought with it a prickle of suspicion. There was something she wasn't telling me.

"Some of my course mates," I said evenly. Another bear trap of a lie. "Where are you going?" My measured tone matched hers.

That's when I noticed the notepad and pen sticking out of her jeans pocket. She *did* think she was in a true crime novel.

"North Tower," she said, studying me even more closely. Her hand twitched toward her phone, but then she seemed to think better of it. "I want to know what's going on." Then, more fiercely, "We have a right to know."

Trying to calm the wild horses galloping in my chest, I asked, "Do they know who it is yet? The body?"

Please don't be Harris, please don't be Harris, please don't be—

"Some girl from the fine arts program. I didn't know her."

Unable to feel any relief, I tossed the duvet off my legs. "I'm coming with you."

Lottie shook her head. "I . . . I don't think that's a good idea."

A beat, in which I tried to figure out the least suspicious course of action.

"You're probably right," I replied slowly. "I should go and clean myself up." I lifted my hand to my nose to support the fell-and-hit-my-face story, only to find that it really did hurt. In fact, I was struggling to find a part of me that didn't.

It was then that Lottie finally caved to her impulses. She grabbed her phone and snapped a picture of me in my blood-soaked clothes.

The flash blinded me temporarily, and by the time my vision had cleared, she was gone.

I waited for the hot flare of anger but it never came. Instead there was just a soft, simple thought:

I don't blame her. I look guilty.

I shook my head in disbelief, almost as though trying to dislodge the anticipated rage, the elastic band snap. But it never came. All that was there was a calm, rational sense of understanding. The clear head I'd envisaged manifesting.

Had . . . had the ritual worked?

With the clear head allowing me to think logically, I knew the first thing I needed to do was wash. Not only was it uncomfortable sitting in my own blood, but it was fairly incriminating too. I changed my top for the walk to the communal bathroom, keen not to let anyone else spot me covered in blood on the night of a suspected murder, and tossed the crimson-soaked shirt into the bin by my desk. It was one of my favorites—a cream silk button-down with billowing bell sleeves—but I suspected it was beyond saving.

The undue sense of calm followed me to the communal bathroom. I carried my toiletry bag and towel with a feeling of peace and well-being despite the aches in my body, breathing in the fake-pine scent of the floor polish.

When I arrived, I was the only one there. I chose my favorite shower cubicle, farthest from the entrance and closest to the old brown radiator, where I could huddle and stay warm. I lathered shampoo into my hair, scrubbed beneath my nails with a bar of lavender soap, worked every inch of myself clean until I felt raw from the heat of the water.

My mind was curiously clear of . . . well, everything. There was no fear about the rumored murder, or residual anger toward Lottie or even Harris. Even the low-level dread when I thought of my mum and her illness was replaced by a general sense of resignation. It was as though I'd meditated with Buddhist monks for a thousand years and emerged totally remade.

When I got back to the dorm room, Lottie was still gone.

But so was the blood-soaked shirt.

CHAPTER 27

Lottie

Nothing can adequately describe the feeling of walking into your dorm moments after a suspected murder to find your roommate drenched in blood.

After taking in the devastating scene at the North Tower—it still wasn't clear who had died, and the police wouldn't let anyone near the spot where they were hoisting someone into a body bag—I had returned to Willowood to grab a hoodie and charge my almost-dead phone for a few minutes so I could take some pictures. As sleazy as it sounded, I wanted firsthand evidence of any potentially supernatural elements of the death, whether a ruby in the throat or something else—hell, even Salem looking particularly pleased with herself would sate me.

In the end I found a shot nobody else in the world got

that night: Alice Wolfe, sitting up in her bed, covered in crimson from lips to navel.

I should have been afraid. I should've run for my life. There was every chance I was mere meters away from a murderer.

But I was calm. Almost *too* calm.

It was as though I was being guided through the night by an otherworldly presence; an invisible hand on my shoulder, steering and soothing in equal measure. Both a warm comfort and a persistent push. My body a shared vessel, borrowed by something that had no reason to be afraid. Distantly I wondered whether it had something to do with the ruby in my throat, with the gloomy shadow of the North Tower and the cold hold it had over me. But that all seemed very far away; a sidenote. For now, all I could do was focus on the murders.

The more I thought about it, the more something about Alice as the murderer didn't quite sit right—it didn't mesh with my own theories about the North Tower being the killer. Despite Alice's vicious streak, it didn't tie into the supernatural pulse in a way I could make sense of. Plus, she was only a kid at the time of the original murders. Perhaps she had wanted to re-create one tonight? But why?

My thoughts were clear—and hungry. I wanted to solve this.

Now I'd been handed a lead on a silver platter, and I wasn't going to let it slip through my fingers.

I had to get Alice's shirt. Even if I didn't think she was capable of murder, what if I was wrong? I had to take it to the police. If the blood down its front belonged to the victim . . .

So I left the dorm with my phone in hand, then waited around the corner until I heard the door open and close again. A peek around the wall showed me Alice in a thick black jumper, carrying a towel and her wash bag. But had she left the shirt behind? Or was she still wearing it under the jumper, hoping to wash it clean of blood in the sink? Part of me wondered whether she was off to bury the shirt in the woods, but that would've been more incriminating than anything. She was smarter than that. If she truly had nothing to hide, she would have left the shirt in the dorm.

As her footsteps faded to an echo in a distant stairwell, I slipped back into the room and found, to my surprise, that she'd just dumped the shirt in her dustbin as though it wasn't a potentially key piece of evidence in what was likely a murder investigation.

I plucked it out and placed it carefully in one of the envelopes I'd bought in case I ever wanted to write to Frankie. The sheer silk fabric was still warm and the blood was mostly dry, but a few patches seeped through the white paper in bright-red blooms. Dimly I noticed my hands were trembling, but they seemed entirely detached from me, as though they belonged to someone else.

Cell phone and envelope in hand, I made my way back to the crime scene. As I walked, my own levelheadedness surprised me. I was someone who felt emotions to their full depth.

So why wasn't I more afraid?

Again there was that invisible hand on my shoulder, at once steady and insistent. I had the vague sense of lagging a few seconds behind reality, watching events unfold while acutely disconnected from them.

Somewhere deep, deep inside my head, a frightened voice told me this wasn't right, but I couldn't seem to bring that voice back to the surface.

The atmosphere around the tower had shifted. The body had been removed from the scene, but hysteria among students was rising. The mild night air rang with cries and shrieks and ringtones as students tried desperately to contact their parents. The moon hung in the starry sky, gazing down at us all with celestial indifference.

I had imagined this scene for so long. I had pictured what it would've been like to be at Carvell back when the murders took place, when the bodies kept falling and the nightmare kept rolling.

And now I was living in it.

It was exactly how I thought it would be, and the almost familiarity offered a sick kind of comfort. Imagination had indeed opened the door and let the terror walk right in.

After a moment's hesitation, I trod over the night-black grass to the nearest police officer. She was young and kind-faced and was holding a walkie-talkie up to her mouth but not speaking into it. Nor was any sound coming out. It was as though she was frozen in place by some existential horror.

I cleared my throat softly, and it seemed to shatter her reverie.

"Excuse me?" I asked, dismayed at how childlike my voice sounded. "I have something you might want to see."

CHAPTER 28

Alice

At the discovery of my missing shirt, the internal peace didn't shatter, per se, but it did splinter.

Had Lottie given it to the police?

Again I waited for the surge of fury.

Nothing. Just more calm understanding. She was probably scared, of the murder and now of me. If she suspected I had something to do with it, she had every right to go to the police.

Seriously. Who am I?

By now the almost impenetrable sense of serenity was beginning to feel oppressive, like a veil I couldn't see beyond, even though I knew there was something on the other side. Something terrifying in its lack of clarity or form. I was detached from myself in some kind of fundamental way.

In an attempt to focus on the perilous situation—someone was *dead*, there were hours of my life missing from my memory, and I'd woken up covered in unexplained blood—I grabbed a notebook and a pen, turned to a blank page, and tried to recall the night as best as I could. If the police were going to come knocking, I needed to have answers.

11:35 P.M.—WALKED TO LIBRARY

11:55 P.M.—ARRIVED AT LIBRARY, SAW AMANDA BELL, KATE FEATHERING, HAFSAH AL-HADI + GINGER FRIEND (THEY CAN ALL VERIFY?)

12:05 A.M.—PERFORMED RITUAL

12:05–4 A.M.—?????

4:15 A.M.—WOKE UP IN DORM COVERED IN BLOOD, BODY FOUND AT NORTH TOWER

This did not look great.

It was immediately and abundantly clear what I had to do next: figure out where I had been in those four hours.

I looked down at my watch: not even six a.m. If I headed back to the library now, would Kate Feathering still be there? She seemed to be sitting behind that U-shaped desk no matter what the hour, but logic dictated she had to sleep too. My own eyelids stung with exhaustion, the black hole of my night having provided little rest.

Yet Feathering might be the only one who could account for my whereabouts during those missing few hours, and the thought of waiting for her to wake up seemed counter-intuitive. Why be a sitting duck by staying in bed? There was likely a detective hunting me down right now, if Lottie had anything to do with it. Hell, Harris probably went straight to the police too, given what I had done to him mere hours ago.

The idea of cold steel handcuffs around my wrists spurred me out the door. Although I knew that realistically I wouldn't be arrested just yet—most likely just brought in for questioning, if *Law & Order* had taught me anything—I wanted to fill in as many mental blanks as I could before that happened.

The beginnings of a plan solidified in my mind. If I couldn't find Feathering in the library, I'd quickly head up to the philosophy section and make sure the ritual book wasn't splayed on the carpet for all to see. Then I'd go to the sheltered glade and bide my time until the black-lipped librarian returned from her rare slumber. I would also attempt to pierce the oppressive emotional veil and psychologically process the morning's events, because feeling so inhumanly detached was wholly unnerving. I had no idea how I would survive cross-examination if I came across like an unfeeling psychopath.

The morning was crisp and dark, although the obsidian sky had started fading to indigo. The almost dawn was clear of clouds. I breathed in great lungfuls of air. It was deep and heady, tinged with rosemary and woodsmoke and something metallic.

The main convent building was stony cold and unrelentingly quiet. My every footstep echoed as I walked as calmly as I could down the cloister to the library. My heartbeat quickened and deepened; an insistent thump as though my body remembered something my mind could not.

To my surprise, Feathering was sitting behind her library desk reading a mammoth tome. She looked much the same as she always did: polished, groomed, achingly aloof. It was not the appearance of the sleep-deprived or the overworked. I briefly wondered whether she might be a vampire.

It was also not the appearance of someone who knew a girl had just died mere yards from where she sat. I decided not to be the one to break the news. It would make what I had to ask her sound even more suspicious.

"Hi," I said, and she looked momentarily shocked as I approached the desk. In the time I'd been coming here, I'd only ever seen one other student go over to her.

"Can I help you?" she said tersely.

"Yeah, erm, I was here last night—a few hours ago, actually—and I need to prove where I was during that time." I swallowed hard, then spouted the excuse I'd come up with on the walk over. "My roommate accused me of sleeping with her boyfriend, and I want to show her it would've been impossible. Does my student record show what times I scanned in and out of the library?"

If Feathering was surprised by the request, she didn't show it. She turned to her computer screen, clicked on the mouse a few times, then typed my name on the keyboard.

"It says here that you scanned in at 11:54 p.m. and left at 3:58 a.m."

Relief flooded me from head to toe. When I first checked my watch back in the dorm, it had read 4:09 a.m. I must have gone straight back there from the library. There's no way I would have had time to go up to the North Tower, quickly murder someone, and then hurry back to my room. I was in the clear. And I could prove it.

There was only one problem: I'd told Lottie I was at the Refectory.

I was so busy focusing on that dilemma I didn't notice something crucial.

Feathering had known what name to search for in the system without my having told her.

CHAPTER 29

Alice

The police were waiting for me by the time I returned to the dorm.

I'd spent the whole walk back from the library convincing myself that Feathering knowing my name was innocent. I'd been at the library so much already this semester, and I supposed maybe my name flashed up on her screen whenever I signed in. Perhaps she'd made a note of it after my altercation with the Chris look-alike.

When I saw the two detectives waiting outside my door, I inwardly sighed with relief. They obviously hadn't secured a search warrant, or they'd already be rooting through my belongings. The blood-soaked shirt was suspicious, but perhaps not suspicious enough. The printout of my library comings and goings should confirm my innocence without too much hassle.

I didn't bother feigning surprise at the sight of them. Instead I smiled pleasantly—not long before realizing that probably made me look even more sociopathic than usual. There had just been a murder. Any normal student would be fraught with worry, with fear that they might be next, with devastation over an innocent life lost. All I had been doing was traipsing across campus in the small hours of the morning, trying to prove my own innocence with little regard for the victim or their family. And with no regard for my own safety, given that there was a killer still at large.

Not great, Wolfe.

"Alice Wolfe?" the taller of the two women asked. She had a severe widow's peak and a hooked nose, with close-together brown eyes and crow's-feet.

I felt oddly calm. "Yes?"

"I'm DCI Wilson, and this is DI Blenkinsopp." She nodded to her colleague, a young blond woman shaped like a pigeon. "Do you mind if we have a quick chat?"

"Do I mind?" I asked, feigning another smile. "You make it seem like I have a choice."

"You do," said DCI Wilson flatly. I couldn't trace her accent. "This is entirely voluntary."

I shrugged, as though I didn't care either way and the entire thing was boring. More classically innocent behavior. "Sure."

"We're happy to conduct the interview in your room, if you're comfortable with that."

Interview. That sounded decidedly more formal than a "quick chat."

"Of course. I just need to check that my roommate is out." I had a vague mental image of Lottie standing on the other side of the door, ear pressed against it. For some reason, the Scooby-Doo of it all made me want to laugh.

But the room was empty—and, now that I was seeing it through the eyes of two police officers, hideously untidy. My nose wrinkled against the tangy effluvia, and I hastily cracked the window, propping it up with my fattest Nietzsche. The cold morning air was instantly sobering.

"Would you like a seat?" I asked, gesturing to the two desk chairs with their backs to each other as though partaking in private study.

"That's okay," DCI Wilson said. "We'll stand. But please, make yourself comfortable. As we say, this is a voluntary interview, and we'd like you to feel at ease."

"Sure," I said, turning my desk chair to face them and taking a seat. Blenkinsopp shifted awkwardly on her feet, arms crossed over her chest, while Wilson rooted around in her pocket for something.

"We'll be recording the interview for internal purposes," she said, pulling out a small black Dictaphone with a snarl of headphone cables wrapped around it. She unwound the wires and pressed a button that made a solid red light illuminate on the top.

"As you may or may not be aware, a body was found at the base of the North Tower in the small hours of this morning. At present, the circumstances surrounding the death are still under investigation."

"I heard. That's awful. Her poor family."

I froze. Had I messed up already? They hadn't mentioned that the victim was female. But the knowledge was already widespread, so this surely wasn't a suspicious thing to say in itself.

DCI Wilson nodded. "Did you know the victim?"

"I'm not sure. I don't know her name. Are you allowed to tell me?"

"Poppy Kerr."

My gaze fixed on the red light of the tape recorder. "No, I don't think I know her. My roommate said she was in the fine arts program?"

"Yes. Now, your roommate, Ms. Fitzwilliam, alleged that last night you returned from the Refectory covered in blood. Is that true?"

The desk chair felt harder than usual; my spine pressed almost painfully into the curved wooden back. "Partially true, yeah. I *was* covered in blood, but I wasn't at the Refectory. I was at the library." I unfastened my satchel and pulled out the printed piece of paper detailing my sign-in and sign-out times. The Carvell logo stood proudly at the top of the letterhead.

DI Blenkinsopp reached out and scanned the page, then passed it to DCI Wilson, whose face remained the picture of neutrality. "I see," said the latter. "And do you normally carry details of your sign-in times around with you?"

My stomach clenched into a fist. "No. I went there this morning, after I showered. I knew the fact I came home covered in blood looked bad, and I wanted to prove my whereabouts."

"So why the initial lie to your roommate?" DCI Wilson's close-set eyes studied me for tells: a bead of sweat on the brow, an averted gaze. I tried not to betray any.

"I was embarrassed. She already thinks I spend too much time at the library and not enough time enjoying myself. She doesn't understand that those two things are one and the same." A tiny attempt to soften myself.

"Ms. Fitzwilliam alleged that you were unaware of what time you returned to the room. Is that true?"

As I nodded, I realized just how heavy my head felt. I was bone-tired, and faintly dizzy. "I fell and hit my head on the way home, hence all the blood. I think I have some kind of concussion, because getting back to my own bed is a little blurry."

I decided to stick with the fell-and-hit-my-face story, because what other narrative did I have? Besides, judging by the ache in my skull, a DNA test of the blood on my shirt would soon return a result in my favor. I was sure of it. Whose else could it be, when I'd been in the library all that time? I must have fallen facedown when I blacked out after the ritual. I should've gone to the philosophy section this morning, I realized. Any large maroon patches there would confirm this theory.

But I'd already said I fell on the way home. The spider's web of lies was snaring me already.

DI Blenkinsopp spoke for the first time. "How long after leaving the library would you say you fell and hit your face?"

I frowned. "I'm not sure. Why?"

"Well, the library is very close to the North Tower, and I wondered if you might have seen anyone coming or going as you were leaving."

I sensed a trap on the horizon, like a looming attack on a chessboard. I didn't seem to be in immediate danger with this line of questioning, but if I specified where I fell and hit my face, they'd likely check that area for signs of blood to corroborate my story. But if I claimed not to remember, that would also look suspicious. I settled for somewhere in between.

"No, I didn't see anyone when I was leaving, but I wasn't really looking. I think I fell around halfway back to Willowood." Hopefully this was vague enough that they'd struggle to confirm it but specific enough to avoid casting unnecessary aspersions on myself.

"Around halfway? Where exactly, if you had to narrow it down?"

My lungs tightened. "There's a tree with a crook in its branch that looks like an elbow. Around there, I think, but like I say it's a little hazy."

"All right. And you're absolutely sure you didn't know

the victim?" DCI Wilson took a photograph out of her shirt pocket. "This is Ms. Kerr."

At the sight of the face staring back at me, it took everything I had not to gasp.

It was the pretty ginger girl I'd seen talking to Hafsah al-Hadi.

She'd been in the library when I was there.

Throat arid, I managed to say, "No. No, I didn't know her."

CHAPTER 30

As much as the thought filled me with nausea, I knew I had to call my parents. They were going to find out soon enough, and better to save them the split-second agony of wondering whether it was *their* daughter who had been carried away in a body bag.

It was a little after seven a.m. Dad would just be waking up with a strong English breakfast tea and three slices of hot buttered toast, our golden Lab pottering around his feet.

Standing in the first-floor stairwell in Willowood—Alice was still talking to the police in our dorm—I folded one arm around my ribs, leaned back against the banister and hit dial. Dad picked up after three rings.

"Hello-o?" His voice was morning chipper, like cornflakes and radio jingles. I suddenly missed him ferociously.

"Dad, hey. It's me."

"Bumblebee? Wow, not like you to surface before nine."
I heard Radio 2 being turned down in the background.
Our lovely warm kitchen, where everything was safe. "To
what do I owe this most enormous pleasure?"

I swallowed hard, the vague tang of bile at the back of
my throat. "Another girl died."

There was a long, rolling silence, stretching out so long
I wondered if he'd been cut off. Then, "The North Tower?"

"Yeah." My voice was small and sad.

"Right. You're coming home. I'm coming to get you."
He was serious; I could hear the jangle of keys in his hand.
"I'll call Dave and let him know I won't be on-site today.
Get everything packed up as best you can and I'll—"

"Dad, no," I interrupted. "I can't. I want to stay."

To any rational mind, this probably seemed absurd.
But again I felt the presence of that unearthly hand on my
shoulder, coupled with a sudden, breathtaking *need* to stay
and solve the case. I needed to solve it more than I needed
water or air. The thought of finding the killer sent a dark
thrill rolling through me, and it was impossible to tell
whether that thrill was excitement or fear.

A strangled sound. "You *want*—? I'm sorry, but no.
I'm your dad, and I'm overruling you."

"What, you're going to tie me up and kidnap me?"

"Lottie! Why the hell would you want to stay there
after . . . Who was she? Did you know her? Do they know
what happened?"

"I didn't know her. And they're not sure what happened yet."

Dad's voice became low and urgent. "There's something wrong with that place. You shouldn't be there."

I know, I wanted to scream. The ruby in my throat, the lassoed-stomach knots, the visions of another life, the cairn of dead bodies. The supernatural pulse that had lured me here to begin with. It was all so cruel and terrifying.

But you can't leave, said something both inside and outside myself. Whether a thought or a threat, I wasn't quite sure.

Furnishing my tone with a defiant tilt, I said, "You wouldn't stop driving on a road just because there had been a few car crashes."

"Car crashes aren't *murders,* Lottie. Jesus. You're young and beautiful and talented, just like Janie and the others. What's to say it won't be you next?" He groaned viscerally. "Please. I can't bear the thought of anything happening to you. It would destroy your mother and me."

I closed my eyes and sighed. "I know."

And I did. I thought of Janie's parents at her funeral, the animalesque hysteria of her mum, the determined stoicism of her dad. How could I risk doing that to my own family? I was their only child. I was Dad's "kiddo" and Mum's "sweetheart." Their bumblebee. Was I being selfish, staying here to investigate? The thought of home was like a warm comfort blanket. I could leave right now, leave all this behind, and let someone else bring Janie's killer to justice.

Suddenly, as though sensing my wavering will, the ruby in my throat seared red hot, and then the roots wrapped around my windpipe, gripping so hard I choked. They loosened a moment later, but the meaning was clear: a warning from the North Tower.

Panic rose in my chest, filling my lungs like smoke I couldn't breathe through.

I had to get away from this supernatural pulse. It would be uncomfortable at first, like it was on the bus when my stomach churned and my vision blurred and I nearly fainted. But then the lasso would snap and I would be free, and I would be alive, and my parents wouldn't have to go through the worst pain imaginable.

"Okay, Dad," I said tightly. "I—"

The ruby's roots seized my throat more fiercely, robbing me of breath. I gagged silently, as though there were invisible hands wrapped around my neck.

The stairwell grew dark and spotty around me as stars danced across my eyes. I dropped the phone to the concrete floor and it skittered away.

I could die. I could die right now, and I would be powerless to stop it. My breathing was shallow and fast.

Is this what happened to Poppy?

To Janie?

Okay, I silently begged the ruby. *Okay, I'll stay, just let me go.*

The grip loosened and I gasped for air, gulping down deep lungfuls as I bent down to grab my phone. I was so weak I couldn't stand back up, so I stayed on the cold concrete on my hands and knees, fighting hard not to whimper.

"Lottie, are you there?" Dad's voice was crinkled around the edges with concern.

"Yeah, sorry, just dropped the phone."

"Look, I'm coming to get you." A door opened and shut somewhere near him. "There's nothing you can say to change my mind."

"Dad, I'm not leaving. Not like this." The words were cold, but they were my own, I thought. I hoped. Truth be told, I didn't know how far inside me the ruby could reach. "If they decide to close Carvell again, fine. But until then, you can't force me to do anything. I'm nineteen." A short, petulant pause, in which I knew I had to close down the conversation with an air of finality. "I'm not your little bumblebee anymore."

I regretted the words as soon as they left my mouth.

A few terrible moments later, Dad hung up, leaving me with the hand on my shoulder and the cold fist in my heart.

CHAPTER 31

Alice

The murder victim had been in the library with me.

I had thought my presence there all night was an alibi, but it wasn't. It was incriminating.

The police clearly didn't have enough to arrest me, but before long they'd check Poppy Kerr's ID card and figure out that our time in the library overlapped. I just had to hope that Poppy left a while before her time of death—and that the inevitable DNA test on my blood-soaked shirt came back as my own.

The knowledge that I had seen Poppy just hours before she was killed should have filled me with dread. I should have been terrified that I was the murderer, but I wasn't. I felt very little and remembered even less. That oppressive sense of detachment lulled me to sleep while still fully clothed, spread-eagle on my bedsheets.

I awoke to a quiet rustling and the acute sense that I was not alone. For a disoriented moment, I thought the police were still here, that I'd drifted off mid-interview. I'd been dreaming of handcuffs and of prison, and of how devastated my parents would be to see their only daughter in chains. My mum in a hospital bed, reaching for me and I wasn't there. Noémie seeing my face on the front page, tossing the newspaper away in disgust. Aidan, my sweet little brother Aidan, scared to come near me. Those images bled into the daylight, and it took me longer than usual to separate them from reality.

When the scene in the bedroom finally solidified, I saw Lottie riffling through the copy of *Thus Spoke Zarathustra* I'd used to prop open the window. It was the book I'd read more than any other, and was filled with my marginalia: musings and offshoots of thought from the original text. An immediate feeling of vulnerability settled on my skin like a sunburn, pink and raw.

"What are you doing?" I croaked.

Lottie looked up at me. "Sorry. I went to close the window because it was cold in here and I didn't want you to freeze, and I ended up flicking through the book." Her forefinger hovered over a page I'd underlined and annotated. " 'I am a forest, and a night of dark trees: but he who is not afraid of my darkness, will find banks full of roses under my cypresses.' That's beautiful." She smiled, with an expression on her face I couldn't read. "As is this rose you've drawn in the margin."

Heat rushed to my cheeks as I grabbed the tome and noticed the open phone camera in her other hand. Had she been taking pictures of my marginalia? Or was she really just casually flipping through the book with no ulterior motive?

She laid down her phone, kicked off her shoes and clambered up onto her bunk, which was still in a state of disarray from her four a.m. departure. "Why philosophy?"

I blinked. "What?"

"I mean, why are you studying philosophy? I don't think I've ever asked you before."

Propping my pillows up against the wall so I could sit and face her, I was struck by how intensely vulnerable it is to share a bedroom with someone. To show them the innocence of you in sleep. Maybe it was that exposure that made me offer my real answer—not just the one I'd parroted to impress Le Conte in my first class. Or maybe it was the ritual, stripping back the hard veneer I'd worked so hard to build.

"Because as much as I love the ideas, the actual philosophers are absolutely batshit *insane*, and I adore them dearly." I smiled. "Like, Diogenes lived in a wine barrel and owned only a cloak and a staff. He walked backward down the street to confuse other pedestrians. Once he overheard Plato define man as a 'featherless biped,' and Diogenes ran out and plucked a chicken. He returned to Plato and shouted, 'Behold! I've brought you a man!'"

I did a grand gladiatorial accent on this last part, and Lottie laughed.

"That's hilarious. Who else?"

"Pythagoras—"

"The triangle dude?"

"Yep, although a lot of scholars don't think his eponymous theorem was even his. But that's a much more boring story. He was actually well-known as a mystic, and there was a cult that embraced his philosophy of living." I could feel myself talking too fast, but the stories were gushing out of me. "The cult had all these bizarre customs, like members couldn't take public roads, eat beans, bake bread, or put their left shoe on first. Some people think he was killed by an angry mob that chased him to the edge of a bean field. Not wanting to touch the beans, he stood at the side of the field until the mob caught up to him and bludgeoned him to death."

"Incredible."

"*Then* there was Jeremy Bentham, who . . . god, sorry." Suddenly the fresh, pink vulnerability was too much, and deep-rooted paranoia told me the entertainment on Lottie's face was built on mockery. That she'd tell her field hockey friends about how much of a loser I was. So I muttered, "This is probably extremely boring for you. I'll shut up."

Lottie's grin spread from freckled dimple to freckled dimple. "No! Please don't. I love hearing you talk like this. It makes a nice change from all the brooding."

Ordinarily I'd take almighty offense at this, but there was something in the playful levity of her tone that made me think she was just trying to be nice.

I smiled back, trying to ignore the pull of my scar as my lips parted. "Okay, so in Bentham's will, he demanded that his remains be publicly dissected by a friend of his. Invitations were sent out to see the great philosopher opened up. He also bequeathed twenty-six mourning rings to his mates."

"Mourning rings?"

"Yeah. They featured a silhouette of his bust and strands of his hair. I'm surprised they haven't caught on."

Lottie snorted. "If you die and don't bequeath a mourning ring to me, I'll be livid."

But somehow, the joke seemed to kill the moment; we both knew we weren't good-enough friends for mourning rings. Lottie looked away, peering out the window toward the North Tower. Shame creeping up my chest like ivy, I followed her gaze. A raven was perched on the highest window and the sky outside was mottled like a bruise.

"I'm sorry for giving your shirt to the police," Lottie said finally.

"Oh."

"I mean, I'm assuming you knew that was me."

"Well, yeah. The subsequent interrogation gave you away somewhat."

Lottie met my gaze once again. "They said you were in the library all night. So you really did just fall and hit your head?"

"I really did just fall and hit my head."

The lie was beginning to feel natural, now, and it

frightened me. I got the sense that every time I recited this cobbled-together version of events, I'd erase the truth of what really happened—because the fact of the matter was that I still didn't know.

There was still every chance that I had killed Poppy.

CHAPTER 32

Lottie

The milky morning light washed over Alice's bare face as we spoke, and I couldn't deny that she was beautiful.

I could've been imagining it, but it seemed like some of the tension had been leeched out of her. Her shoulders sloped downward, relaxed instead of hunched around her ears, and there was no double knot between her brows. She talked about her favorite philosophers with the kind of easy yet unsettling charisma I'd come to associate with Professor Sanderson. She was like a cult leader—except her curves were far more intoxicating than Sanderson's sharp masculine lines, the black silk of her pajamas clinging to her hips and waist.

Something unfamiliar curled in my lower belly, and my throat felt dry all of a sudden.

Oh.

This is what people meant. This is what they meant when they talked about attraction.

Seeing her all lit up like this, bright and funny with her gladiator accent, I couldn't imagine her murdering anyone in cold blood. And yet wasn't that what was so often said of notorious killers? That nobody believed they could do such a thing?

Besides, this was the girl who'd punched someone in the face on our first night here. The same girl who made my stomach cramp with nerves whenever she drew near. Although now I wondered . . . *was* it nerves that made my stomach flutter? Or was it something entirely more terrifying?

But there was *something* sinister there, behind those kohl-smudged eyes. I knew it.

And yet . . . if someone had been watching me closely these past few weeks, wouldn't they say the same? The sleepwalking, the manic clawing at the tower, the ruby in my throat and the nameless dread.

Maybe Alice was falling victim to the same darkness I was.

Long after I got off the phone with my dad, the ruby in my throat still pulsed red hot, a metronomic reminder that something, some*one*, had well and truly sunk their claws in. I knew in my bones that I couldn't leave Carvell even if I wanted to.

So I had to stay. I had to solve this. All of it. Because it was all part of the same snarled knot. And it was what I had come here to do.

I decided to use Alice's unprecedented openness to ask a few probing questions. Something to reveal whether or not she felt the supernatural pulse too. Locking my phone—feeling a little embarrassed that Alice had caught me snooping through her stuff—I laid it down on my desk and climbed onto my bunk.

"Alice . . . ," I started, and she looked up, her eyes a deep lake blue. Wondering how to broach this, I settled for honesty. "I haven't been feeling like myself since I got here. Especially not the last few weeks." My hand went automatically to the ruby in my throat, and her gaze followed.

"In what way?" she asked, a chiming note of curiosity in her voice.

"I don't know," I admitted. "Just . . . darker, somehow. Gloomier. It's hard to put a word to it."

Something passed across her face, and I felt the slightest nibble on the line I'd cast, the feeling that I was about to coax a similar admission out of her, until the moment died and she just said, "You don't seem the type to get depressed."

It would have been easy to give up, but I pushed on. "I mean, first of all, depression can affect anyone. My mum was the happiest person I knew until she wasn't. Second of all, it's not that. I think it's something to do with the North Tower. Living in its shadow." A heavy beat, in which Alice's body went extremely still, as though she was waiting to see where I was going with this. "That's why I submitted the dorm transfer request. It sounds mad, I know. But I'm starting to think the tower is driving me insane. That's where I keep sleepwalking to."

Alice gave a small, seemingly involuntarily smile at the thought that she wasn't to blame for the request, then fought it back down.

She adjusted herself on her bed, propping her head up on her elbow so she was staring up at the North Tower too. It was backlit by the watery sun, the side facing us drenched in shadow. The police tape woven in and out of the Gothic arches flapped in the wind.

"It is . . . ominous, isn't it?" she murmured. "As a presence. But I can't tell if that's just because we all know what happened there. What's *still* happening there." She ran a hand through her hair, and it stuck up in stark red clumps. "Have you ever sleepwalked before?"

I shook my head. "Sleep talked, yes. Loquaciously. Dad used to threaten to stuff his dirty socks in my mouth if I didn't shut up." A pang of guilt as I remembered how I'd left things on the phone with him. "But I've never sleepwalked, no."

Alice shrugged, but it wasn't as casual as it should've been. "Maybe it's just the stress of being here. The academic pressure, making new friends. That kind of thing can exacerbate sleep problems, can't it?"

Yes, I thought, *but that doesn't explain the ruby in my throat.*

I didn't want to tell her about that. Not yet. I didn't know why I feel the need to keep it close to my chest. It made me feel oddly ashamed: tainted, or *dirty* somehow. I remembered how its roots felt as they closed around my windpipe while I was on the phone to my dad, how I knew in that moment it could kill me if it wanted to.

Fear shot up my arms and legs in hot stripes as I thought of the police carrying Poppy away in a body bag. Her poor family.

I didn't want to die. I really, really didn't.

"Are you scared?" Alice asked, and I realized she'd been watching me think. My face had always betrayed me like that, displaying my innermost turmoil like a slideshow at a museum.

"Yeah," I admitted. "Are you?"

She looked up at the North Tower once again, and I studied her face for any flicker of guilt. Her skin was creamy white, like marble, and she was almost as emotionless.

"I'm going to get some sleep," she said finally, leaving my question hanging unanswered between us.

CHAPTER 33

Alice

I managed to catch a few more hours of kip before I felt a hand on my shoulder, shaking me awake. Groggily, I peered up into Lottie's freckled face.

"Hey," she said softly, a messy lock of blond hair floating free from her french plaits. Her breath smelled of apple sweets. "Sorry to wake you, but it's a little after half three. Dean Mordue is addressing the student body in the chapel at four." A swallow. "Attendance is mandatory. Want to walk over there together?"

Despite the awful circumstances, the simple suggestion of walking there together spread an unfamiliar warmth through forgotten corners of my chest.

She hadn't submitted the dorm transfer request because of me. There was still a chance for us to be friends.

Unless you're a killer, of course.

The easy conversation of that morning had dissipated, replaced by a companionable silence as we walked down the cobbled walkways to the chapel. As we passed the crooked-elbow tree, I could've sworn I saw Lottie peer at the ground beneath it, as though searching for evidence of my supposed fall. I wondered how much she knew. What had the detectives told her, if anything? What gaps had she filled in on her own? The tentative peace treaty between us seemed too fragile to ask.

The chapel's scuffed old pews were as packed with people as they had been for the inauguration speech. Beside the ornate brass sconces, thin autumn sun poured through the stained-glass windows, bursts of brilliant-yellow maple leaves visible through Mary Magdalene's open palm. The chapel was deathly quiet. Salem was perched on a window ledge, watching with feline disinterest.

Dean Mordue stood behind the lectern, staring at the sheet of paper in front of her. Her hands were clasped tightly, as though to stop them from shaking. Her features were drawn, eyes lowered.

Students traipsed in silently, sliding along pews with none of the jubilance or fervor of that first day of the semester. Once everyone had stopped filing and was seated, Mordue spoke clearly but quietly into the small microphone at the top of the lectern.

"It is with the deepest sadness that I confirm the passing of Poppy Kerr."

Absolute silence. Even the ancient radiators stopped groaning.

"Poppy's family have been notified, and they ask that students and press alike respect their privacy during this difficult time."

Mordue took a deep breath, steeling herself. "I have already made my official statement to the media, so allow me to be candid with you all for a moment. I cannot believe I am here again, saying these devastating words once more." Her voice was ripe with almost-tears and she spoke softly, heavily. "I cannot believe we are here again."

The air was potent with an alchemical substance I couldn't quite name, a charged feeling, like when the sky is about to rain. The silence played in a minor key: fear, or sadness, or something richer still.

"For now, while the police investigate the circumstances around Poppy's tragic death, Carvell will remain open. This decision has been made in consultation with both the police and the board of governors, and will be under constant review. Campus security will be heightened considerably, and you are urged to report *anything* out of the ordinary either to myself or the nearest member of staff. Should you feel at all unsafe, please reach out. If it emerges at any point that there is a sustained risk to the student body, I will not hesitate to close our doors once more." A shaky nod. "Thank you."

My mind whirred, trying to slot the emotive sentiments

and the facts of the situation into something resembling an explanation. If Carvell was allowed to remain open, there had to be a reasonable chance that the police believed Poppy's death could have been a suicide.

What evidence did they have that pointed that way? It struck me that I knew very few details of her passing, beyond the fact that she had been found at the foot of the tower. What state had her body been in when it was found? Was there anything suggesting she had jumped? Was there any evidence of another person's presence that night?

Maybe Lottie knew more, since she went straight to the scene when she heard the news.

Or maybe . . .

No. Even though Lottie had been sleepwalking, and even though she'd been awake at four in the morning, there was nothing to suggest she could be a suspect. She was the most wholesome person I'd ever met. She was human sunshine. And besides, if she was the killer, why had she looked so horrified at the blood on my shirt? Why would she go to the trouble of taking the shirt to the police, knowing that would only draw attention to herself?

As the silence crept up to an urgent din, I turned to face her in the pew—only to find that she was deep in conversation with the girl on the other side of her.

Hafsah al-Hadi. The philosophy student who'd been with Poppy in the library.

Black hair pulled into space buns on the top of her head, Hafsah looked deeply shaken, her eyes red and raw.

She was making a repetitive finger-snapping motion, albeit silently. I strained to hear what she was saying to Lottie—would my name come up as someone she'd seen at Sisters of Mercy?—but their voices were too low to hear over the sound of hundreds of bodies pushing their way to the exit.

Deciding it would look too suspicious to linger and eavesdrop, I reluctantly headed back to Willowood. The dorm still smelled stale, so despite the cold, I propped the window open again. As I did, something in Lottie's bin caught my eye: a scrunched-up piece of pale-green paper. That particular shade of mint chimed something in my memory, and without thinking, I stooped to pick it up.

The dorm transfer request.

For a hopeful, fleeting second, I thought Lottie might have had a change of heart about me. That after all the nerdy philosophy talk, she'd decided I wasn't so awful after all.

But then the pieces finally fit together—the phone camera, the omnipresent notebook, the stack of true crime novels, her probing questions this morning—and I realized: she didn't *like* me.

She was investigating me.

CHAPTER 34

Lottie

Canceling my dorm transfer request was an illogical decision, on the surface. I should have been mortally afraid of Alice. I should've wanted to sleep as far from her and the North Tower as humanly possible.

And yet if I was going to glean insights nobody else had, this tower-adjacent dorm was where I had to be. If I was going to figure out how to get rid of the ruby in my throat—how to remove its murderous presence from my body—I couldn't just run. All I could do was hope that with Alice locking the door to prevent me from sleepwalking, the North Tower couldn't claim me next. As long as I was in bed before midnight every night.

Still, the guilt over staying ate away at me. If anything horrible did happen, I knew my parents would never survive. For a few moments after I threw the form away, I gripped the bumblebee charm on my bracelet until the silver was warm to the touch.

Dad, I'm sorry. I'm so sorry. But I don't have a choice.

As I was running through what I knew about the murder so far, I kept catching on the question of how Poppy, and possibly her killer, got into the tower. It was locked. Who else had the key, besides Mordue? And then: Was Poppy suffering from the same haunting symptoms I was? Did she ever find herself at the foot of the North Tower with no recollection of how she'd got there?

And above all, how could I possibly find all this out?

My first inroad came later that day. As we were piling into the chapel for Dean Mordue's address, I spotted a dark-haired, olive-skinned girl sitting alone. She looked more traumatized than anyone else, and it drew me to her. She snapped her fingers compulsively while staring up at the rafters.

I slid onto the pew beside her.

"Hey. Are you okay?" I asked.

"Uh-huh." She didn't even break her gaze away from the ceiling.

"It's horrible," I said inanely. "I just keep thinking, like . . . it could have been any one of us."

A strangled noise. "But it wasn't. It was Poppy."

"You knew her?"

"Yeah. I think I was the last person to see her alive."

A horrible choke-laugh. "Well, apart from whoever killed her."

My heart skipped a beat. "You saw her? When?"

"In the library. We . . . we had an argument. It was stupid, but . . ." She trailed off, lost in her thoughts.

I persevered. "I'm sorry. Did you know her well?"

"I mean, as well as you can know anyone you only met a few weeks ago. But yeah, she lived on my corridor in Foxglove." Foxglove was right next to Willowood, and it was the only dorm hall that offered single suites.

"What did you argue about?" I asked, trying to get my tone to land somewhere between consoling and curious.

Her fingers stopped clicking abruptly, and she turned to face me. Her deep-brown eyes were wild, pupils dilated so they almost completely consumed the iris. A look of primal fear. "I talked to the police. They said they found a suicide note. And her body, it was . . . They were asking me all about it, whether she was depressed. I didn't know her that well, but she didn't seem . . . I mean, I know you can never really tell, can you? It just . . . I don't think it makes sense. Especially with everything that happened the last time people died."

My surefooted approach stumbled. I wasn't expecting that. "Did you see the note?"

She shook her head. "No. But it was typed. They asked whether Poppy usually handwrote her essays or typed them."

I swallowed. "And?"

The girl shook her head and dropped it into her hands. "I don't know. It makes you realize how little you pay attention to the people around you. I've been so absorbed in my own shit that . . . ugh."

This triggered something in the back of my mind: the fact that Sam Bowey tried to have Janie committed under the Mental Health Act. A common thread between two of the victims *could* be a possible connection to the hauntings. Demonic possession might look like psychosis to the untrained eye.

Something hideous prodded at my memory—how the field hockey girls had described me on the second night I was drawn to the tower from the refectory. *Then this weird expression came over your face. Like you were doing an impression of someone else, I don't know. Your features just kind of changed.*

Swallowing down a gush of dread, I tucked this thought into my back pocket to examine later.

There was one question I badly wanted to go back to— what Hafsah and Poppy had been arguing about—but I didn't want to seem insensitive or bullheaded.

Before I could ask anything else, Dean Mordue entered the room from a side door by the dais and the whole chapel hushed. I decided not to take notes like I had at the inauguration—it would make it all too clear what I was up to, and potentially make it harder to earn the trust of the girl beside me whose name I still didn't know. Instead I had to try to carry it all in my head: the conversation with Poppy's almost friend, the dean's statement, the general atmosphere, the needling thoughts that arose from all of the above. It took so much mental effort while operating on so little sleep that I clenched my jaw against the strain of it.

When the dean left the stage and people started to gingerly climb to their feet, the girl next to me whispered so softly I almost didn't hear her.

"What if it was me?"

I was sure I'd misheard her. "Sorry?"

She turned to face me again with those frantic eyes, that terrified expression. "I said something really mean to her. About her art. What if she killed herself because of me?"

I put my hand on her shoulder and gave it a little squeeze through her Hello Kitty sweater, and said, "Why don't we go for a drink?"

The Grandstand was almost empty; all the sports events set for that afternoon had been canceled. One solitary guy was throwing dart after dart, alternating between sips of his whiskey and Coke. The fire was crackling and spitting in the grate like a feral thing.

Hafsah was nursing a Fentimans Victorian lemonade. Her skin had taken on a clammy pallor as she spoke.

"Poppy is—god, fuck, was—in the fine arts program. She'd shown me some of her A-level portfolio one night in the Foxglove common room. Her stuff was good, but trying a bit too hard to be angsty. Tracey Emin Light, you know?" I nodded, but I knew nothing about artists. "Anyway, at the time I was nice enough about it. But then last night, we were in the library and she said something flippant about philosophy students. How pointless a degree it is. I think she'd forgotten that's what I study, but somehow her forgetting pissed me off even more, when she'd made me sit through all those derivative paintings. So I just . . . I snapped. I said, 'At least I'm good enough to be here in the first place.' I'm like that a lot. Too blunt. Too direct. It gets me in trouble."

"Wow," I said, not quite knowing what to say. Telling her it wasn't her fault didn't seem entirely genuine. If Poppy had committed suicide, the timing of Hafsah's cutting remark was pretty terrible.

There was a moment of silence between us, in which it seemed like she expected me to comfort or absolve her, but I didn't. It seemed prudent to remain neutral. Instead I asked, "Did you tell the police about this?"

She shook her head vehemently, a lock of hair shaking loose from one space bun.

"I think you should," I said carefully. "Nasty comments aren't a crime. It'll just give them helpful context."

Hafsah put down her drink, stared at the flames leaping in the fireplace and said nothing.

I decided to try to mine the seam of Poppy's mental health further, and how it might have related to my own haunting experiences with the tower. As softly as I could, I asked, "I know the police already asked you this, but did she seem like herself in the days leading up to her death?"

At this, Hafsah's attention snapped back to me, her features hardening. Her fingers started snapping seemingly of their own accord. "I already told you I barely knew her. How am I supposed to know what 'like herself' meant?"

She stood up from the chesterfield sofa and stormed out without a backward glance.

I leaned back in my armchair and mulled over what had just happened. Maybe Hafsah was just a prickly person, but then again, maybe she was hiding something.

What was with all the spiky girls around here?

CHAPTER 35

Alice

After I figured out that Lottie was investigating me, I second-guessed my every move, trying to view it through the lens of suspicion. What would it look like if I disappeared to the library—the potential scene of the crime—for hours on end? What would it look like if I started asking around for more details about Poppy's death?

And so I maintained the air of aloofness I'd spent my entire adolescence honing. I was pleasant to Lottie without ever crossing into keenness. I attended all my classes, but didn't spend too much time in the library after hours. I read books while I ate meals in the dining hall, and smiled politely whenever anyone approached. I was the kind of gentle I'd never imagined I could be.

The strange thing about it was that it didn't feel difficult. After the ritual, the constant imaginary arguments ceased entirely, and so there was no prickly defensiveness in my interactions with other people. The urge to smash a person's head against a wall if they looked at me the wrong way evaporated. In fact, I couldn't even recall what those flashes of anger or violence felt like; it was as though they'd been severed from my psyche altogether.

But the calmer I felt, the sadder I was that I didn't have anyone to share it with.

Encouraged by my new freshness of spirit, I texted Noémie:

> Miss you x

I wished her no ill will when she didn't reply, though I did think wistfully of the last autumn we'd spent together, taking long walks through the Cheviots and drinking homemade hot cocoa made with the darkest chocolate we could find.

The new ease with which I moved through the world was welcome, for the most part. Sure, it was unnerving to feel that I was no longer whole—that so much of what made me Alice had been dug out at the roots—but it made my existence feel so much less fraught. And if the price I had paid for this peculiar peace was a few missing hours and a dead moth, it seemed like a fairly good deal.

Of course, there was always the lingering dread that wondered whether that *was* the whole price.

What if the real cost had been Poppy Kerr's life?

However, when several days passed without another visit from the police, I had to deduce that the blood on my shirt had been proven to be my own. And with the absence of Poppy's blood on my person, what did the police have to tie me to the crime, other than the fact that our time in the library had overlapped?

The logical explanation was that I had passed out after the ritual—maybe the tincture was slightly poisonous?—remained unconscious in the philosophy section for a few hours, and then staggered my way out at 3:58 a.m. as proven by Kate Feathering.

Feathering. The thought of her still sent a flicker of unease through me. She'd known my name without me having ever given it to her, but I kept reminding myself that it probably flashed on her computer screen when I scanned myself in. She would've remembered me, thanks to my altercation with the guy who asked for ink. Another logical explanation I clung to like a raft.

The presiding sense of serenity was a gift to my academic progress. I found that I could achieve a much deeper sense of focus during my study sessions. I could wrap my mind around broader concepts, to think critically about widely accepted principles. My thoughts had a clarity to them that they'd never had before; a pure, singular chime as opposed to a riotous symphony.

It was good timing, because around a week after Poppy's death, I had my first private tutorial with Professor Dacre. Before the ritual, I would have been beyond nervous about meeting with him, especially after his first few impressions of me were less than favorable. Now, though, I felt confident I could win him around with my new composure; my singularity of thought. If he was to be my mentor for the next three years, I wanted his opinion of me to be a positive one. I wanted to *impress* him.

Dacre's office was high-ceilinged and bright, filled with objects of distinct beauty: Persian rugs and porcelain, little paintings of gods and monsters, low bookcases teeming with rare first editions, fine china teapots in Byzantine blue and the bitter botanical scent of Earl Grey. Cut-crystal vases of wildflowers and herbs, the blues and purples and greens of foxgloves and ferns, the citrus musk of marjoram. The rattle-paned window was propped open by an ancient copy of *Roget's Thesaurus*.

"I heard that you keep the window open for the campus cat," I said, taking a seat in the velvet wingback armchair opposite his desk.

Dacre nodded with a tsk of a chuckle. "Indeed. My fireplace is a favored spot for her early-evening nap."

The room had a sweet, heady air to it that I found incongruous with Dacre, with his brown corduroy and tobacco-stained fingers and general air of personal neglect. I still felt on edge around him, the memories of our first prickly interaction needling at the corners of my mind. We exchanged pleasantries about the weather for a few minutes before I decided to grab the thistle by the hand.

"Professor Dacre, I just wanted to apologize for the

anger you saw in me on the first day of the semester." I shifted awkwardly. "I was stressed and flustered and embarrassed. It won't happen again."

Dacre offered me a genial smile, little commas appearing at the corners of his sagging mouth. "Worry not. It calls to mind Aristotle: 'Anybody can become angry, that is easy, but to be angry with the right person and to the right degree and at the right time and for the right purpose, and in the right way—that is not within everybody's power, that is not easy.' From *The Art of Rhetoric*." He crossed one leg over the other, trousers riding up to reveal mismatched socks. "You are still young, Ms. Wolfe, and learning to control your anger is a lifelong pursuit. Yet it is a pursuit worth the effort. Anger left to run free is like wildfire, indiscriminate in its destruction. But if you learn to tame it, to position it, to take aim with it? Then it becomes a candle. And what is the candle but one of humanity's greatest assets? It warms. It nourishes. It shines a light in the darkest of places, and it illuminates the path forward."

I grinned wolfishly. "Speaking of paths forward, I was a little pissed off when you told me such anger was 'unbecoming of a young woman.'" I made pointed air quotes around the phrase.

A grandfatherly chuckle. "Forgive me. I ought not to have said it. I was forged in a different time, a different culture, but it's no excuse. I must move with the zeitgeist. It's fantastic to have such passionate women at Carvell."

Women have been getting degrees for over a hundred

years, I wanted to say, but I was finally back on steady ground with Dacre, and I would try to keep it that way. The man in front of me was going to be crucial to my future as a judge—a personal recommendation from him would secure a place at any law school I wanted.

Suddenly, it all seemed back within my reach, and I smiled to myself. Dead body aside, I was thrilled with how the ritual had turned out.

But things that seem too good to be true usually are, and this was no exception.

CHAPTER 36

Lottie

During the week after Poppy's death, the depths of my amateurishness began to sink in. Having handed in Alice's shirt to the police, alienated Hafsah and royally pissed off Peter Frame, I'd burned through all of my leads. I wrote up everything that had happened in my notebook, which took most of the day after—I found myself scribbling through-out my first Chaucer seminar, barely listening to Professor Wang's ruminations on symbolism in *The House of Fame*.

But once I'd transcribed the events of that tumultuous day, I was at a loss for what to do next. I made conversa-tion with countless other students, both in my classes and at the Grandstand, but none of them had anything of inter-est to offer like Hafsah had. Almost everyone had been asleep at the time Poppy died.

Field hockey practice resumed ten days after the death,

and though the atmosphere was melancholy, we all seemed glad to have an outlet for the grief. There was a catharsis to smacking a heavy ball around a field for two hours, and I felt lighter for the release.

Lighter, but no less haunted.

One thing my brain remained stuck on was how Poppy—and her possible killer—managed to get into the tower. The door was locked, as I knew from firsthand experience, but who else besides Mordue had a key? It seemed a futile avenue to go down when the police had likely already pursued it to its logical end, but it was one of the only avenues I had.

Making an appointment to see Mordue was easier than it would've been before Poppy died. She had cleared her schedule for the week so she could talk one-on-one with any students who were considering leaving. By the time I talked to her secretary, I got one of the last remaining appointments.

Mordue's office had a black Gothic fireplace—all columns and arches—and an antique mahogany desk in front of an enormous bay window. A grandfather clock engraved with rows of peculiar symbols in an unfamiliar alphabet stood in one corner. Upon closer inspection, I realized it ticked backward.

When I entered, Mordue rose from behind her desk, thanked and dismissed her secretary, and gestured for me to take a seat on a sofa. If she remembered me from the North Tower confrontation, she didn't show it, but maybe she just had a good poker face. I adjusted the pashmina around my neck, hoping it covered the ruby, which was throbbing like a wound.

"Thank you for coming to see me, Ms. Fitzwilliam," Mordue said, smiling warmly. She had sharp feline flicks drawn on her eyes in black liner, her smooth hair pulled back in a high ballerina bun.

"Thank you for seeing me," I said, uncertain just how to play this. "I've been really scared, as I'm sure you can imagine. Especially living so close to the tower."

"Yes, now your file says you'd put in a dorm transfer request, but you withdrew it the day after Ms. Kerr's passing—is that right?"

I fluttered with nerves. She'd looked into me. Did she do that with every student? Or was it that she really did remember me from that night?

"Yeah, I withdrew it because I think I'm going to leave," I improvised, praying to hell she didn't call my bluff. The timing did look pretty odd. "This is all . . . it's a bit too much."

"I understand." She nodded. "It's been frightening for us all. Especially those of us who were here ten years ago. It brings back a lot of traumatic memories." Her delivery was slightly rehearsed—she'd probably uttered the same words to countless students already—but I could tell there was real pain behind the practiced lines. It was etched in the wincing crinkles around her eyes and the downward tilt of her mouth.

I looked down at the trembling hands clasped in my lap. "I don't really want to leave, it's just . . . what if I'm next?"

She fixed her hazel eyes on mine. "Please rest assured we're doing everything we can to make sure nothing like this ever happens again. For one thing, it looks like Ms. Kerr tragically took her own life. But regardless, we know how terrifying this is, given the history, so we're upping security measures considerably. There will be a guard posted at the entrance to the tower twenty-four hours a day, and CCTV cameras installed both there and in the observatory."

I stared at the backward grandfather clock; it had an almost hypnotic presence in the room, like a magnetic field.

"But how did Poppy get into the tower in the first place?" I asked, laying some of my cards on the table. "I thought it was locked."

"That's something we're still looking into." From Mordue's measured tone, I guessed this was something other students had asked too.

"Okay, it's just . . . who else had a key, besides you?"

This was crossing a line, and I knew it.

She tilted her jaw upward ever so slightly. "Several other trusted staff members. Those keys have since been revoked. I'm now the only person with access, and the key is on my person at all times. Which is why I'm confident nothing like this will happen again."

At least not in the North Tower, I thought, with a stab of genuine fear that seemed to originate in my throat.

"Who were the staff members?" I asked, chewing my lip. I'd have to play up the nervous student act if I was to coax any answers loose.

She pressed her lips into a flat line. "I don't think that's appropriate for me to answer. Is there anything else you would like to talk to me about?" I shook my head. "Very well. I do hope you decide to stay with us, but if you would like to leave, we'll be happy to provide references for whatever institution you apply for next year."

I left the meeting feeling defeated. I should've known she would never share that kind of information with me, but I was hoping she'd let something slip: gender, department, whether it was a caretaker or a cleaner. Unfortunately she'd been the picture of professionalism, and I was no further than I had been before I went in.

So now the only real lead I had left was the girl I shared a dorm with.

CHAPTER 37

Lottie

It was time to go all in. I had to get as close to Alice as I could, lying in wait for her to put a foot wrong.

As I studied her, I realized there was something tangibly different about her since the murder. She still reminded me of the woods, vast and beautiful and dark, but it was as though all those prickly defense mechanisms—thistles and nettles and hogweed, poisonous mushrooms and gnarled earth—had been dug out at the root. An oddly vacant placidness I found disquieting. Her anger and upset over the dorm transfer request seemed to have dissipated entirely.

At first, I put it down to guardedness; she must know I was watching her carefully. She must know she had to act like nothing had happened, to remain as neutral as possible to avoid arousing further suspicion.

Strangely, though, this misty dissociation made it harder

to talk to her, not easier. It was like half of her was always somewhere else—or missing entirely. We chatted inanely about the weather and about what classes we had that day, but nothing like the textured conversations about imps of the perverse or kooky philosophers or even what we were respectively reading.

I couldn't quite make sense of the changes, or of how they related to the murders, if they did at all. If I was to think the absolute worst of Alice, I'd say that she'd finally acted on her violent impulses, and it had quelled them for now. The idea chilled me to the bone.

And yet she'd left her bloodied shirt lying so carelessly in the dustbin, and didn't seem at all angry or worried that I'd handed it over to the police. Someone who'd just committed a murder wouldn't act like that.

Her newfound impassivity did have some perks, in that her guard wasn't up nearly so high. Whereas she'd usually hunch over her satchel while opening it on the writing desk, angling her body so I couldn't see what was inside, she began to leave it unattended more and more often.

The next night, I waited until she was asleep and opened the satchel as quietly as I could.

Inside was a small leather pencil case monogrammed with her initials, a lined notebook filled with scrawled notes on her lectures so far, a merlot-red lipstick, a plastic water bottle filled with something that smelled like elderflower cordial, a cell phone that was out of battery, and a course reading list I copied down in the back of my own notebook. It wasn't relevant to the investigation or anything, but I wanted to impress her with some casual knowledge of her subject area. It had felt really good to catch her off guard with my Baudelaire and Edgar Allan Poe quotes.

Why exactly I wanted to impress her . . . I decided not to examine that urge too closely.

There were a couple of other random objects in the satchel I couldn't make sense of. First was a small selection of glass vials, all empty. They were notched into the elastic pen loops on the roof of the satchel. The other was a pair of gardening shears, whose sharp blades made my heart thump a little harder—until I remembered Poppy hadn't been stabbed. And yet what use did Alice have for them? She had an oversized monstera plant on our windowsill, but I'd never seen her do anything more than half-heartedly spray it with water.

Unusual as these were, they were also dead ends. Short of asking Alice what she did with them—which would immediately betray my raid of her private possessions—there was no obvious way to figure out whether they were relevant. I just had to keep watching her and hope she slipped up.

In the evenings I often found myself staring out of our dorm window for hours on end, like the North Tower was a magnet my eyes were perpetually drawn to. It was during one of those mammoth staring sessions that I noticed something strange about the dimensions of the building.

Right next to the North Tower was the Sisters of Mercy

Library, which took up three floors. The tower had no windows apart from the open arches of the observatory, but the library had large Gothic windows the height of multiple stories. Inside the library, they started right at the edge of the room, by the bookshelves, and spanned the whole way across the wall. But from my vantage point in the dorm, I noticed that on the outside, it looked like the windows were a few meters from where the North Tower curved outward.

What was between the library and the tower? Was it just dead space?

I drew a sketch of that wing of the building as I saw it from my window, then compared it to the campus map I'd been given with my welcome pack. Sure enough, the campus map showed the library stretching right up next to the North Tower with nothing in between. It didn't make spatial sense.

One Saturday morning when the main convent was quiet, I went into the building to scope it out. On the ground floor, through an ornate stone cloister bolting off from the main corridor, was the entrance to the library, fronted with security gates where you scanned in your student ID. I had always found this hilarious. As if a non-student would have any interest in breaking into a dusty old library run by a white-haired, black-lipped villain from a film about dalmatians.

In the dead space I'd identified next to the library, there was a storage closet, which a cleaner had left slightly open.

It was stuffed with damp mopheads and old bleach and many, many rolls of the industrial blue paper towels found in all schools and universities across Britain.

In the same place on the first floor, there was a varnished brown door with a gold-plated WC sign, but it was locked and looked like it had been for all of eternity; a brass key was jammed into the keyhole and didn't rotate when I tried it.

On the second floor, the space where a door should have been was bricked and plastered over.

The paint—a pale sage green—looked fresh, but that in itself wasn't odd. A lot of the old convent had been given a good old spit and polish before Carvell reopened.

What was odd was that it had been bricked over at all.

What was behind that wall? And did it lead into the North Tower?

CHAPTER 38

Alice

I realized my dark side was returning in earnest a couple of weeks after the ritual while I was eating lunch with Amanda, a girl from my program who was struggling to wrap her head around divine command theory. We were discussing the Euthyphro dilemma when a sudden urge pierced my consciousness:

Stab her with your fork.

The impulse was so sharp, so overwhelming, that I had grabbed my fork and raised it before I even finished the thought. I managed to wrest control of the desire before I brought the fork down against Amanda's neck, but the ferocity of the urge and the utter lack of control I seemed to have over it chilled me to the bone.

It happened again the next evening, when I was passing the Refectory on my way to the library. Two drunk guys stumbled from the booming entrance, their faces slack and happy under the fluorescent green lights, and the visceral longing to slit their throats swallowed all else. My fists clenched of their own accord, and my feet lunged me in their direction as though under some divine command. If I'd had a dagger on my person, there was a very real chance I might have acted upon it.

Before I knew it, the impulses were coming thick and fast, and bridling them became a never-ending battle—one that required intense concentration at all times lest they take full hold. Seemingly overnight, the ability to study, to communicate, to think of anything but bloodlust was entirely lost. The clarity and the innate sense of goodness I'd felt in the first few weeks following the ritual were shrinking, until it felt as though there was a mere pinprick of light left.

I canceled my private tutorials with Dacre in case I alienated him once again. I stopped going to class; I couldn't concentrate anyway. I stopped sleeping, for fear of what I might do when I let my guard down. The effort of holding back a ravenous tide meant I was perpetually doused in cold sweat. I couldn't even eat, because any distraction might be fatal.

It was as though my very soul had been split in two, with Good and Evil battling for control over the fortress of my mind. Only now, the skirmishes that plagued me through adolescence had devolved into a full-fledged war.

And it was not going the right way. Evil had torched

through Good's defenses, and the fortress would not hold for much longer.

One night, in a fit of desperation, I went to the chapel to . . . not to pray, exactly. To find solace? Forgiveness? Something to provide a salve, a balm, *anything* that would ease the monstrous instincts for just a moment so I could think. A voice from above to tell me I was not evil. I was not broken. That I would be saved, somehow.

I didn't find it, of course. No god in any world or any realm would absolve me of the thoughts in my head. But it was a relief to be in a wide-open space with nobody else around; nobody else I could fantasize about killing in vile and vicious ways.

As I sat there in the scuffed pew in the back row, staring miserably at the centuries-old floor, I felt something soft brush against the back of my neck like a fur scarf. Jolting upright, I watched as Salem leaped gracefully onto the pew beside me, arching her back and stretching out her paws.

For the briefest of moment, her presence was the salve, the balm, the moment of fleeting goodness I needed. A tiny speck of relief that almost brought me to tears. There would always be cats. Cats hated you regardless of your thoughts. They *could* judge you, but it was probably too much effort, and anyway, they'd rather be left alone.

And then she looked back at me, and something red and unnatural flared in her eyes.

Unthinking, I grabbed her viciously by the throat.

Her claws gouged the backs of my hands, the red vanishing from her eyes as her normal yellow irises shrank in fear. A spiderweb of scratches formed across my skin, weeping red, but I didn't let go.

Her neck was so fragile, I could feel even tiny matchstick bones beneath my palms.

Stop stop stop stop, pleeeease stop, whimpered the five-year-old girl at the core of me, but I couldn't. My limbs were no longer my own.

Utterly unable to wrest back control, my grip tightened on Salem's neck and made a snapping motion, a violent, right-angled jerk to one side.

Crack.

Her body went limp in an instant.

The horror hit me all at once.

No no no no no no no—

I dropped her to the ground and retched up nothing.

Please please please, it was a mistake please please don't be dead don't be dead—

But her soft black body was still, head crooked at an awful angle. Her eyes were wide, the unnatural red in them faded to dark.

Over my desperate gasps, slow footsteps echoed in the chapel. Self-preservation kicked in, and I hurriedly nudged Salem's body under the pew in front of me.

I'm sorry I'm sorry I'm so sorry, you didn't deserve it I'm sorry I'm a monster I'm—

I stood up, smoothing down my blazer, and dabbed at

my eyes to make it look like I'd been crying. Blood roared in my ears as I turned into the aisle.

Professor Le Conte had stopped a few meters away, all his weight on his back foot as though he was about to turn and leave. He offered a remorseful look, as though embarrassed to have caught me in a moment of private turmoil, and lifted his hands in apology.

My heart thudded in my chest. "I was just leaving." The words seemed to come from very far away.

"Very well," he said in his soft, assured voice. "I do hope everything is all right."

I nodded, a strangled feeling in my throat, and then strode past him toward the exit.

Fuck fuck fuck fuck fuck, I just killed a cat fuck fuck fuck—

As I reached the door, I glanced back to see Le Conte had taken a seat in the front row, far from where Salem's lifeless body lay on the cold stone floor.

Panic rose in my chest like a black tide. Someone would find Salem soon. They'd find her with her neck snapped. And Le Conte would know—surely, he would know—it had been me.

I was every bit as evil as I'd always feared.

CHAPTER 39

Alice

Even through the darkening veil of monstrosity, I knew I had to move Salem's body. If she was found dead, I would be . . . I'm not sure what I'd be. Expelled? Criminally charged? Either way, the thought of anyone knowing what I'd done filled me with obsidian shame, as though the blood in my veins ran pure black. It made me want to tear the skin from my flesh.

I returned to the chapel in the small hours of the morning, praying Salem's corpse hadn't yet been discovered. Mercifully, the place was deserted, and I found her sweet black body where I'd kicked it hours earlier. If I left her in the woods at the bottom of a tree, it might look like she'd fallen badly.

Tears sliding down my cheeks and into Salem's fur, I

picked her up in a plastic carrier bag and stuffed her into my satchel. The feel of her stiffening limbs made me gag.

I went as deep into the woods as I could bear, near the glade where I'd found the tincture ingredients. The moon lit the way until it didn't, and then I had to feel my way over gnarled roots and low-hanging branches with my breath hitching in my throat.

Eventually I emptied her out of the plastic bag at the base of a beautiful old oak.

Rest easy, little one, I thought, but the word *murderer* beat in the back of my head like a pulse.

As the days crunched on, my body sank into deeper withdrawal from the tincture. In the fragments of respite between the psychotic urges, all I could think about was the ritual. It was a craving unlike anything I'd ever experienced; like I was dying of thirst and the tincture was the only thing that would slake it.

There was logic to the bone-deep need too. I believed that if I could go back to the blissful ambivalence I experienced right after taking the tincture for the first time, no matter how impermanently, maybe I would have the headspace to think through my next moves. Because it had become abundantly clear that I needed to find a way to reverse all of this. The post-ritual clarity would give me room to breathe, to plan. To atone.

Because if I didn't reverse the ritual . . . what if Salem was just the beginning?

If my soul really had been split in two—if Good and Evil had become warring forces in my mind—I needed to broker a peace treaty. And the only way I could do that was by returning to the calm waters of those post-ritual weeks. I couldn't think like this. Not when the final defenses of my mind could fall at any second.

I had to take the tincture again.

I still had the elderflower mixture in my satchel, but I was missing blood. Specifically, the blood of someone I had wronged. Yet how could I trust myself to gather more when there was a very real chance I wouldn't be able to stop? The thought of Harris bleeding out on the cobbles filled me with a rich sense of pleasure, and I had never been so afraid.

Before long, the tenuous dam I'd built against the darkness burst.

On bonfire night, campus was rich with the scent of gunpowder, whorls of smoke curling up into the charcoal sky. The fireworks had ended, but students still gathered in knots on the front lawn, drinking hot cider and toasting marshmallows over miniature campfires. The distant sound of them made me sick with envy.

It was almost midnight, the half-moon's pearlescent gleam slicing through the crack in our curtains, and exhaustion had me trembling in my bed.

My thoughts were bleached by pain. I felt something deep within me shudder and then break, and I knew it was over.

Using the last vestiges of light to guide me, I stumbled from my bunk and crossed over to Lottie's, where she was snoring merrily next to a hardcover copy of *My Dark Places.*

I shook her awake, monstrous thoughts churning in me like nausea.

Strangle her strangle her strangle her look she looks so innocent she's defenseless strangle herrrr, she deserves it she hates you it would feel so good—

My hands reached for her throat.

"What? What is it?" she mumbled through the shroud of sleep, pushing my outstretched fingers away.

With every ounce of strength I had left, I pulled my hands away.

Then, with a final, gasping pause, "I need your blood."

CHAPTER 40

Lottie

I got back from town late on bonfire night, having filed a postal request with the National Archives for the most recent architectural drawings of the convent. I claimed it was for a school project, because it never hurts to pretend to be twelve in these situations. Having endured a full day of lectures, seminars and hockey practice, I was so exhausted that I fell asleep reading.

The next thing I knew, I was being shaken awake by Alice.

Alice, wide-eyed, shaking, convulsing, spittle around the corners of her mouth, drenched in bluish shadow, hands outstretched toward my neck, rasping, "I need your blood."

I propped myself up on my elbows, sure I'd misheard. "You—*what?*"

She sank to her knees, jaw cracking repeatedly as she

shuddered like a dying spider. "I did . . . a ritual . . . my soul. It's . . . like it's split in two. Good. Evil. Explain . . . later. Please, Lottie, *ple-e-e-ease*—"

Conflicting emotions rattled through me.

First, excitement. This was a lead. A big one.

Second, genuine concern for Alice, for the cartoon villain, for the girl who made me cry on my birthday. She looked so afraid, and it made me afraid for her. The pang of worry had an unusual texture to it, somehow deeper and grainier than it should have been.

Third, belief. She was in no state to explain why she needed my blood, what this soul-splitting ritual entailed, and yet I knew in the very roots of myself that it was true, and it was important—and it had something to do with what had been happening to me.

Even though I was awake, glimpses of another dream life flitted through my mind: illuminated manuscripts, wooded glades, falling bodies. Stinging nettles, swarms of moths, vials of blood, red spatters on a white cornette.

The ruby in my throat burned hotter than a poker in a forge.

The pain rendered me momentarily useless. I fell to my knees beside Alice, breathless, the taste of blood in my mouth, as though the poker had pierced my neck, a melting blade I had fallen upon. It was so intense, so absolute, that I couldn't even cry out.

I knew, without knowing how I knew, that the only way to stop it was to help Alice.

It was all connected somehow.

It was all in the horrifying bones of Carvell. In its flesh and sinews, ancient and cruel.

I crawled to the small drawer in my writing desk, pulled out the three-inch Damascus-steel pocketknife engraved with my great-grandfather's family crest, tore it from its tan leather sheath and pressed the very tip of the blade into the palm of my hand until it drew a few crimson beads.

Rasping and writhing, Alice handed me one of the vials, which I recognized from her satchel. Those had been empty, but this one was filled with strange ingredients and smelled of elderflower cordial. I wordlessly added the blood and passed it back to her.

She drank it greedily, desperately, as though she'd been walking through the desert for a hundred years in search of this very tonic. For a moment her shaking stilled, her franticness eased, and all the tension seeped out of her body.

Then the screaming began.

It was like nothing I'd ever heard, like her bones were being passing through a meat grinder, like her skin was being flayed strip by strip, like she was watching everyone she'd ever loved die a slow and painful death.

Panic rose in my chest. Had I done it wrong? Had I given her too much blood?

I tried to usher her away from the blunt corners of her desk, worried she'd slam her temples into it in a fit of agony, but her writhing was too intense. I couldn't get a solid grip on her arms, and she whipped the back of one hand into my face with a sharp *thwack*. I struggled to bite back a cry, but my teeth jammed down onto my tongue and made it bleed.

After the longest minute of my life, Alice half slumped on the floor like a marionette doll whose strings had been cut. I eased toward her, holding out a tentative hand.

"Alice?"

Slowly, too slowly, she tilted her head to one side until her bloodred eyes locked on mine.

In a low, monstrous voice, she snarled, "I'm going to fucking *kill you*."

Heart lurching, I climbed to my feet and ran.

But the door was locked.

I rattled the handle, then remembered with a sharp drop of my stomach that as part of the sleepwalking solution, Alice had agreed to hide my key under her mattress.

Alice was slowly climbing to her feet, unfurling her limbs like a baby deer. I took a deep breath and sprinted toward her, knocking her to the floor with a thump of bodies. I scrambled to my feet, shoved my hands under her mattress, and my fingers closed around the key.

By the time I turned back around, Alice was brandishing my Damascus-steel pocketknife, that ferocious red glare in her eyes.

"I'm. Going. To. Kill. You. *Bitch*."

Her voice was a low grind, hoarse and subhuman.

She dived at me, and I spun out of the way just in time, my field hockey footwork drills finally coming in handy.

I dodged her fierce lunges twice more until I'd danced my way over to my stick bag. Wrenching a stick free from the front pocket, I stood with it like a sword.

I hoped this would deter her, but this monster was not Alice, was not capable of rational thought. She pounced, and as she raised her knife arm high and her feet left the ground, I swallowed every ounce of humanity I had and whipped the stick across her temples.

Hard.

She slumped to the floor, knife skittering away under my desk.

With a stifled sob, I dropped to my knees, holding two fingers to her throat to find her pulse.

It was there, fast but steady. Shallow breaths leaked out of her.

Without looking back, I slid the key into the lock with shaking hands, opened the door and slammed it shut behind me, locking it from the outside.

What.

The.

Fuck.

CHAPTER 41

Alice

The first thing I was aware of when I woke up was an acute pain searing through my abdomen in hot stripes as though I'd been branded with a pitchfork. Despite the scorched feeling, I shivered severely, convulsively. The dark room slowly appeared in misty patches, dizziness fuzzing the periphery of my vision, until I eventually realized I was not in my own bed but in Lottie's.

Then I realized it wasn't just my stomach that was killing me; it was my head too. Like I'd slammed headfirst into a brick wall.

"Arghhh," I groaned into the almost black, and seconds later Lottie's little bedside lamp flickered on.

"You're awake," she said, voice filled with an emotion I couldn't quite place.

Her hair was still in french plaits, but only vaguely;

there was a halo of soft blond frizz where strands had worked themselves free. She was sitting on the strip of floor between our two bunks, rubbing her eyes, and I could see she'd made herself a bed out of coats.

My watch said it was half five in the morning. I'd lost even more hours this time.

Through pain-clenched teeth, I asked, "Why am I in your bed?"

Lottie grimaced, then gestured to my bunk. "Um, you bled all over yours."

My bed had been stripped of its sheets, and there was an almost perfectly round patch of dark-maroon blood in the center of the mattress. The sheets balled up at the foot of the bed were sodden, and the entire room smelled metallic, despite the half-cracked window.

I held a hand to my stomach, and was surprised to find soft, warm bandages instead of an open wound. "Dare I ask . . . ?"

Lottie's lips pressed into a flat white line, and again I couldn't read her expression. "You did it to yourself, after I left you alone." Was that disgust on her face? Or pity? Which would be worse? "I patched you up as best I could when I came back."

Unable to stop myself from trembling, I muttered, "Fantastic. At least I didn't hurt anyone else." A pregnant pause, in which I thought of the dead cat in the woods. "I didn't hurt anyone else, right?"

Lottie looked like she was about to say something, then

decided against it. "Well, you threatened to stab me if I called an ambulance. But otherwise, no." She didn't look at me. Was it a lie? Had I actually hurt her? The thought was profoundly awful.

"I was capable of speech?" I asked quietly.

"Yeah. But the voice wasn't yours. It was too low, too hoarse, too . . . monstrous. Like loose screws were rattling around in your throat."

I flinched away from the words, but no subsequent anger came.

I'd fought back the darkness with the tincture. For now.

I heaved myself up to a sitting position, but the wounds on my stomach complained viscerally, panther claws dragging through my middle, and I lay back down. Inside my bruised skull, my mind was back to oppressive blankness and currently assessing the situation with an unnerving clarity. "How did you get me under control?"

"After I came in to check on you the first time—didn't go well, by the way—I waited outside until you eventually tired yourself out."

"So I cut myself? With what?"

Lottie hugged her knees, the dark-green Sevenoaks hockey joggers she often wore to sleep bunched up around her ankles. "My pocketknife. The one I used to give you my blood. I couldn't get it out of the room. I think we should go to the hospital. I tried my best to disinfect your wounds with the antibacterial wipes in my kit, but I can't guarantee I did a great job."

My heart panged in a wholly unfamiliar way. "Why did you look after me?"

Lottie swallowed hard, and then took a drink of water from the tumbler sitting on her desk. "Because I'm a good person. That's what good people do, which is maybe why you can't understand it." The words were neither cold nor fiery, perhaps tinged with jest, but I couldn't quite parse them. Either way, she was much calmer than she should've been.

Instead, I just nodded. "I deserve that."

There was a long, uncomfortable silence while we both sorted through the questions helter-skeltering through our minds. Outside, a bird chirped despite it not yet being dawn. The scent of rosemary and wild garlic floating through the window was a balm, and I sucked in lungfuls of the cold, fragrant air.

Lottie broke the quiet with a fearful whisper. "Alice . . . what the *fuck* have you done to yourself?"

I shook my head. "I didn't . . . I didn't think it would work. The first time. It was just an absurd ritual I found in the library." I dug my fingernails into my palm until they made crescent moons. "Do you believe me? That it was a ritual? This whole supernatural thing . . ."

She nodded slowly. "I do."

"Okay. And now . . ."

"And now." She rested her chin on her knees. "We're going to figure this out."

I didn't need to ask her motivations for figuring it out

with me. She was determined to Scooby-Doo everything that was going around Carvell. And I'd just handed her the biggest scoop imaginable.

Sweeping the duvet off me, I said, "Here. You should have your bed back. I'll take the floor."

Lottie scoffed, pulling a black wool coat over her shoulders. It was one of my coats, I realized, and she was hugging it around her for warmth. "Like hell you will," she said. "You're hurt."

"Okay, well, the least you can do is bunk up next to me." The words were out of my mouth before I considered the intimacy of them. Hastily I added, "You must be freezing on the floor, and I really don't need to add 'roommate developed frostbite because of me' to the list of things I currently feel guilty about."

As Lottie chewed her lip with indecision, I found that my heart was fluttering against my rib cage like bat wings. I wasn't sure whether it was because I was embarrassed for suggesting it, or because deep down I really wanted the comfort of someone lying next to me. I hadn't shared a bed since Noémie left.

After what felt like an eternity, she mumbled. "Fine, but I'll take the side nearest the edge. I don't trust you not to go all *Exorcist* on me. Please try not to scuttle backward down the steps like a possessed spider."

A smile tugged at my lips. "Are you really taking the piss out of me right now?"

She nodded sagely. "A little bit, yes."

The treacherous flurry in my chest only intensified when she climbed up beside me, the mattress sinking under her weight. I pressed myself against the wall, biting my lip to keep from groaning in pain. My stomach *hurt*.

We didn't touch. She immediately faced away from me, balling a corner of the duvet up in her fists and yanking it mostly off me, but the bed felt instantly warmer for having her in it. Something vulnerable and childlike at the very heart of me glowed, and I had to fight the urge to nestle into her back. I *ached* for it.

Her breathing was so soft and steady that it was difficult to tell whether or not she'd fallen asleep, but after there had been a few minutes of silence, I allowed my tense muscles to relax. I didn't think I'd be able to sleep through the hot stripes across my abdomen—would it have killed Lottie to find me some codeine?—so I finally forced myself to look at the terrifying question that loomed in my mind.

Could the ritual be undone?

And then:

What would happen if not?

The thought of spending the rest of my life cycling between the extremes of good and evil was more frightening than I could comprehend. Was this why the ritual fell out of favor not long after it was discovered? Was that what the missing pages in the library book detailed?

Or did they detail the cure?

And either way . . . why would those pages be missing?

Who had torn them out, and what possible motivations did they have for doing so?

"Lottie?" I semi-croaked.

Her voice was muffled and soft with sleep. "Yeah?"

"I'm really, really scared."

CHAPTER 42

"I shouldn't have left you in there alone."

Alice and I were tucked in a quiet corner of the dining hall, stacks of hot buttered toast in front of us. She was shoving slabs of them into her mouth as though she'd never eaten in her life—which was strangely endearing—while I couldn't stomach any food. The red flare of her eyes, the monstrous voice, those violent gashes on her pale torso . . . they haunted me.

She shrugged, crumbs flying everywhere. "I get it. I probably would've done the same."

I gave a good-natured chuckle. "You wouldn't have given me the blood in the first place."

She stopped chewing and studied me carefully. Pre-ritual Alice might have snapped at me for that, but this neutralized version seemed to weigh the statement with pure, emotionless logic and reasoning. "You don't know me as well as you think you do."

Looking around, I noticed Salem wasn't in line for her kippers. That was strange. She was usually here at nine on the dot.

I cupped my coffee mug with my hands, letting the heat burn through my palms. Having spent the night with Alice's warm body pressed against mine, I couldn't seem to shake the cold this morning. "You're right, I don't."

Alice had told me on the way over here—our heads pressed together as we talked in a hush—that the ritual was the reason she had that gap in her memory on the night of Poppy's death. She'd performed it for the first time and blacked out. That in itself should be incriminating; I had seen firsthand how murderous she became while in the throes of it. At first I wondered whether she had found Poppy, found a way into the tower and killed her. She certainly had it in her when she was in that state.

But a few things about this didn't add up. First, I had to assume that the police had discovered that the blood on her shirt was her own, otherwise she'd be in prison right now. Second, how would she have found her way into the tower? The door had been locked, and as far as I knew, none of the faculty members who used to have keys had reported being attacked by a psychotic, red-eyed first year. There was a chance I'd found another entrance, but it was currently bricked over, and I was still waiting for the National Archives to get back to me with a blueprint.

None of it quite fit.

Alice popped a crust of toast into her mouth, then flipped her claret-red hair over her head so the side part was even deeper. Her hair was unbrushed and unkempt, but it looked right on her. She looked like she was about to respond when her eyes snagged on a spot just below my chin.

"When did you get another piercing?"

My stomach somersaulted. In all the drama and exhaustion, I'd forgotten to wear my pashmina. The crewneck sweater wasn't high enough to cover the ruby.

As I lifted my hands defensively to the jewel, dread seized my heart.

It was no longer just one ruby. There was another.

No wonder it had hurt so much last night, in the throes of helping Alice. Was that the sensation of another one piercing my throat? I hadn't been conscious for the appearance of the first one.

It was impossible to describe the creeping terror this second gem caused. Would they just keep appearing until they circled my neck like a noose?

Would the rubies' hold on me only intensify now that there were two of them? One ruby already had a hold over me, could choke me into submission if I didn't behave the way it wanted me to. What would another sentient jewel do? I thought of how those invisible roots had curled around my throat and squeezed when I'd tried to tell my dad I wanted to go home. I thought of the intangible hand on my shoulder, guiding me around campus, and of the lasso around my stomach whenever I got too far away.

Dread grabbed me by the ribs. Why was this happening to me?

I knew I had to tell Alice the truth—about the haunting, or the possession, or whatever the hell this was. After what I'd witnessed last night, I knew she was the only one who wouldn't doubt that something paranormal was happening here. We were both falling victim to the Carvell curse, whatever that curse might be. We could help each other figure out how to free ourselves.

Breath hitching in my chest, I whispered, "They're not piercings." I gulped. "They're from Sister Maria's statue."

Alice blinked. "I—what? How? Did you steal them?"

"No." I bit my top lip. "They just appeared on my throat. One a few weeks ago, and one . . . at some point last night, I guess."

Alice blew air through her lips. She took all of this at face value—which made sense, given the completely absurd things that had been happening to her too. "That explains why you immediately believed me about the ritual. Does it hurt?"

I looked away, focusing instead on a painting of a rolling wheat field dotted with hay bales. "It's okay." An outright lie—they hurt like hell, and I felt like I might throw up from the fear.

"No, it's not," insisted Alice. Through the corner of my

eye, I saw her lean over the table to get a closer look. Then she whispered, "Can I see?"

For a goth this was probably an incredibly exciting and erotic turn of events, so I swallowed hard, turned back to face her and nodded. She reached out a long, elegant finger and traced it over the rubies. The roots in my neck curled with pleasure, and I fought the urge to shiver.

"Wow," she breathed, then sat back on her bench. "They're really in there."

"Yeah." I reached over and grabbed a piece of now-cold toast to dissipate some of the weird tension that had gathered between us. "So I feel like we have a lot to tell each other."

And so, over several cups of steaming coffee—mine milky and sweet, hers black and bitter as the Northumbrian night—we told each other everything. I explained how I kept waking up at the foot of the tower, hands bloodied as I clawed at the stones, my run-in with Mordue, the lassoed-stomach feeling, the visions of wooded glades and illuminated manuscripts and bloody vials. I told her about how I'd wanted to go home right after Poppy died, but the ruby had started choking me until I fell back into line.

It felt good to finally tell someone about everything that had been going on. Someone I knew wouldn't judge me, because she'd succumbed to the strange supernatural pulse too, albeit in a different way. It made me feel less alone, less of a monster. That sensation of being tainted, compromised . . . it eased off, if only for a moment.

Then Alice told me about the ritual—the book in the library, the missing pages, the wooded glade filled with ingredients. Her description matched what I'd been imagining perfectly.

"So, to sum up," I said, "we're fucked."

Alice grinned.

"What?" I retorted. "It doesn't seem particularly funny."

She snorted, taking a long sip of black coffee. "No, it's just nice hearing you be negative for once. The whole sunshines-out-of-my-butt thing gets old."

"I'm not positive all the time," I replied, folding my arms.

Alice fixed me with an amused glare. "Name one thing you dislike."

After a long pause, I said, "Cola bottles."

She arched a villainous brow. "You ate a bag of cola bottles literally yesterday."

"Okay, I dislike *some* cola bottles."

"All cola bottles taste the same."

I shook my head vehemently. "Not the one my friend Frankie dared me to eat when I was fourteen. It had been stuck to the bottom of her shoe all day."

"So let me get this straight. Of all the people, places and things that exist in past, present or future, the only one you actively dislike is a specific cola bottle you ate half a decade ago?"

I nodded sagely. "Sounds about right."

Alice shook her head, and a lock of red hair fell into her eyes. "Unbelievable."

"Anyway, back to the life-threatening situation at hand. How do you think any of this fits in with Poppy's death?" I mused. I was warming up now, thanks to the toast and the coffee and the conversation. "Like, could she have performed the ritual? Or did the North Tower have Poppy in its grasp too?"

Alice shook her head. "I don't know. As awful as it sounds, I'm more focused on how the fuck I'm going to fix this. I can't . . . god, what happened last night can't happen again. It wasn't just the pain, it was . . . what if you hadn't helped me? What if the darkness had won before I could take the tincture, and I hurt someone? What if I'd hurt *you*?"

Somehow, I got the sense that she was holding back. There was something she still wouldn't tell me. Was it about Poppy? Had she done something awful in the throes of monstrosity?

"Well, first of all, you'll never be in that situation again," I said. "Now that I know, I can be on the lookout for the signs of transformation. We can be prepared with the tincture ready to go as soon as it starts happening. And we'll find a way to restrain you while it's happening so you can't hurt anyone, including yourself. You're not in this alone anymore."

Alice looked as though she might have been touched by this if she had been a normal person with normal emotions.

Something seemed to bob in her throat, but she swallowed and looked away. "And second?"

I drained the dregs of my coffee, put down the mug and got to my feet. "We have to find those missing pages. I think they have our answers."

CHAPTER 43

Alice

Feathering was in her usual spot behind the library's entrance desk, and I began to seriously consider whether she might be some sort of supernatural being. There were never any other librarians here, and no matter what time you called upon the books, Feathering was here. When did she sleep? I'd never seen her eat, and there were no empty coffee cups or glasses of water littering her desk. The whole thing left me slightly unsettled, as though I might be dealing with a vampire or a werewolf or a particularly humorless poltergeist.

Today she wore a black turtlenecked poncho and a silver necklace with an amber pendant shaped like a lily of the valley. Her black lipstick was so perfectly applied it cut a neat line across her face, and her sheets of white-gray hair were so smooth they could've been a wig. I tried offering her a smile—maybe if she smiled back I'd be able to tell how pointed her canines were—but it was no use. She was as cold, distant and unidentifiably paranormal as ever.

"Hi," I said, attempting to imbue my voice with strength despite the fact that the walk here had left my wounds hot and sharp. I pulled my tweed blazer tighter around myself, folding my arms across my abdomen to stop my hands from shaking. I couldn't stop thinking about the way Salem's body felt in my hands: soft and rigid and awful. It felt like I might die from the shame of it.

"Can I help?" Feathering asked in her usual blunt manner.

My heart began to pound, though I couldn't pinpoint why, exactly. "I was wondering whether the library had any books by T. A. Renner?" Of course, I already knew it did, but I was hoping there might be more than one copy— one without missing pages.

Feathering's long emerald-green nails clacked on the keyboard as she ran the search. Then, impossibly, she shook her head. "No, sorry. What's his subject area?"

I frowned. "Erm, philosophy, I think?"

She arched a thin, dark brow. "You think?"

"Yeah. Yes. Philosophy. There's a book about divine command theory in nineteenth-century convents. I can't remember the title, though." A lie and a slightly off-pitch description so that she wouldn't know how important the book was to me.

Feathering shrugged impassively. "Sorry. Nothing here."

Disappointment crested in my chest, shortly followed by the sensation of missing a step. Why would the system say the book didn't exist when I knew for certain that it did?

"Oh," I said. "No problem. And you've never heard of the author?"

"No. Sorry." The words were slow and deliberate, as though she were speaking to an idiot.

I waited for the prickle of irritation, the righteous annoyance that a reference librarian would treat me like a moron when it was her literal job to provide the information I'd requested, but of course the irritation never came. I was fresh from the ritual, all traces of malevolence vanished from my psyche, and all that came out was a bright smile and a "Thank you so much for your help." I was practically Lottie. All I needed was a packet of sweets in my hand and an infuriatingly luminous grin.

Since Feathering had insisted neither the book nor the author existed in this library, I figured it was fair game to go and take the book for myself once again. If it wasn't in the system, what was the harm? And while the pages I needed were missing, perhaps there would be some clues inside that would help me track down another copy—an author bio maybe, or at the very least information about which imprint had published the book. It hadn't appeared out of thin air, so it was a simple case of following the bread crumbs.

I climbed the winding spiral staircase to the philosophy section, running my hand over the cool wrought iron banister in an attempt to distract me from the searing wounds on my torso, but when I arrived at the relevant shelf, the book was nowhere to be seen.

How could it have gone? It didn't formally exist, so how could it have been checked out of the library? I thought of the small, round bloodstain on the corner of the ritual page, of my suspicion that someone else at Carvell had performed it too. Had they come back to get the book—also desperate for answers? If so, how could I find that person? If we put our heads together, we might have more luck.

As I headed out in the direction of my late-morning seminar, I felt uneasy. Something about the whole exchange with Feathering felt off, but I couldn't put my finger on why. Traipsing over the dew-slicked cobbles, I ran over the conversation in my head until I found it.

She'd said, "What's *his* subject?"

Unless she'd just defaulted to male pronouns without thinking, Feathering knew the author was a man. So why did she pretend she'd never heard of him?

The Ancient Ethical Theory seminar took place in a drafty old classroom next to the patch of cobbles beneath the North Tower where Sister Maria fell to her death—as had all the other victims thereafter. Great efforts had been made to brighten the room up: windowsills lined with potted peace lilies and asparagus ferns, framed paintings of

Northumbrian landscapes by Carvell alumni, a dusty record player with its matte gold arm permanently raised.

Dacre looked even more disheveled than ever, with the pink-rimmed eyes and sour scent of the painfully hungover. He fumbled every sentence and paused for too long after a student had answered a question, as though he might have been taking a brief nap while they spoke. My newly minted good heart felt a bit sorry for him. I couldn't imagine having to teach Plato while perilously hungover.

As he waffled on about Socrates's aporetic writings in *Euthyphro*, I glanced over at Hafsah, whose seat was adjacent to mine. She seemed to be breathing more heavily than was really required of the situation, and her skin was clammy with sweat. She was muttering under her breath with the ferocity of an incantation, but I couldn't make out the individual words.

"Hafsah?" I whispered, trying to get her attention, but she didn't hear me. Her hands gripped the sides of her desk, stretching her knuckles taut. "Hey. Are you okay?"

"Please please please please, not now, no no no no," she muttered, and there was something familiar in her tone that sent a cold wave of dread shoring through me. Her eyes were wide and unblinking, and she shook her head wildly as though trying to vanish an unwelcome voice.

I thought of the small, round splotch of blood in the ritual book, and I just *knew*.

Before I could really process what was happening, she got abruptly to her feet and sprinted from the room, leaving all of her belongings behind. A loose sheet of paper drifted to the floor. I picked it up and turned it over as though it might contain some kind of clue, but it was blank except for some ragged blue holes; by the looks of things, she'd been stabbing into her notepad with her fountain pen.

I'd seen her in the library on the night of the murder, I remembered. Talking to Poppy Kerr, who had been gripping her notebook like a weapon.

Poppy Kerr, who was found dead hours later.

"Fuck," I groaned, louder than intended.

Dacre looked at me in puzzlement. "Is everything all right?"

"I'm going to go and check on her," I said, my voice hoarse even to my own ears as I gingerly hauled myself out of the chair and grabbed my satchel. The painkillers Lottie had doled out like jelly beans were wearing off fast.

As I crossed the room to the door, I felt dozens of eyes on my back, and none more potent than Dacre's. He'd stopped teaching entirely and was staring at me like Hafsah and I had made his morning far more interesting.

The classroom was situated opposite a harsh stone staircase that led up to the art studios, and beneath the staircase was a small ladies' bathroom with two wooden cubicles and a single sink. I found Hafsah on her hands and knees in the middle of the floor, panting as though undergoing some kind of werewolf transformation.

It's how I imagined I'd looked right before I begged Lottie for her blood.

CHAPTER 44

Alice

Hafsah was in the throes of hell in front of me, and the only way I knew how to save her was to perform the ritual. I still had a few vials of elderflower tincture in my satchel, but none contained the blood of anyone she had wronged.

The door croaked shut behind me, and she slowly turned to face me. Her dark eyes were burning scarlet red, and her teeth were clenched together in a vicious snarl.

A split second passed, and then she lunged at my throat.

I let her.

I let her clamp her stone-cold hands around my neck until my vision swam.

And then I lifted a thick book from my satchel and swung it as hard as I could at the back of her head.

She fell to the ground like a deadweight. My throat

throbbed in protest as I coughed uncontrollably. When I finally recovered, I knew what I had to do.

Hafsah was out, but not quite out cold; she writhed and frothed on the ground like a dying thing. Now that she had harmed me, I could perform the ritual for her, but I had to act fast.

After retrieving a vial of tincture from the notches in my satchel, I lifted the hem of my navy satin shirt and looked down at the wounds Lottie had so carefully bandaged up. I tore away the topmost bandage to reveal a seething red cut spanning from one side of my torso to the other. There were faint streaks of faded pink where Lottie had gently rubbed at it with an antibacterial wipe, and the thought sent a curious flutter through me. Lottie's hands had been on my stomach, her fingertips working their way over soft, exposed skin.

Gritting my teeth against the impending pain, I pinched the edges of the wound and dug a fingernail into the cut until it reopened. Hot blood trickled out in fat globules, and I caught them into the unstoppered vial. Grimacing, I rewrapped the bandage, dropped my shirt and hunched down to Hafsah.

She was beginning to convulse as though in a seizure. Her fingernails gouged at her eyes, pulling down the lower rims so the fleshy pink was visible. When she sensed me nearby, she swung an arm in my direction, but I ducked back just in time to dodge the blow.

I swallowed my terror, grabbed her viciously by the jaw and all but threw the contents of the vial down her throat.

As I tried to pull away, she bit down hard on one of my fingers, and I let out an involuntarily shout of pain.

As the liquid hit her gag reflex, she released her bite, coughing and spluttering helplessly. I used the split-second advantage to grip her by one ankle and drag her into the nearest cubicle, her head juddering dangerously against the floor as we went.

With the sliding mechanism on the inside of the door, I couldn't lock her in, but the door opened outward, so I was able to block her in by sitting in front of it. It was an old, full-length door, so she couldn't lash out at me through any gaps underneath. I sank to the floor, pushing back against the door as my ragged breathing slowed.

Hafsah slammed and slammed and screamed and screamed, throwing her full weight against the door, but still I held on, pain in my stomach, throbbing in my bitten finger, cold sweat dripping down my brow, and horror in the deepest, darkest parts of me.

And then she stopped hurling and started to talk.

And just as Lottie had said, it was too low, too hoarse, too monstrous.

"I'm going to fucking kill you, I'm going to fucking kill you, I can't wait to kill you, it's going to feel so good, you horrible piece of shit, my hands around your throat as I feel the life seep out of you, I will be here waiting and waiting until you slip up, you fall asleep, and then it's over, and then I get to *kill* you, get to drink your blood forever, watch your parents weep over your lifeless corpse—"

I clamped my hands over my ears like a toddler, but it was no use. I could still hear her. The voice was just as Lottie had described it—loose screws rattling in a throat.

There was every chance I was shut in a bathroom with Poppy Kerr's murderer, and yet all I could think about was the fact that Lottie had heard me talking like this.

What did she think of me?

And why did it *matter* so damn much?

The hours inched disquietingly by, with a constant soundtrack of dark threats. The voice never let up. It told me of the thousand ways in which it could kill me, what it could do with my skin and my organs, how good it would feel to tear my muscles from my bones, how much my loved ones would suffer at the sight of my mangled corpse.

Every few minutes, Hafsah threw herself at the door with her full strength, the whole thing shuddering and reverberating through my spine. Twice it almost gave out, a few inches opening between door and frame before I could shove backward with all my might and close it again. Sweat poured down my neck and face, both from the effort of keeping her in and the fact that the painkillers were rapidly wearing off. Gritting my teeth, I forced myself to sit strong. If she got out, there was no telling what she might do to me.

Still, I didn't have the strength to hold on for much longer. Dread held me in a viselike grip. How long would this last?

I couldn't stop thinking about Lottie. She'd felt the same fear, and she'd still bandaged up my wounds. She'd still offered me her bed. She'd still let me fall asleep with my face pressed against her arm.

Was she just *that* kind? That brave? Or that stupid?

A few people came into the bathroom while I was stuck with my back against the door. They frowned at my position on the grotty linoleum floor, but I made some needlessly detailed excuses about my friend's food poisoning and they soon left us alone.

Finally, after nearly three hours, the voice trailed off into silence. I was relieved for a moment, but what if Hafsah was trying to trick me? What if she was pretending to have stopped so I'd open the door, and then she'd rip the arteries from my neck with her bare teeth like she'd been threatening to do? I was exhausted, listless, pain searing across my stomach. I couldn't fight her off even if I wanted to.

But then a small, frightened voice said, "Hello? Is anyone there?" And I knew immediately that the ritual had worked. Hafsah had been brought back around.

Through the relief and the exhaustion, one question chimed with the clarity of a single church bell: Had Poppy Kerr succumbed to the fate I'd so narrowly escaped?

CHAPTER 45

Lottie

Alice and I parted ways after breakfast, and I headed to my Gothic literature seminar with Professor Sanderson. Usually I looked forward to it, but my reality had become so frightening that I found myself wanting to escape, not journey deeper into the belly of darkness.

As I walked into the classroom, I spotted an Edgar Allan Poe quote in one of the morbid obituaries on the wall: "Deep in earth my love is lying; / And I must weep alone." It made me think of my parents, and of Janie's parents, and of Poppy's parents. I ached for my dad. We hadn't spoken since I told him I wasn't his bumblebee anymore. But it was true, wasn't it? There had been a swift and perilous change in me. I dreaded the thought of him seeing the rubies studded in my throat, of him hearing the way they choked me if I disobeyed.

Would the power over me be stronger now there were two rubies?

Rain rapped on the high, loose windows as Sanderson stood in front of them, staring out onto the sprawling woods. Once we were all seated, he started talking without turning around.

"Sister Maria Dunn was a lover of gothic fiction," he said, voice halcyon clear and almost pastoral, as though he was delivering a sermon. "It was a filthy habit, pardon the pun, and one that distracted her from her worship. As such, not many knew she could read—the stack of novels and magazine serials was only found after her untimely passing—but she was known among her fellow sisters for her excellent work decorating manuscripts."

My heart beat faster.

Those half dreams of illuminated manuscripts held in age-spotted hands.

"The abbess at the time, a Sister Catherine, found a slim volume called *The Two Magics* tucked under Sister Maria's pillow on the night she died. The volume contained two stories, the best known of which is *The Turn of the Screw,* by Henry James—a story of spiritual possession, of haunted grounds, of the terror of the supernatural. It was, for its time, deeply frightening." Sanderson turned to face us, eyes black and shining, dark hair combed and parted on the side with oily precision. "Once again, I would like us to hold up a magnifying glass to that shimmering thread between author and reader. Between Henry James and Sister Maria Dunn, who died shortly after reading this story."

The fine hairs on my forearms stood to attention. Nobody knew for certain whether Sister Maria had been murdered, or had fallen, or had taken her own life. Sanderson's theory about *The Turn of the Screw* was bound to be pure conjecture, and yet my body thrummed in response. The rubies in my throat twirled their roots almost in pleasure—in recognition of something.

"In the late eighteen hundreds, there was a cultural fascination with the supernatural. Scientists and psychologists took ghosts seriously. Spiritualism—a religious movement based on communicating with the dead—had taken hold. And of course, the church had long believed in demonic possession. At some point in the early Middle Ages, priests began to be trained to perform clergy-sanctioned exorcisms, which has continued right through to modern day. Yes, modern day—I have a friend who makes decent money from a particularly paranoid parish in northern Wales.

"Now, we already know that Sister Maria was somewhat . . . rebellious. With her long habit—again, very sorry for the pun, shan't happen again—of hoarding books, she had somehow procured a highly sought-after ghost story that had only been in print for a month. She also had a reputation at the convent for her somewhat fiery personality; she regularly butted habits—*my sincerest apologies*—with the abbess over her overall mardiness. She had unsavory quirks and foibles, a predilection for cursing and a fascination with fire. A local historian recently uncovered a letter from the abbess to the diocesan bishop in which she wrote that Maria 'seethed with a godless energy.'

"And so why Maria's obsession with gothic horror? My theory is that she saw herself in it. She saw the erratic behavior of the haunted and the possessed, and she believed herself to be so. She believed there to be something fundamentally wrong with herself. She was the monster from the stories."

Something clicked into place with such precision that it almost took my breath away.

I wasn't possessed by the North Tower.

I was possessed by Sister Maria.

How hadn't I made the connection sooner? They were *her* rubies, after all. My fingers brushed them tenderly, prickling with a sudden kinship.

What *was* this? Her ghost? Her spirit, her soul?

And then the most burning questions of all: Why me? What did she want?

CHAPTER 46

Alice

Hafsah and I left the old convent building and came to the woods for some privacy. The air was heavy with the scent of moss and earth, and I breathed in deep gulps of it. It settled my nerves somewhat, as did the painkillers I'd swallowed after we left the bathroom, but all I could think of was Salem's body lying nearby. How long until she was found? Had Dacre already noticed her missing? He told me she slept in his study every night, after all. Guilt clutched at my insides, and I had to fight the urge to cry.

"I saw you in the library that night," I said to Hafsah, clearing my throat. "When Poppy died, I mean. That was the night I did the ritual."

Hafsah grimaced, staring down at her baby-pink Converse as they crunched over the undergrowth. She held her hands near her waist, snapping her fingers methodically. "I did the ritual the next day. So it seems like the effects last almost exactly one moon cycle. Love the werewolf journey for me."

I smiled darkly. "Why did you do the ritual?"

"It was the day after you saw me with Poppy. I'd said something awful to her that night. She didn't deserve it, and bless her, she was so fucking upset. I don't think I even meant it. It just came from a place of anger. And I used to be able to dismiss that, to be able to say, 'Oh, I didn't mean it, I was angry.' But it had got to the point where I didn't know where my anger ended and I began." Her words chimed in my chest like a tuning fork. "The next day, I found out Poppy was dead, and something deep in my gut told me it was because of me."

My feet were leading us in the direction of the glade where I'd foraged most of the ingredients for the ritual. Imagining Hafsah treading the same path, gathering weeds and wildflowers in her satchel and finding a moth to kill, made me feel less alone. Yet the fact that I felt kinship with Hafsah troubled me. What if she *was* Poppy's murderer, and here I was identifying with everything she was saying? What did that make me?

Then again, there was only a small chance that she was a killer. I *definitely* was. I could still feel the snap of Salem's neck reverberating through my palms.

Even if we managed to reverse the ritual, how would I ever live with myself?

Turning over Hafsah's account in my head, though, I

realized the timing didn't quite work. If Hafsah hadn't performed the ritual until *after* Poppy died, it seemed unlikely she was the killer. Unless she'd done it in cold blood, fully cognizant of what she was doing. The idea didn't strike me as particularly realistic, but stranger things have happened.

"What happened after your fight with Poppy?" I asked.

Hafsah laughed airily. "Are you asking if I killed her? I didn't, but I was terrified I might have, in a way. I thought what I said might have caused her to jump." As she passed below the wooded canopy, fragmented sunlight and shadows shifted across her face. Clear glitter eye shadow was slicked over her lids, glimmering like morning frost. "And don't worry, I've already talked to the police. I have an alibi. I was off my face in the Refectory all night, with hundreds of lucky people witnessing my sick dance moves. No jail for Hafsah! Yay for Hafsah!"

We reached the glade, and she promptly slumped onto the stump of an old tree, as though her very bones were tired. I felt similarly exhausted.

"What did you say to Poppy that made you so worried she could have jumped?"

She grimaced, but there was a mischievous undertone to it; she didn't seem as ashamed of her anger as I was of mine. "Promise you won't judge me?"

"Hafsah, I once genuinely considered running someone over with my car because their bike swerved ever so slightly in front of me while I was driving. Trust me, you're fine."

She kicked at a cluster of grubby mushrooms with the

toe of her shoe. "I told her she was talentless. That she didn't deserve to be here." A shrug as she buried her chin in her yellow scarf. "I mean, true enough. But I probably didn't need to say it. Story of my life."

I scoffed. "That's tame."

I killed Salem, I almost found myself confessing, but I swallowed the words before they reached my tongue. I had just found someone I felt a connection with. Someone who could be a friend. I didn't want to scare her away so soon.

At that Hafsah snorted. "I'm glad I found you. Utterly hilarious that we're currently studying ethics, isn't it?"

"What made you choose philosophy?"

"I've always had a strong sense of justice. Of right and wrong." She gave me a dark look. "Don't worry, the irony is not lost on me."

I fought the urge to laugh. I knew exactly what she meant; it was why I wanted to be a judge. "Maybe that's *why* we're so angry. We're just furious at all the wrongs in the world."

"Or we're just bitches," Hafsah suggested.

"That too. What do you want to do after uni? Be a philosopher?"

"Yeah, I'm one of those rare freaks who actually wants to be an academic. A really, really eccentric academic, with *Space Invaders* wallpaper all over my office. And none of that hideous *teaching* malarkey. I would like thinking to be my entire job, without the need to converse with other human beings." She grimaced. "I mean, no offense. You seem fine."

I really did laugh, then.

She swallowed, rocking back and forth slightly on the tree stump. "How awful was I? When . . . you know. In the bathroom."

There it was. The steely glint of shame she was trying so hard to bury beneath jokes and bravado.

"Well, at one point you mentioned making a skipping rope out of my intestines. I sort of had to admire Dark Hafsah's creativity."

"Dark Hafsah. Love it. Big fan."

I leaned back against a tree, staring into the branches above. The beeches surrounding the glade were old and huge, taller than the convent, with sprays of curling maroon leaves clinging on for dear life. "This is not especially funny, is it?"

"No," Hafsah admitted. "Who would've thought that violently splitting your soul in two by drinking the blood of your enemies might end badly?"

Despite myself, I chuckled once more, and the impulsive peal of laughter sent waves of pain lancing through my abdomen. I knew I should get my wounds seen to, but I couldn't even begin to explain to a doctor how they came about.

I slid roughly down the tree, its coarse bark rustling against the back of my coat, until my knees were bent and my bum was inches from the damp earth. The burn in my thighs gave me something else to focus on. "So what do we do now?"

"Call an exorcist?"

"Funny."

"I'm not kidding. We are kind of being possessed. By, erm, ourselves."

A red squirrel darted up a nearby tree, paying us no mind. Our problems seemed both enormous and irrelevant in the simple context of the woods.

"Do we even need to do anything?" Hafsah mused. "I mean, don't you kind of *like* how you feel right now? Calm, kind, good? Like, I just want to reach over and hug you. Usually I would be mentally critiquing your every word, as well as every aspect of your physical appearance. So maybe, if we keep on top of it, and we never run out of blood . . . we could just live like this? As genuinely good people? And perform the ritual once a month? I'm already a weirdo, by most standards. What's one more insane habit?"

The thought was so briefly and viscerally appealing that it took my breath away, but at the same time, I knew it was wrong. It was so deeply irresponsible, and potentially dangerous.

The darkness would always come back to us, and what then? What if we messed up our doses? What if we couldn't find any moths one month? What if our blood sources dried up? The risks were too high. I told Hafsah as much.

"Besides," I added, "I feel like . . . there's more to all

of this. That it's linked to the North Tower murders, and to Poppy." I thought of the rubies in Lottie's throat and shuddered.

Hafsah said. "I guess you're right. So you want to find a way to reverse the ritual. You know those pages of the book are missing, right? I already looked."

"Not just those pages," I said grimly. "The whole book is gone. I couldn't find it last time I went searching. You didn't take it, did you?" Hafsah shook her head. "Okay, so we need to find either another copy of the book or the author. The answers have to be somewhere."

Hafsah sighed and nodded. "Where do we start?"

I climbed to my feet, sending the murder of crows resting on a nearby branch flapping up into the canopy. "Fancy taking a road trip?"

CHAPTER 47

The next day we went to Edinburgh by train, since Alice was still too knackered to drive.

As the shuttle bus into town pulled away from Carvell, the familiar lasso sensation in my stomach was so tight I actually vomited into a pick-'n'-mix bag. My vision went black, and I passed out for several seconds, during which time I had incredibly vivid hallucinations about illuminated manuscripts and wooded glades. Screaming started up in the darkest recesses of my mind—a high, female shriek of pain and fear, growing louder and louder the farther from the campus we got.

Finally the invisible tether snapped and I came back to myself, but my heart was pounding fiercely, the creeping tide of a headache lapping at my temples. I guessed this answered the question of whether two rubies had more power than one; I was left shaking and acutely fearful about what would happen if I tried to leave Carvell for good.

Did Sister Maria know we were investigating the Carvell curse? Is that what she wanted from me all along? Is that why she was allowing me to leave campus without choking me to death?

In any case, I'd warned Alice and Hafsah about the effects of the lasso, so they watched the whole thing unfold with an almost comically casual apathy that frightened an old man a few rows behind us.

An hour later, we were on the Royal Mile. Edinburgh was all rain-slicked cobbles and smoking chimneys, wonky stone town houses and faded storefronts painted siren red and forest green and thistle purple.

Torquil's Tomes was a rabbit warren of a bookshop nestled on one of the side streets. It spanned three floors and a low-ceilinged attic, little corners and nooks created by the too-many bookshelves. All the wood in the shop was painted a wine red, and the carpet was a faded brown.

Alice had been there several times since she was a kid, and I practically heard her bones sigh as soon as we walked in. Nostalgia misted her eyes, warming her usually hard facial features into something sweet and childlike. I could've watched her like that for hours. After the pain and fear of the last few days and weeks, she deserved the soft glow of contentment.

While Hafsah and Alice browsed the literary fiction, I

approached the front counter, feeling like a mother on an outing with her sullen teens.

A jolly-faced man with a ginger-and-gray beard and thick-framed glasses beamed at me. He all but glowed with sheer delight that someone had entered his shop.

"Afternoon. I'm the eponymous Torquil. How can I help yous?"

Before I could even respond, Alice chimed in without looking up from the copy of *The God of Small Things* she was flipping through. "Well, she's a jock, so she could do with an explanation as to what a 'book' is."

There was no venom in her words, just a lightheartedness I liked on her. I nodded earnestly. "And it would help if you defined the word 'eponymous' while you're at it."

Alice snorted, and Torquil looked momentarily dumbfounded until he realized we were kidding. "Oh, ha ha, very good."

"She's actually a bigger nerd than me," Alice said, laying down the Arundhati Roy and picking up *The Secret History*. "Seriously. She wears tracksuits completely unironically, and yet she can quote Baudelaire. Like, in French."

I angled my face toward the door so she couldn't see me blush.

Torquil smiled tightly, as though he had no interest in being in the middle of our banter but didn't want to lose customers. "So are yous just looking then, or?"

"Actually, it's a particular author we're looking for," I explained, grateful to be back on track. "T. A. Renner?"

Hafsah was gripping a bestseller table tightly, as though about to faint at any moment. Her Pikachu backpack had sloped off one shoulder, and her eyes were squeezed shut.

Alice nudged her upper arm, whispering, "You okay?"

Hafsah nodded jerkily. "I just get overwhelmed sometimes. I'm gonna wait outside." She stumbled out into the street, fingers clicking at her sides, and Alice looked after her worriedly. It was nice seeing her like this; the kindhearted soul at the core of her finally able to surface. It pained me that it wouldn't last. Not unless we found the book.

Torquil frowned. "Never heard of a T. A. Renner. What sort of thing do they write?"

"Oh, just some super-mainstream stuff about how to split your soul in two using ancient blood rituals." Alice's delivery was flat and deadpan, but it made me laugh.

"Let me just have a look," Torquil said, typing the name into a fat beige computer that moaned in protest. "Renner, Renner . . ." He shook his head. "Nope, nothing."

"Nothing as in, nothing in stock in this shop?" I asked.

"I mean nothing as in I cannae even order it in. The fellae doesn't seem tae exist."

I glanced over at Alice. We exchanged grim looks.

After purchasing a few books to make up for tormenting the poor chap with our terrible in-jokes, we headed out to check that Hafsah was okay.

"Yeah, my senses just get overloaded really easily," she said, fiddling with the straps on her backpack. "New sights, sounds, smells."

"Is that because of the ritual?" I asked.

She laughed. "No. My brain just works differently from most people's. It's like being trapped inside a pinball machine. I'm either autistic or an alien. I go back and forth on which is most likely."

We hiked around the massive Waterstones on Princes Street, several other indie bookshops and even the National Library of Scotland, but nobody had ever heard of T. A. Renner or the peculiar book on soul-splitting rituals. And the more we were told no, the more frustrated I got. Because the more I heard Renner's name, the more and more I was sure that I'd heard or read it somewhere before. I just couldn't for the life of me figure out where, and the internet had been zero help whatsoever.

On the train ride home, we shared some fondant fancies from a little bakery near Waverley Station. Hafsah immediately started playing her Nintendo Switch with a dazed expression on her face, and when Alice called her antisocial, she simply said, "I like *Super Mario* more than I like people."

I nodded. "Fair. I like books more than I like people."

Alice frowned. "What does it even mean, to 'like' something?"

Hafsah and I both glared at her.

She laughed at herself. "Yeah, no, I heard it. Pretentious as hell. My apologies."

While Hafsah played *Super Mario Bros.*, I showed Alice a chapter in *The Devil and the Divine*. It was a pamphlet dated ten years after the one detailing the Loudun exorcisms, printed in seventeenth-century France shortly after the Wars of Religion. This one was an account of the Louviers possessions, and it had bothered me ever since I read it.

"Madeleine Bavent was an orphan born in the early 1600s," I said, scooping chocolate goop out of a cake with my fingernail. "At the age of twelve, she was bound to a linen worker as an apprentice and drugged with *Atropa belladonna*, i.e., deadly nightshade. Did you know, by the way, that *Atropa* means 'unturning one' and *belladonna* means 'beautiful woman' in Italian?"

Alice stared at me, strawberry fondant caked around the corners of her mouth. "You know, sometimes you're so cheerful that I forget you're smart."

"Hey, just because I'm sunshiny as fuck doesn't mean I'm an idiot."

Hafsah sighed, without looking up from *Super Mario*. "Continue, please. So we have Madeleine what's-her-face. She's being drugged. Then what?"

"So, the confessor started having his way with her by the time she was thirteen or fourteen. Then, when she was sixteen, he got her pregnant. Madeleine decided to tell the authorities that she had been abducted and taken to a witches' Sabbat, where she was married to the devil and committed sexual acts with him on the altar."

"Fucking the devil sounds like a classic trauma response to me," Hafsah said, frantically pressing a button on the Switch. Then she added, "My mum's a psychologist. Apparently a lot of kids do this when they've been abused. Make up elaborate stories to cope with what happened to them. And that's what Madeleine was, right? Just an abused kid."

"Pretty much. What then?" Alice asked.

"Madeleine's confession encouraged a lot of other nuns to come forward and say the same thing, so they were exorcised in a public spectacle. Then Madeleine was sentenced to the rest of her life in the church dungeon."

"What?" Alice said, aghast. "But she was the victim!"

"I know."

Hafsah's Switch bleeped as she ran out of lives, and she finally looked up. "And, erm, how is this relevant to our current mindfuckery? I feel like you're saying a lot of things without actually *saying* anything."

"I'm not sure it is relevant," I admitted. My fingers went to the rubies in my throat. "But right now I may or may not be haunted by the ghost of a malevolent nun, so I want to understand what she might have been going through. Anyway, it was at this point that the French authorities decided to catalog the supposed signs of demonic possession. They're included in the pamphlet."

I pointed to the page that troubled me.

To think oneself possessed.

To lead a wicked life.

To live outside the rules
of society.

To be persistently ill,
falling into heavy sleep.

To utter obscenities and blasphemies.

To be troubled with spirits.

To show a frightening and horrible
countenance.

To be tired of living.

To be uncontrollable and violent.

To make sounds and movements like an animal.

To deny knowledge of fits after the paroxysm
has ended.

To show fear of sacred relics and sacraments.

To curse violently at any prayer.

To exhibit acts of lewd exposure or abnormal
strength.

Once Alice had finished reading, she looked up at me with an expression of almost understanding. "So what are you thinking?"

I met her clear blue gaze. "I'm thinking that almost all of these could simply be described as anger."

CHAPTER 48

Alice

By the time we got back from Edinburgh it was nine in the evening, and the sky glittered with white-silver stars. Pulling up the oak-lined drive toward Carvell, tiredness dragged at my eyelids. Was it really only two nights ago that I performed the ritual and gouged vicious cuts into myself? The freshness of the wounds confirmed it, although the sheer length of the days made time feel warped and unreliable.

Saying goodbye to Hafsah outside her dorm in Foxglove Hall was strangely emotional. Despite the horrific circumstances under which we'd come together, something in me glowed at the thought that I might have a friend. A friend who would never judge me for my darkest impulses and urges, because she shared them.

Lottie and I, on the other hand, climbed the two flights

of stairs to our dorm in silence. There was so much hanging between us that idle chitchat seemed absurd. I had no idea how I was supposed to feel in her presence now. Guarded and defensive, knowing that she was likely still investigating me? Grateful and humbled that she had saved me? Embarrassed, or ashamed? Whenever I thought of her hands on my bare stomach, heat spread across my cheeks. And yet despite the circumstances, I'd laughed more today than I had all year.

Either way, there was the clear sense that we were no longer just background characters in each other's lives, passing through the periphery with mutual disdain. Our roots had suddenly and irrevocably knotted together.

As ever, our dorm room was an utter mess. I put my satchel down on one of the few remaining bare patches of carpet and got to work changing my bloody bedsheets. Wordlessly, Lottie helped me stuff pillows into their covers and fluffed them up before laying them on my bed. I struggled to fight the wincing as I worked. The pain in my stomach wasn't fading; if anything it was growing hotter and sharper.

"Let me see," Lottie said sternly.

"I'm fine."

"You're not. Don't be a twat." She put a hand on my shoulder and pushed me down into my desk chair. I whimpered involuntarily on impact, and she softened. "Sorry. I'll be gentle."

The intimacy of lifting the hem of my shirt was as raw

as the wounds beneath. As she started to dab at them with another antibacterial wipe, I sucked the air between my teeth. Her head was so close to mine that I could smell her green apple shampoo.

After examining and dabbing for a few more painful minutes, she pulled away again. The air where she'd been felt instantly cooler. "I'm not sure. They're looking very angry. We should really go to the hospital."

We.

A simple word, but it meant more than I could say.

"I'm not going to the hospital," I said in a low voice. "How would I even explain it? It's fine. Time heals all wounds."

Lottie looked at me like I was a prize idiot. "But not the ones you leave infected."

This chimed with a deeper resonance—something poignant about anger and forgiveness—than she likely intended, but I didn't want to look at the revelation head-on. Not yet, when I already felt so fragile.

I groaned as she cleaned the cuts and applied new bandages, then dropped the hem of my shirt with relief. I shivered at the thought of how the cuts got there in the first place. I had dragged a knife across my own skin, filled with such all-consuming rage that I would destroy anything in my path. Even myself.

Without warning, Lottie unfastened her jeans and dropped them to her ankles, kicking them away and grabbing her pajama shorts off the side of her bunk. I averted my gaze quickly, but not before I caught a glimpse of fuchsia underwear and long, muscular legs. She had a tattoo I'd never seen before: a black Celtic ring wrapping around her upper thigh. I swallowed hard. Being a woman attracted to other women was confusing; a constant game of comparison and lust. You never quite knew whether you were jealous of their body or just jealous of the person who got to touch it.

After I'd changed into my own pajamas in the small bathroom down the hall—I still hadn't plucked up the courage to undress my own curvy, pale body in front of Lottie—I came back to find she was in bed reading a book. The main light had been switched off, and she lay in a pool of golden lamplight that illuminated the frizz of her hair like a halo.

I followed suit and climbed gingerly into my freshly made bed, picking up *The Conscious Mind* to flip through, but my eyes were too heavy and trying to focus made them sting. I closed them instead, hoping for the sweet respite of sleep, but my mind was still racing from the events of the last few days. I tossed and turned, unable to get comfortable.

Noticing my restlessness, Lottie threw the duvet over the edge of her bunk and sat up, shoving her new copy of *Shot in the Heart* down the side of the mattress in a manner I found very disrespectful to literature as a whole.

"Have a drink with me," she said simply.

The freshly ritualized heart in my chest told me I should

oblige, because it would make her happy and I owed her at least that much, but every bone in my body ached at the prospect. I shook my head and rubbed my eyes. "I'm too tired. Sorry. I'm not trying to be a dick for once. It's just . . . I can't stand the Refectory. All the noise and the sweat and . . . it's just not me. I'm sorry."

"Who said anything about the Refectory?" She hopped lightly off her bunk and crossed to the window, which she grabbed by the bottom of the frame and hauled all the way to the top. As she stretched up on her tiptoes, a strip of toned stomach appeared over the crinkled band of her plaid pajama shorts. She was always too warm. "Let's drink here."

The ledge jutting out of the stone wall was wide and deep and smattered with yellow-green moss. Lottie perched herself bare-legged on the lip of it, then reached back into the room to grab the bottle of wine off her desk. She took a deep, thirsty swig and gestured for me to join her.

Stiffly clambering out, I tried not to look down. We were only on the second floor, but I was deathly afraid of heights. She handed me the bottle, and I shook my head automatically. "I don't drink white."

She shrugged. "I don't drink red. And last I checked, you were all out."

I took a reluctant sip, the mouth of the bottle wet from Lottie's lips, and begrudgingly admitted that it tasted pretty good. Lighter and drier than my beloved merlot; fresher, somehow. Citrusy sharp.

Despite the cold night air, I sighed into the gentle burn down my gullet, then handed the bottle back to her. The uncertainty between us was still there, a rocky terrain of fundamental mistrust, but I found myself wanting to chart a path across it.

Lottie spoke first, quietly and clearly into the night. "Why did you do it?"

"The ritual?"

"Yeah. Was it because of what happened with Harris?"

Despite the warning siren in my gut—she was investigating me, tricking me somehow, and I shouldn't trust her—I answered before I could stop myself. I felt like I owed her an explanation, after everything she'd done for me.

"Partly. I just . . . I've always had this *anger*. This violent streak that scares the hell out of me." For all the awful, painful flaws in the ritual, I was grateful to be sitting up here without the lingering fear that I would shove Lottie off the ledge in a sudden seething fit. "I'm so angry. I always have been. And I don't know why."

"It's not your fault," Lottie said, neither softly nor comfortingly, just matter-of-factly. She took a deep sip from the bottle, the smell of the wine apple crisp on her breath.

I shook my head. "But in the movies, the murderous psychopaths always have some kind of tragic backstory, an abusive childhood, an unresolved trauma . . . *something* that made them this way. Yet apart from the fact that my mum is ill, I don't have any of that. My life has been good.

So I think I'm just evil. Or broken. Or both. I was just born angry."

Mosquitoes fuzzed around us and I knew we must be being bitten alive, but in the golden backlight of the room they looked almost beautiful. Pops of laughter echoed from a dorm party below. An owl hooted somewhere in the obsidian sky.

Lottie looked up with a kind of misty reverence at the North Tower looming above us. "Alice, we all have the violent streak. We all get angry. It's like Raskolnikov argues in *Crime and Punishment*: extraordinary men like Napoleon are allowed to act on it, simply by virtue of being extraordinary. They wage wars and build empires and are celebrated for it. But what about the rest of us? Especially women? Where does *our* anger go?"

I stared at her. "You feel it too? The existential anger?"

"Why do you think I thwack hockey balls around a field all day? It's a release. And it makes me feel powerful, if only fleetingly."

I ruminated on this for a few moments. "You think that's what this is about? Wanting power?"

"Everyone wants power, in some form. You want to be a judge, right?"

The statement snagged on my suspicion. I couldn't remember ever telling her that. Had she built some kind of case file on me?

"Yeah," I said carefully.

"What is that aspiration about if not power?"

I mulled this over. "But the violence . . . it doesn't feel like I want power for power's sake. It's feral. It's *physical*."

"Well, when was the last time you felt physically powerless?"

Staring out into the night, I remembered the moment viscerally. It coiled around in my gut like an adder through wild grass. I swallowed hard.

"With my ex-boyfriend, Chris. I . . . I cheated on him. Emotionally, at least. I was in love with my best friend, Noémie." Her name still tasted ripe and heavy in my mouth. "He went through my phone and found texts between us. We crossed the line, and I knew that. I tried to apologize, to say I was sorry, but when I went to kiss him, he shoved me away so hard I fell and hit my face on the coffee table."

Lottie looked up at me. "Is that where you got your scar?"

I nodded, feeling my cheeks pinken. She'd looked at my mouth long enough to notice the scar. "So I got up, blood everywhere, and I tried to lash out at him. I lunged with my full weight, went to smack him right in the face, and he just grabbed my wrists and held me back as though I was nothing."

Lottie took this in for a while, turning the new knowledge over in her mind. "Do you think that's why you punched Harris when he grabbed you by the wrist?"

"Maybe. Or maybe I really am a supervillain."

She laughed in a kind of half snort. "Would we say 'super'? I feel like you're not doing a very good job."

"Fuck you," I chuckled, not meaning it in the slightest.

There were a few moments of silence between us as we drank, and I realized that this was my first true experience of peace since I'd arrived at Carvell. And it wasn't just because of the ritual. It was because of Lottie, and how I felt when I was around her. It was her innate sunshine, the warmth and glow of it spreading to me. I liked who I was when I was around her. And for someone who'd never liked who they were—not really, beneath all the pretension and snobbery—this was significant.

For the briefest of seconds, some part of my subconscious told me to lean my head against her shoulder.

But the moment was shattered with an almighty feline screech.

Before I could even process what was happening, claws dug into my shoulder, a feral hiss in my ear.

"What the fuck!" yelled Lottie, dropping the wine bottle to the ground below with a smash.

I turned to face the cat, only to be met with a fiery red glow in its demonic eyes.

Salem.

CHAPTER 49

Just as Salem was about to lunge for Alice's ashen face, I grabbed the cat by her hips and flung her down to the ground, right where the wine bottle had shattered moments before. She landed sure-footedly on the broken glass, then glared back up at us with a look of pure hatred in her scarlet eyes.

The hiss that came out of her was straight from the mouth of hell.

Then, with a final flick of her long black tail, she disappeared around a corner.

"Are you okay?" I asked Alice, who was staring after Salem as though she'd seen a ghost. One shoulder of her black silk top was torn, and smears of poppy-red blood surrounded the puncture wound.

"I don't understand," she whispered slowly.

"Cats are weird," I said. "They see threats where

humans don't. They dislike people for no reason. Don't take it personally."

"No, Lottie," she murmured, shaking her head. "I *really* don't understand." She turned to face me, her eyes wide with something awful and terror-shaped. "I killed Salem last week."

I stared at her. "You're confused. Why would you have . . . ? No."

Her voice trembled as she said, "It was before I asked for your blood. Before I did the ritual again. I . . . The violent impulses, they were an onslaught. I found myself alone in the chapel one night, and Salem was there, and I don't know what happened, I really don't, but the next thing I knew I was snapping her neck with my bare hands." She swallowed hard, gingerly lifting a hand to her scratched shoulder. "I took her to the woods and left her at the foot of a tree so that whoever found her would think she'd fallen badly."

I frowned. If this was true, it was awful, but how could it be true? Salem had just attacked Alice moments ago. She was very much alive, if not particularly well. "Alice, are you . . . are you sure that really happened?" I bit my lip. "Maybe the ritual withdrawals made you hallucinate?"

Alice turned and stared out into the middle distance, looking troubled. As though she had no idea what was real and what was not.

Over the next few weeks, we made no further progress tracking down Renner, and each day flipped by with a sense of looming dread over the next transformation. I was finding it harder and harder to focus on the things I was supposed to be here to do. Studying Chaucer and hitting hockey balls into a goal seemed utterly arbitrary in the context of Poppy's death and Alice's predicament.

We didn't talk about Salem again, and I got the sense that it was because there was no unterrifying answer. Either Alice really had killed the cat, only for Salem to come back to life, or she'd imagined the whole thing, and Salem's vicious attempted assault was entirely unrelated. Neither option was great, and so I tried not to dwell on them either.

When my essay on *The Strange Case of Dr. Jekyll and Mr. Hyde* came back with a high first and complimentary feedback from Professor Sanderson, I scanned through what I'd written and found a disturbing parallel to what was going on at Carvell. The plot was almost exactly what Alice and Hafsah were going through: a soul carved down into the middle into good and evil, both sides constantly warring for command of the physical vessel.

See me after next class! Sanderson had scrawled in the margins, next to a row of extravagant ticks in green Biro. For some reason, the thought of being alone with him sent invisible ants scurrying up my arms. His intensity, his jarring rhythms, his cultish grin. He was a brilliant lecturer, but a chilling presence.

And yet, he knew a lot about Sister Maria. Maybe if I

could get him alone, I could uncover some clues as to why she had dug her roots into me in the first place.

We'd just wrapped up a harrowing session on *The Castle of Otranto* and I lingered by his desk, waiting for him to say goodbye to the other students. Today he was wearing a moss-green button-down rolled up to the elbows, and for the first time I noticed a tattoo snaking around his inner forearm, though I couldn't quite make out what it was. The sharply studded leather cuffs remained on his wrists, as though threatening anyone who might try to shake his hand.

"Ms. Fitzwilliam," he said once we were alone, his voice feathery soft. "I was so impressed with your essay. Please, sit."

He gestured not to one of the classroom chairs but to his own, a burgundy leather wingback with clattering gold wheels and time-cracked arms. The idea of sitting in it while he remained standing made me uneasy, like it was too intimate an act, so I leaned back on a small, rickety school desk instead.

"You wanted to see me?" I asked, mouth dry as dead autumn leaves.

"I did, I did," he said, staring intently at the blank blackboard. He rolled a piece of chalk between his thumb and forefinger. "I think you show a lot of promise."

"Thank you."

"Your personal tutor is Professor Chiang, correct?"

I frowned carefully; I'd never told him that. "Yeah."

He laid down the chalk and rubbed his hands together. The residual white dust erupted in gentle puffs, disturbing the sleepy drift of sun-dappled dust motes. "How would you feel about entering under my mentorship instead? I think you have a knack for the gothic."

You have no idea, I scoffed internally.

"I'm . . . I'm not sure," I replied, not wanting to hurt his feelings. "I'm enjoying the unit, but I don't think I want to study gothic horror long term. Like for my dissertation."

Sanderson raised his eyebrows as though he didn't quite believe me, like he could tell I was lying. It made me bristle. "I see. And what *do* you want to write your thesis on?"

"Golden age crime fiction. Or maybe even earlier, like Arthur Conan Doyle. He literally hated Sherlock with every fiber of his being. He's hilarious."

He shook his head with a dismissive smirk, then crossed the room to one of his amber-suspended insects. He held it up to the light, illuminating a milky exoskeleton. "Woefully unoriginal, quite frankly. But to each their own. I simply think it a waste." He put the unusual arthropod back down, then turned to me. "Tell me, do you have any grand writing ambitions of your own?"

Irritated at his condescension, I snipped, "Maybe."

"Then you would do well to study the golden thread—if you have any hope of weaving one of your own, that is." A soft, knowing smile, a silky gaze, like a spider weaving a web. "You're a talented girl, Charlotte. Don't fritter it away on the same lazily trodden path as everyone else." He took a slight step forward and leaned intently on the back of a chair. "Your mind is more pliable, more open than most. Let me take it to the next level."

For a shameless split second, I felt myself being carried away on the tide of flattery, the idea that I might be exceptional as heady and intoxicating as incense.

But I knew what he was doing. I knew that the unease creeping up and down my limbs like black rot was trying to protect me.

"I actually was interested in what you had to say about Sister Maria," I said, pushing through the discomfort. "Do you have any theories as to how she died?"

Sanderson gave me a victorious look, as though he'd known exactly what I was about to ask. "Theories? Many. Answers? None."

"What are your theories?"

A slithery expression. "Enter into my mentorship and perhaps I'll tell you."

I fixed a neutral expression on my face. "I'll think about it." I turned to leave, then hesitated and turned back. He was studying me as though I was a museum exhibit. "One more question. Do you believe in demonic possession?"

He gave a sharp bark of laughter, gesturing to the arcane paraphernalia scattered around his classroom. "What do you think?"

I chewed the inside of my cheek. "And what do you think makes people particularly susceptible to it? As victims, I mean."

His eyes locked onto mine. "I believe I already told you the answer to that."

It took me a beat to figure out what he meant.

Your mind is more pliable, more open than most.

I'd been a willing vessel from the start. I'd literally thought, *What if it was my imagination that could open this long-sealed door? And if that key let the terror walk right into my own life, so be it.*

Hell, I'd practically invited Sister Maria to a tea party.

As I left Sanderson's too-warm classroom, the sickly feeling of mold and decay still clung to me, and I didn't think it had anything to do with the long-dead nun. Sanderson was more unsettling than I could've ever imagined, and not because of the sheep skulls and Baphomet figurines. It was in his lecherous gaze, the cloying way he spoke to me.

Had I been a fool to dismiss Peter Frame's theory about a professor grooming students? Sanderson had taught both Dawn Middlemiss and Fiona Taylor before their deaths. Perhaps he had ensnared them too with satin-soft flattery, like a silkworm. But what about Sam Bowey and Janie Kirsopp? Or was this just an almighty leap?

Walking down the grand hallway in the convent, something came back to me—something so obvious and so significant that I kicked myself for not remembering earlier.

I'd seen Sanderson in the Grandstand on the night of Poppy's death.

Within *minutes* of Poppy's death.

It was four in the morning, and he was staring into the dying fire with something amber in a crystal tumbler.

Why was he awake then? Why had he looked so macabre?

I waited for a hot pulse in the ruby, a writhing of the roots, *something* to show me I was on the right lines, but nothing came. Sister Maria had many opinions, but on the subject of Professor Sanderson, she was silent.

One afternoon in late November, the sun hung low and languid in the sky, burnishing the deciduous woods a dying bronze—the last gasp of autumn before the choke of winter took hold. I was in a Critical Practice seminar thinking of Janie Kirsopp when I suddenly remembered where I'd seen T. A. Renner's name before.

I couldn't say for certain why the lightning bolt struck then. Nothing Professor Mellor was saying related to the author or the ritual in any way. It was more like my brain had been rifling through my memory in the background, searching through the dusty boxes in the archives of my mind to find the source. It was in one of those dusty file boxes that I knew I'd seen the name Renner.

The newspaper archives.

I didn't know in what context, but I could picture his

name in that very specific serif font beloved by local newspapers the world over.

As soon as the seminar was over, I caught the next shuttle bus into town—grimacing through the tightening lasso and the starry vision—and faced off against the disgruntled gentleman at the archive's front desk once again.

It took around an hour to find the piece containing Renner's name. At first I scanned all the coverage of the murders, assuming that's where I'd seen it, but it was actually in a very small column near the back of the paper that I'd barely registered at the time: *Local historian reviews the latest books about nineteenth-century Northumberland.*

Renner's bio at the end of each column read:

> *T. A. Renner has an MRes in 19th-century literature, and self-published his own work of nonfiction, Soul-Purification Rituals in 19th-Century Convents. Fantasy Prints on West Street printed the work, and copies are available to purchase from the author directly. Please write to: T. A. Renner, Kittiwake Keep, Little Marmouth, Northumberland, and enclose a check for two pounds plus postage.*

My heart raced. Not only did I have an identity for our mystery writer, I had an address.

And it was only one mile from Carvell.

CHAPTER 50

Alice

After the night Salem attacked me on our window ledge, my sense of reality swirled and eddied.

Had I really killed her, only for her to come back to life?

Or was the whole thing a pain-addled hallucination?

And which would be worse?

Despite the concern for my sanity, things between Lottie and me finally felt on a semi-even keel. There was still wariness between us—a shared understanding that we could hurt each other horribly if we chose to. She could keep investigating me until I slipped up badly enough for her to go to the police, while I could quite literally murder her in a red-eyed rage. Regardless, we sank into a pleasant almost-friendship, asking about each other's day and, a couple of nights a week, reading in our separate beds in the golden lamplight. The intimacy was a salve to the worry over the ritual, but in my darkest moments, I found myself thinking I didn't *deserve* the salve. Not after everything I'd done—or *hadn't* done.

Twice Lottie asked for a lift to the nearest post office—once to drop something off, and once to pick something up—but was vague about why she had to go in the first place. A glimpse at the manila envelope clutched in her hands yielded only a stamped return address: The National Archives, Richmond. I assumed it must've been something to do with an assignment.

One of the most troubling things about this period was how much I began to enjoy her company. We had another night of drinking wine on the window ledge—my merlot, this time—when her field hockey team suffered a spectacular defeat in a derby match. She was a soft, easy presence; a sunny glade to my darkened forest. Eventually I started to enjoy being around her more than I enjoyed being alone—something I hadn't experienced since Noémie left for Toronto.

Speaking of Noémie, the unexpectedly prescient wisdom from Lottie turned over and over in my mind: *Time heals all wounds, but not the ones you leave infected.*

Over the ensuing days, I realized that's what I'd been doing with Noémie: hoping the simple passage of time would stitch together the flesh I'd left exposed. But in truth, I'd left the wound infected with my lack of apology, my lack of acknowledgment of what I'd done to her. If I truly wanted the wound to heal, I had to endure the sting of cleaning it. Which first meant admitting to myself what I had done.

In truth, I had needled away at her for so long that, in the end, she turned down her place at Carvell. Her first-choice university, the place she'd always dreamed of attending. She gave that up because she couldn't bear to be around me anymore. My barbed comments and impatient snapping, my long stretches of stubborn silence.

It only got worse after my confrontation with Chris. We broke up, and I was free to be with Noémie if I wanted to, and yet something innocent inside me had been shattered. A person who claimed to love me had hurt me, physically and viscerally. He had thrown me to the ground like I was nothing, and I had been powerless to fight back. How could I trust her not to do the same?

And so I pushed and pushed and pushed, determined to find the outer limits of her love, the point at which she too would lash out, the desperate need to draw a boundary for myself, an area in which I knew I was safe.

She left before I ever found it.

It was only now, months later, that I could bring myself to apologize.

> I'm sorry, Noémie. I'm sorry for everything. X

She didn't reply, and maybe she never would. Maybe a simple sorry would never be enough. But at least now my own wound could start to heal.

I also spent more time with Hafsah, hunched over the antique writing desks in the library as we scribbled our assignments side by side, chatting about the reading list as we ate lunch in the cafeteria.

"So I think I've come up with an original theory," Hafsah said, clicking her fingers rapid-fire. "About the relationship between modern philosophy and the rise of insane asylums, and how they coexisted and contradicted each other before the Madhouses Act of 1774. The link between autonomy and identity. 'I think therefore I am,' sure, but what if a person is considered unable to think adequately? Do they thus not exist?" Her lips quirked. "Very mainstream stuff, I know. Can you think of any journals I might submit the paper to?"

"I don't like not being the smartest person in the room," I grumbled, but I pulled out my laptop and started researching places for her to send her irritatingly great theory.

"Many apologies," Hafsah said, deadpan. "I know how foundational it is to you as a person that you're better than everyone."

I pressed my lips together. "Do we think we know each other well enough to take the piss quite so savagely?"

"It's sort of my default setting," Hafsah admitted. "Even post-ritual. A love language, if you will."

We luxuriated in the thought of a full month of kindness and ease before we had to go through the transformation again, but in the back of my mind a dark spot loomed on the horizon.

Hafsah had managed to find two blood sugar monitoring kits that came with pinprick needles to draw small amounts of blood from a fingertip—a relatively painless way to secure the final ingredient. But there were other logistics to consider, and not all of them had such a simple solution.

Where could we go to perform the ritual so that we couldn't hurt each other—or ourselves? The wounds in my stomach became less sore as the days wore on, but the purpling scars were a stark reminder of what I'd done to myself the last time. Yet the campus was not a psychiatric facility. There was nowhere we could be locked in padded rooms until Dark Alice and Dark Hafsah handed the reins back.

With two weeks to go until the ritual had to be performed again, I started to feel Dark Alice creeping back in.

Only this time, it happened much more swiftly and severely than before.

It started out tamely enough. I snapped at Hafsah over the slightest misunderstanding. I blared my car horn over the most minor traffic infraction. I rolled my eyes when Lottie talked endlessly about field hockey as though the team's wins and losses were in any way important to the world.

Then, too soon, the violent impulses once again became an onslaught, the desire to hurt a constant in my head and my bones. The ability to study, to communicate, to think of anything but bloodlust vanished.

It was happening too fast. I should've had more time.

By day nineteen, I was pacing the carpet between our

two bunks, willing Lottie to come home soon. I needed her blood far quicker than I'd thought I would. I wasn't prepared.

I crossed to the window, heaving it open and gulping down the frigid air. The sky outside was charcoal gray with storm clouds. A crow sat on an open arch in the North Tower, looking down at me. Its eyes were hard, cold beads, unblinking, unyielding.

I tore my gaze away, and that's when I noticed the manila envelope peeking out from under a weighty textbook on the Romantics. Unable to fight back the devious urge, I pulled the envelope out—and recognized the stamped return address instantly.

The National Archives.

This is what Lottie had retrieved from the post office that day. My fingers slid out the stapled sheets of paper, and I frowned.

Blueprints. What looked like architectural drawings of Carvell from when it was a working convent. Neat pencil lines and pristine printed room labels, with black smudges and blemishes from where the originals had been photocopied.

There was one sheet of paper for each floor. On the third page, which outlined the second floor, Lottie had circled a room and written *What is this??* in chicken-scratch pencil.

The room was sandwiched between the North Tower and the library, right by the philosophy section. The blueprint clearly showed there was a relatively large room with doors opening onto the first floor of the library and into the tower itself. There was also a door leading to the corridor in the main building, but when I tried to picture the spot where it should be—adjacent to Le Conte's classroom—all I could see in my mind's eye was a stone wall.

Had the door been bricked over? If so, why?

And what *was* that room between the library and the North Tower?

I thought of whom I might ask for the answer, and vague pieces of a shadowy puzzle rearranged themselves into the silhouette of Feathering.

She was always there, always in the library—somehow.

She knew who I was when I went to seek out my alibi. And she knew who T. A. Renner was, and she lied to me about it.

Why, why, why?

But I barely had time to process these revelations and what they might mean.

The feral thing inside me finally awoke with an ominous yawn, a black dread unrolling in my gut, spilling into my organs like shadows. Tendrils of anger climbed up my throat, jagged claws dug into my lungs, my whole chest convulsing in pain.

No no no no please no I can't do this please no—

The opening of a door, in another world. Lottie's ragged shriek. "Alice? *Alice!*"

Fuck her fuck her she doesn't care about you, you

should just kill her to get it over with, everyone you love leaves you anyway, slit her throat and drink it all—

I fell to the floor with an animalistic groan, clawing my fingernails into the emerald-green carpet.

"Is it happening already?" Lottie asked urgently, from the other end of a long, dark tunnel.

Throw her out the window, we're not high enough to die but high enough to hurt, and don't you want that, don't you want to see her hurt, how good would it feel to see her—

My duality waged war in my heart, and only one side was ever going to win.

"Alice, stay with me, okay?" Lottie said, dropping to her knees and opening my satchel to find a vial.

"It's too soon," I heard myself whimper from very far away. "I should have had more time. It's not even been three weeks, I—"

Hurt her hurt her hurt her before she can hurt you—

I thrust the thoughts back with all my internal might.

Fear slalomed through me.

What if the transformations kept getting closer and closer together?

What if the darkness eventually consumed me entirely?

I watched in acute horror as Lottie used the blood sugar kit to take her own blood and add it to the vial.

There were just moments left before Dark Alice wrested control of my body. Every inch of me hurt, and I cried out.

As my vision began to turn black, I murmured, "Lottie, you have to run. Lock me in. So I can't . . ."

"I'm not leaving you," she said fiercely, gripping my shirt collar where it gathered at the nape of my neck, blazing blue eyes just inches from mine. "I told you, you don't have to suffer this alone."

A long, low groan leaked out of me, along with the last wisps of my consciousness. In the final moment before the darkness took over, I tried to move my mouth to beg. Beg her to go, before I hurt her, or worse. But I bit down on my tongue, and the world disappeared.

CHAPTER 51

Alice

After my transformation ended, we found Hafsah just in time.

Mercifully, she didn't have a roommate. Her parents were both doctors and so could afford the almost double-rent premium on the Foxglove single dorms with en suite bathrooms.

I could barely walk from the residual aches and pains caused by the transformation. My wrists were red raw from yanking fiercely at the handcuffs Lottie had used to restrain me, and my throat was like sandpaper from Dark Alice's hostile takeover.

Pure adrenaline propelled me down the corridor to dorm 3-14, the vial filled with tincture clutched in my palm so tightly that the glass was warmed through. I'd already pricked myself with the blood sugar needle and added the metallic crimson to the elderflower so that it was ready to administer the second we got to Hafsah. It was the last vial; we'd need to make more.

Sure enough, her groans seeped through the old wooden door.

"Hafsah?" I said in a low voice, mouth inches from the keyhole. "Hafsah, it's me and Lottie. We have the tincture. Open up?"

No response, just the sound of a weary body dragging itself along the carpet toward the door.

"Stand back," I whispered to Lottie. "You've already done enough. I'm not letting you put yourself in any more danger."

"Whatever, I can take her," Lottie said measuredly. "Neither of you work out." She flexed her biceps, which popped up beneath her pink Ellesse sweater. I couldn't hold back the smile, despite the situation. She was *such* a jock.

Hafsah's expression when she opened the door would haunt me for the rest of my life.

Fear and hatred waged a violent war behind her dark-brown eyes. Her face was slick with rivulets of mascara, and her chest heaved with pain and desperation. She was on her hands and knees on the emerald-green carpet, limbs trembling and convulsing. Her room was filled with childhood paraphernalia: *Avatar: The Last Airbender* posters and Marvel Funko Pops, stacks of manga and Studio Ghibli figurines, kawaii plush animals and an art print of Goku from *Dragon Ball Z*.

"Hey, it's okay," Lottie said, voice gentle and calm. "We're here. Can we come in?"

The question was rhetorical. Lottie pushed the door open farther and offered Hafsah a hand, but when it became clear Hafsah didn't have the strength to take it, Lottie hauled her to her feet, tossed her over her shoulder as though she were a sack of potatoes and carried her to the cabin bunk in a fireman's lift. Hafsah watched in vague terror as Lottie cuffed both of her hands to the sides of the bed.

Slipping the tincture down Hafsah's throat was easier than it had been in the bathroom last time—we'd arrived before she was entirely consumed by the darkness. No sooner had it hit her stomach than the shaking stopped abruptly. A black veil went down behind her eyes, and Dark Hafsah emerged. She turned her head to stare at us, and the coldness of her glare bore right into my soul.

"I'm going to kill you fucking *bitches*," the voice uttered, a grinding of metal and a crunching of bones.

"Cool," Lottie said nonchalantly, settling herself cross-legged on the floor. "Let me know when you're done?"

"Where did you get the cuffs, by the way?" I whispered to her. "Youngman's Hardware?"

She looked at me with a mischievous twinkle in her eye. "Who says I didn't already have them?"

Feeling my cheeks pinken, I had to forcibly banish the thought of her in her fuchsia underwear from my mind.

Seeing that I looked flustered, she laughed and said, "I'm kidding. I got them at Youngman's last time I was in town." An odd little smile. "I've never even kissed another person before."

This caught me off guard. "Really? Surely you could've had your pick of anyone you wanted." I gestured to her face and general physique.

She bit her lip. "Did you just compliment me?"

"Absolutely not," I rebutted, my cheeks growing even hotter.

She shrugged and picked at a thread in her ripped jeans. "I just never felt any desire to kiss anyone. At least not until . . ."

When she didn't finish, I quirked an eyebrow. "Until what?" I racked my brain, trying to remember whether I'd seen her go out on any dates.

"Never mind," she said, just as Hafsah muttered something about using tendons as toothpicks.

"Why did we have less time?" Hafsah asked a few hours later, watching as Lottie uncuffed her from the bunk. The mascara had dried down her cheeks like crude black veins. "It was supposed to be a month. Why wasn't it a month?" She rubbed at her wrists, her red welts matching my own.

"I don't know," I admitted. I sat in her desk chair, elbows resting on the desk and my forehead slumped into the heels of my hands. Pain and exhaustion and a deep pit of hunger had rendered me weak.

Hafsah climbed unsteadily down the stairs of her cabin bunk and crossed into the en suite bathroom, where she plucked a baby wipe from a freshly opened packet and rubbed the mascara from her cheeks. "Thank you," she said quietly. "You've saved me twice now."

I shook my head. "It was all Lottie."

Lottie literally puffed her chest. I would have laughed or made a sarcastic comment, but I didn't have the energy. The helplessness of the situation weighed heavily on my lungs.

How were we ever going to escape this cycle?

How could I become an esteemed judge if I spent half of my life trying to fight back my own murderous impulses?

How could I find love—and keep it?

My soul had been carved in two, and my whole life had been torn out from under me.

"Hafsah," I moaned, tears sliding down my cheeks. It felt alien and vulnerable to cry freely in front of other people, but exhaustion had made the tears impossible to suppress. "What have we done?"

"That paper idea I had, about the madhouses and modern philosophy . . ." Hafsah scrubbed at her eyes with the wipe long after the mascara had gone. "An editor reached out about my pitch, literally within a day of emailing. And they were seriously interested, and they wanted a draft, but now . . . how am I supposed to deliver it? I can't concentrate on anything but the ritual." She dropped the wipe on the floor and gripped the edge of the sink with clawed hands. "I wanted to make a career out of my brain, and now I've set fire to it instead. What have we fucking *done*, indeed."

Lottie tucked the handcuffs into her scruffy purple backpack and zipped it shut. "Do you guys want to mope around for a bit, or shall we skip straight to the part where I save the day with my unparalleled genius and resourcefulness?"

I lifted my head from the palms of my hands. "What?"

She lifted her chin and met my gaze, eyes twinkling with that trademark blend of mischief and triumph.

"I found T. A. Renner."

CHAPTER 52

Lottie

Kittiwake Keep was a decommissioned lighthouse at the end of a sweeping redbrick promenade. Along the seafront were clinking amusement arcades, candy-striped ice cream kiosks, pastel-colored beach huts and a bustling fish-and-chip shop that smelled of salt, vinegar and joy. The air had been bitten by a winter crispness that felt delicious in the lungs.

After parking Alice's car nearby, Alice, Hafsah and I approached the lighthouse with trepidation. The white and red paint was flaking away, and rust crept up from the bottom of the structure. The whole place had a general air of neglect I found desperately sad.

Suddenly it seemed incredibly naive of me to assume that Renner would still be living in the same place he had over ten years ago. And yet people who lived in lighthouses didn't seem the type to hop from one home to the next, so I had to hope we were in luck. It was beginning to look like Alice's last chance, and I was willing to do anything to never have to watch her in that kind of hell again.

"I assume you'll be doing the talking," Alice said in a low voice, as though reading my mind. She wore a calf-length houndstooth coat and burgundy-and-gold-framed sunglasses that made her hair look even wilder. "On account of being sunshiny as fuck."

I snorted. "Yeah. I don't think threatening to stab him is the way to go."

"Coward," muttered Hafsah sardonically, still rubbing her wrists. She'd covered the welts with a stack of colorful beaded bracelets—chunky purple stars and poppy-red cubes—from Claire's. Somehow, she was kind of rocking it.

I knocked on the door, politely at first, then when there was no response, I rapped more insistently. After we'd waited a minute or two, Alice's shoulders visibly sank.

"Let's just go," she muttered, pushing her sunglasses farther up on her nose as if trying to better mask her disappointment.

But then there was the faint shuffle of footsteps, and a grumble as a key turned in the lock.

T. A. Renner was both exactly as I expected and not at all as I expected. He wore a long velvet night-robe with a fur-trimmed collar and suede slippers with sheepskin lining, and there was an unlit tobacco pipe in his mouth. So far, so eccentric.

But his manner was far more jovial than I'd imagined. He had two perfectly round spots of red flush on his cheeks, as though he'd been drinking a lot of wine, and an utterly euphoric expression, eyes wide and glistening.

"Frances! How utterly incandescent you look!" He shoved straight past me and kissed Alice twice on each cheek. "Do come in, do come in! I'll have Crispin rustle up some tea. Crispin!" He picked up a little silver bell from a sideboard in the hallway, tinkled it insistently, and then shuffled through the house in his slippers, gesturing for us to follow.

Alice lowered her sunglasses and peered over the top of them, utterly aghast. I quickly raised my phone and took a picture of her astonishment. It was simply too perfect not to capture. With the clear cerulean sky behind her and the edge of the rusting lighthouse to the side, it looked like a *Vogue* editorial.

She was so beautiful it was a little painful to look at her. Just like I'd almost explained in Hafsah's dorm, I'd never experienced real attraction before. Asexuality had been a coat that fit perfectly until I met Alice. Now I wasn't entirely sure what I was—or whether a label mattered at all. All I knew was that the last thing I thought about before I fell asleep every night was the way her silk pajamas clung to her curves.

"Come on, Frances," I said with a small smile, trying to tamp down the unwelcome embers. Alice was still violent, after all. She may or may not have murdered a cat who may or may not be immortal—and she may or may not have been losing her mind. Thoughts about running a finger down her tilted pixie jaw were not particularly useful at the moment.

Renner led the three of us through to the kitchen: a semicircular hodgepodge of tables, chairs and sideboards. Mugs and saucers covered every available surface, and there was an aubergine-colored stove in the center of the room that was smoking lightly. Renner did not appear at all concerned by this.

No butler by the name of Crispin had appeared.

"Now, Vanessa, how can I be of service?" he said to me, rustling in a cupboard for some tea bags. "I trust you're here to execute the estate." He plopped a tea bag into each mug and filled them with cold water straight from the tap.

We all took a seat at the rickety kitchen table as the cups of non-tea were handed to us. "Actually, my name is Lottie," I said. "Lottie Fitzwilliam. We haven't met before. I just wanted to ask you a few questions about the book you wrote, if that's all right?"

"I wrote a book?" he asked, eyes widening with awe. "How marvelous. Did anyone read it?"

I'd envisaged this conversation playing out in many different ways, but this was not one of them. "Well, yes. We did. That's why we're here."

"Wonderful." He beamed broadly. "Now, here's a good one. What did the cuckoo say to the ox?"

"I don't know," I said politely.

"You're running late!" he cried, before utterly exploding into laughter. Great gulping roars echoed around the curved walls, and fat tears rolled down his cheeks. He slapped his thighs with so much vigor that I was vaguely worried he might shatter a femur.

I offered a courteous smile, and once he'd finally calmed down, I gently nudged, "Would you mind talking to us about your book, Mr. Renner?"

"Gosh, it's funny, isn't it?" He got to his slippered feet, sloshing cold tea water over the stained wooden table, and crossed to the sink where he began some miscellaneous clattering. "That all books are just different combinations of the same twenty-six letters, and the hallucinations in your brain vary wildly depending on what those combinations are."

"That's true," I conceded. "We would love to know more about the combination you used in your book, specifically."

At this Renner gasped and clapped one hand to his mouth, staring out to sea from the kitchen window.

"Is everything all right, Mr. Renner?"

"Could you even imagine what it would be like if a dolphin could ride a bicycle?"

I stared at Alice and Hafsah helplessly. Neither looked like they could bear to converse with Renner, which made sense on account of their not possessing a single shred of patience between them. Then again, they did have a lot at stake here, and a mad hatter of an author spewing bilge and nonsense was probably not what they'd been hoping for.

"Do you mind if I have a look at your bookcases?" I asked, desperate to gain some control of the situation. I'd spotted two cluttered units in the adjacent living room when we came in. Surely there was a copy of his own book there somewhere—a copy that still contained the reversal or cure.

He shrugged as he turned back to us. "Certainly, but I'm not sure you'll find any sausages. Bacon, perhaps. Oh, why don't you crack some eggs, there's a chap! But can you make sausages without breaking any—no, no I suppose not."

As I left the room, I could see Alice trying very hard not to put her whole fist in her mouth. Perhaps the ritual had its limits.

Wishing I was a fly on the wall for the conversation she and Hafsah would be forced to have with Renner, I got to work searching the bookcases. The purple cover Alice had described should've stood out, but the shelves were triple stacked, books on bird-watching and marine conservation shoved haphazardly into spots alongside *Moby-Dick* and *Ulysses* and *The Grapes of Wrath*. I couldn't imagine the man I'd just met reading any of these, but maybe he was more lucid when it was just him and the page. Or maybe the madness was a recent affliction.

His delusions unsettled me. It didn't seem like a simple case of dementia, which my grandfather had suffered from.

He wasn't just forgetful—he was stark raving bonkers. And his bizarre statements weren't incoherent clumps of random words. They followed proper sentence structure, for the most part. In short, it wasn't a type of madness I'd ever encountered before.

Had it been the result of a ritual gone wrong?

After trawling every inch of the bookshelves, as well as every side table, drawer and other cranny in the ramshackle living room, I admitted defeat.

I traipsed back to the kitchen, where Renner was enthusiastically performing the "Y.M.C.A." dance for an extremely discerning audience.

"Mr. Renner? Does the lighthouse have an attic? Maybe some dusty boxes of old books up there?" I asked.

He stopped mid-*M,* so it looked like he was doing an impression of a gorilla. "No, madam. Ask Crispin, he'll confirm it."

I wasn't ready to give up on the only person who could help us find those pages. "Is it okay if I have a little look around the other rooms? We would really love to find that book."

"Could you find my good slippers, while you're at it?" He kicked the suede ones off his feet with sudden disgust, as jerkily as though he'd just noticed there was a large spider crawling up his leg. "I'm loath to don these impostors."

I searched the lighthouse high and low, but I found neither the book nor another pair of slippers. After swallowing down the most horrific "cup of tea" I've ever had the misfortune of drinking, we said our dejected goodbyes to Renner and headed back up the pier toward the promenade.

"Poor guy," I muttered, staring at the scuffed toes of my Nikes.

"Poor guy?" retorted Alice incredulously. "Poor us!"

"Maybe he's gone crazy because of a ritual gone wrong," I pointed out. "Surely you can sympathize with that?"

Alice made a little tsk noise. "You're assuming my emotions operate in a logical manner."

"Sorry. My mistake."

When Hafsah finally spoke, it was with quiet, burrowing dread. "What are we going to do?"

Before I could answer, I saw something that made my spine tingle.

Mordue, in her black peacoat and red lipstick, walking up the promenade toward us.

Some unconscious instinct led me to grab Alice and Hafsah by the elbows and steer them into Carr's Fish 'n' Chip Shop before Mordue spotted us.

"What the—?"

"Mordue," I muttered, right as the dean passed the steamed-up chip shop window we were huddled behind.

From that spot, we watched her walk all the way up to the lighthouse and let herself in.

And then the rubies in my throat pulsed white hot, their roots coiling around my windpipe until all I could do was scream.

CHAPTER 53

Alice

Seeing Mordue at Renner's lighthouse made perfect sense, and yet it made no sense at all.

We drove back to Carvell with the windows down, letting the flow of crisp sea air wake us up. The adrenaline of rescuing Hafsah had long worn off, and all I could think of was resting my aching body in a warm bed. Yet Lottie's screams in the chip shop reverberated through my skull, through the dark and dusty corners of my chest. I never wanted to hear her scream like that again. Some strange protective instinct had come over me, and for a fleeting moment, all I wanted was to hug her to my chest and keep her safe.

Absurd, of course. She was a six-foot-tall athlete; she could take care of herself. She didn't need me.

Lottie, who sat in the front passenger seat beside me

as I drove, plucked a chip from a limp newspaper wrapper and bit into it with a sensuous groan. Food always made her feel better, and so the finest delicacy Northumberland had to offer felt like a fair reward for surviving the afternoon.

"Maybe Mordue performed the ritual too," she said, licking salt from her fingertips. "God, what if Mordue killed Poppy? And all the original victims? It would kind of make sense. She even admitted to me she was the only one with the key."

"I'm not sure," I confessed, looking out at the caravan park we were driving past. "I don't know why the very sensible dean of the university would feel the need to dabble in petty occultism. Though it would explain why she was coming to see Renner—she's searching for the reversal ritual as well."

Lottie finished her final chip, scrunched up the vinegar-soaked newspaper and tossed it into the messy footwell. "So what do we do now? Tell the police about Mordue visiting Renner and leave it to them to investigate?"

Hafsah snorted from the back seat, clicking her fingers in time to the upbeat pop song on the radio. "I mean, telling them about Mordue would also involve telling them about the existence of a secret supernatural ritual that goes back hundreds of years, the fact two of us performed said ritual for no good reason, that we practically stalked a mentally ill old man and badgered him into giving us instructions for a counter-ritual that may or may not exist, and that we

314

think the dean of our university murdered a student in a fit of evil rage linked to the above, and while telling them all of this, we would have to keep a straight face. So that feels like a not-great course of action."

Lottie nodded sagely. "Point taken. So how about we do a little Sherlocking of our own?" She patted the notebook and Parker fountain pen in the front pocket of her backpack.

"Sherlock?" I scoffed. "Don't flatter yourself. You're one hundred percent Scooby-Doo."

She smirked at me sideways. "Which makes you Scooby-Doo's sidekick, does it not?"

"*Sidekick?* In what world am I—"

Hafsah sighed, flinging sideways in her seat as I took a roundabout slightly too fast. "Would you two consider not flirting for one single second so I can concentrate?"

I gripped the steering wheel tightly and waited for Lottie to object to the accusation that we'd been flirting, but the outrage never came. She did, however, fall completely silent.

It had been weirdly intimate seeing her in Little Marmouth, a place that felt like an extension of myself: the hot sugar scent of frying doughnuts, the clinking of old copper pennies in the arcade, the fragrant hops of the nearby brewery mixed with the unmistakable salt tang of the North Sea. A place that was so viscerally mine, shared with her.

Heat stung at my cheeks the whole way back, and not even the frigid sea air could cool them down.

Lottie must have performed some kind of witchcraft of her own, because the day after our trip to the lighthouse, I found myself standing at the side of a freezing-cold hockey field, in the bare depths of November, ready to watch her play. Voluntarily. Of my own free will.

She'd come back from practice the previous evening with a fiery glow in her eyes, despite the icy rain hammering at our window. Her number fourteen jersey was drenched through and clung heavily to every long, muscular line of her body. She smelled of cold, fresh air.

"I made the first eleven!" she exclaimed, beaming at me as she waited for my reaction. I wasn't sure what to say, on account of not understanding the statement, but she persevered in search of praise. "I mean, it's not that amazing an achievement for a first year when there are no older years here to compete against for places . . . but still. I'm starting tomorrow!"

"Starting," I repeated. "As in, when the game starts, you will be standing on the pitch? I was operating under the assumption you did that already."

She rolled her eyes and tossed her sodden stick bag on the floor. "I've been a sub up until now. Haven't played more than ten minutes of any given match."

"Oh. Then I retract all of my historic sympathy for previous defeats."

"Sympathy? Alice, you said, 'I'm sorry your team was not as good as the other team,' and then handed me a bottle of wine."

"Yes," I said pointedly. "Sympathy. And I retract it."

She laughed, shaking her soaking-wet hair free of its high ponytail. "You're unbelievable. Anyway, I'm off for a hot shower. Do you mind if I borrow a towel? I forgot to hang mine up last night, and I think it's growing a new towel."

For some godforsaken reason, I found myself blushing as I handed her the soft, dry towel I'd already used once. It had touched me, naked, and now it was going to touch her, naked, and why did she not realize how intimate that was? Then again, maybe I was overthinking it, as I was wont to do.

Anyway, in a fit of chaotic and unprecedented decency, I found myself asking Hafsah if she wanted to come along to Lottie's starting match to support her. It seemed like the least we could do, since she'd been repeatedly flinging herself in harm's way to save us from the transformations.

The sky was gray and mizzling—what Northumbrians called that omnipresent half-mist, half-drizzle situation. The hockey pitch was surrounded by trees, and the muddy ground was crunchy with yellow-brown sycamore seeds. There was a winter coarseness to the breeze that hadn't been there a few days ago.

Lottie had yet to spot us in the crowd, but as she and her teammates swarmed onto the pitch under the harsh white glare of the floodlights, I felt a strange prickle of awe. Playing sports was not something I'd ever particularly aspired to, but I respected the way Lottie was willing to put herself out there like that. To be watched by hundreds of people as she ran around, sweating and shouting at her teammates to pass her the ball, the whole time risking that she might look like an idiot if she messed up, or might get hurt in front of a crowd, and that this many people could see her in pain and defeat. There was a bravery and a vulnerability to it I'd never considered before.

I wasn't going soft on sports, I told myself. Just Lottie.

She played center midfield, which even I understood meant she did most of the running around. I did not understand the physicality of how she could sprint the length of the field so many times and not require the aid of an oxygen tank. I felt breathless just watching her.

"It's impressive," I said to Hafsah. "Lottie, I mean."

She looked up from her Switch and gave me a knowing smile. "Mmm. Especially if you're secretly in love with her."

Heat rushed to my cheeks. "I am not—"

Hafsah held up a palm. "You know, a lot of people think autistics can't read people, but I'm the opposite. I read people very, very well. So well that it makes me overthink every minor shift in their mannerisms."

"Okay . . . ," I said slowly, still mortified at being perceived.

"For example, I am currently having casual sex with the captain of the rugby team."

I gaped at her. "You kept that quiet."

"I have a lot of sex with a lot of people. I'm just a slutty, slutty alien. Would you like a weekly digest?" She smirked, pressing the A button on her console with far too much vigor. "But yes, unfortunately the rugby dude is falling in love with me. He has that same hapless look you do right now. Like all the tiny creases and crinkles in your face have softened and smudged. Glazy eyes. The whole works."

"It's probably just the ritual," I argued, wrapping my scarf tighter around my chin.

Hafsah smiled, a sloping grin that fell somewhere between sly and condescending. "You're right. It's probably just the ritual. And absolutely nothing to do with the fact that her thighs could crush a man."

Just before the halftime whistle blew, the score was 1–1. One of Lottie's teammates passed her the ball and she took off up the field, weaving between the opposition's players like they were nothing, doing fancy little dribbles and dance-like skips. It was beautiful, in a way. Hardly *Swan Lake,* but in comparison to the brutishness of the thugs ramming up and down the pitch, Lottie had a certain elegance to her play. She deserved to have made the first eleven.

I gave my head a shake. It was absolutely *nothing* to do with her thighs.

Then, just as Lottie approached the D in front of the other team's goal and poised herself to shoot, a defender lifted her stick to make a tackle.

But she lifted it too high, too fast, and she was in the wrong place, and it hit Lottie's skull with a sickening thud.

I screamed as she fell lifelessly to the ground.

CHAPTER 54

Alice

Lottie crumpled like a rag doll, limp and awful.

Her teammates downed sticks and rushed over to where she lay.

Before I knew what I was doing, I was hopping over the barrier and running over too.

Carvell's head coach was crouched on the ground beside Lottie, two fingers to her wrist. "She's breathing and she has a pulse, but we need an ambulance." She pulled a phone out of her tracksuit pocket. "Tell them it's a brain injury with loss of consciousness, at least a grade-two concussion."

"Shit," muttered Hafsah somewhere behind me.

Blood roared in my ears. I couldn't get anywhere near Lottie, since she was so swamped with teammates and a first-aider who'd run over with a crate of water bottles. Nearby, the opposing team huddled around the tall, spindly player who'd hit her.

"If she 'adn't run straight at me, it wouldn't've happened." She spat on the ground, a thick glob of white spit. "She 'ad it coming."

Then, despite the ritual, despite the fact I was supposed to be Good Alice right now, something tore through the veil separating the two sides of my soul.

A red dagger of anger so sharp it obliterated anything in its path.

I saw crimson, and I charged.

Straight at the defender, who was easily a head taller than me.

I planted a palm on each of her collarbones and shoved with all my might. She fell back onto the squelching ground, letting out a shriek of shock.

"How fucking *dare* you," I hissed, my voice low and hoarse and cruel, and this time, this time I was fully aware of how monstrous it sounded.

Something had broken.

A mass of hands clawed at my arms and hair—the defender's teammates pulling me back. Distantly, I heard Hafsah swear profoundly.

With a strength I never knew I had, I stood firm, rooted like a tree, immovable despite being vastly outnumbered. I felt invisible roots burrow down into the earth, and the dragging grasps were nothing more than a gentle breeze among my leaves.

"Apologize," I rasped. "Apologize now."

"To who, you?" the defender snarled, hands pressed into the mud as she pushed herself up. Her badly bleached hair was plastered to her forehead, and there was a salt crust of sweat along her upper lip. "Or to 'er? Because it don't look like she's waking up anytime soon."

And then she smiled. A proud, hateful grin.

As though my hands were no longer my own, I lunged forward and grabbed her by the throat.

With her skin and muscles and arteries wriggling frantically beneath my iron grip, I stared her straight in the muddy-hazel eyes and said, "If you ever, *ever* touch Charlotte Fitzwilliam again, I will snap your neck like a twig."

Her eyes bulged as I tightened my grip and then flung her back down to the ground. She coughed and heaved in the mud, elbows buckling beneath her weight.

When I turned back to see if Lottie had woken up, every single member of the Carvell team was staring at me. Not with disgust, nor with awe, but with genuine bewilderment.

Nobody approached me. Neither to reprimand— although the head coach looked like she was considering it—nor to make sure I was okay.

Because what I smelled on them was fear. And it smelled fucking delicious.

"Ward sixteen, bed A," the nurse told me from behind her semicircular station.

I'd been in the hospital waiting room for thirty minutes while Lottie was examined. I wasn't allowed to travel in the ambulance with her—something about having grabbed her attacker by the throat mustn't have screamed *calming presence*—but some of the urgency of the situation eased when she regained consciousness a few minutes after being struck. She was groggy and confused, but she was awake. It was likely a concussion, albeit a serious one.

Once Lottie had been lifted into the ambulance on a stretcher, Hafsah and I jumped in my car and drove full throttle to the nearest hospital, which was fifteen miles away. I tried to use the time on the road to clear my head, to figure out what the ever-loving fuck had just happened.

"Are you okay?" Hafsah asked. She had actually put her Nintendo down in the cupholder, which is how I knew things were quite serious.

I shook my head. "I don't know. Something's shifted."

There was a darkness jutting through my soul veil like a mountain range. The veil fluttered around it in rags, and gusts of evil drifted through on the breeze.

I couldn't get the smell of the players' fear off my skin.

"Shifted how?" Hafsah asked, firing off a text to someone saved in her phone as "Brick."

"Like . . . okay, so I don't feel feral like I used to. Not like I might attack anyone at any given moment. But I no longer feel that oppressive calm of post-ritual fog either." I swallowed hard, swigging from a bottle of water that had been in my footwell for far too long. "But my thoughts are . . . cold. And murderous. I still really, *really* want to hurt that girl who hit Lottie. I want to flay her alive. I want her to *suffer*."

"Fan-fucking-tastic," Hafsah muttered, staring out at the skyline of redbrick terraces and balding trees.

Something darker had taken root in me, something that felt more sinister and more permanent than the fleeting bursts of anger I experienced before I came to Carvell. This was a calm, almost indifferent knowledge that I would hurt anyone who hurt me—or Lottie.

I would hurt them, and I would enjoy it immensely.

Ward sixteen was mostly empty of patients. It was a dated hospital, with lacquered pine furniture and linoleum floors that might have once been a cheery mint green but were now faded beige. The pale-blue curtain that enclosed Lottie's bed had come loose from several hooks and slouched defeatedly at one end.

Lottie was propped up in bed with an impossible smile on her face. There was a misshapen lump on her left temple, and her blond hair was loose around her shoulders, wavy from where her french braids had been. Her easy laugh carried around the whole of the ward as she told the nearest nurse what had happened.

I smiled to myself.

Just because I'm sunshiny as fuck doesn't mean I'm an idiot.

A teammate who'd ridden in the ambulance occupied the chair beside Lottie's bed, and the two of them were laughing with the nurse when I entered, but they quickly fell silent at the sight of me. I shifted my weight from brogue to brogue, unsure how to begin.

After an awkward beat, Lottie laughed again and said, "Oh hey, Jack Unterweger."

I frowned. "Jack . . . ?"

"The Vienna Strangler. I hear you got a bit . . ." She held her hands up to her throat and mimed strangling herself, then she dropped them and looked at me pointedly. "As much as I'm grateful to you for defending my honor, dearest knight in shining armor, I really don't want you to murder anyone on my behalf."

Her tone was light and airy, likely for the benefit of her teammate, but there was an intensity in her stare that only I could read.

She was scared for me. I shouldn't have wanted to hurt anyone at this point in the cycle.

Hafsah gestured to Lottie's bump. "How's the head?"

"S'okay. They've given me some pretty excellent pain meds." A lopsided grin. "I'm off for a CT scan in a bit, but they're not too worried. I seem to largely be making sense." She turned to her teammate. "Hey, can you give me and Alice a minute alone?"

Her teammate gave her a coy smile, and Lottie rolled her eyes.

What had she told her team about me? Or was the reaction based solely on me leaping violently to Lottie's defense?

Hafsah looked smugly at me. "Guess I'll be going too, then."

Lottie blinked. "Oh no, you don't have to—"

"No, it's fine." Hafsah pulled out a large pair of purple cat-ear headphones and arranged them over her space buns. "I'll be out in the corridor." Then she mouthed something at me that looked horribly like *thick thighs save lives*.

Once Lottie and I were alone, though, there was nothing tender or romantic between us. I perched on the edge of the nearest chair, tension pulling the ridges of my shoulders taut.

"Alice," she said in a low voice, the vowels elongated thanks to her meds. "What the hell happened?"

Slowly rotating my silver serpent ring around my index finger, I couldn't meet her eye as I answered.

"Something bad. My soul is no longer split, but it's not mended either. I think . . ." I swallowed the dry-ice lump in my throat. "I think I tore through the veil."

PART III

Woods

CHAPTER 55

Lottie

The lingering aftereffects of my concussion made it difficult to investigate either Mordue or Sanderson for the following week. I couldn't stand up for too long without feeling dizzy and nauseous, and I was dog-tired by midafternoon most days.

My weakened state allowed Sister Maria and her two rubies more control over me than ever.

The memory dreams were more vivid and intense than ever. There was a feeling of fully inhabiting them, walking around and affecting the scene around me, as opposed to drifting aimlessly through. They often bled into daytime; I'd be sitting in class fully cognizant one minute, and hallucinating about dead moths and bloodstained manuscripts the next. It was as though she was trying desperately to show me something, but my brain was too woolly to process any of it.

In one of the memories—more of a nightmare—my hand was being held over a burning candle until the skin blistered in agony. I screamed myself awake, only to find that my palm hurt in real life too. There were no blisters, but it throbbed for days, a kind of phantom pain that I couldn't explain.

Though the rubies' roots didn't try to choke me to death again, they were not afraid to make their feelings known. One morning I was waiting for Alice outside one of her seminars when the roots twinged and tugged until I was gagging. I had no idea why. Were they annoyed that I was wasting time instead of investigating Sister Maria's death? In any case, Alice and Hafsah found me crouched on the floor, hand clasped desperately around my neck. Professor Dacre, who had the demeanor of a toffee-toting grandfather, escorted us to the medical office only for the retching to stop as soon as the nurse saw me. It was a relief to excuse myself—I didn't want to have to explain the rubies to anyone.

Often I would wake up thrashing in my bed or clawing frantically at the dorm door in a bid to escape. Alice's hands would be gently coaxing me away as she talked in a low, soft whisper so as not to wake me too suddenly. I would wake to her skin on mine, and the quiet thrill of it would jolt me from any nightmare. I was afraid to interrogate too closely what that might mean.

Alice provided excellent nursing in general, bringing me bacon rolls and hot coffee from the dining hall, making sure I was drinking enough water and letting myself rest. This couldn't have been easy for her—knowing that all the while I was laid up in bed, her internal ritual clock was ticking ever forward—but she seemed to genuinely want to do it.

One thing I found particularly touching was when she returned from a trip to town with a small, midnight-blue paper bag and handed it to me somewhat gruffly. I was in plaid pajama shorts, and I could've sworn she was trying not to look at my thighs.

"This is for me?" I asked, propping myself up on my elbows. I was lying in bed reading some course material, trying to make the room stop spinning and eddying whenever I moved the slightest fraction of an inch.

"I mean, it's nothing, really. An early Christmas present." She immediately busied herself folding the stack of laundry that had been mounting up on her side of the room.

Inside the bag was something very small, wrapped in silver tissue paper and secured with a precise square of tape. I peeled it open as carefully as I could.

It was a black velvet choker, with a neat silver clasp at the back.

Alice glanced over her shoulder. "I know it's more my style than yours, and it doesn't really go with joggers and hoodies, but I thought you could use it to cover the rubies. Better than being constantly hot and bothered in that huge pashmina." She shrugged. "It's okay if you hate it."

A smile tugged at the corners of my mouth, spreading a

warmth through my cheeks that I didn't fully understand. "No. I love it. Thank you." And I really did. True, it wasn't my style, but it was Alice's—a style she took great pride in. I took it as a token of trust and friendship that she'd willingly shared that style with me.

I wrapped the choker around my neck and tried to fasten it, but the clasp was tiny and fiddly, and my hands still trembled from the head injury. Alice crossed over to me without saying a word.

She tenderly swept my hair over one shoulder, then took the clasp from me. Her fingertips brushed the back of my neck as she worked, and I could feel her warm, slightly quickened breath on the top of my spine. I shivered despite myself, an odd flutter that extended from the depths of my chest to the tips of my fingers.

"There," she said, stepping back and handing me my makeup mirror.

My reflection was, for the most part, hideous. My skin had a pallor I hadn't seen in years—I usually spent so much time outside that I had a permanent tan—and there were purplish bags under my eyes. My hair was frizzy and unwashed, with a halo of fuzz around my crown, and my lips were dry and chapped.

And yet the choker, which covered the rubies perfectly, made me feel beautiful. Not the whole dark woods—not like Alice—but maybe a particularly glorious blackberry, the ultradark kind that bursts with sweetness when you bite into it.

"Thank you," I murmured, my voice thick with an emotion I couldn't quite name.

As the days wore on, though, I could no longer deny that something had once again shifted in Alice. The torn veil—whatever that meant—was going to be a problem.

She, Hafsah and I were sitting at one of the big group tables in the library one morning in early December, working on assignments. The library was busier than usual since most courses had essays due at the end of the semester, and it rustled with the sound of shuffled papers and turning pages, cleared throats and stage whispers. The space had been decorated for Christmas, with an enormous fir tree in the center of the ground floor. It dripped with warm white fairy lights, red-gold baubles and glass snowflake ornaments, and the golden angel at the top was holding a book. The sullen librarian, Kate Feathering, looked at it with withering hatred approximately every thirty seconds.

I was forcing my milky gaze to focus on the passage of *The Picture of Dorian Gray* I was trying and failing to annotate. Hafsah had big purple cat-ear headphones over her ears as she scribbled away on her madhouse research paper, while Alice was reading something in a Confucius reference book and frowning intently. The trance music Hafsah was listening to was so loud we could hear every beat.

"Hafsah," Alice muttered, looking over at her with unfettered irritation. I knew from the timbre of her voice that the darkness was talking, but what could I do in such a public place? "Hafsah." The word seethed with vicious energy.

While most people would've nudged a noisy neighbor with an elbow to get their attention, Alice reached into her black leather pencil case, picked out a math compass with a sharp golden point and stabbed it straight into Hafsah's forearm.

Hafsah jumped and hissed in pain, shale-dark eyes flaring with fury. She ripped the headphones from her head as the compass clattered to the floor. "What the fuck, Alice!" She pulled back her sleeve, but there was only the slightest bloody puncture; her jumper had cushioned most of the needle.

Other students had turned to glare at us. Alice was staring at her own hand as though it had betrayed her in some fundamental way.

The next day, she arrived from an impulsive jaunt into town with a small object wrapped in brown parcel paper.

"What's that?" I asked, sitting up in bed with a wince. Frustration over my injury was really starting to build. All I wanted was to be running around a muddy field thwacking balls with a stick, and instead, for the first time in my life, I was what some would describe as "irritable."

Alice's eyes sparkled, but not with mirth; lined in more black kohl than usual, there was a sinister incandescence to them. "A knife," she replied calmly.

"A what?" I practically yelped.

"A knife," she repeated, unwrapping the brown paper

to reveal a smooth olive wood penknife with the initials A.K.W. engraved in a cursive font. "I had it customized, because I am nothing if not pretentious."

"Why do you need a knife?" I asked, unease rubbing up against me like an arched black cat.

I hoped the answer would be something innocent, something easier to dismiss—maybe because she was jealous of my pocketknife, or because she wanted to protect herself from the murderer at large. But instead she just curled her lip and said, "I'm going to kill Kate Feathering with it."

My stomach dropped. "The librarian? I . . . *Why?*"

A nonchalant shrug. "She looks at me the wrong way."

"She looks at everyone the wrong way!" I said, urgency creeping into my voice. "I think that's just her face!"

"So you agree she needs to be dealt with?" Alice asked calmly, her villainous brows hooking upward. Her demeanor, so mild and composed, was somehow far worse than the monstrous voice of the transformations. A cold and calculated killer had replaced the feral, desperate girl.

I knew we needed drastic action, and I knew we needed it now.

CHAPTER 56

Every night since the lighthouse, I'd watched the North Tower from our dorm window. Every night Dean Mordue arrived just a few minutes before midnight and headed inside.

Only now I realized she wasn't just doing a quick security search. She stayed there for hours on end, usually reappearing around three in the morning.

Had she been there on the night of Poppy's death?

Even if she wasn't responsible, she must have seen something. And yet the police were all but certain it was suicide.

Then there was the strange dead space that the architectural drawings had confirmed the existence of. What was in that space? And was that space the reason for Mordue's midnight visits?

Mordue was hiding something. And after seeing her at

Renner's lighthouse, I was convinced that that something had to do with the ritual book. Somehow, the book was the key to everything, and it was time to tie all those loose ends together into one knot that would both solve Poppy's murder and free Alice and Hafsah from the confines of hell.

And so it was between those hours of midnight and three a.m. that I decided to break into Mordue's office.

My reasoning was this: various other faculty members had, at the start of the semester, a copy of the key to North Tower. Mordue told me that those keys had been revoked in the wake of Poppy's death, and so she was the only one with access. She'd also told me that she kept her key on her at all times. But what about all the other keys, from the other staff? Surely she wouldn't have had them destroyed, because what if her own was lost or damaged?

Those keys must still be in her office, which was locked whenever she wasn't in it.

But that locked office had a window. And windows could be broken.

As I left our room while Alice slept, I locked the door from the outside, taking her key and knife with me. I'd managed to distract her from her murderous crusade that evening by taking her to the Grandstand for a game of backgammon, but I couldn't risk her waking up, finding me gone and heading over to the library to stab Feathering in the chest. Just normal roommate things, you know.

A little after midnight, I smashed into Mordue's office window with a rock I'd found in a flower bed. It made a dull crack, the glass fissuring but not smashing. The second blow shattered the window, glass tinkling around my feet. But the hole was jagged and treacherous and not large enough for me to climb through, and it took several more perilous seconds to remove the worst of the massive glass shards before I could haul myself into the room over the festive poinsettia garland laid along the windowsill.

Once inside, I peered back out from behind the brocade curtain, checking to see whether anyone had heard the commotion and come to investigate. But the night was still quiet, with just the distant bass of the Refectory and a couple of pops of laughter hanging on the breeze. Hopefully if anyone had heard the glass shatter, they'd assumed it was a pint glass broken among the drunken, festive debauchery.

The rubies in my throat thrummed with something like pleasure, almost as though Sister Maria was telling me I was close.

Mordue's office was dark but for some final embers glowing orange in the fireplace. There was a streetlamp just outside the window, so there was plenty of light to see by. I immediately began to rummage through every conceivable hiding spot for the keys, but found to my dismay that all of her desk drawers were locked, and there was no key handily taped to its underside. An old-fashioned Father Christmas figurine peered curiously at me from beside her computer, as though the fact I was anything less than jolly in the month of December was utterly incomprehensible.

Giving up on the desk, I crossed to one of the tinsel-decked bookshelves with cabinetry on its bottom half. The brass-handled doors opened to reveal a squat gray safe with a black, six-digit combination lock.

Fuck, I thought. If I had Alice's encyclopedic memory of all things Carvell, I would've had plenty of important dates to try: the date it first opened, the date of Mordue's appointment as dean, the date of Sister Maria's death. Mordue's birthday and graduation date. I tried the dates of all of the North Tower murders, which I found I was able to recall, but none of them worked.

Just as I was racking my brain for other ideas, there was the sound of footsteps approaching the door to Mordue's office.

And then, awfully, impossibly, the sound of a key in a lock.

She was supposed to be in the North Tower.

Quickly as I could, I slammed the cabinet door shut and tucked myself behind one of the thick brocade curtains like they did in movies, pressing my back as tightly against the bay window paneling as possible.

The door opened, and then came the crackle of breath hitching in a nervous throat.

"Whoever's there, I can see you behind the curtain." It was a shaky female voice I didn't recognize. "Come out or I'll shoot."

Shoot?

Fear twisting in my gut, I stepped out.

It was Mordue's secretary, wielding an enormous

hunting rifle with trembling arms, a look of wild terror on her mousy face.

If I was Alice, I'd make a dry remark about how unnecessary and escalatory the gun seemed, but my voice box was paralyzed. I held up my hands as though under arrest.

"What are you doing here?" she asked. "I've already called the police."

Oh god.

Desperation had led me down some reckless paths, and now I was about to pay heavily. The police would be here in minutes; any call from Carvell would be treated as an emergency.

Would they think I was the murderer? Breaking and entering was hardly innocent behavior.

There was no lie that could get me off the hook. And so the truth would just have to do.

One final gambit.

"Listen, Alison—it's Alison, isn't it?" I said, taking an ill-judged step toward her until she raised the rifle and pointed it at my face. "Whoa, okay. The reason I'm here is because I think the dean has something to do with the murders. She goes to the tower at the same time every night, for hours on end." A beat. "You've seen her, haven't you? You've wondered what she's doing too?"

I searched her clammy face for a glint of recognition, and I found it in the subtle rearranging of her mouth. I pressed on. "I know the police have already talked to her, and they've found nothing. But I can't let any more of my friends die. I need to know what she's doing, and I need to know if she was there when Poppy was killed." A pause, in which I strained to hear for sirens. None yet. "Look, just tell me if you've seen her going to the tower?"

Alison reached up to brush a lock of pale-brown hair out of her face, and the sudden downward jerk of the gun made me almost crap myself. Then, finally, a nod. "I've seen her."

I nodded. "Did you tell the police?"

Another agonizing beat. "No."

"Why not?"

A shaky shrug. "I need this job. My husband's on long-term sick and can't work anymore. We've got four kids to feed. What would we do if Carvell closed again?"

"Okay," I said, forcing patience into my voice. "But kids are *dying* here, Alison. Kids just like yours, with parents who love them." I fought back images of my own frightened father, our final hug on the day he left me here. I'd been ignoring his calls since my bumblebee comment, in part because I was so ashamed of how I'd made him feel, but mostly because I didn't want to have to say no to him again. I *couldn't* say no. Sister Maria made sure of that.

"All I need is the North Tower key," I urged. "I'll slip away before the police arrive, and you go back and wait outside. Say you were too afraid to go in. They'll find the office empty, and hopefully they'll write it off as a prank.

And I'll do everything I can to make sure nobody else dies."
I softened my voice. "We're just kids, Alison. None of us
want to die."

Alison looked like she was considering this, and I
wanted to tell her to hurry the fuck up, but I knew that
rushing her would force a decision that might not go in my
favor. "Vanessa will notice there's a key missing."

I nodded. "Maybe. But hopefully we can find answers
before that happens."

There were still no sirens, but blue and red lights illuminated the semidistant sky.

"Okay." Alison put down the rifle, crossed to the safe
and deftly entered a combination I didn't manage to catch
over her shoulder.

She handed me the key with a final stoic nod.

I climbed out of the window and disappeared around
the corner of the convent just in time to see the police car
rolling quickly but silently up the drive.

Adrenaline and residual fear made me so dizzy I had to
take a brief pause by a tree with a crooked-elbow branch.
Blood roared in my ears, and purple spots muddied my
vision. The rubies were pounding so intensely it was like
having three pulses. It took everything I had not to throw
up all over the cobbles.

But it was worth it. I had the key to the North Tower.
Now all that was left to do was get past the guard.

CHAPTER 57

Alice

Lottie came up with the plan to distract the North Tower guard remarkably fast.

If it was successful, we might be in, with a chance of figuring out why Mordue went to the North Tower every night at midnight. Lottie's hunch was that it had something to do with the mysterious room beside the Sisters of Mercy Library, since the original architectural drawings showed a second door halfway up the tower's spiral staircase. All we would have to do once we got past the guard was lie in wait for Mordue to arrive and see whether she went to the circular observatory at the top of the tower—or to the hidden room Lottie was sure was central to this whole thing.

What was Mordue doing for those three hours? I had my ritual-shaped suspicions.

The night after Lottie stole Mordue's spare key, we

made our move. It was hasty—maybe too hasty—but the transformations were hurting Hafsah and me more and more, gripping every inch of us in full-body cramps and spasms, as though a fork of white-hot lightning was shredding the skin from our muscles and the muscles from our bones. Almost as though the effort of cleaving our goodness from our darkness was taking more and more from us. It left us ragged and gasping, incapable of anything but sleeping shakily for a whole day afterward. The thought of an eternity of this fear and pain was so overwhelming I couldn't let my brain consider the idea for more than a few seconds at a time.

I was also bitterly disappointed that the latest vial of tincture had not repaired the ragged hole I'd somehow torn in the veil at the field hockey match. The kind, gentle instincts were still there—I longed to reach over and tuck a lock of stray hair behind Lottie's ear, or make her one of my favorite whiskey cocktails—but they were twisted by the cold, violent thoughts, like smooth tarmac warped by tree roots. I stalked around campus accompanied by a cold, calm voice that said: *You could kill them. You could kill all of them, and it would feel amazing.*

There was no longer a separation between me and the vicious killer on the other side of the transformation. I found myself plotting Kate Feathering's murder with an indifference that chilled me to my core—as though I was planning a birthday party, not an assassination. Worse, I knew in my bones that I couldn't stop it. I had to rely on

Lottie to keep me in check, or before long there would be blood on my hands.

And it would feel so good.

The night of our attempt at the plan was a Friday, and Carvell's campus hung with the scent of mulled wine, woodsmoke and clove. The darkness had soft edges to it, blurred by fairy lights and tinsel, Christmas carols and teddy coats. Bats swooped and dived among the branches of the now-bare trees. Moth cocoons hung in neat rows down the elbow-crook branch of an old ash, and I found myself wondering how many vials of ritual tincture I could harvest from them.

The murderous voice that had taken root in me made mental note of all the potential weapons: the crackling fires and sharp metal skewers, dangling tartan scarves and the neat little penknife I'd bought and had engraved. That night it was tucked in the inside pocket of my coat, nestled close to my chest along with a freshly made batch of tincture already mingled with Lottie's blood. She'd let me carry the penknife in case anything went wrong and we got into real danger, but her eyes darted over to me every thirty seconds to make sure I wasn't trying to withdraw it.

It was around nine p.m., and the night guard had just taken over from the day guard. The two men looked almost identical—middling height, thick brown-and-gray beards and stocky frames. They exchanged a few muffled words, which we couldn't make out from our window perch.

Soon enough, it was time to put the plan into action.

I left Willowood first, wrapping around the building until I was concealed around the corner closest to the guard. Lottie and Hafsah would enact the first part of the plan. All I had to do was watch, listen and be close enough to sprint if and when the guard ran from his post. I gripped the key to the tower between my thumb and forefinger until the timeworn brass was hot to the touch.

Lottie and Hafsah came out the front entrance of Willowood, embroiled in a fake argument, and started walking slowly in the opposite direction from where I stood. I slipped my boots off, wincing as the soles of my feet met the freezing cobbles, but it was important that I be able to slip silently across to the locked door.

"Lottie, please, I didn't mean to," Hafsah faux pleaded, her voice taking on a whiny pitch I'd never heard from her before.

"How could you do this to me?" Lottie all but yelled. "Fuck you. Just . . . fuck you, Hafsah."

I peeked around the corner. The guard was indeed watching them, although he seemed to be trying hard to pretend not to be.

My heart beat audibly through my satin shirt. What would happen if I got caught? Would suspension from school be better or worse than what we were currently going through every time we had to perform a ritual?

I tried not to think about the fact that if we were expelled, we might never find the counter-ritual. We'd be doomed to this dark half existence forever.

How would I explain what was happening to me to my family?

"What will it take for you to forgive me?" Hafsah moaned, the words wobbling with fake tears. She was a decent actress, I'd give her that.

Lottie was striding ahead as though she didn't want to hear more, and Hafsah was scurrying to keep up. They were almost at the corner of the building when Lottie swung maniacally around, grabbed Hafsah by her petite shoulders and slammed her against the wall, forearm pressed to her throat.

"You could let me hurt you as much as you've hurt me," Lottie growled. I shivered involuntarily as she pulled her ornate penknife from her back pocket and held it against Hafsah's stomach.

That's when Hafsah started to scream for help.

After a few split seconds of indecision, the guard strode over, shouting, "Oi!" in a brisk Borders accent.

Now or never.

As quickly and quietly as I could, I sprinted straight toward the tower door, shoes in one hand and keys in the other, not bothering to turn and look at what was going on with the guard and the girls. If he saw me, it was all over, whether I saw him see me or not.

Feet screaming at the freezing cobbles, I made it to the door and jammed the key in as softly as possible. It took a few juddering attempts, but it finally gave. I turned the ribbed brass handle and winced as the mechanism clicked conspicuously, but before I knew it I was inside, panting hard as I eased the door shut. I locked it behind me for good measure so the guard wouldn't be alerted to the presence of an intruder if he tried the handle.

I eased my feet back into my shoes, pulse jackhammering against my skull. The air in the North Tower's stairwell was dank and freezing, with almost no light. I could barely make out where the spiral staircase began. I touched my fingertips to the circular stone wall—it was cold and slick with a miscellaneous moisture—and followed it carefully around until the pointed toe of my boot met something solid. And then I began to climb.

I kept my fingertips on the wall, feeling for the place where it gave way to a doorway. Sure enough, around what must have been halfway up the tower, the stones abruptly became smooth, slatted wood. The door must have been absolutely flush to the ground, because no light poured from a crack beneath the frame. The whole place was sinisterly, absolutely black.

Feeling around with my feet, I found a small ledge jutting out into the staircase. I climbed softly onto it, breath rattling in my throat, and pressed my ear up against the door.

For a few seconds, I strained and strained to hear what might be on the other side, but there was nothing but silence. I couldn't even hear any commotion from outside the building. I had no idea how the rest of Lottie and Hafsah's plan had turned out, or whether the guard had returned to his post. It was almost as though the entire North Tower was muffled beneath a great blanket, allowing no light or sound to breach its round stone walls; like time itself operated differently here.

I was about to creep up the stairs to hide in the observatory when the halfway door opened.

My heart hitched into my throat as I stared in horror at the person on the other side.

Kate Feathering grabbed me by the faux-fur lapels of my coat and dragged me inside the secret room.

I staggered across the crooked threshold, clipping the toes of my boot on the stone step. Feathering shoved me to the ground, my soft palms scraping against the hard, rough floor. For a split second, I felt like a debauched thief being tossed from a medieval tavern onto ale-soaked cobbles. My grazed hand went to the knife in my pocket.

Behind me there was the sound of the door being closed again. Then, a key in a lock. Slowly, fearfully, I raised my head and took in where I was.

A narrow, windowless room. Vaulted ceilings with beams hung with moth cocoons of sickly silver gray. A long mahogany table topped with twisting silver candelabra lit with flickering flames. Several wooden sideboards like you might find in a Renaissance apothecary, with neat little drawers with ornate silver handles. From the cabinet nearest me, I was sure I could pick out the scents of sage, rosemary and elderflower.

Atop one sideboard were rows of miniature test tube

racks in dark wood, with cast-iron wolf heads on either end. Notched inside the racks were dozens of the same small vials I'd been using for my own tinctures, and four of the racks had a name carved into each of them: FEATHER-ING. MORDUE. BAPTIST. SANTOS. The vials in those racks were full of preprepared tinctures.

There were doors in three of the four walls. One was the North Tower entrance from which I'd just entered. The second was directly opposite, and, if I remembered the architectural drawings correctly, led to the library. On the third wall was a row of three identical doors with keyholes that locked from the outside.

On the fourth wall was a portrait of Sister Maria in a gilded frame. Despite the traditional bust style of the painting, it was unlike any portrait from that era I'd seen. Her eyes were jet black, as though her pupils had swallowed her irises. She wore her familiar ruby rosary beads around her neck, but they were painted in such a way that they looked more like bloody gashes on her throat. She was surrounded by moths, and cocoons hung from the dark folds of her habit. In the bottom right corner was a signature in off-white: *Maria Dunn*. A self-portrait.

Understanding hit me like the whipcrack of a tree branch thrashing in the wind.

It all started with her.

Hung above the antique sideboard was a large forest-green plaque, like the one champions pose beside at Wimbledon. On it were more than a dozen names in gold leaf. I recognized a handful of them:

KATE FEATHERING

VANESSA MORDUE

JANIE KIRSOPP

DAWN MIDDLEMISS

FIONA TAYLOR

ALICE WOLFE

HAFSAH AL-HADI

Something cold and creeping pooled in my gut.

I turned slowly back to Feathering, who was watching me carefully for a reaction. For the first time since I'd known her, a lock of white-silver hair was slightly out of place, and her black lipstick was smudged in one corner.

"What the hell is this place?" I asked, almost breathlessly. My pulse sang thin and fast in my ears. "It looks like some kind of . . . clubhouse."

Her hard green eyes bore into my own. "Welcome to the Society for Soulless Girls."

CHAPTER 58

Alice

"The Society for Soulless Girls?" I swallowed hard. "That kind of raises more questions than it answers."

"Aren't you supposed to be bright?" Feathering said irritably, with a dismissive wave of one manicured hand. "We all performed the ritual. Just like you did. This is where the surviving members of the original society come each night to perform the ritual." She pointed to the row of doors at the opposite end of the room. I noticed for the first time that they had gold-plated letter boxes beside their ornate handles. "They lock from the outside. I post the vial through a slot and wait for the transformations to run their course. Then we swap places."

There were a thousand other questions on my tongue, but before I could give form to them, the door from the North Tower opened. Dean Mordue entered, a look of furious indignance on her face. She wore claret lipstick and a long black peacoat that blew out behind her.

"Kate? How is she here?" She glared at me with an expression I couldn't quite parse—it wasn't disdain, but perhaps something fear-shaped.

Feathering peered at me with sudden interest. "Yes, how *did* you get past the guard? The locked door?"

"I have a fearless friend." There was a proud tilt to the words; a strange weight on the final word. In a bid to look nonchalant, I shrugged—despite the fact my heart was pounding through the too-tight skin on my chest. "We wanted to know why the dean came here every night. We saw her at Renner's lighthouse. What's going on?"

For a split second, the dean seemed torn between anger and understanding. Her shoulders dropped as she chose the latter. "I suppose you have a right to know. You're one of us, after all."

Even though the situation was terrifying, something in me glowed at the sentiment. I'd never belonged anywhere before. The kinship felt dangerous and doomed, a wounded ship on a violent black sea.

As I stood up I suddenly felt weak and dizzy. I pulled out a chair from the long table and slumped into the worn velvet seat, clutching my knife so hard my knuckles went ghost white.

"Start at the beginning," I said faintly, both my mind and the dark room reeling.

Mordue sat down in a chair opposite me, gesturing for Feathering to do the same.

The dean spoke first. "When I first came to Carvell, I was just like you. Young, and smart, and *angry*." A laden pause, hung with the shadows of moth cocoons. "During my time at Oxford, while I was studying for my doctorate, I was assaulted by a tenured professor. He cornered me in his office, pinned me against a wall, and kissed me against my will. It didn't go any further, thank god. A cleaner came in at that very moment. But I was never able to shake that powerless feeling. The sheer imbalance of our physicality. The awful inevitability of it." A bitter laugh. "The real reason they encourage little girls not to fight. So that we won't know how."

She stared at her hands, and I could tell that right now, she was young and scared once again. "Over the years that followed, my thoughts grew more and more violent. All I thought about was hurting my attacker. *Killing* him. It took over my life. I couldn't focus on my work—or anything else. I really thought I was going to do it. I was going to drive to Oxford and cut his throat. It's difficult to fully explain, but this completely destroyed my sense of self. I'd always been religious, you know? I'd always had a deep personal connection to God. Church every Sunday, prayers every morning and night. Yet according to everything I believed in, that wrath was a sin. *I* was a sin. I couldn't love my neighbor, I couldn't turn the other cheek. I was burning up inside. It became more and more difficult to fully devote myself to my faith with that anger hanging over me, and without that deep personal connection . . . I didn't know who I was anymore."

My throat had gone scratchy and thick. "So you performed the ritual."

Mordue nodded. "I found the book in a knickknack shop in town. Renner had only printed a handful, and it was the last one left. Back then it still had all of its pages, but to begin with, I didn't *want* to reverse the ritual. I'm sure you remember that at first, the feeling of liberation and relief is astounding. I was able to focus on my teaching and my research without having my thoughts obscured by violent impulses. For a glorious few weeks, it was like all my problems had simply evaporated. There was no anger, only patience and reason. Then came the first transformation. The pain . . . it's like nothing else, isn't it?"

She squeezed her eyes shut against the memory, her fine wrinkles deepening. "It was once I realized that the time between transformations was narrowing that I finally wanted to reverse it. But the pages were gone."

"What happened to them?"

"I kept the book on the desk in my office, and I can only assume someone tore them out while I wasn't around. Who, and for what reason . . . that I still haven't been able to figure out."

My mind vaulted and somersaulted over the facts, trying

to find a place to land. Each one was as terrifying as the last. "But you said the author printed a handful of copies," I pointed out. "So there must be others out there."

Mordue shook her head. "I've searched the area for years, including every inch of Renner's lighthouse. I've never been able to find one. But I visit him once a week, just in case he's lucid enough to remember."

He called me Vanessa, I dimly recalled. I'd dismissed it as senile confusion, but Mordue's name was Vanessa. He knew who she was, even if he couldn't help her.

Helplessness stung at my eyes. My brain swam with the magnitude of it all. I was looking at my future, and my future was confined to a locked room every night, clawing at the walls like an animal.

I forced words into my mouth. "So then . . . the North Tower murders."

"Of this I am truly ashamed." The dean rested her hands on the table in front of her and clasped them together, knuckles stretched taut. The skin around them looked dry and cracked. "Before I realized how dangerous the ritual was, I encouraged others to do it with me. Two colleagues and a student."

"Who was the student?" I asked.

Kate Feathering cleared her throat, and my heart sank. It was her.

"Earlier in the semester, I had confided in Vanessa about my anger issues," Feathering said quietly. "There was no real reason for it, no origin story. I was just born pissed off." A sour laugh. "I had sought counseling through the NHS, to no avail. My old, male GP practically laughed in my face. And I couldn't afford private therapy. So Vanessa recommended the ritual to me in good faith."

"What about the others?" I gestured to the plaque, where the names of the murder victims stood starkly in gold leaf.

"Friends of mine," Feathering mumbled, the words clipped with pain and guilt. "Fellow students. I told them about the ritual, before I knew it would ruin their lives."

Janie Kirsopp. Dawn Middlemiss. Fiona Taylor.

They were Feathering's friends.

They were like *me*.

Mordue sighed. "It was a few months later, once we were all in the thick of it, that we came together and formed the society. We met in the observatory back then, and we tried our best to restrain each other during the transformations. We didn't have the facilities we do now—we created this clubhouse while the university was closed—so we made do with crude supplies. Handcuffs and old pipes. But we weren't infallible, and neither were the old pipes. Accidents happened."

My jaw clenched. "Accidents? Or murders?"

"Or suicides," Mordue said quietly. "Janie jumped. It's the only one I remember. She'd killed her boyfriend, Sam, while lost in the unfettered darkness. The guilt ate her alive. As for Dawn and Fiona . . . none of us can remember. By the time they died, the darkness had pretty much consumed us all. Maybe they jumped. Maybe they were pushed. We don't know."

"Their bodies were ravaged," I whispered. "Dawn and Fiona. Slit throats and stabbed torsos, claw marks up and down their arms . . ."

Mordue and Feathering said nothing. I felt cold to my bones.

I was sitting in an enclosed room with possible murderers.

Worse, I was sympathizing with them.

"What happened when Carvell closed?"

Feathering grimaced. "We lived here in secret for a decade. We're estranged from our families, our friends, our loved ones."

As I watched Mordue press the heels of her hands into her eyes, I suddenly couldn't believe that I'd never noticed the unbearable grief they both carried. They seemed laden with it, pressing down on their shoulders and chests, drawing the corners of their mouths down, misting their pupils like fog over the North Sea.

They had lost their lives to Sister Maria's ritual. And before long, I would too.

CHAPTER 59

Bile filled my mouth as I sat on our window ledge and watched Mordue enter the North Tower after Alice.

It was too early, just after ten. Had the guard suspected the breach and alerted the dean?

I suddenly wished I'd been the one to go instead. The thought of anything happening to Alice was unthinkable.

What if I had to watch her fall to her death, red hair swooshing up behind her, the sickening crunch of impact, those ice-blue eyes snuffed out forever? What if she would never wear her silk pajamas again, or light up as she was talking about wacky philosophers, or ill-advisedly fight for my honor?

If she was hurt, I would never forgive myself. What if she was the next Poppy? The next Janie?

Anger began to simmer at the very core of me. It was

the world we lived in that ultimately led Alice here. That pushed her to the ritual in the first place. A world that made her think that to be angry as a woman was fundamentally wrong; something that needed to be exorcised or carved out by whatever dark force necessary.

Rather than running from it, I leaned into the anger, felt its righteous arms welcome me in.

The rage churned in me until it was all-consuming, until it was larger than myself, until nothing else existed. I became vaguely aware of a struggling sensation beneath my ribs, in the corners of my lungs, in the pulsing atria of my heart.

Then there was a sudden, searing starburst in my throat.

A blinding light threw me back into the room.

A pain in my skull so intense I thought I'd been shot.

For a moment, everything went from hot white to absolute black, and I was sure, in that moment, that I was dead.

But slowly, slowly, my eyes pushed open like moth wings unfurling from a cocoon, new and bright and strange.

As the room came into soft focus, I realized I was no longer in the dorm.

I was in the observatory.

It was dark and cold and empty; a round, stone-floored room at the top of the North Tower, with open Gothic arches around its circumference. The stars in the sky were brighter than I'd ever seen them—swirling sprays of silver white across a black canvas. The convent was crypt quiet but for the sounds of the nearby forest.

I knew at once that this was not the present day. This was a century ago.

And I was not Charlotte Fitzwilliam.

The other-life glimpses that had dogged my dreams for months were no longer shutter-click images; they were rich, full memories I could swim around in like lakes.

Age-spotted hands—my own hands—were illuminating a manuscript about devil possession, painting a little demon behind the chapter heading with a tiny brush and potent-smelling oils. Reading the script secretly as I worked, and recognizing the signs in myself.

> To think oneself possessed.
>
> To lead a wicked life.
>
> To live outside the rules of society.
>
> To utter obscenities and blasphemies.
>
> To show a frightening and horrible countenance.
>
> To be tired of living.
>
> To be uncontrollable and violent.

I, Sister Maria, had learned of the soul-splitting ritual through that manuscript. I'd hunted high and low for the tincture ingredients, taken cuttings, planted them all in the same wooded glade for ease. I stole blood from Sister Elizabeth's discarded bandages when she tripped and fell on uneven cobbles. Then I performed the ritual; the temporary relief, the eventual unraveling. The wolf wildness in my heart.

With a lasso yank, my memories flung me back further. Years earlier, little-girl Maria slapped in the face by her father for a minor indiscretion, and slapping him right back.

The punishment: the palm of my hand held over a candle flame, anger churning in my gut.

My retribution: burning his study to the ground, and taking half the house with it.

Being sent to a convent at twelve.

Only God can save you, you monstrous thing.

Now I was on my hands and knees in the observatory, the stone freezing cold beneath my shaking palms, the sound of my shallow breathing echoing around the room. Fear and shame and desperation seized me, a vise, a guillotine, and I found myself begging the Lord's forgiveness for what I was about to do.

It was the only way. It was the only way. It was the only way.

The abbess had called me into her chambers after Nones. Sister Catherine was in her sixties, brown-eyed and gray-haired, warm yet stern, with absolute authority over her nuns, but still a fraction of the power of a bishop or a priest on account of her being a woman. I wondered if it ate at her like it ate at me.

Distantly, as though from underwater, she told me the diocese were concerned about my episodes, about the jaw-snapping violence, and that it was abundantly clear what was going on, and it was not my fault, it truly was not, for the devil can take any one of us, but it was in my best interest—and those of the wider parish—to arrange an exorcism, which would be held in public so that tickets might be sold to pay the exorcist, who was not cheap and would be traveling all the way from North Yorkshire, and I should be grateful, really, when all was said and done.

The fear gripped me for real then, for I'd read stories of exorcisms in my manuscripts, how frightened and tortured and shamed the women were, how none of them ever truly recovered from it, and many were locked away forever, and I knew that it would be futile, because there was no devil in me that was not myself, and anyway, the transformations were getting closer and closer together, and so, when all was said and done, could anybody save me at all?

And that was not the point really. It was that I did not want this exorcist—this witch doctor, this con artist—to profit from my suffering, the satisfaction of a jeering crowd and ticket riches, a pamphlet about my agony as though it was cheap entertainment for the masses.

Taking one's life was a mortal sin, and I would never make it to heaven if I went through with it, but after everything I had already thought and said and done, I was unlikely to make it anyway.

Wrath is a sin.

I am a sin.

With grim determination I climbed to my feet, doggedly dusted the grime off the heavy folds of my habit, and took three purposeful strides toward the northernmost arch. I turned and shuffled backward onto the narrow ledge, gripping the carved stone frame with my tired hands.

Father, forgive me.

And then I fell backward, black fabric flung up all around me in a final, wrathful display.

I fell, and I fell, for what felt like eternity.

The impact never came.

With another sickening jolt, a bang of white pain, I came back to myself in the dorm, lying on the floor as though I'd just pushed myself from the window ledge.

There was a ring of fire around my neck as though I'd been hanged by a flaming noose.

I knew before I lifted my hands what I'd find, but it was worse than I ever could have feared.

There were not three rosary rubies in my throat, but dozens and dozens, encasing my neck in a single terrible circle.

A voice screamed in my head, shrieking and echoing in every temple and every bone:

Make them pay.

CHAPTER 60

Alice

Anger was rising in me now; anger I had condemned myself to the same terrible fate as Mordue and Feathering.

"Why did you leave the book out in the library when Carvell reopened?" I asked Feathering, flares of anger bursting across my chest like flash-bangs. "Why would you want anyone else to have to go through this?"

Feathering shook her head vehemently. "I didn't. I have no idea who did. I was telling the truth when I said there were no copies in the library. Or at least there shouldn't have been."

"My copy went missing right before the final North Tower murders," Mordue said, pain etched around her eyes like a linocut. "I have no idea who has it now—or who planted it in the library for a student to find."

A kind of paranoid dread slicked up my spine.

Who would want to do this to me?

There were plenty of people I had wronged. Harris, Noémie, a thousand others I'd snapped and snarled at since arriving here. But none of them would have had the insight to do this. How would they have known about the disastrous effects of the ritual?

Unless . . .

Lottie.

She was tapped into the supernatural pulse in ways I could never understand. And I had hurt her plenty over the last few months.

What if Sister Maria had channeled her spirit through Lottie? What if she had planted the book in that terrifying sleeplike trance that kept leading her to the base of the North Tower?

But . . . *why*? Why would the dead nun's spirit want more girls to meet the same fate?

I turned to Mordue, my nose itching with the strength of the spices emanating from the sideboard. "And Renner is a dead end? He definitely doesn't have the missing pages?"

"I've visited the lighthouse every week for years. Still no answers."

Resting my elbows on the long mahogany table, I dropped my head into my hands. The life I so badly wanted for myself was disappearing. I would never be a judge. And yet that was not what concerned me the most—and nor was the idea of suffering the pain of transformation every single day of my life.

What frightened me most was a life without love. Without intimacy or affection. Without my family.

Without letting myself fall for Lottie the way I so badly wanted to.

Unless I found the answers, it would only ever be this. This room, these people. For however many months or years or decades it took for me to hurl myself from the North Tower and put an end to the misery.

Yet I had one more question. One that I'd almost forgotten through all the despair.

I raised my head and looked at them both, noticing with vague surprise that Mordue's hand was resting comfortingly on Feathering's.

"What happened to Poppy Kerr?"

There was a long, heavy silence. And then Mordue spoke. "I killed her."

Horror unfurled like gossamer insect wings in my stomach, slow and strange.

"What happened?" I asked, feeling the weight of every syllable.

Mordue let go of Feathering's pale hand and rubbed her face until mascara smeared down her cheeks. She didn't look sad or remorseful, just exhausted to her bones. "I . . . I can't." Her voice was tight and small. "Kate? Please."

Feathering climbed shakily to her feet, gripped the back of the chair she'd been sitting in, and stared up at the portrait of Sister Maria. When she spoke, her words were weighed down with sadness.

"As you know, it was the night you performed the ritual for the first time. I was already running late to meet Vanessa for her ritual—I'd been caught up helping a professor with something—and I could feel my own darkness flaring dangerously. I hurried up to the second mezzanine to use the clubhouse door behind the philosophy bookcase. That's when I saw you convulsing on the floor, the book splayed out beside you. I dashed over, planning to pull you into the clubhouse with me, but you were stronger than I thought. *Angrier* than I ever remember being. And so we fought."

My fingers went to my face of their own accord, remembering how the dark crimson felt crusted on my skin, how it made my shirt cling to the curves of my chest. "That's where my bleeding nose came from?"

Feathering nodded. "I eventually managed to knock you out. Blow to the head from the heaviest book I could find."

Fear coated my insides like soot from a chimney, cold and black and choking. "Then what happened?"

"I managed to drag you into the clubhouse without anyone seeing, then scrubbed the library floor clean of your blood. You stayed here in a locked room for a few hours, then when you started to come around, I pushed you back out through the library exit and hoped you'd find your way to your dorm. That's why your library card provided you with a time-stamped alibi. The police don't know about this secret room."

Several small mysteries were solved, but not the question I'd originally asked. "Right. But what happened to Poppy?"

Mordue's head was in her hands, shoulders quaking as she sobbed silently. Everything about the last twenty minutes had turned my stomach, and it was all I could do not to throw up.

"By the time I got you into the clubhouse and cleaned up the blood, Vanessa had gone. I'd left her waiting too long, and the darkness had taken over. She went up to the observatory, where we used to have our society meetings. By the time I sprinted up there, Poppy's body was crumpled at the bottom of the tower. I helped Vanessa back down here—with great difficulty, as she was near feral by that point. By the time the ritual brought her back to herself, she couldn't remember a thing."

So there it was.

Poppy's final moments, her unbelievable fear as she was shoved over the window ledge, her last fleeting thoughts before she went into free fall. The starburst of shattering pain as she hit the ground. Had she died on impact? Or had she lain there on the cold ground and suffered before the life in her eventually blinked out?

I shivered, goose bumps flickering up my arms and down my spine. With its stone floor and lack of light, the clubhouse was freezing. Something deep in the belly of the building dripped incessantly.

"What was Poppy doing in the observatory to begin with?" I whispered.

"Investigating," Mordue croaked. "The next morning I found her notebook stuffed in my pocket. It was full of notes on the North Tower murders."

My blood ran cold. It could so easily have been Lottie.

"What happened to the notebook?" I asked.

Mordue sniffed, wiping her nose on the back of her sleeve. "I burned it."

"You didn't give it to the police?"

"What, and incriminate myself?" Her tears had dried, and her words prickled defensively. "As much as I'd love to come clean, what would happen to us then? We can't go to a general prison with our souls still split like this. We could kill our cellmates, or our guards. We're too dangerous."

"So go to solitary," I snapped, struggling to keep the heat from my voice.

Mordue shook her head wildly. "Without the tincture, it'd be a life of eternal suffering. Can you imagine that pain, day in day out, with no escape, no way to end it for good? Literal purgatory. And it wouldn't bring Poppy back."

Something else Lottie had told me weeks ago reared in my mind. "But the police found a suicide note in Poppy's dorm." I gritted my teeth. "It was typed. Hafsah found that odd, because Poppy handwrote everything."

Mordue grimaced. "I planted it. I knew from her student record that she had a long history of depression."

I felt my lips curl in disgust. "How do you live with yourselves?"

"We know we'll go to prison eventually," Feathering said, her soft voice at odds with her harsh appearance. "But we need to bring our souls back together first. And for that we need you."

CHAPTER 61

Hafsah and I met Alice at the Grandstand to hear about the events in the North Tower. I listened to her talk about the Society for Soulless Girls with a thick, cloying horror inside me, black tar oozing between my ribs and setting around my lungs.

I had been right. Carvell was rotten to its core.

Just how deep that core went, I had yet to find out.

"So you don't know who laid the book out in the library for us to find?" Hafsah asked. Her eyes were pink and shining as she sipped at a lemonade.

Alice pursed her lips and looked at me with something like suspicion. "Actually, I wondered whether it might've been Sister Maria." She swallowed hard, a visible lump in her throat. "Through Lottie, I mean."

My stomach plummeted for a split second, until I

realized the timing didn't work. I shook my head vehemently. "No. You said you found the book in late September, but the first ruby didn't appear in my throat until the first week in October."

Alice was paler than I'd ever seen her. "But you'd been sleepwalking before that."

Heart tightening, I shook my head again, more fiercely this time. "How would that have worked? How would I have got into the library in a trance without Feathering noticing? You said yourself, she's always there."

Alice's shoulders seemed to relax a little when she realized it couldn't have been me. As though I was her last safe house, and she had been on the verge of losing it. She clasped her hand even tighter on the knife, digging the blade into the side of the wooden table. "These women . . . they're husks. They're consumed by their own pain and fear. I've just taken a look into my own future, and I . . . can't. I *can't* let my life end here."

At first I found it a little strange that *this* was what Alice was sad about—the fact that the female professors were locked away at night—rather than the revelation that Poppy was killed by the dean of the university. I'd been rocked to my core to find out Janie had killed Sam and then herself—let alone the misty, savage circumstances surrounding Dawn's and Fiona's deaths. Then the shocking and untimely murder of Poppy Kerr just meters from where she slept. Yet it seemed like Alice was brushing over the killings as though they were minor details, set dressing in the tragic play of her life.

Then again, she hadn't obsessed over the North Tower murders for as long as I had. She was still very much fixated on the fact that she and Hafsah were likely to meet the same fate if they didn't find a way to reverse this hellish ritual.

I still suspected there was something more to all of this. A bigger picture we were missing somehow.

I'd stayed quiet for the last ten minutes, listening, theorizing. I hadn't yet told Alice and Hafsah about my astral visit to the observatory, nor did I reveal the furious band of red rubies from beneath my choker. It wasn't that I was ashamed or embarrassed, or even that I doubted they would believe me. I knew they would. It was more that I wanted to let all the puzzle pieces shift and settle in my mind for a little longer before I offered them up for dissection.

I felt on the brink of understanding, as though the shadowy smudge in the middle distance was about to come into sudden, sharp focus. I was zooming out, examining not just the individual branch or tree but the woods as a whole.

Sinking into my mind palace with fingers steepled in my lap, the warm, tinkling Grandstand faded into the background, disappearing somewhere beyond the misty crags. There was something in the periphery of my memory that I felt was paramount to this whole thing, and I stayed mentally very still in the hopes of coaxing it out—or of zooming out far enough to see it.

My mind had snagged on something as I was recovering from Sister Maria's fall, sorting through everything she had shown me. It was in the way she thought about her impending exorcism:

I did not want this exorcist—this witch doctor, this con artist, to profit from my suffering, the satisfaction of a jeering crowd and ticket riches, a pamphlet about my agony as though it was cheap entertainment for the masses.

It hit the same infuriating note as *The Devil and the Divine* had, with its graphic depictions of the possessions in Loudun. Had Sister Maria guided me to that book? Was she trying to show me what had happened to her without having to *show* me?

Why? Why did she need me to know?

I suspected that it was more than just a vague sense of wanting her life to be known and understood. She wanted to be known and understood because it was relevant to the North Tower murders. It was relevant to the ritual. It was relevant to whoever the hell had stolen those pages from the soul purification book. And she wanted me to solve this thing once and for all, to break Carvell's curse before it turned any more angry women into monsters.

Make them pay.

Make who pay, Maria?

Several pieces shifted, a parting of clouds, a rearranging of shadows, revealing something that should've been obvious all along.

The why of it all.

I shot to my feet and sprinted in the direction of the Sisters of Mercy Library.

CHAPTER 62

Alice

As Lottie rushed out of the Grandstand without a word, I realized how utterly exhausted I was. The thought of following her was borderline impossible; I couldn't get my limbs to move the way they should. And yet the room felt instantly duller without her in it.

Still, I wanted to sink and sink into the delicious armchair, kick my feet up on the claw-foot coffee table, and sleep for approximately a thousand years. The fire was crackling and smelled of woodsmoke, and the whiskey in my throat burned so sweetly. There were iced cinnamon cookies in little bowls while traditional Christmas songs played in the background, and the massive fir tree in the corner shone with multicolored fairy lights and the fake gold-wrapped presents at its feet.

As I looked around the bar—at the oak-paneled parlor

room walls, the antique dartboards and marble chessboards and faded snooker tables, the enormous oil paintings of sunshine-yellow fields—it seemed to me that the whole place felt like Lottie. Warm and open and fun.

"Come on, we should humor her," said Hafsah, hauling herself up from the burgundy chesterfield sofa just as "Silent Night" started caroling through the speakers. "She thinks she's Scooby-Dooed *real* good this time." A half-hearted laugh. The bags beneath her eyes told me she was as tired as I was. Splitting your soul in two and dealing with the dramatic consequences was apparently harder than it looked.

"Fine," I sighed, draining the rest of the whiskey and placing the tumbler on a round glass side table. I felt very young and very old all at once. "But you don't have to come with me. Escape to Foxglove while you still can. At least one of us should get some rest. And you have your madhouse paper to work on, okay? For the journal." A heavy beat. "We have to hold on to the things that make us *us*. While we still can."

She nodded. "Thanks. Listen, I . . . I'm sorry. That you're the one who had to go up there tonight."

I exhaled sharply in an almost snort. "It wasn't as bad as you think. They're just like us, really."

Hafsah stared at me. "They're killers."

Nodding fearfully, I replied, "I know."

I traipsed out to the library alone.

It was violently cold outside, and my breath plumed

around me. By the time I passed through the cloister and scanned into the library it was after midnight, but Feathering was behind her desk as usual. Now that I understood the source of her angst, I no longer felt the need to slit her throat. Her stony expression gave nothing away, but I knew that just a few hundred feet away, in the secret room beside the North Tower, Mordue was undergoing the transformation in a locked room. When would Feathering complete her own ritual?

I found Lottie kneeling on the floor of the philosophy section, where Feathering had knocked me out all those months ago. She leafed furiously through a large, leather-bound volume I didn't recognize, searching for something only she understood.

"Everything all right?" I asked, flopping into the chair nearest her. Every muscle in my body ached with exhaustion.

"*There!*" Lottie exclaimed triumphantly, stabbing a title page with her forefinger.

I frowned at the oversized serif font. It read:

THE FALLACY OF FEMALE VIOLENCE
A STUDY IN DIVINE COMMAND THEORY, DEMONIC POSSESSION AND THE SIXTH DEADLY SIN

BY ALISTAIR E. DACRE

"Read," Lottie ordered me, shoving the book into my hands. She sank backward onto the ground, kicking her long legs out in front of her. I shook away a mental image of Feathering scrubbing at the old wooden floorboards to remove every last trace of my blood.

Forcing my stinging eyes to focus, I started to read. It was dense and heavy going; Dacre had an old-fashioned writing style, one that smacked of pretension. But after a few paragraphs of meandering intro, I hit the meat of the text, and my heart began to beat a little faster.

It was a philosophical essay on why women are so often violent when violence itself is an inherently male trait. Violence, Dacre posited, was fueled by testosterone, which activated the subcortical area of the brain that produces aggression. Because women produced relatively little testosterone, it followed that they should also produce relatively little violence.

He then went on to clumsily interrogate the societal, cultural and religious factors that could account for this "unnatural" phenomenon of female anger. Could divine command theory explain it? Were violent women acting according to God's will? Because God was male and thus his anger was physiologically sound? If this was the case, then surely it followed that the only acceptable place for women to exhibit anger was in spreading the Lord's message.

His conclusion was this: all angry women were either godly or possessed.

The whole essay was pathetically binary and reductive. I felt a kind of oily repulsion settle in my stomach.

Such wrath isn't very becoming of a young woman, you know.

When I looked up, Lottie was studying me intently, gauging my reaction. The cogs of my brain cranked begrudgingly into action. "I mean, why did you even read this in the first place?"

Lottie's cheeks flushed a furious red. "I found your course reading list. And I knew you thought I was stupid, so I wanted to prove you wrong by casually dropping philosophy references into conversation."

I smiled, warmed to my bones by the idea of her sneaking into the library to read philosophy books so she could prove herself to me. "Okay, let's skip over that for now, on account of how embarrassing it is for you." I held up the book, noticing distantly that my hand was shaking. I couldn't remember when I'd last eaten. "What are you thinking?"

"Right, this is going to be an almighty stretch, but hear me out?" Lottie asked.

She was intellectually streets ahead of me at this point, and yet she was still asking me to hear her out. All I managed was a nod.

"Dacre's book was published before the murders," she said, gesturing to the imprint. "So let's say Mordue then discovers the ritual book in a little shop in town, brings it back to her office and leaves it on her desk. At this point, we know that female violence in a religious setting is already a specific research interest of Dacre's. So maybe he's waiting in her office for a meeting, and he sees the title of this book about soul purification and anger and possession and religious rituals, and he's intrigued. He flips through it, finds it interesting but probably dismisses it as hokey nonsense. It's about a supernatural soul-splitting ritual, after all.

"But then, over the next few weeks or months, there's a change in Mordue. Like you, she must have always been tightly coiled. Always *simmering* with anger, but then suddenly she's placid and cool. Dacre wonders if maybe she performed the ritual—and, impossibly, that it *worked*. He starts to study her movements, his interactions with her, tries to fit it into his own quite frankly batshit musings on divine command theory and demonic possession. He doesn't want this incredible research opportunity to end, so he tears the reversal pages from the book."

From her seat on the floor, Lottie looked up at me expectantly, almost nervously, and I was momentarily stunned by her brilliance. She had made connections that seemed so obvious now that she'd made them, but that I would never have put together no matter how long I agonized over it.

Really, it should have been me who pieced it together. Dacre had even requested to be my mentor. It was right there from the start. And yet it was Lottie who had figured out that Dacre packaged his own disdain for angry women into a religious missive, and was now exploiting it to further his own career, to make money, to raise his profile. He was no better than the exorcists and witch doctors of

Loudun—or the male writers who turned those stories into cheap entertainment for the masses.

Lottie's brain was fierce and bright, and loath as I was to admit it, I was jealous. Not just of her brain, but of her goodness, her kindness, her sunny smile. That easy zeal. That fearlessness.

I was jealous, or something else entirely.

"So you think Dacre still has the reversal ritual pages?" I asked, barely allowing myself the glimmer of hope.

She tilted her jaw up, eyes shimmering. "I think he has much more than that."

CHAPTER 63

Lottie

By the time Alice and I got back to our dorm, exhaustion tugged not just at my eyes and limbs but also at my heart. I felt emotionally wrung out from the mortal fear I'd had for Alice, and from my experience with Sister Maria. The adrenaline from the Dacre theory and the burn from the ruby noose around my neck were all that kept me awake, kept me rooted in reality.

"What a day," Alice mumbled, tossing her coat over the back of her desk chair.

"Yeah," I said. "What a day."

She turned to face me, leaning against her bunk. "What now?"

"Honestly?" I swallowed hard. "Sleep. Sleep is what now. The rest we'll figure out in the morning."

She studied my face, her gaze flitting from my eyes to my lips to my choker and back again. "You know what I loved?"

"What's that?" No part of the night we'd just endured seemed an appropriate guess.

She bit her lip, her front teeth nibbling into her scar, and then said, "Forget it."

"No, what?"

A half laugh, then a shake of the head. "You'll think I'm soft."

I pulled my hoodie over my head and tossed it to the floor. "There are worse things to think."

"Not for me."

I sighed and rolled my eyes, but there was no tension in it. "I promise not to think you're soft, Alice."

Alice looked at my newly bare arms, my hands, my choker once again. Finally, my eyes. Hers shone in the lamplight. "That night I shared your bed. It was just . . . it was nice. It didn't really feel weird. I don't often feel comfortable with people."

My stomach did a funny twist. She hadn't said the moment was "nice" at first. She'd said she loved it. The knowledge stoked those unfamiliar embers deep in my belly. I had the sudden urge to cross over to her, to wrap my arms around her and bury my face in her neck. To find that kind of warm physical comfort again. But I didn't. Because it was Alice, and I might get stabbed.

"I felt the same," I admitted carefully. For some

reason, this conversation felt more vulnerable than any of the trauma we'd been dragged through hand in hand. "Despite the fact I'd just given you my blood as part of a sinister soul ritual and then listened through a door as you carved into yourself with a knife. Maybe I just don't scare easily."

Alice smiled. "You don't. It's impressive. The way you've handled this whole thing . . . it's like you have no fear."

I gave a little snort laugh. "I was scared of you, to begin with."

"Good." She nodded. "That was my intention."

As charged with emotion as the conversation was, one thing kept stealing my attention—the searing rubies around my neck. I knew I had to show her.

"And I'm scared . . . I'm scared of this." I reached my hands behind my neck and undid the choker's delicate silver clasp.

As it fell away, Alice gasped, clapping a hand to her mouth. Then she closed the gap between us, so her face was right up close to mine. I could smell the late-night whiskey on her breath. She dropped her hand from her lips and traced a finger along the brutal necklace. I managed to suppress the shiver, but not the awkward lump bobbing in my throat.

She pulled away, looking like she might cry. "I—I feel like this is all because of me. You're hurt because of me."

"No," I said fiercely. "This started happening before you and I got close."

She raised an eyebrow, still every inch the cartoon villain. "You and I are close?"

"Oh, piss off." I pushed her backward playfully, my hand on her clavicle. "You know we are."

She started to laugh, but it died on her tongue. Instead she gazed out the loose-framed window at the tower that had tortured us both. Then she looked back to me with a newfound urgency, and something else, something softer, something gentler. Something shimmering and ephemeral. Something that carried a magnetic charge.

"Lottie . . . ," she whispered, and for a split second, I thought . . . I don't know what I thought. That she might close the distance between us. That maybe, just maybe, I wasn't the only one feeling the burn of those embers. She'd hated me on sight, all those months ago, but surely she felt this too. Something rich and soft knotting between us.

But instead, the black shutters went down behind her eyes with a dangerous flash, and she rasped, "Help."

No, I found myself almost praying. *Please, no. Not now.*

Alice nearly sank to her knees but managed to clamber up onto the bunk before her back started to arch with agony. She held out her pale wrists to restrain at the same time as a long, ear-shattering scream tore out of her chest.

Despite the exhaustion, despite the distress, I sprang to action.

Cuffing her to the bed and force-feeding her the tincture we'd already prepared had never felt more devastating.

This girl, who was soft at heart, who was both the vast, dark woods and the glorious light of a full moon, who was angry at all the thousand tiny ways she'd been hurt in her life.

The moment we had almost shared, stolen by a world that would punish her endlessly for that anger.

It was too soon. Not even ten days since the last ritual.

Alice was almost out of time.

I thought of her fingertips on my neck as she fastened the choker clasp, of the way she'd told Torquil the book-seller how smart I was, of the way she'd defended my honor to the hockey player who nearly killed me. I thought of all the unexpected ways in which she had become important to me, and all the ways in which I'd failed to save her.

When the monster started talking with its hoarse, awful timbre, detailing all the ways in which it wanted to kill me, I didn't stay for long. I wrapped myself in Alice's houndstooth coat, drinking in the red wine and rosemary scent of her, and left Willowood with a singular purpose in mind.

I'd had enough. My Dacre theory may have just been a theory, but it was the only one I had.

Now I needed evidence, and I would stop at nothing to find it.

CHAPTER 64

Alice

I woke up from the worst transformation yet to find Lottie holding my hand.

The touch was so warm and pleasurable that for a few minutes, I didn't let on that I was awake. I lay in my bunk with my eyes half-closed, listening to the sound of her breathing, the gentle patter of icy sleet on the window.

Last night, something had almost happened between us. And it fucking terrified me, for so many reasons.

First, because of Noémie. I had let myself feel these things for her, and she had left. And it was only now, with distance from the situation, that I really realized how much it had hurt. How much of a chasm she'd left in my heart. What if Lottie left too? She was human sunshine, and I was the deep, dark woods. She was bound to grow tired of the shade.

Then there was the obvious fact that I was a monster.

A cold psychopath still roamed free in my mind, leaving ragged flaps of the veil blowing in the breeze. I thought calmly of shoving Dacre from the North Tower observatory, imagined the sickening thud of a body splattering over the cobbles below, how good it would feel to exact revenge for something he may not have even done. I thought of the girls who had mocked me in high school, and imagined taking a knife to their skin, how satisfying it would be to cause death by a thousand cuts. I thought these things with a casualness that disturbed me to my core.

Because these were not just hot, fleeting impulses as they once were—like when a cyclist would swerve in front of my car, and in that split second I'd picture ramming into him with my bumper. These thoughts were cool and enduring, surviving long beyond the heat of a moment.

And now the transformations were closing in, and I didn't know how much more lucid time I'd have before I became like Feathering and Mordue, gritting my teeth through each day until I could take myself away to a locked room and go through it all over again. How long had there been between this one and the last? A week? The walls were closing in like something out of a nightmare. Soon there would be nothing left of who I used to be.

So I couldn't let Lottie get too close to me. If I hurt her, I would never forgive myself.

Still, I could indulge myself this single sweet moment.

Her hand in mine, sleet on the window, and something pillowy and peace-shaped in my chest.

I heard her shift in the desk chair she was perched on, and then felt warm, soft lips pressing against my knuckles, so lightly it threatened to unravel me.

I couldn't let this happen. I opened my eyes and pulled my hand away.

"Morning," she murmured, stretching her arms above her head and cracking her shoulder joints. "Are you ready to bring your soul back together?"

Frowning, I propped myself up on my elbows. "What? How?"

"I will tell you," she said. "But first, Hafsah."

"Shit, Hafsah!"

Lottie rubbed her bleary, red-rimmed eyes. "Don't worry, I went to check on her last night. I stayed with her until it was over. But we should take her some coffee."

Hafsah was propped up in bed when we arrived with three lattes and several cold slices of toast from the dining hall. There was a stack of manga on her bedside table, and she was leafing through one volume looking thoroughly exhausted.

"I might never leave this room again," she said, taking the coffee from Lottie and groaning as she sipped. "I'm just going to stay here and read comics about monster sex. Just let Dark Hafsah come and go as she pleases."

"Dark Hafsah may not be around for much longer." Lottie stuffed a hand into the back pocket of her jeans and pulled out a flash drive. "I got this from Dacre's office last night."

I frowned. "What is it?"

"I'm not a hundred percent sure. I took it to the library and slotted it into a computer, but it's encrypted. But check out the label."

Written in ink on a white label, in Dacre's clearly recognizable handwriting, was one word: SOCIETY.

"*The* society?" I murmured. Then, a vivid memory came back to me, and I kicked myself for not recalling it sooner. "Fuck, I saw Dacre and Le Conte on the night Poppy died! They were walking with their heads together as though they were discussing something private. I remember thinking it was weird they were out so late."

"I feel like I'm missing several links here," Hafsah said slowly.

Lottie quickly filled Hafsah in on the findings from the library while I nursed my hot, sweet coffee.

"And Alice saw them together on the night Poppy died. Which means . . . hang on," Lottie said. She grabbed the investigation notebook from her desk and uncapped her blue fountain pen. "What time would that have been?"

I racked my brain. "Maybe five minutes after midnight?"

She nodded, scribbling the time and the note on a blank page. Then she stared at it, as though trying to slot it into the picture slowly growing in her mind. "What could they have been doing? We already know Mordue killed

Poppy—and we're one hundred percent going to the police about that once her soul is intact. So how else could Dacre and Le Conte fit into it? Unless it was just a coincidental midnight stroll about an unrelated private matter . . . do you think they might be boning?"

Clicking her fingers rhythmically, Hafsah said, "Le Conte's research area . . . it could fit with Dacre's. In our first lecture, he said something like, 'We natural theologians provide arguments for the existence of God based on reason and rationality, and where better to do so than a former convent?' Remember that, Al?"

"First of all, we're not going to be doing 'Al,'" I said. Like a sudden burst of light, something Feathering told me in the clubhouse came back to me. "Oh! And Kate said last night that she was late to meet Mordue on the night Poppy died because she'd been delayed helping a professor with something. That's pretty weird given it was midnight. What if Dacre or Le Conte was intentionally holding her up?"

Lottie nodded slowly, then very quickly. "Because by then they knew Mordue needed Feathering to perform her ritual at the same time each night. They wanted to see what would happen if the ritual couldn't take place at the right time."

Hafsah squinted as though blinded by something. "Why would Dacre want to see that?"

Lottie's eyes were ablaze with excitement. "Because he's studying the society. This is all part of some wider experiment on female violence. He's old and crusty and almost irrelevant in the field of philosophy. Such unprecedented research would bring him back to the forefront. *And* validate his hideous views on women as a whole."

I nodded passionately. "It fits. He saw me snap with anger when I first arrived, and literally days later he chose me as his mentee, even though I'd requested another professor. He delivered the news to Le Conte himself." I shuddered with retrospective understanding. "He must've known I was a prime candidate for the society. I wouldn't be surprised if he knew I attacked Harris too." I pictured him and Le Conte salivating over my actions and felt sick with loathing. "And if all this is true . . . I bet *he* planted the book in the library, hoping I would find it since I was the only student going to the library so early in the semester."

Lottie gasped. "Remember when I was waiting for you outside Dacre's seminar room, and the rubies were thrumming so hard they were making me gag? It was most intense when he was leading us to the nurse's office, and it eased off almost as soon as he left me there. I think Sister Maria was trying to warn me about him." She held two fingers to her throat. "Sorry, babes. I should've listened."

I laughed despite the situation. Only Lottie could find herself possessed by the spirit of a wrathful nun and call her "babes."

There were still a few threads left hanging—like Le Conte's possible involvement—but it had started to feel like we were nearing a conclusion.

I picked up the flash drive. "So what do you think is on here?" At that point, I was rapidly beginning to trust Lottie's instincts over my own.

Fiddling with the zipper on her hoodie, she said, "My thinking is that he's fully aware of what the Society for Soulless Girls has been up to. If my theory is correct and he's been watching Mordue for all these years, then he's bound to have kept close enough tabs on her to know where she goes every night. So maybe this flash drive contains notes on all the society's members. Or maybe . . ." She bit her bottom lip, and it flushed dark purple. "Maybe it's surveillance."

My blood ran cold. Mordue had told me there weren't any security cameras on campus, but that didn't mean they didn't exist. What if they were hidden? Worse, what if they were unofficial—installed by Dacre for his own private use?

What if Dacre had seen everything that happened in the library when I first performed the ritual? In the clubhouse when Feathering had dragged me in unconscious? In the observatory when Mordue had pushed Poppy to her death?

If he had footage of all that, and he hadn't turned it over to the police, it meant he had his own agenda. Lottie's theory fit that agenda perfectly.

But these were several big ifs, based on nothing but academic theory.

I pulled my coat tighter around me. I was still freezing from the night before. "What do we do now?"

"Well, the flash drive is encrypted, so that's a dead end for now." Lottie tucked her heels up onto the chair and hugged her knees to her chest. "I think we need to focus on getting those missing ritual pages back first."

"If Dacre still has them," I pointed out.

Lottie pursed her lips. "When I flipped through the calendar on his desk, I saw he's meeting 'the Chamber' tonight at a pub in town. The Red Lion. I don't know what the chamber is, exactly, but it could mean an assembly or council. A regulatory body. What if the thing they're regulating is *us*?"

My stomach churned at the thought.

"It's a stretch, but we should go," said Lottie definitively. "Confront him, if the opportunity arises."

I shook my head at her, but not in a disdainful way, more in disbelief. "You really do just barrel into situations without any regard for your own safety, don't you?"

She grinned, displaying white, slightly overlapping teeth and the two deep dimples in her cheeks. "I have my murderous goth to protect me."

My stomach clenched at this, but I disguised it with a smile so tight it pulled at my scar. "How *did* you get the flash drive from Dacre's office, anyway?"

"The old crank always has his window wedged slightly open. For Salem, remember? He props it up with a thesaurus."

I stared at her. "His office is on the second floor."

Another broad smile. "Drainpipes."

CHAPTER 65

Lottie

The Red Lion was a low-ceilinged old man's pub. The carpet had a red floral pattern stained with decades of spilled dark ale, and the tables were ring-marked and scratched. There were dartboards and a pool table, a little DJ booth with a frosted glass panel around it, and a slightly raised stage with dirty black floorboards. The air was thick with cigarette smoke and an unnamed body odor that made my stomach turn.

It didn't seem the type of place an upper-middle-class university lecturer like Dacre would frequent, but perhaps the incongruity was the point. Nobody would expect to find him here, and so he was free to conduct his potentially sinister meetings in peace.

The car ride there had been hell. With a full noose of rubies around my neck, the lasso-stomach feeling was so intense I bent at the waist with agony, as though I was being sawed in half. My head exploded with white-silver sprays of stars, like the ones above the observatory in Sister Maria's visions. I heard myself scream as though from the end of a long, dark tunnel, and then I passed out. When I woke up, Alice was stroking my hair.

"Calm down, babes," I muttered to Sister Maria. "We're on the case." Alice seemed to find this laugh-worthy.

The chamber session appeared to have already begun by the time we arrived at the Red Lion. Dacre was nowhere to be seen, but there was a private function room at the rear of the pub that rumbled with men's voices and low laughter. Alice, Hafsah and I parked up at the table nearest the entrance—partly so that we could confront Dacre when he left, partly so that every time the door opened, the influx of fresh air would dissipate some of the stale smoke.

I ordered us three pints of cider and black currant, which we nursed in our dingy corner.

As I slid into the booth beside Alice, I felt an urge to wrap an arm around her shoulders or lay a palm on her thigh; something intimate and familiar. The moment right before her last transformation played over in my mind on a frantic loop—the charge in the air, the heat of our bodies, how I longed to press mine against hers. I'd never understood the appeal of tongue-kissing, of the clashing of teeth, of nibbling on exposed necks and roving hands over the peaks and planes of another body. When I saw it on TV, it left me entirely cold, but now I felt that burn of desire whenever I was around her.

Those fucking silk pajamas.

So I was definitely not asexual, but I had no idea what I was instead. Wolfesexual?

It wasn't just raw longing, either. The urge to wrap an arm around her came from a far deeper place. It was romantic, and protective, and, if I was being truly honest with myself, a little possessive.

"What do you think they're doing in there?" Alice asked, staring at the door of the back room.

"Honestly, I'm not sure," I admitted, giving my head a shake. "There's a chance Dacre is acting as a lone wolf, and this is just an innocent game of poker or something. But there's also a chance these men are in on the whole sinister thing. What you said about Le Conte and his theology research . . . I don't know. I just have a hunch that this is all connected. It's the word 'chamber' that rattles me."

The rubies in my throat throbbed like a wound.

Where was the bone-deep desire to solve these mysteries coming from? Was it still from watching my parents mourn Janie? Or had it become something else entirely, borne of the centuries-old wrath of a hotheaded nun?

Or did I just want to save Alice?

Either way, I would solve this it if it killed me.

I strained my ears for anything that might float through the walls, but I was out of luck. I had just about been able to pick out Dacre's voice from the bar, but the walls of the old building were thick, and I couldn't be certain. I had better luck from the ladies' loos, however, which were back-to-back with the function room. Hunched over a toilet without a seat, with my ear pressed to the wall, I got much clearer snatches of conversation:

"Ritual."

"Feathering."

"Hysteria."

"Devil."

And then, finally, the one that made me see red, "Wolfe."

Alice. They were talking about Alice, in the same breath as the devil.

Then, clearer than all the other voices—perhaps he was seated closest to the bathroom wall—I heard Dacre. "This is all evidence that the anger of females is a plague to be eradicated. Curse the society, the culture, that gave it credibility. It should never have been afforded free rein. It must be purged."

There was a great burst of heat in my ruby necklace that brought me to my knees on the filthy tiles.

Pure, unfettered fury; not just mine but Sister Maria's too.

She was the devil because they made her so.

I thought of angry women exorcised on stages, burned at the stake as witches, strapped down to metal tables and tortured with electrodes in private asylums. I thought of all the women I knew who'd been called hysterical for daring to raise their voices.

I will make this right, I thought, with a desperation that robbed my lungs of air.

The scorch mark in my neck settled into an almost pleasant pulse of warmth, as though Sister Maria was saying, *Thank you, thank you, thank you,* and I vowed to do her justice. To do them all justice.

Around an hour later, the session was adjourned, and the men filed out of the room. I recognized Le Conte, as well as a tall, black-whiskered man I was sure was on the board of governors. He'd attended Mordue's chapel address after Poppy was killed. He'd listened to the dean's trite sentiments and barefaced lies just like the rest of us, and he hadn't said a word.

As the men started to file out, Le Conte offered Alice and Hafsah a nod of recognition as though he hadn't just been discussing them in a filthy back room. If he was at all suspicious about why we were there, he didn't show it, although he was surely aware this was not a regular student haunt. The others followed him, shuffling arms into black wool coats and exchanging inanities about the muffled snow falling on the street.

Dacre, however, stayed at the bar, resting his elbow on the sticky varnished wood and leaning over to talk to the blond barmaid. She was young and slim, and from her expression looked like she'd much rather he wasn't there.

There was a wooden *thunk* just to my right, and I swiveled to see that Alice had withdrawn her penknife from her pocket and slammed it blade-first into the rickety table. Her face was paper white with rage as she stared at Dacre with a red-tinged glare. She stood up suddenly, knocking her almost-empty pint glass over. I grabbed her wrist and yanked her back down.

"Stop. You can't kill him until we have the missing pages." I swallowed the addition of *or even after that*. I had to give her hope of a release for her murderous rage. "Let me handle this."

As I approached the bar, Dacre didn't look up—he was too engaged in his conversation with the barmaid. I cleared my throat.

"Professor Dacre?"

He looked up irritably. "Can't you see I'm talking to—"

His vexation vanished in an instant when he saw what I was brandishing in my hand: the flash drive labeled SOCIETY.

I smiled sweetly. "Perhaps we'd better talk in private."

CHAPTER 66

Alice

The private function room smelled of stale beer and even staler academics. Dacre paced up and down the faded patterned carpet with an expression I both recognized and feared: that of a cornered animal who might lash out at any minute.

Despite there being three of us and one of him, I was afraid. Because even though I'd let the cold murderer in my soul loose, and even though I'd have no qualms over hurting him, I still didn't have a clue how to fight. How to physically overpower someone twice my size, twice my strength.

What if he attacked Lottie? How would I protect her?

My fingers closed even tighter around the smooth handle of my knife. We had one thing going for us, and that was the element of surprise. Dacre hadn't come to this chamber meeting expecting a confrontation, and so he likely was not armed.

Not armed, I thought bitterly. *His entire body is a weapon.*

As he paced, his eyes kept flitting to me, and something in his skittish expression told me we were bang on the money. He knew how dangerous I was, which meant he'd been watching me. He'd been watching the society.

But he didn't know how much we knew—after all, the flash drive was encrypted. All he knew was that we were suspicious enough to steal it in the first place. He still had plausible deniability.

With her usual bravado, Lottie took control of the situation. "You have something we want. And we have something you want."

Dacre sneered. "Oh yes? And what would that be?" He was shooting for condescending but landed somewhere closer to panic.

Hafsah stepped forward, gripping the back of the nearest chair so hard her knuckles turned bone white. "Ten years ago, you tore some pages out of a book outlining a soul-splitting ritual. We need those pages. We'll give you your highly incriminating flash drive back in return." A beat. "Obstruction of justice is a crime, just as an FYI."

"I have no idea what you're talking about," Dacre replied haughtily, but faint spots of pink had appeared on his cheeks.

Lottie grinned. "Yes, you do. Because you wouldn't be in this room with us otherwise." She wagged the drive in his direction, and her deliberate taunting set me on edge. She was waving a red flag at a bull. A bull who had a *lot* to lose if this situation didn't turn out the way he hoped.

Dacre took the bait.

He lunged straight at Lottie, so fast none of us had time to react, and grabbed her by the throat, slamming her against the peeling wallpaper. She dropped the flash drive in shock, eyes bulging, mouth opening soundlessly.

"Listen here, you little *rat*," he hissed at Lottie, face contorted in a gargoyle snarl. "If you don't keep your nose out of—"

She could not breathe.

I pulled out my knife and started forward, but then, with a howl, Dacre yanked his hands from Lottie's neck as though he'd been burned.

Lottie raised a hand to her throat and gasped.

The black choker had been torn away, and the rubies beneath seared red hot and ember-like.

Dacre's hands were already blistering, the skin bubbling and melting. He stared down at them and moaned a low, terrible moan.

In Dacre's split second of recovery, I leaped toward his back and stabbed him as hard as I could in one shoulder.

Pleasure rolled through me like thunder.

He roared like a monster, and swiveled to face me, his expression towering with rage.

With a guttural growl, I tried to stab him again and again, but he held my wrists with minimal effort.

Just like Chris had.

Only this time, I was not alone.

Hafsah picked up the chair she was gripping and swung it hard at Dacre's head. He dropped my wrists and fell backward to the ground, beast-like eyes glaring up at me with the hatred of a thousand scorned gods. But he was also dazed, if only for a few precious moments.

Now or never.

Kill him kill him kill him, said the coldest part of my soul, and I had to fight the urge with everything I had left. If I killed Dacre, we'd never get the pages back—and I'd spend the rest of my life in prison, in the solitary purgatory Mordue was so afraid of.

And yet the veil was torn, and the psychopath roamed free, and I no longer had the energy to resist.

I wanted Dacre's blood more than I wanted anything. More than I wanted to live.

I lunged, knife held high above my head, the real Alice watching from afar with a kind of detached, existential horror.

I was going to do it. I was going to kill.

Until I caught Lottie's wide, pleading eyes, the oceanic depth of them, and something poignant and rich passed between us, and for a moment, just for a moment, the surge of love outshone the feral hatred in my heart.

It was fleeting and transient, but it was more powerful

than the hate, than the violence, than the anger. It stopped me dead, stealing the breath from my lungs.

That was what I wanted more than being alive. What I had always wanted, at the very heart of myself.

To love and be loved—for who I really was.

If I killed Dacre, I would never have that.

I took a ragged step back, and Lottie all but collapsed with relief. Hafsah let out a strangled sob. The murderer in my brain cried out for blood, and I knew I couldn't fend off the desire for much longer. I twitched forward again, preparing to have the same existential debate with myself all over again.

Kill him it'll be worth it nothing could feel better, do it for Lottie he hurt her he hurt her so bad—

Then came a voice from the doorway.

A frightened, female voice.

"Dad? What's going on?"

I swiveled on my heel, and a pit opened in my gut.

It was the barmaid, shattered pint glass around her feet.

She was Dacre's *daughter.*

The horror on her face as she took in the situation should have cleaved me in two, but it didn't.

The cold psychopath in me saw the final gambit before my rational brain could protest.

Swiftly as I could, I pivoted away from Dacre and tore across the room toward the barmaid, grabbing her from behind and cupping one hand over her mouth. I lifted the penknife to her throat. Squirming in my arms, she started to scream, but I clamped down on her mouth even tighter.

"Leave her alone!" Dacre bellowed, clambering desperately to his dazed feet, and I wished he was dead, I wished I had killed him, I wished I had felt his warm blood spurt across my face as the blade went in, I wished—

Focus.

"One more step and I'll slit her throat," I growled, pressing the knife harder against the delicate skin of his daughter's neck. Dacre stopped in his tracks. I shot him a meaningful stare. "You know I will."

And he did. He knew I was a Soulless Girl. He knew what I was capable of.

His breath hitched in his throat, and his eyes widened with fear. "Jess. Jess, don't move."

Despite Jess's whimpering, Lottie did not flinch at my crude display of cruelty. She just massaged her own throat, grabbed the flash drive from the floor and hoarsely muttered, "Give us the reversal ritual or your daughter dies."

A perverse impulse to laugh came over me, and it took all my willpower to tamp down the temptation. There was just something so hilarious about hearing literal human sunshine issue a death threat.

But Lottie didn't need to sound convincing, because *I was.*

And Dacre knew it.

His cheeks turned beetroot red with anger, and spittle

foamed at the corners of his sagging mouth. He kept raising his hands to go to Jess, then reminding himself she would die if he tried to save her, and in those few moments he was just an old man again, an old man scared for his daughter's life. Her hot, wet tears slid over my hand.

The place in my chest where guilt should have lived was empty.

Realizing his back was against the wall, Dacre's shoulders sagged. "There are scans of the pages on the drive. The password is 'zygaena.'"

The name chimed in my memory: the same breed of moth I'd first performed the ritual with.

Dacre had been watching from the start.

After waiting until Lottie and Hafsah were safely out the door with the flash drive, I shoved Jess toward Dacre with a final, hateful growl. She folded into his chest with a heaving sob.

The glare he threw in my direction would have terrified me, but I knew there was no way he could kill all three of us. Especially not in front of his daughter.

Instead he drawled, "If you go to the police about the contents of that drive I'll go to the police about the fact that you assaulted me and my daughter."

With a smile I knew was ugly, I snarled, "Don't worry. We'll all get what we deserve in the end."

CHAPTER 67

Lottie

After haring back to Carvell, we went straight to the library and dragged three chairs around one of the computers that had a USB port.

The password worked. Alice seemed outraged by this.

My neck still ached—not just from the rubies but also from Dacre's thick fingers squeezing all the air from my windpipe. I didn't scare easily, but I had to admit, I'd been scared then. Still nowhere near as afraid as I was in the beat before Alice decided not to kill Dacre. If she'd done it, she'd have spent the rest of her life behind bars. I would not have survived seeing her like that.

The first and most important thing we found on the drive was a JPEG file named RITUAL PAGES. It was a scanned version of the missing pages from Renner's book.

Alice nodded stoically as though afraid to get her hopes up. There was no guarantee that the reversal would work, but Renner's research had been flawless thus far. Even if Alice wasn't optimistic, I was.

"There's an end in sight," Hafsah murmured, a glazed expression on her face. "Everything is not lost. I might get *me* back. Alien brain and all." A small laugh. "I didn't realize how much I loved my pinball thoughts until I lost them."

Sorting through the rest of the documents took time, but we did so diligently. The fury built in me with every file we opened.

What we discovered was that I was right: Dacre's "chamber," mostly made up of male professors from Carvell, had been founded eleven years ago—before the original murders. From the impassioned manifesto written by Dacre himself, it seemed their ultimate goal was to return women to the social and cultural chains we so desperately belonged in. To reduce us to concubines. And the way they wanted to do so was to prove that a woman left unfettered is a woman feral.

There were notes upon notes upon notes from weekly meetings, transcripts of conversations with Feathering, Mordue and the other ritual victims, followed by reams and reams of annotations, hypotheses and further experimental ideas—all to prove that female violence was both fundamentally unnatural and existentially dangerous.

There were bone-chilling suggestions for how to neutralize female anger for good, using a barbaric surgical procedure not dissimilar to a lobotomy. There was an account of how Le Conte had poisoned Renner with an archaic tincture that wrought madness—all to keep the reversal ritual hidden from Mordue and the society.

Worst of all, there were long-range photographs of the original North Tower murders. There was the moment Janie threw Sam from the observatory. A few days later, there were the vague silhouettes of the society members midepisode, hitting and clawing and kicking each other senseless. And there was Janie climbing onto the window ledge in the few dreadful moments before she jumped. In that photo, she was in the tower alone.

Why had they kept this evidence from the police?

A few moments later, the question answered itself.

Dated a week later, there were pictures of a limp-limbed Fiona being shoved by a faceless shadow; moments later, Dawn. But in the latter photo, the silhouette of a familiar profile could be seen, illuminated just enough by the stark moonlight to remove any doubt.

I gasped. "Son of a—"

It was *Dacre*.

"Mother*fucker*," whispered Hafsah.

"No, yeah, I should've killed him," Alice groaned.

It was him. Not the society. Not Mordue.

Him.

He hadn't just been observing the deaths from a distance. He hadn't just been twisting them for academic gain. He'd been orchestrating them himself.

Dacre was the killer.

He had murdered innocent girls to prove that angry women were fundamentally dangerous. To give substantial cause to implement the "cure" for anger he had outlined: a lobotomy designed to carve out something essential and human in order to keep us compliant.

"I want to gut him like a fish." Hafsah grimaced. "With the bluntest knife I can find. And a teaspoon."

I looked to Alice for a reaction, but she had gone white as snow. The revelation was likely ten times as shocking for her; Dacre was her mentor. She had sat in his office just feet from him and told him that she wanted to be a judge. And the whole time, he'd been a killer. Had he still felt Dawn's throat squirming beneath his hands while he was talking to Alice? Could he still hear Fiona's screams in the darkest recesses of his mind?

Finally, there was a folder of more-recent video footage. Low-quality CCTV cameras rigged up in some dim rafter of the observatory, recording Poppy's final moments as she grappled fearfully with Dacre.

Not Mordue. Dacre.

It was always him. From the very beginning to the hideous end.

He had pushed Poppy from the North Tower in a bid

to make it look like suicide—a story Mordue had inadvertently corroborated with her planted note.

"*Why?*" I was almost breathless with fury. "Why kill Poppy when he'd gotten away with so much already?"

"Didn't you say that Poppy had been investigating the murders?" Hafsah asked Alice. "Maybe she'd figured it all out, and he knew she was going to go to the police. And maybe Mordue didn't read Poppy's notebook before she burned it."

"Yes, that," said Alice bitterly. "But also because with every passing day, with every step forward for women, he felt himself becoming more and more irrelevant. His views more and more outdated. And he wanted to prove that we had it right decades ago. Centuries ago. That it was wrong to ever give us the rights we have now. That we should be stripped back to silent vessels for their children."

I could barely watch the footage, my stomach clenching like a fist as Poppy was hurled from an open arch by a man she should have been able to trust to keep her safe.

I'm going to make them pay for this, I told myself, the blood roaring in my chest and ears, and as I thought it, as I let the ferocity of the desire grow in me like a guiding light, I felt some invisible grip on me loosen, a long-held sigh exhaled, a hundred years of suffering finally passing through some liminal boundary.

Sister Maria's rubies didn't vanish immediately, but they lost all their heat. They no longer felt too tight around my throat, no longer felt like a noose that could kill me at any second. The roots retreated, albeit slowly. I knew, somehow, that they wouldn't be there much longer.

Bye, babes, I thought, knowing I wouldn't miss the salty old bitch in the slightest.

"It wasn't us," said Hafsah numbly. Her whole body had gone rigid, as though moving a single inch would somehow shatter the truth.

Alice's emotions finally surged through, and she collapsed forward. "It wasn't Mordue. It . . . it wasn't the society. I can't wait to tell them. I can't wait to . . . It wasn't *them*. They're innocent." A meek little sob. "*We're* innocent."

Wanting to go to her but fearful of intruding on a private moment, I fought the urge to throw my arms around her. She was innocent. And I didn't know which of us was more relieved.

After she'd been silent for a few minutes, I felt Alice's fingers lace through mine, hers cool and elegant, mine clammy and calloused from hockey. I gave her hand a squeeze and gazed out the arched library window at the vast, dark woods outside.

Hafsah looked down at our interwoven hands and smirked knowingly. Silently excusing herself, she grabbed her bags and took off toward the exit. Probably to cathartically rail someone named Brick. I smiled to myself. I'd grown very fond of our local slutty alien.

"This is going to make a hell of a story," I said to Alice,

with a half-strangled laugh. I dimly realized that I was crying too. For everyone who was lost, and everyone we still might save.

"Yeah," Alice snorted, her eyes streaming with tears. I turned back to her. She still looked so beautiful: wine-red hair flipped over in a wild wave, cat-eye liner slightly smudged around the edges. "And I think you should write it."

"What?" I asked.

"Come on." Her hand squeezed mine. "I see how you look at those stacks of true crime books on your desk. *You* should be the one to tell our story. Let's take the power back from the exorcists. Let's *own* the demons in our throats." A defiant upward tilt of her chin. "I'm tired of feeling like a monster."

"You were never a monster, Alice," I whispered. "Not even close."

"No?"

"*No.*" My voice hitched. "Do you remember a couple of weeks ago, when I told you I'd never wanted to kiss anyone before until . . . ?"

She gave the slightest nod, with the general expression of someone who's just stopped breathing.

"It was until I met you."

Her eyes brightened so suddenly it was like the sun coming out from behind the clouds.

For all the times I went barreling into situations without fear, I suddenly felt extremely vulnerable. I had never put myself out there like this before. Hell, I'd never even entertained the concept of romance before, let alone declared it in such a brazen way. It felt like every nerve in my body was standing to attention.

My voice thrummed with quiet electricity as I said, "Do you feel the same?"

Please feel the same.

Another tiny nod as a tear slid down her cheek. "This semester ostensibly should have been the worst time of my life," she said softly, "yet some of my all-time best moments are tucked inside it. Because of you."

My heart burst into a thousand glittering pieces.

Then, cupping her pixie jaw with my free hand, I leaned in and kissed her; the softest brush, my lips against her scar, the salt of her tears, and the gentlest moan escaping her throat. Everything in me sang. A slow, sad ballad, but a song nonetheless.

"I want you to write the story with me," I whispered. "It's yours too."

She swallowed hard, lips still inches from mine. "Okay. I trust you."

We kissed again, and it was so deep and so right, and yet I was terrified all over again—just for very different reasons.

I was falling in love with Alice Wolfe.

"Hey," I said softly, pulling my phone from my pocket. "I just need to make a quick call, okay?"

Alice nodded, wiping her cheeks on the back of her

sleeve as I walked toward the enormous Christmas tree in the center of the library.

My dad picked up on the second ring.

"Lottie," he said, voice gruff with emotion. "Is everything all right?"

"Yeah, Dad, everything's all right." I swallowed hard. "It's just . . . I have some news about Janie."

CHAPTER 68

Alice

Gathering the ingredients for the reversal tincture was, for the most part, simple. Allium and hyacinth, thyme leaves and chestnut, broom and baby's breath.

Elderflower cordial. The blood of a moth. A ground-up cocoon.

And finally, the blood not of someone you hurt, but someone who loves your soul as it truly is.

At first I was concerned I would have to go home and somehow try to wound my own mother, until I realized—or rather hoped beyond all logic or reason—that the answer was simpler.

Lottie and I were in our dorm, preparing the botanicals on my desk, when I finally plucked up the courage to ask. After we'd turned over the flash drive to the police, Dacre had been arrested that morning, boarding a ferry to Amsterdam, and all the other members of the chamber were being rounded up for questioning. We were due at the police station the next day to give our statements. But first, we had a reversal ritual to perform.

"I'm really sorry, but I need your blood again," I said matter-of-factly. I was wrapped up in a cashmere jumper, yet I still couldn't stop shivering—whether from the winter chill or the vulnerability of the situation, I did not know.

I was hoping Lottie wouldn't question my request, that she was so used to giving her blood that she'd just pick up the blood glucose kit and prick her finger as usual, but I should've known that her infuriatingly efficient brain wouldn't be so easily fooled.

She frowned, looking down at the notes on the ritual she'd made in blue fountain pen. "It says here you need 'the blood of someone who loves your soul as it truly is.'"

My stomach churned with doubt.

"Erm, yes." I smiled awkwardly.

She looked at me in shock, then burst out laughing. "You're such a narcissist."

I bit my top lip with my bottom teeth. "I am, yes."

"Like, truly unbelievable."

"It's not a big deal, all right? You've done it so many times before. Just a quick scratch and it's done."

She pressed her lips together into a flat line, not with anger, but with suppressed hysteria. "That's not the point."

"Why not?"

Another explosion of laughter. "Someone who *loves your soul as it truly is*."

I folded my arms and looked down at the neat row of freshly washed allium beside her investigation notebook. "Look, if you're going to be a dick about it . . ."

"Alice! You are essentially asking me if I love you! Incredibly flippantly, I might add!"

Sighing, I forced myself to look at her. Her bright eyes were crinkled with mirth, and the corners of my own mouth quirked treacherously upward. "Would it help if I said it first?"

Her laughter stopped abruptly, and her cheeks turned pink. "Said what first?"

"That I love you," I muttered irritably.

There was a long, agonizing pause, in which acres of vulnerability rolled out before me.

And then she rolled her eyes, grinned her dimpliest grin, and picked up the blood glucose kit.

As she squeezed a tiny droplet of blood into a glass vial, I smiled to myself.

Mordue wanted to go first. It had started with her all those years ago, and while she was relieved beyond words that she hadn't murdered anyone, she still felt responsible for the ritual's spread through Carvell.

Feathering offered her blood for the tincture; someone who loved Mordue's soul as it truly was. I thought of Mordue's hand on hers in the clubhouse, and of Lottie's on mine as I slept, and of how such a small gesture betrayed so much.

Lottie and Hafsah looked around the clubhouse in wonder. It was a space unlike any other: moth cocoons pinned to vaulted ceilings, the overwhelming scents of rosemary and clove, the eerie self-portrait of Sister Maria with a ruby-crusted gash across her throat, which Lottie understandably stared at for a long while. Her own rubies were fading fast.

And yet despite the lack of light and the cold stone floors, there was a certain warmth to the room. The warmth of intimacy, perhaps. Of kinship, and of shared pain. Of knowing that despite everything, we were not monsters. We never had been.

Lottie played the role of apothecary to perfection. She laid out each neatly prepared ingredient on the long mahogany table: little piles of thyme leaves and hyacinth petals, washed and trimmed allium, lively sprigs of baby's breath. Feathering killed the moth, extracted its hemolymph and ground the cocoon with well-practiced precision. Then, because Feathering was shaking too hard, Lottie laid out the test tube racks, assembled the right doses of each ingredient in each vial, and squeezed a droplet of blood from Feathering's index finger into Mordue's vial.

Mordue watched all this unfold with an impenetrable

expression. She sat silently in a chair at the head of the table, hands clasped in front of her, staring at her test tube rack. Was she trying to steel herself? Did she think the reversal ritual would work? Or was she too afraid to hope? Then there was the unbearable weight of the lives we had to mourn. Even though Poppy's soul would be brought back, her life could never be. Neither could Fiona or Dawn, or Sam or Janie. No wonder Mordue looked so thoroughly hollowed out.

Once the tincture was ready, Mordue stood stoically in high-heeled boots, her black peacoat hanging heavy on her shoulders. She held out one hand to Lottie and nodded. Lottie gave her the vial, then exhaled deeply. She had played her part. Now all that was left to do was watch and hope.

Mordue raised the vial to her mouth, but Feathering suddenly said, "Wait. Stop."

The dean looked at her wearily. "What is it?"

Feathering simply threw her arms around Mordue, squeezing tight and whispering something inaudible in her ear. Mordue didn't reply, just pressed her eyes shut and hugged Feathering back.

Then it was time.

Mordue drank.

For a few seconds, nothing happened. Mordue looked around at each of us, mouth twisted in displeasure at the taste of the concoction. She was halfway through a shrug when her eyes flew open in a dreadful bulge, and a blood-curdling scream erupted from her lips.

"Vanessa!" Feathering cried, grabbing Mordue by the elbow as she sank to the ground.

The screams went on for what felt like hours. Mordue writhed, gouging at the stone slabs with her bloodred nails, gagging and retching and heaving.

My own stomach turned at the sight. Because if this didn't work, the pain was all for nothing.

And if it did work . . . I would have to go through it too.

Lottie sank into the chair next to mine and laid her arm across my shoulders. Before my body could flinch at the unexpected intimacy, before I could throw up all of my worldly guards, I was resting my head on her chest and fighting back tears.

Eventually, Mordue went quiet and still. It was almost worse than the screams. I lifted my head again.

"Vanessa?" Feathering whispered, voice lifted with fear. She wasn't wearing her black lipstick, and her white-silver hair was pulled back in a low bun. Her cheeks were pink and her eyes were raw with worry. I could hardly believe this was the same woman who so intimidated me when I first came to the Sisters of Mercy Library.

After another few moments of awful stillness, Mordue groaned, unraveling herself from the fetal position she'd found herself in. Pressing one hand against the ground, she lifted herself up gingerly, as though she'd just been beaten to within an inch of her life.

"It worked," she murmured. Then her voice hitched with tears. "It . . . it worked."

"*Oh,*" moaned Feathering, and threw her arms around Mordue. The two shared a long, trembling embrace.

"How can you tell?" Hafsah asked curiously, squinting at Mordue like she was a particularly puzzling level of a video game.

"I'm me again," Mordue said simply, sniffing back an errant stream of snot. "It's been so long. I almost forgot who . . . I almost forgot. But I remember now. I can't explain. I'm just . . . I'm me."

"I'll go next," said Hafsah briskly.

"Whose blood are you using?" I asked curiously.

"I've been fucking a bartender from the Grandstand." A casual shrug. "He's way more into it than I am. Told me he loves me last night, so I did a little cut on his arm while he slept. Just normal psychopath things."

Laughter erupted from me before I could stop it. Even Mordue and Feathering gave weak smiles.

Hafsah's ritual went as harrowingly as Mordue's did— the writhing and the clawing and the retching. I felt every bloodcurdling scream in my own rib cage.

Then the stillness, followed by the opening of her eyes like a newborn foal.

Hafsah gave a stoic nod as she dusted herself off. "Thank fuck for that. George's blood came through. He must *actually* love my soul as it really is." A slight nod. "Poor bastard."

Lottie squeezed my shoulder and then unwound her

arm. I looked at her, and she looked at me, and a thousand unspoken words passed between us.

I wanted to get this over with.

Soundlessly, she retrieved the vial containing her blood from the pocket of her hoodie. She added the ingredients from the makeshift apothecary in front of her, topped it up with elderflower cordial, then stoppered it and gave it a hearty shake. She clasped it tightly before relinquishing it to me.

Not allowing myself the luxury of hesitation or forethought, I held the vial up to my lips and drank.

And then everything went black.

As my soul was woven back together, the pain was larger than anything.

All-consuming agony in my rib cage and skull and limbs; a fishhook repeatedly thrust through bone; a thousand dull knitting needles stitching every fiber back together.

Far away, I heard myself screaming.

As blood roared in my ears and my vision gave way to fragmented oblivion, I wanted to die. I lost awareness of my body, my surroundings. I became consumed by the pain, fell into it like it was a physical abyss, a gaping chasm where no life could survive, where I would fall and fall for eternity without ever hitting the bottom.

It was another plane, another dimension, one that should not exist in any reality.

But then slowly, slowly, miraculously, the raging storm

clouds faded, and the abyss began to dissipate, and a slice of sunshine shone into the darkness.

Lottie.

The clouds parted. The sun spread.

I was on my hands and knees on the stone floor of the clubhouse, shaking uncontrollably, still racked with residual pain. Lottie was crouched in front of me, one hand cupped around the back of my sweat-slicked neck, whispering, "It's okay, it's okay, you're okay, it's okay."

And as I came fully back to myself, I knew it was.

There was no longer a cold psychopath stalking the darkest corners of my mind. There was no more veil, torn or otherwise.

There was just Alice. Spiky, angry, hurt—but Alice, nonetheless. A girl who could hope and love again.

It felt like the first day of my life.

As I started to cry, I looked up at Lottie, embarrassed beyond reason, only to realize she was crying too.

How did she still look like human sunshine when she was crying?

"I love you," I whispered, the words, mixed with fat, salty tears, slipping through my lips before I could stop them, and it felt so vulnerable and yet so inevitable, and I knew she loved me too, and mainly I was just relieved that I no longer had to worry about accidentally murdering her in the night. "And thank you."

"I love you too," she said, every syllable a balm. She

was laughing through her sobs, her dimples deep enough to stick a penny in.

And then she kissed me, and it was warm and wonderful and right, a sweet-scented yellow field in the summer, and every shaking inch of me melted into her, and then she ruined it all by cupping my jaw with both hands, gazing into my eyes and whispering:

"I told you I was Sherlock. Scooby-Doo can fuck all the way off."

CHAPTER 69

Alice

What surprised me most about pulling my soul back from the brink of darkness was how much I came to miss teetering. Because on the edge of that darkness, my anger had no longer roiled around inside me, unspent. It was given free rein. It had been let loose, and bridling it again proved harder than ever.

As life returned to normal—as normal as it could be on a college campus plagued by arrests and murder convictions—my fuse shrank back to an inch long. I once again snapped at the people I loved, wished ill on bad drivers, physically prickled with irritation over minor inconveniences. Even with Lottie I lost my temper, stormed out on arguments, said things I didn't mean in the heat of the moment. Afterward I'd be filled with the familiar self-loathing that had plagued me since the day Chris threw me to the ground in his parents' living room.

Eventually I realized that my anger would never leave me unless I gave it somewhere to go. It was a fundamental part of me, and I had to honor it—to exist alongside it.

Because contrary to everything Dacre had argued about female anger, there was nothing in the world as natural. As far back as my ancestral tree could branch, there were women who had been overpowered by men, underestimated by men, controlled by men, dominated by men, all the way back to the very roots of humanity. That anger had woven itself into the fabric of our beings. And instead of giving it room to breathe, we let it fester like an uncleaned wound, destroying us from the inside out.

And the few women who fought back, who embraced that anger, that violence, that raw power . . . they were burned as witches, exorcised in front of jeering mobs, labeled hysterical and committed to sanatoriums, bound and gagged and poked and prodded and electrocuted and studied as lab rats, shunned by friends and family and teachers and students and colleagues and peers, treated as something crude and ill-disciplined.

So the choice became this: let anger fester, destroying you from the inside out, or set it free and let the world destroy you instead.

As Sister Maria had over a century ago, I began to wonder whether there was another way. Not electric rods or a sinister soul-splitting ritual, but a means of embracing the anger without letting it overpower us. Of refusing to *let* ourselves be overpowered, of luxuriating in the thrill of the fight the way men did.

I thought again of my brothers grappling on the living room floor, wolfing down their dinners and falling into easy sleep, and I wondered how different my life would have been if I had done the same. How could we break those generational cycles? How could we stop what happened to Sister Maria—and to our grandmothers, and our mothers, and to the smart, brilliant women like Mordue and the other original members—from happening to us? How could we reject the internalized shame that was passed down to angry women throughout history? How could we own it instead?

We had to break the cycle.

For all Dacre's flaws, he had shared one powerful thing in our first private tutorial, and it had stuck with me: *Anger left to run free is like wildfire, indiscriminate in its destruction. But if you learn to tame it, to position it, to take aim with it? Then it becomes a candle. And what is the candle but one of humanity's greatest assets. It warms. It nourishes. It shines a light in the darkest of places, and it illuminates the path forward.*

Which was how Lottie, Hafsah and I found ourselves back in the society's clubhouse several weeks later, crash mats laid out on the smooth stone slabs, armed with padded head guards and mouth shields and taped-up knuckles. The long mahogany table had been taken to the Grandstand bar, where it had been thoroughly rehabilitated as a beer pong table.

Both the emerald-green plaque and Sister Maria's unsettling self-portrait still stared down at us; reminders of why we were here.

A female boxing trainer we'd recruited from Edinburgh was hanging a large punch bag from a newly installed hook on the vaulted ceiling beams. The moth cocoons were long gone. The air still smelled of rosemary and clove, but also of gym halls and fusty boxing gloves.

Attendance at the first Soulless Girls Fight Club was better than expected. There was Hafsah's hall mate Alicia, a handful of girls from Lottie's field hockey team, a young barmaid from the Grandstand, as well as Mordue and Feathering. Everyone was taped up, guarded up and ready to learn how to fight. Ready to learn how to *love* the fight.

The anticipation in the air was palpable.

Public speaking and rallying battle cries weren't really my scene, so even though the Soulless Girls Fight Club had been my idea, it was Lottie who stood at the center of the room addressing the girls she'd soon be learning to beat up. Her throat rubies were gone now, leaving behind the faintest trace of a scar.

Her voice was strong and clear; she was every inch the field hockey captain I knew she'd be one day. "Welcome to the new and improved Society for Soulless Girls." Mordue smiled reassuringly at her. "As some of you may know, I recently sold the story of the Carvell murders to a major newspaper for a significant amount of money."

There were whoops and hollers and wolf whistles, mainly from the field hockey girls, but I couldn't resist a little air-punch myself. We'd told them *everything*, no matter how ugly, no matter how unflattering, no matter how impossible for the average reader to believe. The rituals, the throat rubies, the ghost of a furious nun—everything except my brush with Salem, whose fabled immortality had somehow saved her from my wrath. I didn't want anyone to know I'd killed an innocent being. It would forever change the way the world saw me.

"Thank you to everyone who worked with me on that piece, who gave interviews and insights, who helped claw back our power in some small but vital way. We have channeled our anger into something good, something that will help build a better world, and I want that to continue. Which is why we are pouring the money we earned straight back into the society.

"As well as these training sessions, we've also hired Dr. al-Hadi, Hafsah's mum, to provide counseling to all members of the society. A healthy space for us to work through our anger and our pain, and to learn how not to let it destroy us."

Hafsah beamed proudly; it had been her idea. Between this and having her Madhouses Act paper accepted by a prestigious journal at the ripe old age of eighteen, things were definitely looking up for her. I had no doubt she'd be the eccentric academic of her dreams one day.

Lottie shot me a wide smile—sunshine-yellow fields and chin dimples so deep you could stick a penny in them. Writing the piece with her had been hard. Not just because it meant reliving it all over and over again until we got it right but also because it illuminated the holes in our story that we'd probably never be able to fill.

I would never know whether or not I had killed Salem, only for her to resurrect herself days later.

I would never know how the ritual was possible in the first place.

I would never know why the clocks in Mordue's office ticked backward, or whether the stained-glass windows in the Refectory changed shape, or whether Lottie's creepy Professor Sanderson really could conjure golden threads between the gothic and reality. Call it the Carvell curse; call it madness. All I knew was that those dark spots would haunt me for the rest of my life.

Lottie turned back to the enraptured faces around her.

"One of my favorite quotes in *Crime and Punishment* is this: 'Power is only vouchsafed to the man who dares to stoop and pick it up.'" As she looked around, I could feel the coiled energy in her, the palpable fizzing. The anger in me felt different, somehow—a leaping excitement rather than a fearful snarl.

Lottie bashed her boxing gloves together with a final, rousing grin.

"Let's stoop, bitches."

ACKNOWLEDGMENTS

Publishing a book takes a village, and I feel very lucky to work with such talented and passionate teams on both sides of the Atlantic. Special thanks to . . .

AGENTING: Chloe Seager, Suzie Townsend

ASSISTING: Sophia M. Ramos, Kendra Coet

EDITORIAL: Hannah Hill, Liz Bankes, Asmaa Isse, Aleena Hasan

MANAGING EDITORIAL & COPYEDITING: Tamar Schwartz, Heather Lockwood Hughes, Colleen Fellingham, Alison Kolani

DESIGN: Ray Shappell, Megan Shortt

MARKETING & PUBLICITY: Dominique Cimina, John Adamo, Kelly McGauley, Elizabeth Ward, Adrienne Waintraub

PUBLISHING: Beverly Horowitz, Barbara Marcus

RIGHTS: Juliette Clark, Kim Yau

ABOUT THE AUTHOR

Laura Steven is an award-winning author from the northernmost town in England. She has published several books for children and young adults; her debut novel, *The Exact Opposite of Okay,* won the inaugural Comedy Women in Print Prize, while *The Love Hypothesis* was optioned for TV by an Emmy-winning team. Her books have been widely translated, and her work has appeared in *The i Paper, The Guardian,* and *BuzzFeed.*

LAURA-STEVEN.COM